**Avail**
**from M**

# OUT OF CONTROL

## "I want you to kiss me again. Really kiss me."

Her request seemed to open up a throttle, turbo-charging the leisurely, languid connection between them. Without ever letting her feet hit the ground, he turned her – using the truck and the friction of her curves bunching against his harder angles to keep her suspended in the air and aligned against him in a way that was sending every red blood cell in her body charging hard into the tips of her aching breasts and down to her full, weeping centre. And then he kissed her. And kissed her. His kisses consumed her.

# HOT UNDER PRESSURE

## David's finger stroked down her back, following the arc of her spine

Ashley smiled, but kept firmly to her side of the bed.

"You make me feel cheap," he finally said, no trace of hurt, only humour in his voice. David continued to talk, his finger trying to coax her closer. "I know you're only here to use and abuse me, but I have needs, too."

At that, Ashley stared at him suspiciously.

"You think of me as just a fast-action pump and drill, variable speed settings and excellent torque, but I have feelings, and when you turn away from me…" He looked at her, hazel eyes dancing, and sniffed.

"What do you want?" she asked cautiously, not quite trusting appearances, but willing to go with it, because he made her take chances she didn't want to take.

He grinned. "I don't know. But I need to feel you respect me."

Ashley scooched close to him. "I respect you."

He sniffed again. "I need you to like me for my mind, not just the awesome sex."

All the characters in this book have no existence outside the imagination of the author, and have no relation whatsoever to anyone bearing the same name or names. They are not even distantly inspired by any individual known or unknown to the author, and all the incidents are pure invention.

First published in Great Britain 2010
Harlequin Mills & Boon Limited,
Eton House, 18-24 Paradise Road, Richmond, Surrey TW9 1SR

*Out of Control* © Julie Miller 2009
*Hot Under Pressure* © Kathleen Panov 2009

ISBN: 978 0 263 88127 1

14-0410

Harlequin Mills & Boon policy is to use papers that are natural, renewable and recyclable products and made from wood grown in sustainable forests. The logging and manufacturing processes conform to the legal environmental regulations of the country of origin.

Printed and bound in Spain
by Litografia Rosés S.A., Barcelona

# OUT OF CONTROL
## BY
### JULIE MILLER

# HOT UNDER PRESSURE
## BY
### KATHLEEN O'REILLY

MILLS & BOON

# OUT OF CONTROL

### BY
### JULIE MILLER

While **Julie Miller** has never driven an actual drag racer, she has written more than thirty-five books and won several awards for her work, including the National Readers' Choice Award. Some of her books have appeared on the *USA TODAY* and Waldenbooks bestseller lists. Julie lives in Nebraska, where she teaches English and spoils her dog. Find out more about her at www.juliemiller.org.

For Lori Borrill, Alison Kent and Jennifer LaBrecque.

FROM 0–60 has been a great collaborative effort
and a lot of fun to boot!

Dahlia, Tennessee, really came to life for me,
working with you guys.

I feel I've been to that town and I know
those people living there.

I appreciate you sharing your knowledge of
drag racing with a novice like me.

I appreciate your humour and your creative
energy fed my own.

And thanks to Brenda Chin for introducing us!

# *1*

———

*Nashville, Tennessee*
*Seven months ago*

"GET OUT OF THE VEHICLE. Get *out* of the vehicle!"

Detective Jack Riley pulled his Glock 9 mm and pointed it, along with his flashlight, at the three-hundred-pound behemoth who ignored his badge and his command and started the engine. Shit.

As the drug dealer shifted his customized Chevy Suburban into gear, Jack jumped back inside the cab of his pickup and slammed it into reverse, hoping to block his target's exit from the convenience store parking lot. But Lorenzo Vaughn slipped past him, burning an acrid trail of black rubber onto the pavement as he swung out into the street.

"Screw that."

Silently apologizing to the truck's big bruiser engine, he shifted into drive and ruthlessly gunned it.

Jack flipped on the siren and warning lights of his unmarked truck, praying Vaughn would take this pursuit to the open road. With a long, straight stretch ahead of them, Jack's years of training behind the wheel would give him the advantage. But it might already be too late. There were too many hills, too many trees and houses blocking his line of sight—too many things wrong with this takedown.

The original plan he and his drug enforcement team had worked weeks on had gone way beyond south.

"Come on, baby." He urged as much speed out of the engine as he dared this time of night with so many cars still on the streets.

"Jack? You in trouble?" His partner Eric Mesner's voice crackled over the radio. "We're hung up in traffic at least five minutes away from your location."

Jack swore, yanking his steering wheel to the left to swerve around a car pulling out of a driveway. "We're already a day late and a dollar short, buddy. Vaughn didn't stick to his regular schedule. He got away from me. I'm in pursuit."

"Son of a bitch. Did you see the drugs?"

"Didn't get a chance to. But the Chevy he's driving has been modified like the others. Looks like a monster-sized race car. If it's street legal, I'm your Aunt Fanny. Whatever he's selling was either transported in there or is still hidden inside."

Rather than risk their lives or any innocent bystanders' lives by confronting Vaughn at his house—where guns, drugs, lieutenants and a reputed fighting dog stayed—they'd wanted to arrest him when he slipped out to pay a nightly visit to one of his girlfriends. "You watch your back, Jack. Don't take this guy on by yourself."

"Too late for that." Jack had been spying on Vaughn's house, tracking his routine for weeks. The closest they could figure was that Vaughn was getting his drugs stashed inside one of the new vehicles that seemed to show up at his house about once a month. The plan had been to grab the man, grab the car, and break both down until NPD had the proof necessary to bring down one of the city's biggest drug rings. But their precisely timed plan was turning into a flat-out road race. "You're coming to save my ass, right?"

"We're coming," Eric assured him. "Let's get moving. Now!" he shouted to the other team members who were closing in on Jack's lead position.

Jack switched his radio to an all-call channel and reported his location. "Officer in pursuit. I could use some backup."

Flying through intersections and leaving streetlights and startled drivers in the dust, Jack needed to think fast. He glanced at the name of a side street, pulled up a map inside his head. Hell, yes. Flexing his fingers around his truck's taut leather steering-wheel cover, Jack took a deep, steadying breath…and jerked the wheel to the right. He cut through an alley, skidded around the corner and pressed on the gas, his eyes peeled for any sign of pedestrians or civilian vehicles as he zoomed ahead of Vaughn's position on a less-populated parallel street. He couldn't safely outrace Lorenzo Vaughn, but he could damn well outsmart him.

Spotting the cross street he wanted, Jack spun left. By the time his two left wheels hit the pavement again, he had his target in sight. He floored it. "Gotcha."

Forty damn years old and Jack Riley could still play a gutsy game of chicken. Vaughn's head turned. He saw the inevitable rushing toward him and Jack grinned. He was either going to turn Vaughn toward the highway entrance ramp or T-bone him.

Only Vaughn didn't understand the rules of the game he was playing.

"Turn, you son of a bitch. Turn!"

Vaughn's SUV loomed larger and larger. He was close enough to see Vaughn's *oh, shit* expression now, close enough to count down the seconds until impact or victory, close enough to—

A blur of blue and red flashed through Jack's peripheral vision. In the same instant a bold, taunting voice blared across his radio. "I've got this one, old man! Back off!"

A black-and-white unit whipped around the corner in front of him, almost clipping Jack's right fender. Adrenaline whooshed out of his body as Jack stomped on the brakes to avoid the crash. "Shit. Billington!"

Vaughn jerked his vehicle to the left as Jack skidded through the intersection behind him. In the seconds it took Jack to regain control of his truck, Vaughn's SUV and the black-and-white unit had careened onto the highway ramp. He was blocks behind the chase already. But Paul Billington kept his speed steady, falling into close pursuit.

He'd asked for backup, hadn't he? But Jack had been looking for his seasoned drug enforcement team to show up and save the day—not this fast and furious wannabe who'd answered the call from street patrol.

Cursing the young hotshot, Jack closed the distance between them, slipping into the unfamiliar role of playing backup on the arrest *he* was supposed to have made. "Damn it, Billington!" Jack watched the black-and-white police car slide into position to tap the rear of Vaughn's vehicle and slam him into a spinout. They were going too fast. Too damn fast. "Billington!"

The kid was cocky. Reckless.

Perfect.

In a matter of seconds, the perp's car had rolled to a stop in the ditch and Billington was dragging a dazed Lorenzo Vaughn from behind his deflating air bag. Jack pulled up in front of the wreck and climbed out. "Nice driving," Jack conceded. "I appreciate the help."

"Happy to save your ass anytime, Grandpa."

*Damn schmuck.*

With Eric Mesner and the rest of the team finally reaching the scene to set up traffic control around the accident, Jack lowered his voice and reprimanded the young officer for the unnecessary risk he'd taken upon himself. "Speeding through a residential neighborhood where collateral damage is a definite possibility is not the way to prove you've got the cajones to make the drug squad."

Billington jerked Vaughn to his feet and turned him toward the black-and-white. "Back in the day, when you set the police course driving record I've been trying to break since my rookie year, you would have gotten the job done yourself instead of calling for backup and giving me a lecture. Maybe it's time to step aside and let some new blood into vice."

"Back in the day?" Jack winced at the mix of awe and sympathy in Billington's tone. "I'm hardly ready to retire."

"Oh, yeah?" Billington's expression blazed with an arrogance all too reminiscent of Jack's earlier days on the force. "Who just made this arrest?"

"Good work, buddy." Eric Mesner patted his shoulder as Jack eased the tight clench of his fists. "It's good to see that bastard finally going to jail."

Nodding, Jack replayed the night's events in his head, trying to figure out where he'd lost that half-second advantage to Vaughn—and Billington—and wondering just how many other young bloods in NPD had taken to calling him *Old Man* and *Grandpa*.

Eric nodded his approval to Billington as he closed the back door of the official vehicle on Lorenzo Vaughn. "I've got the rest of the team securing the Suburban. We'll check the accessible places for any hidden drugs. Otherwise, it'll be up to the lab to break it down. In the meantime, I'm looking forward to putting him in an interrogation room and finding out how he's getting his supply into Nashville in the first place."

"You still coming over to the house for barbecue tomorrow afternoon?" Eric switched topics as smoothly as Jack eased through the gears on his truck. "I figure it'll be the last weekend we can be outside before the cooler weather sets in. The kids and the missus haven't seen you for a while. Not since you and Rosie broke up."

Hell. His ego was taking it in the shorts tonight. There was no woman at home for him anymore, waiting to listen to his troubles, willing to ease his doubts and frustrations with the lush warmth of her body. Jack's live-in lover of over a year had moved out a month ago because her job offer in St. Louis had been more tempting than a marriage proposal from him.

He liked Eric's kids, was godfather to his oldest son. Even Eric's wife welcomed him like a long-lost brother. But he didn't feel much like celebrating with the family right now. Jack turned and headed back to his truck. "I don't know."

"Don't know what?" Eric followed. "Hey. We got our guy.

We'll find where the cars and drugs are coming from. The rest will fall into place. We did good."

"No, Eric, we sucked." Jack pulled up and turned to his partner. "*I* sucked. If it wasn't for Hotshot's help back there, Vaughn would have gotten away. He could have dumped the car and the drugs and we'd have zilch. Nada. Nothing."

"So we had an off night." Eric propped his hands on his hips at the hem of his flak vest and shrugged. "How many times in the past have we had to punt and go to Plan B—or C or D— because Plan A didn't work out?"

Jack raked his fingers through his hair. "Yeah, but we were always able to make B, C and D work for ourselves. We never had to have some punk ride in to save our asses before."

Eric's dark eyes narrowed in that wise, patient way of his as he tried to assess Jack's surly mood. "We may be slowing down, but our glory days are hardly over."

Slowing down? Shit. Just the kind of pep talk he *didn't* need.

"BACK IN THE DAY, MY ASS." Jack thumped the truck's steering wheel with his fist. It was late. He was tired. And his patience with himself had worn down to the driving need for an ice-cold beer or a long, hot lay to purge the restless frustration that gnawed at him.

But he was still on the clock, and there was no sweet, sophisticated Rosie waiting for him back home.

He couldn't keep a woman. Couldn't do the job. Eric had said it was an off day. That they'd crack the case tomorrow. Damn optimist. Probably why Eric's wife had stuck with him for almost twenty years. Probably why Jack respected his partner so much. Eric could see the promise of tomorrow. He believed in it.

Meanwhile, Jack…? Well, hell. Even with the windows down and the damp autumn air blowing in his face as he cruised along Interstate 40, he couldn't seem to cool down. Something was eating at him tonight.

And it damn well wasn't the fact that he was forty, unattached and horny as hell with some adolescent need to prove he was still the man he once was. Yeah, right.

Exiting the highway, Jack veered onto Broadway— Nashville's brightly lit, noisy magnet for tourists, partygoers and country-music star wannabes. Maybe there'd be a purse snatcher or scam artist he could haul in to headquarters. *That's it. Make an arrest. Protect and serve.*

That'd get his mojo back. Then maybe he'd believe in tomorrow again, too. Jack inhaled deeply, feeling a surge of renewed confidence.

Scanning Broadway from sidewalk to sidewalk, Jack watched for anything out of the ordinary. Neon lights blinked on and off in modern contrast to the old brick buildings they adorned, marking open-mike joints, dance clubs and honky tonks. Despite the chill in the air, every door stood open to let the music inside pour out into the street.

With a beefy bouncer standing guard at every bar, he suspected there wouldn't be anything to worry about there. Instead, Jack turned his attention to the crowds milling up and down the sidewalk. He took note of the tourists strolling toward a line of horse-drawn carriages, hoping to catch a leisurely tour of the capitol building and other historical and musical landmarks in the downtown area. He spotted a trio of derelict musicians hauling their instruments, bedrolls and backpacks in and out of doorways, looking for work and a place to sleep. Jack nodded to the two uniformed bicycle cops who'd pulled off their helmets and stopped to chat with a street-corner huckster who was probably selling over-priced tickets to something that didn't even exist. Their answering salute told him the two men had the situation well under control.

Soon, he'd run out of road—and opportunities—and hit the Cumberland River that looped through the city. Jack rolled to a stop at the next light. He drummed his fingers against the wheel, thinking his apartment and a cold shower were his best bets to save this night, when a shrill voice pierced the night air.

"You touch me again and you'll take back a stump."

A swirl of honey-gold hair drew his eye to the street-corner commotion in front of Jasmine's Saloon.

Petite yet stacked in a way that reminded him of country-music icons and teenage fantasies, a young blond woman marched down the sidewalk, bumping her way through the crowd. Her makeup had been applied with a heavy hand, and the little black dress she wore was far too short—her strappy silver stilettos way too high—for that sexy get-up to be anything other than an invitation for trouble.

*Trouble* followed in the form of two college-aged boys who hurried along behind her. "What if we pay you double?" the taller one shouted.

The blonde spun around on wobbly legs. Before Jack could wedge his truck into the entrance to a parking alley, Blondie drew her arm back and swung. He winced in sympathy at the slap that connected with the cheek of the gangly, red-haired young man. The young man's buddy laughed, but quickly fell silent as both Red and Blondie turned and glared at him.

There was a story behind that assault, and Jack intended to find out the details before Blondie struck again or the two men retaliated. Closing the door behind him, Jack jogged down the sidewalk for a closer look.

While Blondie tottered on her heels in a less-than-dignified retreat, the red-haired kid massaged his cheek and made some kind of suggestion to his shorter companion. With a nod of agreement, Red and Shorty hurried after their target, perhaps intent on taking what she hadn't been willing to give them.

"Easy, boys." Jack quickly caught up to the boys, stopping them with a low-pitched warning. "Nashville PD. Now turn around nice and slow."

Shorty thrust his hands into the air and whirled around, completely ignoring the *slow* part of the command. "We didn't do anything wrong."

"Shut up, Duane."

The tall one turned, as well, and Jack looked him straight in his bleary eyes.

Hell. Not one wrinkle on the kid's face. And clearly they'd already had a few. Were these two even legal? Jack pulled back the front of his leather jacket to give them a look at his badge and gun. "Let me see your IDs."

As eager to cooperate as he'd been to laugh, Duane handed over his driver's license. It looked authentic enough. Red's ID showed he was old enough to hit the bars, as well. Just barely. Jack did some quick math before returning their licenses. "Celebrating your twenty-first birthday?"

"Yes, sir."

Jack looked between their shoulders to see the young woman hugging her arms around herself for warmth as she paused outside the doorway to the next bar on the block. "What about Blondie over there? Is she part of the celebration?"

The tall one with the fading hand print on his face shrugged. "I thought she wanted to be. She hit on us inside."

Duane slurred his words and blinked sporadically, trying to send a double entendre with a wink as he tucked his license back into his wallet. "She asked Isaac if he had a phone in his pocket. I sure had one in mine when I got a load of those gazongas."

"Yeah. It was a come-on line if I ever heard one."

"I told her that money was no object—that we'd pay the going rate. But she said she wouldn't take our money—"

"I thought she meant she was gonna give me a birthday freebie."

"Maybe she doesn't do two at once, man. I don't mind waiting. It's Isaac's birthday, anyway."

"All right, boys, I've heard enough." Jack raised his hand to end the discussion. These two were clueless but apparently harmless. "Move along. Make sure you call a cab when it's time to go home. I don't want to see either one of you behind the wheel tonight. Understood?"

Both young men nodded with obvious relief. "Yes, sir."

They quickly turned and tottered back into the saloon. "I mean it, boys—" Jack called after them. "No driving tonight."

"No, sir."

Now, back to the real trouble.

Despite her lack of height, Jack easily spotted all that pale bare skin and golden hair as Blondie gave up the idea of going into the bar and, instead, joined the stream of partiers and tourists heading on down the street. Jack picked up speed as he threaded his way through the crowd in pursuit. The woman walked with a purpose. Though if she was running *to* something or running away, he couldn't tell. He supposed Isaac and Duane back there weren't up to her standards or they just hadn't been willing or able to meet her price.

The spaghetti straps on the little black dress she wore had no chance of holding up those puppies if she continued to bounce along at that furious pace. Jack tried to ignore the rush of masculine appreciation that bubbled through his veins and pooled behind his zipper. Hookers weren't his thing, but Blondie was hot, in a trashy sort of way that made him long for a fast car and a one-night stand. No commitment. Nothing complicated. Just pure, any-way-he-wanted-it sex. He wasn't the only male in the vicinity to notice the possibilities, either.

"Ah, hell."

Now she moved to the edge of the curb, stumbling backward in those spiky heels, her thumb in the air. She shouted something obscene to one car that slowed, then sped away without stopping.

Hitchhiking was just as illegal, and no safer than turning tricks. Jack needed to get to her before she got herself in a train wreck that would completely ruin what was left of this night.

"Miss?"

The instant he touched the cool skin of her arm, she started. Before he could identify himself, she jerked away, tilting her chin up, ready to do battle. "If you ask me for a blow job, too, I swear I'm gonna smack you."

He crushed the erotic image of honey-blond curls at his crotch that instantly leaped to mind, and did his damnedest to remember he was a cop. Jack pulled his badge from his belt. "Well, that would be assaulting a police officer, and we frown upon that here in Nashville."

"You're a cop?" Instead of expressing relief or laughing at the joke, she muttered a curse. "This is not happening to me."

# 2

WAS IT POSSIBLE for one woman to be any stupider about men than she'd been tonight?

Alexandra Morgan briefly flashed back to the crippling knowledge that she'd once proved the answer was *yes*.

Still, there was little comfort in knowing that tonight could actually be worse. She'd shunned the idea of dating for so long that she'd known it wouldn't be easy, but she thought she'd get *something* right. After that awful night in high school, and the handful of doomed attempts in the nine years since that had turned her into a closed-up, guarded, spinster tomboy, she'd finally gotten frustrated enough to try embracing the sexy, feminine side of her nature again. She was anxious to learn about all the good things she'd been denying herself. The intimacy. The trust. The orgasms. She'd wanted this.

But nothing had changed. Wanting wasn't the same as knowing. Her feminine instincts—or lack thereof—had failed her once again.

College had given her confidence in other aspects of her life. Her four years of the University of Tennessee made her rethink how she handled the small minds that had dictated the course of her life. She'd gone to work for her father, outlined new ideas to improve the family auto-repair business. She'd made a success of her life despite the concessions survival had forced her to make. But a degree in business management couldn't prepare her for nights like this one.

Tears began to chafe like grit beneath her eyelids again, and Alex blinked them away along with the painful memories from her past. She was smart enough now to grab hold of the anger that gave her the strength to bear the disappointments of her life. Like tonight.

The big bruiser with the badge here was just the icing on the cake. Her feet were blistered. She was cold, embarrassed. Accepting a blind date with the friend of a friend hadn't proved to be the fresh start she'd hoped for. "What did I do wrong?"

He clipped his badge back beneath his black leather jacket, giving her a glimpse of a gun and a rip of muscles that warned her getting away from him wouldn't be as easy as getting away from Dawson Barnes had been. "Relax, sweetheart. I'm not necessarily taking you in. But we do need to talk about what you're selling."

"Selling?" Alex planted her hands on her hips in a defiant pose. "Do you see a purse? Pockets? A suitcase? I don't have anything on me to sell." Dawson had left her with nothing but the clothes on her back. She'd thought his offer to drive all the way to Dahlia to pick her up for dinner had been a gentlemanly gesture.

But when he'd started tearing at her sweater before they'd even gotten inside the restaurant, she'd fought her way out of the car without thinking about her phone or purse or the fact he might drive off and leave her.

Oh. My. God.

The blood rushed from her head down to her painted toenails. Those two boys in the saloon who'd seemed harmless enough to approach? That jerk in the car? Mr. Tall, Dark and Serious here? "You think I'm a hooker?"

"Well, that dress doesn't exactly say all-American sweetheart now does it." His sarcasm burned through her.

Alex glanced down at the twin curses bulging over the low-cut neckline, seeing for the first time just how close she was to popping out over the top of the tight rayon knit. She quickly hugged her arms around her chest as if she could hide her assets.

But the cop's gray eyes, dark as steel and just as hard, said it all. "I look like a hooker."

She was going to be sick.

Alex rubbed her hands along her skin from her elbows to her shoulders. Her father had assured her that her late mother had always put on makeup when she'd gone out. She'd always worn a dress and heels like a "fine lady." Every fashion magazine Alex had picked up over the years talked about how a woman could never go wrong with a little black dress.

She'd managed to go wrong.

Despite the good intentions of the military father and workaholic brother who'd raised her, Alex had managed to go way wrong.

All she'd wanted was a date. One date with one decent guy who'd treat her like a lady and maybe teach her a thing or two about the intricacies of a physical relationship with a man. But Dawson hadn't wanted to teach. He'd wanted to take.

And, by damn, Alexandra Morgan was done letting men take what she'd be willing to give the right one.

At five foot three, she didn't have much to work with in the intimidation department, but she tipped her chin up, way up, to look this cop in the eye and set him straight. "Just so we're clear on this. I am *not* a hooker."

"Then I expect you're either in trouble, or you're well on your way to finding it. Either way, you need my help."

"I can take care of myself."

"Yeah, I can see that." More sarcasm? He raked his fingers over dark hair that had enough silver in it to give the short, crisp cut a smoky cast. "Come on." Making some sort of decision, he cupped a hand beneath her elbow and turned her back in the direction she'd come from. "Let's get you off the street before I have to arrest you for public indecency."

"Are you kidding me?" She jerked her arm out of his grasp. "This is a perfectly good dress." At least, it had looked fine on the girl in the catalog. Of course, that girl was probably taller, and no way did a fashion model have a pair of 38 EEs to work with. "It's not my fault I lost the sweater that goes with it. You take a look for yourself, pal. Everything I own is covered."

But even Alex could look down and see that wasn't far from a lie. Oh, God. She was blushing hard enough that even her boobs were turning pink. Quickly, she tugged the square neckline up half an inch. But then she felt a distinct breeze down between her thighs.

What she wouldn't give for one of her brother's big T-shirts— or a hole to crawl into—right about now.

Alex didn't know whether to give NPD here credit for patience or perseverence. She saw the officer's gaze go *there,* then politely move back up to her face. He nodded toward a half-ton black pickup parked in an alley at the end of the block. "I'll give you a ride to headquarters where we can sort this out."

"There's nothing to sort out. I'm going home."

"Excuse me?"

She shook her head. "Unless you *are* arresting me, I am not going anywhere with you."

His gray eyes grew even steelier. The cool leather of his jacket brushed against her cheek as he took a step closer and pointed over her shoulder at the cars passing by. "You won't accept a ride from a police officer, yet you'll get into the car of a complete stranger?"

*"You're* a stranger to me," she countered, feeling suddenly surrounded by his heat and strength, and fighting the urge to either turn tail and run or throw herself against that wall of black T-shirt and pray his offer to help was a legitimate one. "How do I know I can trust you?"

He was going for his badge again. "You see this? This means you do what I say."

"I don't have a particular fondness for cops." And though this one with the jeans and the leather and the shoulders was a sight better looking than the good ol' boy who ran her hometown, she wasn't inclined to put her faith in any man right now.

"I wasn't giving you a choice, Trouble." He grabbed her arm firmly enough make her understand he wasn't letting go. "You're coming with me."

"Hey!" The crowd parted in front of his long, determined stride as he escorted her back to his truck. Alex tapped along in double-time beside him, struggling against his grip every step of the way. "Did you just call me *Trouble?* This is police harassment. I've got a good lawyer." A big brother who'd be indignant on her behalf, at any rate. "I'll sue."

"Sue away, sweetheart."

He kept right on walking, ignoring her protests, ignoring curious stares and pointing and laughs that made part of her wilt inside. The one man who stepped forward to help quickly changed his mind and backed off when the cop thrust his badge in the guy's face.

"You're a big bully, you know that?"

"You're a pain in the ass."

"Is that any way to talk to a lady—"

The sidewalk ended. The cop turned. Alex tugged. His grip slipped. But escape was short-lived. Her heel caught in the seam of the curb, snapped and pitched her forward.

A rock-hard arm shot around her waist to catch her. "Easy."

Alex shoved it away. Why the hell should anything go right? She stumbled sideways, plucked off the traitorous shoe and tossed it. "Get away from me."

Two big hands closed over her shoulders now, saving her from falling. "Let me help."

"I don't want any help. I just want to go home." She wanted to crawl under the covers and hide her head and heart in shame.

He pulled her back. "I'm not the bad guy."

"Let…" Alex's vision had reduced to a blur of black leather and neon lights. But she had the presence of mind to put that surviving shoe to some good use tonight. She stomped down hard on his instep. "…go!"

Cussing up a blue streak, he did just that. Alex lurched forward, nearly splatting on the concrete. Her pulse roared in her ears. Her eyes burned.

"That's it." Before she could right herself, a straight-jacket came down around her shoulders. Its warmth and softness were almost a shock to her system. But there was nothing soft about the wrap-around bands of masculine strength that pinned her arms to her sides and lifted her feet clear off the pavement.

Alex shrieked. Twisted in his grasp.

"Stop it!"

Tears clouded her vision, burned down her cheeks. "No!"

"Don't fight me."

She writhed and kicked. The second shoe flew into the shadows. "Please," she sobbed. If anything, his hold on her tightened. He locked one arm beneath her breasts, the other farther down, around her hips. She was moving through the air. He was carrying her away as easily and ignominiously as a sack of potatoes. And then she was trapped, her whole body cinched up tight, unable to wiggle anything besides her bare feet, which dangled in the air beneath her.

The humiliation of her evening was complete. She was grappling in an alley with a full-grown man who was neither her brother nor her date…nor her enemy.

The fight drained out of Alex and she sagged inside the prison of the cop's arms. She was breathing hard, her chest pushing against the jacket's silky lining. The cocoon of fiery warmth surrounding her finally pierced the blind haze of fight-or-flight emotions that had turned her into a crazy woman for a few minutes. She could finally blink enough tears from her puffy eyes to see that she was facing the bed of a black pickup truck. She was pinned against the side, wrapped up in a leather jacket and sandwiched between cold steel and warm man.

As her breathing returned to a more normal rhythm, Alex became aware of a hushed, deep-pitched sound murmuring against her neck. "Shh. There's nothing to be afraid of. Just quit fightin' me. Okay?"

Alex nodded slowly, hearing the cadence of that soothing voice more than the actual words. "I'm…sorry."

She exhaled on a surrendering sigh and instinctively leaned her ear closer to the seductive sound. Smooth like whiskey, and just as intoxicating, the deep, soft tones warmed her from the inside out.

"That's it, sweetheart. Relax. I'm not going to hurt you." The rough pad of a finger was surprisingly gentle against her skin as the man who held her wiped the tears from her cheeks. "Shh. Now, come on. Don't do that. You don't want to be cryin'."

The tears of frustration and humiliation quickly dried up beneath his tender ministrations. For a few moments, there was simply fatigue—and gratitude that there was a man whose will and strength were stronger than her own—a *good* man whose will and strength hadn't been used to hurt her. But as her sensibilities returned, Alex became aware of other things. Interesting things. Things that were as male and intriguing and unsettling as that voice.

The muscled forearm wedged beneath her breasts. The rasp of beard stubble that tickled her ear and neck. The buttery softness and furnace-like warmth of the jacket he'd wrapped around her body. Alex breathed in deeply. The jacket smelled like heaven.

She felt the belt buckle pressing into her rear, and the thigh that had been forced between her legs. In their struggle, her short dress had ridden up to an embarrassing level, leaving only her cotton panties between them. But shielded from curious eyes by the truck and the man's big, muscular body, she didn't feel exposed or embarrassed.

Instead, Alex felt…female. Vulnerable.

But not afraid.

The roughness of denim rubbed against her most sensitive

skin. And a rippling response of pressure seemed to be gathering at the juncture between her thighs, building with each flex of hard muscles against her there.

"Let's try this again." He adjusted their positions, shifting her higher onto his hip. Alex closed her eyes, her thighs clenching at the friction of his leg sliding between hers. How could being trapped—helpless—like this feel so good? "I'm a detective with Nashville PD. It's too chilly for this dress and too late for a woman to be walking the streets on her own. I'm here to help you. How old are you?"

"Twenty-five."

"Before I got to you…" He paused, went still around her—as if the next question was hard for him to get out. "Have you been assaulted?"

*Grabbing hands. Buttons popping. Pushing her down in the seat. "I heard you did it for all the boys in Dahlia. Let's see those tits."*

"Shh. Easy."

Something in Alex had gone rigid, defensive. But his mesmerizing voice calmed her into breathing easy again.

Alex answered. "I was on a blind date. There was a little miscommunication. I thought he'd be interesting—he thought I'd put out."

"I'm sorry." He adjusted his stance, pulling the prop of his leg from between hers, relaxing the intimacy of his hold on her without releasing her entirely. "Did he force you?"

Alex squirmed in his grasp, wanting to turn around and ease away the concern—or was it fear? Anger?—that eroded the seductive timbre of his voice into a predatory growl. But she was at his mercy, and all she had to give him were words. "No. I wasn't raped if that's what you're asking. But his plans for the evening didn't match up with mine. When I got out of the car, he drove off with my purse and sweater and cell phone inside."

He cursed. Apologized. "And you've been walking ever since?"

"Yeah. It's been a long night."

"And I thought I was having a bad one. Sounds like yours might have been worse." He adjusted his arms around her, softening his hold. Though there was still little chance for Alex to escape, it felt more like an embrace rather than a takedown maneuver. "Sometimes, it's hard to get it all right."

Alex nodded. "Sometimes, it's hard to get anything right."

"Sometimes."

This man made it so easy to sink into his strength. He was still pressed against her, his cheek to her ear, his chest to her back, his... Alex's cheeks colored with warmth. There was something more than his belt buckle pressing into her bottom. But he wasn't rubbing himself against her or demanding she do something about it. His restraint, despite the hell she'd given him, created a whole new world of confusion inside her.

But oddly enough, *this* felt right.

Even though she was the one being held captive, he was letting her be the one in control of the unexpected, yet obvious, attraction simmering between them. Control was a whole new experience for Alex. And she was beginning to think she wouldn't mind if the handsome detective asked for something more than answers from her.

She tried to ignore the strange impulse and explain what had led her to this moment—pinned against a truck by what had to be the sexiest man who'd ever had a hard-on for her. "I swear I haven't committed any crime. Although, if Dawson Barnes complains that he can't father children for a couple of weeks, then I'll argue it was self-defense. And I'm sorry that I kicked you and hit you. I didn't mean to flake out like that." She squeezed her eyes shut and sent up a quick prayer. She might have really gotten herself into some trouble here. "Are you hurt?"

Laughter danced against her ear and vibrated from his body into hers. "By a little bundle of dynamite like you?"

"Is that a yes or no?"

"Relax." His lips brushed against her nape as he pushed her hair out of his face. "I'll heal."

"You're sure?"

"I'm fine." He exhaled slowly, tickling the fine hairs on the back of her neck. A riot of goose bumps rose on her skin, despite the heat from his jacket and body. "Now. If I set you down, nice and easy, will you tell me your name?"

No. No name. Alexandra Morgan was a failure when it came to men. And she was feeling something, wanting something so badly with this man that she didn't want to blow it. Maybe anonymity would give her a safety net, confidence she normally lacked. And maybe a man with no preconceived notions of who she was, a man who saw her as a desirable woman and nothing more or less, could give Alex what she wanted—a chance to be a normal, sexual, cherished woman.

Even if it was only for one night. Or one hour.

Or one kiss.

"Just like you said, Detective," she finally answered. "It's *Trouble*."

"I believe that. Okay, so no names. Are you flirting with me, Miss Trouble?"

"Would that be a crime?"

"Depends on if you're playing me or if this is really going somewhere."

Alex breathed out the last of her doubts. She might not know exactly what she was doing, but she understood exactly what she wanted. "I don't like playing games."

"Then this is definitely going somewhere." He let go with one arm to feather his fingers into her hair and lift the curling strands to his nose. "You smell so good. Like gardenias carried on a distant breeze."

Alex's breath locked in her throat as the atmosphere around them grew heavy. This man could read a grocery list and make it sound sexy in that voice. A compliment like that was pure poetry.

"You…smell good, too," she whispered. Ugh. Not so poetic. What was she supposed to say?

But the words didn't matter. He angled his head and pressed a hot, openmouthed kiss against the nape of her neck.

Her startled gasp tensed through her body. But when she exhaled, any surprise flowed away and settled with a purr of contentment in her throat. "That was…nice. Better than nice. I didn't know there was a bundle of nerves back there."

"You like that?" he whispered, warming the same spot with his tongue.

She trembled. Nodded.

"You want me to stop?"

They were strangers. She was needy. He was willing. And he was being so…patient. Such a gentleman. And yet, this gentleman's erection was nestled in the seam of her bottom, telling her she wasn't the only one interested in exploring whatever was happening between them. It was damn crazy to want a man so badly. A stranger, no less. But when had an opportunity like this ever landed in her lap? Or rather, when had *she* ever landed in Detective Opportunity's lap?

"Don't stop."

He nibbled the sensitive spot on her neck gently, making her jerk in his arms. Then he worked his way down her spine to the collar of his jacket, discovering nerve after nerve that leaped to life beneath his warm, moist touch.

Alex squirmed between the man and truck, trying to free her hands to grab on to something to steady herself—to try to take part in the embrace. But all she managed to do was work her dress up even higher—exposing more bottom, more damp, slick heat that desperately wanted to feel the press of his leg again.

"Careful," he warned. His arm constricted around her ribcage. His fingers clenched in her hair, pulling slightly at her scalp. But the pinpricks of pain quickly blended in with the pleasure of his moan vibrating against her skin, his teeth nipping at the taut muscle where her neck and shoulder joined. His thumb inched higher, testing the weight of one breast, hooking around the taut nipple that strained against the band of her dress. He flicked the tender nub once, twice, a third time, forcing Alex's mouth open in a gasp of need and want that matched his own. "I'm not getting my signals mixed up, am I, Trouble? Tell me what you want. It's yours. Or tell me to stop."

She'd come to Nashville, expecting to learn a thing or two about this man-woman mystery that other women her age seemed to enjoy. She was looking for the *good* part of sexual experience that had been frightened out of her by a cruel act, denied her by a small town that would never let her forget her mistake. She'd thought she'd failed in her quest.

Maybe she'd just been looking for that experience with the wrong man.

"I want you to kiss me again. Really kiss me."

Her request seemed to open up a throttle, turbocharging the leisurely, languid connection between them. Without ever letting her feet hit the ground, he turned her—using the truck and the friction of her curves bunching against his harder angles to keep her suspended in the air and aligned against him in a way that was sending every red blood cell in her body charging hard into the tips of her aching breasts and down to her full, weeping center. And then he kissed her. And kissed her. His kisses consumed her.

His jacket fell away from her shoulders as her fingers crept around his neck, then raked up the back of his head, tugging his short, silky hair into her greedy grasp. His tongue reached into her mouth, caught hers in a twist and pulled it between his lips for a light nip between his teeth.

Alex returned the bold move, his groan of approval matching the restless cries in her throat. There was nothing soft about this meeting of lips, nothing reticent about the deep, ragged breaths that moved their bodies against each other. He slid one hand down to her bottom, slipped his fingers beneath the elastic band of the cotton and squeezed, branding her, skin to skin. Alex hooked her heel behind his thigh, instinctively opening her body to the hard, thrusting need of his. The truck rocked as he pushed his body closer, drove his tongue deeper.

A wolfish whistle from the entrance to the alley was the first glitch in Alex's mindless need to fulfill tonight's quest. A familiar panic button tried to break through the haze of passion. She should reconsider this impulsive encounter.

But the dectective had other ideas.

"Stay with me, sweetheart." He kissed away her doubts, turned and carried her to the cab of his truck. With an uncere-monious shifting of grips and digging into pockets, he unlocked the door, opened it and dumped her inside. "Move over," he commanded. As soon as Alex scooted backward across the bench seat, he started the engine and took off. "We need some privacy."

His growly pronouncement spoke not only of his need, but reassured a bone-deep fear inside Alex that this was a good choice. That *he* was a good choice. This man would save the night—he'd save her lovelife—for her.

Alex held on tight as they jerked around corners and sped on a straightaway. Then they squealed through a parking lot and swerved into an alley where the neon lights and music and crowds of Broadway couldn't reach. About the time she'd worked her arms into the sleeves of his jacket and had pulled her dress down to a relatively modest level, he stomped on the brake, killed the engine and turned to her.

"You still game?" he asked. The glow from the dashboard shadowed the rugged lines of his face, but his eyes reflected a need, an intent, that rivaled her own.

Alex reached for him. "Yes."

As he wrapped his arm behind her back and laid her down on the seat, the truck plunged into darkness.

Perfect.

For a brief moment, his shadow loomed over her. But Alex felt excitement, not fear. She felt his palms on her thighs, his thumbs sliding up beneath the elastic of her panties. The heady weight of his body pressed her down into the upholstery as he sought out her bruised, swollen mouth for a tender kiss. "I can't believe I'm making out in my truck like some kind of randy teenager." His beard stubble abraded the underside of her chin. His kiss followed. He blazed a trail down her neck, arousing, soothing. "God, I need this, sweetheart. I need this."

And then, there really wasn't much talking.

Driven by instincts, directed by his responsive moans, sometimes guided by the instruction of his hands and mouth, Alex became more powerful, more certain of herself, more demanding.

He pushed the jacket off her shoulders. The straps of the dress followed. The strapless bra offered no resistance. When he closed his mouth over the throbbing peak of her breast, she moaned. When he blew softly across the damp tip, she twisted. And when he pulled the straining nipple into his mouth and suckled her with the rasp of his tongue she bucked beneath him.

Her fingers flexed convulsively in his hair, wanting to pull him closer, wanting to share his attentions with the other breast. As frantic as they'd been outside his truck, he seemed to be taking his own sweet time transforming her into a heavy, quivering, raw nerve of pure desire. He brushed his rough jaw over the other nipple in a caress that made her cry out, yet savor the healing touch of his tongue against her all the more.

She wasn't sure which happened first, the mindless panting or the fist of pressure building up between her thighs. She snatched at his T-shirt, tugged it from his belt as his kisses moved lower. She was desperate to touch the warm skin and the hard muscles underneath, but he moved beyond her reach. She was sitting half upright again, leaning up against the door. He shoved her dress up and kissed her belly, nuzzled her belly button, traced the sensible waistband of her panties with his chin, making muscles clench and stretch and contract. Before she could steady herself, his hand was inside her panties, cupping her bottom, lifting her to drag the underwear completely down her legs and toss them to the floorboards.

And then he was back, his kisses moving lower still. He brushed his lips through the thatch of golden curls and pressed a kiss to the swollen mound beneath. Alex dug her fingers into his shoulders and heard him laugh. The sound vibrated against her inner thigh.

"Easy, sweetheart." He stroked his thumbs along the seams where her legs joined her hips, each stroke getting longer, opening her wider and taking him closer to her slick, pulsating center. "I'm just thinking about how good you smell. All over."

Back home in Dahlia, she would have frozen up at the wanton intimacy of their position. She would have second-guessed. She never could have relaxed enough, felt safe enough, to lose her inhibitions like this. She would have failed to know and give pleasure.

But this wasn't Dahlia, she reasoned. She wasn't Alex Morgan, pariah of gossip turned extreme tomboy. Tonight, she was this man's mystery woman. And she was all woman—all whole, sexually confident woman.

"What are you waiting for?" she gasped into the darkness. And then she tunneled her fingers into his hair and pulled his mouth against her.

Alex's head fell back and she cried out almost instantaneously as he ran his tongue between her folds and thrust inside her. Wave after wave of sensation rolled down to her core and blossomed back like shock waves through her body. He gently bit down against the hard nub, stroked his thumb along her aching crevice, kissed her and licked her and made her come again and again with just his mouth. Alex bucked and moaned and clutched him against her, her body weeping at the newfound experience of having a man bring her to orgasm.

When he was done, when she was spent, he pulled away,

crawling up over her body to reclaim her mouth in a full, deep kiss. She inhaled her own release on his skin, tasted it on her tongue. Alex Morgan had never had a night like this. "You're good."

She felt him smile against her lips. "I kind of got that idea. Thanks."

But she wasn't done. She pushed against his chest. "Your turn."

He gave her one last kiss and pulled away. "You're sure?"

"You'll have to arrest me to stop me."

He pulled off his badge and gun and set them on the dashboard.

While she hurriedly redressed, he gingerly dropped one foot to the floor and stretched his other leg out behind her, opening himself up just as she'd offered herself to him. His deep voice coaxed her across the seat. "However you want."

Alex curled her legs beneath her and scooted closer. The jerk of his leg when she braced her hand against his knee told her he might be as primed for this forbidden encounter as she'd been. "Do you have protection?"

"Shit." She'd take that as a no.

But not as a *never mind*. Alex slid her hand along his thigh, crawling closer, massaging away any noble instinct to stop her wandering hands. His shoulders were broad enough, near enough, to blot out any light from her vision. But her sense of touch worked just fine. She palmed him through his jeans and she heard the creak of leather where he squeezed the seat back in his fist.

Interesting. Alex's pulse kicked up a notch in anticipation. Maybe there were other ways to feel the strength of her femininity that had nothing to do with her own release. She rubbed her palm down the length of his zipper and traced the seam of denim that ran between his legs. He groaned. "There are ways, right? Safe ones?" she asked.

His deep breath stirred the hair beside her ear. "Don't you know?"

All the innuendoes over the years didn't mean she knew what

she was doing. But she was a quick study when given the chance. She dragged her hand up, tracing the same path. "I'm learning."

His shoulders rose and fell in the shadows. "You weren't a virgin. Were you?"

Unfortunately, no. That honor had been stolen from her long ago, trampled on, laughed away as meaningless.

Tonight had meaning. Alex pressed her fingers to his lips, easing his distress as well as her own. "Shh. Enough about me. Talk me through this."

"You are one serious package of trouble, aren't you." He made it sound like a good kind of trouble. An irresistible kind of trouble. He pulled her fingers from his lips and guided her hand down to join the other one. For several moments, he simply cupped her hands over the bulge in his jeans and rocked against her. Her breathing quickened along with his. And then he gave her a command. "Unzip me. Careful. That's it."

The trembling of her fingers lessened with each hint of praise or pleasure. She unhooked his belt buckle, slid the zipper gently downward. He shifted slightly to help her ease his jeans off his hips. She smiled at the bright white cotton that poked through the opening they'd created.

Plain white cotton? A kindred spirit. The detective *was* the right man for the job tonight.

"Pull it out." She did as he asked, stroking his length through the tight tent of cotton, then reaching inside to capture the hot, pulsing hardness of him in her hand. "Oh, yeah." His hand tightened around her wrist, holding her still while he thrust inside her grip. The moisture at the tip caught in her palm and smoothed the friction between them. With a gasp that sounded like a tight breath through clenched teeth, he released her. "You do it. Just like that. Don't stop."

While Alex slid her hand from tip to base and back again, he framed her face with his hands, sifting his fingers into her hair, holding her as tenderly as he'd been firm with her a moment ago.

"I want to kiss you," he whispered at the corner of her mouth. "I can't seem to get enough of kissing you."

And then he seized her mouth with the same vigor that Alex used on him. She braced her hand against his shoulder and worked him as his tongue thrust into her mouth. The harder he kissed, the firmer her touch. He went deeper; she stroked harder. He gentled the brush of his lips across hers; she lightly teased the ridge of skin beneath him.

He was pulsing, throbbing, driving into her grip, mimicking the same rhythm with his tongue in her mouth. As she continued to caress his silken length, something deep inside Alex began to pulse in response. He moaned into her mouth, reached down and wrapped his fingers around hers, squeezing tightly as he came up off the seat and pushed himself one last, long time into her hand.

The power of his release triggered an answering satisfaction in her own body and Alex collapsed against him. For several long, timeless minutes, he wrapped his arms around her and she burrowed against his chest, marveling at the warmth, the exhaustion, the contentment she felt.

No encounter had ever been like this for her. She felt safe. Satisfied. Serenely pleased with herself and grateful to this man. Her night in Nashville had turned out to be a success, after all.

As she became aware of the soft, patternless lines he was tracing against her back, Alex noticed the time on his dashboard clock: 2:14 a.m. Her brother would be worried about her by now, her father up, pacing the living room, trying to decide whether to call the sheriff or get into his own car and drive into Nashville to search for her.

And with those concerns, the first frissons of worry marred her contentment.

"Restless?" the detective asked.

Alex pushed away from the tempting haven of his chest and slid back to her side of the seat. She pulled his jacket more tightly around her, but couldn't seem to ward off the chill of

reality that had wormed its way into her thoughts. "I'm just remembering that I'm stranded, that I don't have any way to get
home or even call there."

He sat up straight, pulling up his jeans and tucking everything
back into place. He reached for his gun and badge. "I'll take you."

"No." Alex shot her hand out to touch his wrist. An armed man
would hardly reassure her father and brother. She pulled away
just as quickly, distracted by the warmth of his skin. "I don't
usually do anything like this."

"Neither do I." The gun and badge found their place on his
belt. He started the engine. "I haven't had an enounter like
this…for a while."

He fastened his seat belt, and while Alex did the same, he
shifted into reverse and backed out of the alley.

Alex tucked her tangled hair behind her ears. "An encounter
sounds like a clandestine rendezvous. Like we were supposed to
meet. I'm…"

He checked for traffic and pulled onto the street. "You're what?"

"Confused."

"Join the club."

"Yeah, but you're…older."

"So I've been told." The lights from the street and other cars
let her read the hard expression that deepened the lines on his
face. "Doesn't mean I've got women all figured out."

Her laugh sounded more like a snort. Yeah, she was a real
femme fatale. Not. At least not outside that alley. "I sure don't
have men figured out."

"I'm not going to apologize for what happened."

"I don't want you to." The old Alex's doubts were quickly re-
sufacing. "I know we didn't do…everything. But, you enjoyed
it, didn't you?"

"Hell yeah, sweetheart. I enjoyed it a little too much."

Alex frowned. "You can enjoy it too much?"

He swore and Alex jerked in her seat. "There are rules and

regulations to life. To my job. I think I've broken about every last damn one of them with you tonight."

"I'm sorry."

He headed up a hill, picking up speed. "Don't be sorry. Be mad. Get that lawyer of yours and sue me."

"Why?"

"I was supposed to be rescuing a damsel in distress, not gettin' my rocks off with her. You can report me for that. In fact, I'll give you the form to fill out and introduce you to the officer where you can file a complaint against me."

After a moment's hesitation, she smiled. "I don't have any complaints. No one's ever called me a damsel in distress before. That's kind of girly, isn't it?"

"I suppose." She didn't understand the 180 degree shifts in his mood from hero of the hour to angry cop, but she had a feeling she was going to be okay. "So, milady—will you let me drive you to precinct headquarters before something worse than me happens to you?"

He maneuvered them smoothly through the late-night traffic and pedestrians. "Is that where we're going?"

"Yeah."

"And you're not arresting me?"

"I'm the one who screwed up tonight, not you. Here." He pulled out his cell phone and handed it across the seat to her. "The call's on me." He stopped at an intersection and watched her punch in a number. "Contacting a friend? Family? That lawyer of yours?"

Alex smiled, feeling extraordinarily relieved and comforted by the simple gift of a phone call. "All of the above. My big brother. He'll come get me."

"Tell him to meet you at the downtown precinct station."

She slid a glance across the seat to her knight in shining armor while she waited for Nick to answer. "You won't tell my brother what we did tonight, will you?"

He scoffed. "If you don't tell my deputy chief."

Nick Morgan picked up after the second ring. "Alex? You okay? I saw Buell and his buddies yukking it up at the track tonight, and I couldn't help but think… I called your cell a dozen times. You've got me scared shitless here."

"I'm okay." The truck slowed and turned into a parking garage. "My date with Drew's friend didn't go as well as I expected. And I lost my purse."

Her brother swore. She could hear her father in the background now, asking questions. "She's okay, Dad." Nick explained a few details to their father, George Morgan, then turned his attention back to the phone. "You're not hurt?"

She'd been embarrassed, angry, frustrated and a little afraid before this smoky-haired detective had literally picked her up off the street. But she hadn't been hurt. "I'm okay, Nick. I met…" Detective Galahad was watching her, hanging on to every word. "Nashville PD has been very helpful." In ways that made her blush and turn away. "Just come get me, okay? I'm at the downtown precinct station."

"I'll be there in forty minutes. I love you, Shrimp."

"I love you too, Nick."

They were parked beneath the precinct offices by the time she handed the phone back to the detective.

"Thank you." She offered him a hesitant smile. "Big brother will save the day."

He nodded. "So now I know this infamous lawyer-slash-wonder-brother of yours is Nick. You ever gonna tell me your name?"

"Look, Detective…" She unfastened her seat belt and reached for the exit handle. "Don't get me wrong, I enjoyed tonight, but…"

She laughed. It was a sad sound, really—a sound that revealed just how much this *encounter* had been an aberration for her, for both of them, perhaps.

"This isn't reality. Let's forget the names so we can skip the embarrassment of you mentioning tonight to anybody who happens to know anybody I happen to know. Okay?"

"Okay. Your call. Tonight never happened."

So why did it hurt that he'd agreed so easily to her request?

# *3*

---

"MMM. YEAH. RIGHT THERE."

Alexandra Morgan caught her tongue between parched lips as her thoughts drifted away from the fan belt she stretched between her hands and took note of how the fender of the '94 Buick she was repairing pressed against the juncture of her thighs. A pocket of pressure was gathering where hard steel met soft woman, fueled by an errant fantasy that seemed to keep cropping up at the most inopportune times.

Normally, she relegated her secret fantasies to the privacy of her bedroom or one of her late-night bubble baths where she washed away the grime of a day spent in the family garage where she worked as a mechanic. But this was a routine fix on a slow day, just maintenance stuff for a local customer. The real excitement of her job wouldn't start until tomorrow or Thursday, when the drag racers who frequented the Dahlia Speedway across the parking lot started showing up for replacement parts and tune-ups in preparation for the regular weekend races.

In other words, Alex was bored. And when she was bored, her mind wandered. Wandering into something as pleasant as her fabricated forbidden affair with the big-city cop with the wide shoulders and hushed, seductive words was a welcome respite from the grief and anger over her brother Nick's recent death that normally filled her head these days.

Outside the open doors of Morgan & Son's Garage, the afternoon air was heavy with the promise of a spring rain. Maybe the green scents of budding trees and flower blossoms hanging in the mist and dappling her bare arms with moisture had reminded her subconscious mind of those bubble baths where a cop with stormy gray eyes had had his way with her time and again in an assortment of imaginary story lines.

Her imagination took her to places far removed from tense, worrisome reality.

*"You like that, milady?" her knight in shining armor drawled, sliding his hand between her legs and cupping her warmth.*

*"Yes," she moaned, closing her eyes against the pleasure of his strong hand reaching into the water and rubbing against her clit. "Please don't stop."*

*"Ah, my damsel is in distress, is she?" Broad shoulders filled her vision as he bent over her to gentle her soft cries with a kiss. "You don't have to beg with me."*

*Her diaphanous bathing gown floated in the water, its sheer material hiding nothing from his eyes. The smoky gray orbs lazily looked their fill, each visual caress like the stroke of his hand on her body.*

*He was unlike the other men in her kingdom. This one came from a far-off country. He served her willingly, while the treacherous knights of her own kingdom were not allowed to touch her. Her mystery knight, the Silver Fox, spoke in hushed, seductive tones. He ruled his own lands with an iron fist but always treated her as nothing less than a lady.*

*"Will you join me, good sir?"*

*"You only had to ask." His tunic and breeches became a taut black T-shirt and jeans as he peeled off his clothes and slipped into the tub with her. Water sloshed over the sides and she laughed as his big frame displaced all the bubbles. Alex's thighs clenched*

*together when he wrapped his viselike arm around her waist and pulled her onto his lap. A well-honed warrior, he'd fought many battles. But each evening he returned to her chamber to take her in any number of ways. Tonight's seduction was to be slow and sensuous. And merciless, she thought with a gasp of pleasure, as the bulging evidence of his arousal poked against her bottom.*

"Milady should never have to beg for pleasure."

*He kissed the back of her neck as he palmed her breasts. His big hands lifted them and kneaded them with a gently urgent reverence—like the patient, mature man he was, not some grabby, greedy teen who could earn ten bucks on a bet if he touched them.*

Teen? Eeuw. Reality tried to nudge its way in and mess with her fantasy.

Alex squeezed the humiliating memory from her mind and tried to *feel* the hardness of the grown man pressed against her.

*"You don't think I'm common, do you?"*

*"You talk too much, milady. Let me show you my appreciation."* No. She smiled wickedly. This time she'd show him. She *spread her thighs slightly, boldly catching his arousal and squeezing it.* "Alexandra…"

How did he know her name? *That was one of the rules between them. No names. Ever. She squeezed him again, gently punishing him for forgetting.*

Alex squirmed in his lap, *guiding him closer and closer to where she wanted him to be. Inside her.*

"Alexandra…" No names. *She adjusted herself over him. He moved beneath her. This time they'd come together. He wanted it, too. She was a lady.* His *lady. The kingdom need never doubt her fine qualities again.*

*The pressure was building. The water on their skin—lapping between them, surrounding them—simmered with heat. Their heat.*

"Alexandra…"

Someone was shouting her name.

But not in passion.

"Alexandra Morgan!"

Alex jerked at the drill-sergeant shout, bumping her head on the open hood of the Buick. "Ow. Damn." She slid off her perch on the fender and tugged her tool belt back into place, embarrassed to think that an errant monkey wrench and a tan sedan had triggered one of her stupid fantasies.

"Daddy?" Alex rubbed at the sore spot beneath the yellow bandanna wrapped on top of her head, clearing her brain of naughty thoughts and ignoring the male laughter coming from underneath the car in the next bay. She quickly scanned the length of the garage, from the lube pit to the office hallway door, trying to account for each of the employees who hadn't gone on lunch break yet. No one had seen her squirming on top of the car, had they?

But she had bigger problems.

"Alexandra!" Her father's deep, booming voice—as crisp and quick as his military stride—announced she was in trouble. Again.

The door to his office slammed, jolting through Alex's body with dread. "Oh, no. He found it."

"Found what?" Winston "Tater" Rawls, a longtime employee of the garage and the closest thing to a big brother she had now that Nick was gone, rolled out from under a Ford hybrid in the next bay. "What'd you do this time, Alex?"

She grabbed a rag off her tool chest and wiped her hands, mentally shaking her head at the lanky blond goofball's question. "I was thinking for myself again."

He made a tsk-tsk sound behind his teeth. "That'll teach you. I think I'll just listen to the fireworks from here, if you don't mind."

"Thanks for having my back, Tater." Sarcasm dripped from her voice.

"Anytime." He rolled back beneath the Ford, his laugh echoing from under the chassis. "Anytime."

Alex dashed toward the exit leading to the business offices. She made it all the way around the sedan before the stale smells of body odor and cigarette smoke stopped her in her tracks. *Not now.*

She tipped her chin to the black-haired mechanic who blocked her path. Artie Buell was nothing if not persistent. Of course, she wished he'd also learn how to wash his stained coveralls, use a little less gel in his hair, and take no for an answer.

Using his tongue, he rolled a toothpick from one side of his mouth to the other with a suggestive swipe. "I'll watch your back, Alex," he drawled. "You need me to smooth over anything between you and your daddy, I'm your man."

Right. Ever since their sophomore year of high school, when dating his older brother hadn't worked out so well for her, he'd tried to be *her man*. She'd grown up, moved away and learned to dream of bigger things than small-town stereotypes. She'd come home again because her father and brother had needed someone to manage their home and feed them. She couldn't cook as well as she could fix a car. She couldn't sew or garden as well as she could grow a business. But she loved the men who'd been her only family from the time she was a toddler, and for right now—especially now that Nick was gone—she'd be whatever her father needed her to be.

Artie Buell, however, hadn't changed a bit in nine years. If he wasn't such a good mechanic—and the sheriff's son—she'd have raised a stink about him working here. But she had her own reasons for wanting to stay on the Buell family's good side now. The truth might depend upon their cooperation. And for that reason alone, she summoned a smile. "I can handle my dad just fine. Thanks."

"I think I impressed him when I won the Moonshine Run last month." Damn. The polite chit-chat wasn't over. Alex froze her smile into place and endured. "You know, I didn't see you at that race. I kind of thought you might want to root a friend on, especially seeing as how I rebuilt most of that car right here in your daddy's garage. Remember I ran some of those last-minute calibrations by you?"

"Sure. I'm glad they helped. Gotta go."

When she would have scooted around him, Artie's hand snaked out to grab her arm and halt her beside him. "You should have at least helped me celebrate at the party afterwards."

Working with Artie was one thing. Anything more personal would be like reliving a nightmare. *Keep it nice.* "I told you I was busy that weekend. Congratulations again, though." She tugged against his grip. "Dad's waiting."

Instead of releasing her, he pulled her close enough that she got a whiff of the cigarettes on his breath when he leaned down to whisper. "You haven't even been down to the pit to see my trophy. It's a bigun."

Right. Like she'd ever venture down into that sunken room that reminded her of a burial chamber unless she had a damn good—work-related—reason to do so. The fact that it was Artie's main work space at the garage probably added to the eerie claustrophobia she got whenever she went down there. "A bigun? That's a pretty lame line, even for you."

"C'mon, Alex. I'm not the bad guy in the family. Remember?"

"Artie." Tater was out from underneath the Ford again. This time, he wasn't laughing. "I thought I asked you to get the specs for this car off the computer for me."

Artie winked one dark eye at Alex but spoke to Tater. "I got 'em."

"Then move it."

"I'm movin'."

When he pulled the printouts from his pocket and released her to deliver them, Alex glanced down at her forearm. She didn't know which bothered her more, his grimy fingers on her skin, or the memory of another Buell's touch. Both turned her stomach.

"Alexandra!"

The steel door connecting the garage to the office corridor swung open. Alex jumped as her father's barrel-chested physique filled the doorway.

For a moment, his stern green eyes looked beyond her into the garage. "Get to work, Artie. I need you back down in the lube pit to change the oil on Jeb Worth's car before he stops by at one to pick it up. I don't pay you to stand around and flirt with my daughter."

"Yes, sir."

As Artie handed off the papers to Tater and both men returned to the cars they were working on, Alex hurried on over and greeted her father's ruddy expression with a wry smile. "Thanks for the rescue, Daddy."

But Staff Sergeant George Montgomery Morgan, USMC, Ret., didn't smile back. Instead, he waved a bill at her face. "What is this? What new scheme are you cooking up now? You know I don't like surprises. I told you I wanted to be cautious about expenditures now that the Fisks are selling the track to Whip Davis."

Alex's relief came out as an embarrassing snort. Thank heaven. He hadn't found the papers she'd taken from Nick's things, after all. She stuffed the shop rag into the back pocket of her baggy denim overalls, using the moment to compose her thoughts before she gave away what she'd been working so hard to hide. "I thought something serious had happened."

"This *is* serious," he groused.

"Right. The money. Of course, it is." She should have known her father wouldn't go snooping through her personal things. But if he'd found the stash of notes she'd been sorting through regarding her brother's death, he'd be in a whole new world of hurt. She'd worried and confounded him enough over the years. Not enough of a lady. No husband. No man. She knew he didn't blame her for their trouble with the Buells, but still, it had to be disappointing for him to know how Artie's older brother had forever changed her view of men and relationships. Causing her father more pain was the last thing she wanted. In fact, she was doing her best to help her father climb out of the emotional pit he was already trapped in by investigating the truth behind Nick Morgan's car crash.

Artie's father had declared it a tragic accident—said Nick had probably fallen asleep at the wheel and careened off the country highway into the bottom of a ravine. Maybe she was grasping at straws, but Alex had seen two sets of tread marks on the muddy shoulder before winter rains had washed the evidence away that night. *"Somebody probably stopped there to see if they could help him,"* the sheriff had suggested. So how did he explain away the twin sets of skid marks on the road near the crash site? Sleeping drivers didn't slam on their brakes. And what was the likelihood of a second driver laying tread in the same exact location?

Sheriff Buell had come up with many plausible scenarios to explain away Nick's death, but Alex wasn't buying them. The rain hadn't started until after the crash that January night. The family business was taking care of cars, for God's sake, and Nick's had been in top-notch condition. Nick had raced at the speedway before heading to law school. He knew how to handle a car. Knew how to handle any road condition. The crash made no sense. His death made even less.

Though George Morgan seemed to accept walking through life with his son in the ground and his heart buried there beside him, Alex wasn't ready to let this town deal her another cruel blow. Especially not when, in Nick's last phone call before his accident, he'd told her that he'd be missing their traditional New Year's Eve game night because he was working on something for the state attorney general's office—and that that *something* could have serious consequences if the wrong people found out what he was up to.

*"Wrong people?"* she asked. *"Here in Dahlia? Who?"*

*Nick laughed at her curiosity and ignored her concern. "Don't worry, Shrimp. It's just some paperwork I need to finish up. Boring stuff. I'm afraid you'll have to find someone else to play that marathon game of RISK with this time. But I'll be looking for a rematch next year. Okay?"*

*"Okay. I'll give Dad the message. Happy New Year, Nick. I love you."*

*"Love you, too, Shrimp."*

The next time she saw her brother was at the county morgue. That night Alex had wept with her father and vowed to uncover how *boring paperwork* could get a good man killed.

But right now she had to deal with whatever current crisis she'd brought into her father's world. "Is there a problem?"

"A five-hundred-dollar problem." He smacked the paper with his hand. "I appreciate you stepping up to help with the business side of things now that—" Alex's heart twisted at the hesitation "—now that Nick isn't here. But the racing season has only been going for a couple of months. I don't want to be spending money we may need to see us through the rest of the year."

Alex reached out and wrapped her fingers around her father's fist where he clenched it at his side, holding on until the tension in him began to relax. When he turned his hand and squeezed hers in return, Alex knew he was going to be all right. For now. Her secret was safe. Suspicious bills she could argue—suspicions about Nick's death she could not. Not until she had something more to back them up with, at any rate.

"This doesn't have anything to do with the Fisks or Mr. Worth or changes at the speedway. You're afraid I'm going to screw something else up. But I've really thought this through, Dad." Alex pointed out the letterhead on the paper. "The Nelson Racing Team is making a name for themselves on the circuit. Skyler Nelson won the Missouri Flats in 4.89, running with an LSX 427 iron block motor. Exactly what we specialize in building. If he puts our name on his car, just think of the advertising. Our business could grow exponentially. We might have to open a second garage."

"I suppose you'd want to manage it?"

Why not? Nick had been the lawyer. *She* was the one with the business sense. "During my internship my senior year at Tennessee, I worked in that auto parts store in Knoxville. In six months' time, my business plan saved a struggling business and helped put them in the black."

Her father scratched his fingers over the top of his silvering crewcut, gradually transforming from the grizzly bear who'd stormed into the garage into the gruff teddy bear who might love her, but who rarely understood her. "I'm not interested in opening another garage or going nationwide. We have a thriving business right now, right here in Dahlia, growing as attendance at the track grows. I hope we'll continue to turn a profit once the speedway changes hands, but during this transition time, I can't guarantee what kind of cash flow I'm going to have. I want to see how things pan out with Davis managing things before I start dipping into our cash reserves."

Alex used his perfunctory explanation as an opportunity to steer the conversation away from anything remotely personal. "What about sponsoring a local driver, then?"

"This is five-hundred dollars out of our budget already. And you want to spend more?"

"We have to spend money to make money, Dad. We need to sponsor a car, not just service the cars whenever the driver needs something. If we hook up with a big name and he or she is successful, then we'll be successful." Oops. Open mouth, insert foot. Retreat to the brig. "I mean, we'll *continue* to be successful and you won't have to worry about our future, no matter who's running the speedway."

But his eyes shuttered and the debate was over. Her father drew back his shoulders, silently reminding her that it was his experience and own two hands that had started this business twenty-two years ago. Nick and Alex's mother had died and George Morgan—former chief mechanic at the Camp LeJeune motor pool—had left the marines to settle in one spot and raise them. The garage had been built from a small military pension and big dreams. "My decision stands. I can absorb this bill. Just don't surprise me with any more new ideas." He reached out and tapped the point of her chin in a gesture he'd used as far back as she could remember. "Okay?"

But Alex wasn't Daddy's little girl anymore. When he opened

the door to the office corridor, she followed right behind him. "Drew Fisk and his father and grandfather have poured a lot of money into the speedway to bring it up to code, modernize the track and add the amenities that racers and fans want nowadays." Her father's sigh told her she wasn't making any headway, but he held the door to his office open for her and let her keep talking. "Those upgrades brought in the Farron Fuels Racing Series, and Dahlia is turning into a booming little town again. We can do the same—increase our promotional budget, sponsor a team and take advantage of the influx of business and money."

He swiveled his leather chair forward, pointing to the door as he sat behind his big walnut desk. "I want to be careful about who we sponsor and where our logo shows up, honey. Remember, it's my name on this company."

Alex's hands fisted at her hips when she glanced back at the red-and-white logo painted on the safety glass. Morgan & *Son*'s Garage. It was a sad reminder of dashed hopes—for her father, and for herself. That sadness painted her voice when she turned back to face him. "It's *my* name, too."

"Ah, honey, I didn't mean…" A powerful engine gunned outside the front of the garage, loud enough to be heard in the interior offices. But George Morgan ignored the potential customer and reached for his daughter's hand, pulling her closer as he sat on the corner of his desk. "I didn't mean you aren't an important part of this family. Or this business. Or that it hasn't meant the world to me to have you close by these past few months. It's just…"

"Dad—"

"Let me say this." He grasped both her hands now, and Alex willingly held tight to his strong grip, wishing she knew the right words or actions to ease the pain that deepened the grooves beside his eyes and mouth. She couldn't be hurting any more than he was. "I had it in my head all these years that Nick would be taking over the garage and running it with me one day. Even when he became a lawyer, he always found a way to stay involved." He brushed his knuckles beneath her chin, and Alex did her best to summon a smile for him. "You've always been my little tomboy. But I hoped you'd grow up to be a fine lady like your mama was. I guess I'm still hoping to see you in a dress, with a good man at your side and little ones running around your feet."

Work boots, overalls and dirty hands hardly lived up to that legacy. "I'm sorry, Daddy. I've tried. I just don't seem to have much success when it comes to being that lady you want." Besides the fact she'd been raised by a marine, and hadn't had much feminine influence growing up, most of the eligible men of Dahlia—like Artie Buell—didn't see her as much of a lady. One man had created the lies about her being a teenage tramp, but it took the well-oiled gears of small-town gossip to perpetuate them. "But I do know my way around cars and business. I'm good at this. Please give my ideas a little thought, okay?"

He leaned in and pressed a kiss to her forehead. "I'll think about it, honey. I promise. In the meantime, just run it by me first before you spend five-hundred dollars on anything besides car parts. Okay?"

Not exactly a victory. But Alex wrapped her arms around his neck and hugged him tight, anyway. "Okay."

A sharp knock on the door ended the father-daughter moment. George stood as Alex pulled away.

"You two open for business?"

"Well, look who's here. Drew Fisk." George reached out with a smile. "Where have you been keeping yourself, son? You weren't at the track during last weekend's races."

Alex tilted her head to welcome the blond-haired man in the tailored blue suit and white dress shirt. As usual, the tie was long gone. "Hey, Drew."

"Alex." He winked by way of acknowledgment and reached

in front of her to shake her father's hand. "George. How're y'all doing? I've been in and out of town, taking care of business."

"For your father and grandfather? How are they?"

"Fine. Dad's in India, trying to work out an agreement to build an aluminum fabrication plant there like the one we have here. Grandfather is as cantankerous and crusty as ever."

"I can't imagine him slowing down, even now that he's retired."

"He seems to keep his nose in everybody's business, for sure." Drew turned his attention to Alex, his bright blue gaze traveling up and down her body, appreciating her curves in the same way he had from the day he'd realized his best friend's younger sister had sprouted breasts, and was no longer just a tagalong for his adventures with Nick. "Alex. You're looking as pretty as that spring day outside."

"And you're full of it," she scoffed, burying her dirty hands deep in her pockets. Though he used that same smooth BS on every female, it was nonetheless good to see an old family friend again. She smiled, knowing he liked talking about his cars almost as much as she liked working on them. "I thought I heard a seven liter V8 engine driving up. Did you get that new sports car you were bragging about?"

"I did." He arched a golden brow in a devilish smile. "As I recall, somebody here wanted to know how the engine runs on one of those. Care to find out for yourself? It's clouding up outside, but we can take it for a spin before the storm hits."

Alex shrugged, appreciating the invitation, but knowing she had too much on her plate right now to have time to fritter away. "I've got Mrs. Stillwell's Buick out in the shop that I need to finish."

She felt her father's hand in the middle of her back, nudging her toward Drew. "I'll put Artie or Tater on it. I think I can spare you for a half hour or so."

"But Dad, I—"

"Go. With his grandfather selling the track, Drew might not be around quite so often. Better seize the moment, as they say."

His hopeless matchmaking wasn't obvious, was it? She had responsibilities here. "Oh, by the way, honey." He reached back across his desk and picked up a pink slip of paper. "I took a phone message for you. From a Daniel Rutledge?"

*Dan Rutledge?* As in Nick's friend from the state attorney general's office Dan Rutledge? The man whom Nick had been going to see that awful night? Alex snatched the memo from her father's hand, her fingers trembling. "Thanks."

"He a friend of yours?" her father asked, no doubt hoping for news of a decent man in her life.

"I've never met him." Technically, that wasn't a lie. She only knew Daniel Rutledge through Nick's notes and a series of phone messages and e-mail inquiries she'd asked him to return. Alex stuffed the note into her pocket. "I guess I'll have to call him to see who he is and find out what he wants."

She couldn't reassure her father with a better answer than that? Especially with a mixture of excitement and fear that was no doubt stamped all over her face. Did Rutledge have suspicions about Nick's death, too? Answers for her? Alex lowered her head, feeling her cheeks steam with her lousy cover-up.

Fortunately, her father was perplexed enough by the mystery to miss her reaction. "The name's familiar. Wasn't he a friend of Nick's back in school? Did you ever know him, Drew?"

Drew shook his head. "Must be from law school. Nick and I lost touch for a couple of years when Grandfather sent me off to Princeton to finish my education."

"I hope he wasn't looking for Nick." George sank back onto the corner of the desk. "Maybe he doesn't know about the accident, and he was trying to reach him. Oh, hell. Somebody else I didn't tell."

"Daddy?" Alex reached out, but he was already drifting away from her, shrinking back into the distant shadow of the man he'd been before grief had ravaged him. "I'll take care of it. Don't worry."

George Morgan barely nodded. Tears burned behind Alex's

eyelids. Some son of a bitch was going to pay for what they'd done to this man. "Daddy?"

A long arm wrapped around her waist and pulled her into the hallway. "Let's give him his privacy." Drew closed the door softly behind them and turned her against his chest for a hug, pressing her nose into the scent of designer cologne at the open collar of his shirt. "He'll be all right, Alex. Give him some space."

When she felt his lips brushing against her temple, she pushed away. "No. I want to fix this."

"You can't."

"Watch me."

"Alex." His familiar, indulgent smile stopped her from retreating across the hall into her own office. "I miss Nick, too. I thought he and I would be a team forever. You can't make your father's hurt go away for him. You have to let him grieve."

"In my head, I know you're right. But…" Drew Fisk was no fantasy knight in shining armor. But he was a friend, and he drove a fast car. And right now, Alex needed some speed to drown out the frustrations roiling inside her. She mustered up an answering smile. "Maybe I could use a little fresh air, after all. Give me a few minutes to find Tater to tell him I'm leaving. Start your engine, Drew. I'll be right there."

# 4

Jack Riley leaned back against the wall at the Headlights Ice House, a bustling food and drink establishment where picnic tables and stacked crates formed eating areas that were anything but private. The lights were bright, the noise was loud, but with thunder rumbling in the night sky outside, it offered a warm, dry place where a man could fill his belly and get a crash course in who was who in Dahlia, Tennessee.

Stretching his long legs out across the bench seat of his table, he took a long swig from his second bottle of beer.

He'd come here to catch a criminal. Or two. Or six. Or however many sons of bitches it took to stop the flow of drugs and money that he'd traced from Nashville back to this deceptively innocent spot on the map.

Located about thirty miles east of Nashville, Dahlia had once been home to plantations, horse breeding and tobacco. According to his current investigation, Dahlia had nearly died during the Great Depression. But one of its founding families, the Fisks, had built the Dahlia Speedway in the 1960s, and the town was reborn. Now, instead of racing thoroughbreds, they raced cars.

The Chevy Camaro he'd been working on since he was a teenager—a lifetime ago, it seemed—was Jack's ticket into town. Secured in the trailer he was hauling behind his pickup, the modified street car would qualify him as an entrant in the track's Outlaw 10.5 Division Drag Racing Series.

He needed to become a part of the track.

He needed to become a part of this town.

Because someone here had murdered his partner.

When Lorenzo Vaughn had agreed to reveal his source for the drugs he'd sold in Nashville, in exchange for a reduced sentence, a fatal chain of events had been set into motion.

Vaughn had sent Jack and Eric to a chop shop. The business of tearing down racing cars from across the country and selling parts on the black market had also been a front for the even more dangerous business of smuggling heroin and other drugs inside some of the vehicles. But by the time the task force moved in to make an arrest, the business had closed up and moved its location. To ferret out the new distribution center and the men behind the drug import scheme, Eric had gone in undercover as a buyer looking to make a purchase. He'd stayed with the job, perfected the role of a new dealer in town, worked his way up through the hierarchy of thugs and lieutenants to the men in charge of the operation—who made him as a cop and had him gunned down in the street. Whoever was running the Dahlia-Nashville smuggling connection was going to pay.

The cop bleeding out on the pavement three months ago could have been Jack. Should have been Jack. He had no wife to grieve over him, no children in shock, no family left in ruins.

Eric had started this investigation.

Now Jack was going to finish the job.

He was going to find the drugs. Find the smugglers.

He was going to find Eric's killer.

Despite plenty of hotshots on the force who could drive their cars fast, Jack had volunteered for this undercover assignment himself. He could drive. Billington was still gunning for his record on the police academy driving course, but Jack had the experience. He knew the S.O.P. (Standard Operating Procedures) of the drug game—when to step on somebody, when to make nice, when to duck for cover. A young stud like Billington wouldn't have the patience for the nuances of undercover work. Besides, this assignment was personal. For almost twenty years, his partner's family had been *his* family. Nobody hurt one of his own without there being hell to pay.

According to an Internet search, the name Jack Riley was almost as common as John Smith. With thousands of Jacks to blend in with, no personal link to Dahlia, and the driving experience to back up the role he had to play, he'd decided to simply become a civilian version of himself—Black Jack Riley, an over-the-hill racer staging a comeback.

He was here to find out who was shipping the drugs and how it was being done without the local cops and track officials putting a stop to it. They were either unaware of the problem or they were unwilling to deal with it.

But Jack would.

And if he found the Glock 9 mm that had taken his partner's life, as well, in this hamlet, then the owner would be taking a trip with him back to Nashville.

He intended to get *this* job done. And done right.

*Son of a bitch.* Jack squeezed his fist around the neck of his beer bottle and weathered the punch of grief and anger that hit him in the gut as he remembered his partner's children weeping, and the weight of Eric's casket on his shoulder as he helped carry him to his grave. *Double-ass son of a bitch!*

Jack tipped the bottle and let the tang of the icy liquid slide down his throat, forgetting for a moment how important it was to bury his emotions and keep his wits about him. It was the key to any undercover operation. Especially one as personal as this. Eyes open. Be tough.

He eased his death grip on the bottle and set it back on the table. He wouldn't fail Eric Mesner because he couldn't keep his emotions in check.

"You ready for another one, big boy?"

Jack turned his gaze to the waitress who'd shown up at his table. She smacked her gum a little too loud, wore her blue-jean skirt a little too tight, but her friendly smile was just right.

Jack smiled back. He remembered her introduction when she'd first taken his order. "Sandy, is it?"

"You bet." *Smack.* Smile. She propped a hand on her hip and nodded toward his drink. "How many can a big fella like you hold?"

Draining the bottle must have been the cue she'd been looking for to come back to his table. Though she didn't appear to be much over thirty, Sandy walked and talked as if she'd been a fixture at this place for years. She was probably a good source of information about the town and its residents. At the very least, she was a friendly face. The service had been as good as the food. He'd remember to leave her a big tip. "One more, at least."

"Comin' right up."

As she cleared the bottle and headed for the kitchen, Jack heard a slurred voice from next table over. "Hey, Sandy—ain't you gonna ask me how much I can hold?"

Hoots and laughter from the drunk's table applauded his clever come-on.

Jack glanced over to see a man palm the waitress's butt. She swatted away the offending hand with a laugh. "The problem with you, Hank, is that you *can't* hold your liquor."

The stained cuticles on Hank's fingers marked him as a man who worked with his hands. "Maybe I wasn't talkin' drinks."

"Honey, you are nothin' *but* talk." The laughter turned to oohs and verbal jabs and more laughter, deriding Hank's failure to score points with the lady. "Why don't you run along home before you get yourself into trouble, Hank. You've had enough."

"Now Sandy, you aren't shooing us all out, are you?" A short man with a shaved head, wearing a jacket that matched the silver Fisk Racing jacket that handsy Hank wore, draped his arm around the awestruck brunette sitting beside. "As far as I'm concerned, this party's just getting started."

Most likely a "drag hag," a woman fan of drag racing who followed the circuit to get close to her favorite driver or top mechanic, the brunette curled her body into Baldy's. "I'll go home with you anytime you're ready, Jimbo." She trailed her finger over the dome of Jimbo's head. "You just say the word and I'm yours."

Jack's beer soured in his mouth at the shameless invitation. Give him sass and fire over that coy crap anytime. Like the blond mystery woman who'd turned him inside out that night in Nashville—and had haunted his most erotic dreams ever since.

*Don't go there.* With a ruthless denial of any distracting emotions, Jack forced his thoughts to the job at hand. He'd do a damn sight better by his partner if he concentrated on figuring out all the players at the track in Dahlia. Starting with Hank and Jimbo and the crew at the next table.

Jack looked back in time to see Jimbo break off a liplock with the brunette. Then he pointed across the table to Hank. "Now that's how you get a woman in line."

"Shut up," Hank drawled. He tucked his fingers into the waitress's pocket and tugged her back to his side. "Come on, Sandy. You and me. We've been dancing this dance for years now. When are you gonna give in?"

"When are you gonna grow up?"

"Burn." The youngest man at the table, a ringer for Hank with his black hair and downhome drawl, had his cell phone out. But he wasn't so busy texting that he couldn't trade a high five with Jimbo. "She nailed you, big brother."

Hank didn't miss a beat. "No. *Nailed* is what she wants me to do to her. Ain't that right, Sandy?"

The table erupted with laughter. Even the fourth team member sitting with them, a silent giant with a full beard, joined in. The quiet redhead cozied up next to him giggled. Another fan from the track, no doubt.

Jack sat up a little straighter, appalled, but not surprised, by the crude innuendoes. Those boys and their babes had probably won big at the races, and were drinking their way through the celebration. Something had given them plenty of profit to allow them to set a stack of bills on the table, bold as brass. They were showing off their momentary wealth to the other patrons and making sure everyone in the restaurant noticed that they were the big men in town.

Jack noticed. It might just be pay day for the locals. But he'd seen the same kind of behavior working undercover in the drug world. Show the world that you were top dog, and nobody messed with you. Hank and Jimbo, Text Boy and the big guy were all going on Jack's list of possible suspects.

As the laughter waned, Sandy deftly slipped away as though she'd had plenty of practice avoiding that table already. "Down, boys. I'll bring you all a cup of hot coffee."

"Don't tease me, woman. I don't want coffee." Hank nearly fell off his bench seat, shouting after her. "Unless you're gonna put a little of that sugar in it."

Jack admired the waitress for ignoring the taunt. He relaxed back against the brick wall, feeling confident that she had enough experience to take care of herself. Besides, the noisy table with the Fisk Racing team wasn't the only group he needed to assess.

As his eyes swept the room from his corner table, he knew he'd made a good choice in stopping here for drinks and dinner. The perfectly grilled burger and the generous slice of home-baked apple pie he'd eaten were only partly responsible for the mental pat on the back he gave himself. Even for a Tuesday night, the joint was hopping. If he wanted a quick introduction to the town, he'd come to the right place. The clientele here at Headlights provided a clear cross-section of the people who lived in and moved through Dahlia.

Besides the crew from the track, there were yuppies at another picnic table. Still wearing their suits despite ditching their ties and high heels, they sipped margaritas and discussed art galleries and business investments.

But most of the place was filled by locals dressed in jeans and other casual work clothes. With one obnoxiously tipsy exception, they were more subdued—probably feeling at home, relaxed, and therefore they had nothing to prove. He saw everything from Southern belle housewives with proper, pretty dresses and proper, pretty children, to farmers and factory men. There was a table of silver-haired retirees, probably all descendants of Dahlia's founding fathers.

Then he took note of a final table, with two men wearing tan shirts and brown slacks. He didn't need to see the badges on their shirt fronts or the wide-brimmed felt hats with the plastic rain covers hanging off the corners of the table to know that they were the law in this town. He pegged the fiftysomething man with the slicked-back hair and evidence of a growing pudge as the one in charge. The younger man would be his deputy.

Jack imagined the balance of customers would shift come the weekend, when the drag races were in full swing at the track, and the number of visitors to the town tripled or quadrupled. Then he'd see more drivers sporting their sponsor's ball caps and jackets. More women, following their favorite drivers.

The faded black ball cap on the table beside him winked at Jack. Nashville Paint & Glass wasn't a racing sponsor so much as a secret tribute to Eric. Jack and Eric had coached Eric's son and his middle-school baseball team to a city championship a few years back. Now the cap was more than a prop in his quest to find the drug runners in Dahlia. Like an ever present conscience sitting on his shoulder, that cap represented Eric, and the justice Jack was determined to find here.

SMACK. JACK GRINNED as he heard the waitress's approach. "Here you go. Enjoy." She served his beer and carried her tray to the next table. "And here's your coffee."

For a few seconds, Jack toyed with his drink, running his fingers up and down the cold glass, catching the icy condensation with his fingertips. He preferred the feeling of soft, warm skin beneath his hands, but ever since Rosie had left him—with the exception of one amazing, unexpected encounter in a Nashville back alley—he'd been without a woman.

It wasn't the eight months of celibacy he minded so much. After all, when the right woman came along, he'd be primed and ready and it'd be worth the wait for both of them. His nostrils flared as he inhaled to soothe the tightness that suddenly constricted his chest. There'd been too many times these past weeks when he'd been crazy with anger and grief, and had longed to bury himself deep inside the heat and solace of some sweet, willing woman, and escape into a night of passion.

He'd even cruised the late-night streets of downtown Nashville, wondering if he should pick up a woman at one of the honky tonks, or even pay one for a night of nameless, mindless sex. In the end, he'd gone home alone and eased his frustrations in other ways. Maybe it was the cop in him, hating the idea of victimizing a woman or breaking the law for his own pleasure. Or maybe it was just the fact that no one had piqued more than a passing interest.

Not one woman had awakened his senses or jump-started his hormones the way one had that crazy night when he'd run into a tiny blonde with too much makeup, too few clothes and a mouth that wouldn't quit.

That night he'd been twenty again. He'd felt strong. Whole. Hell, the way she'd responded to him had made Jack feel like some kind of Don Juan superhero. But with no name, a protective big brother with a law degree and a truckload of guilt over how he'd bent the rules with her, Jack knew the passion of that hour they'd spent together wouldn't be repeated.

No more real to him than a pinup girl or celebrity, green-eyed Trouble should have been filed away with the embarrassing mistakes of his past that he knew better than to repeat. Because, all these months later, even the memory of her scent and those curves and that mouth could still make his blood simmer with want when he shouldn't be thinking about anything except his investigation.

"Hank." A smack—not gum, but hand against hand—startled Jack from his thoughts and drew his attention back to his surroundings.

"Five'll get you ten that you're gonna strike out again, big brother."

"Shut up."

"Artie, don't egg him on." The waitress was having trouble at the next table. "I said to keep your hands to yourself, or I'll have Eddie come out from the kitchen and put you in your place."

"Come on, Sandy. Eddie's busy cookin' right now." Hank was nothing if not persistent. Jack dropped his feet to the floor and sat up straight, trying to determine if the waitress's expression reflected annoyance or fear. "It's Tuesday night. What are we gonna do for fun if you don't help us out?"

"Drink your coffee." When she turned to walk away, Hank's hand latched on to the hem of her skirt and pulled her back to the table. She swatted at his grip. "Damn it, Hank. Let go. Your father's sittin' right over there."

Hank laughed. "He knows that boys will be boys."

Jack glanced across the room to see if the sheriff would intervene, what passed for law enforcement in this town seemed more interested in carving up the chicken-fried steak on his plate.

Jack fought the urge to flash his badge and haul the drunk to jail. But he couldn't do that without blowing his cover. Now, Hank's entourage was daring him to make good on his attempted conquest. Hank obliged by pulling the waitress onto his lap. She shoved his lips away from her cheek and pushed to her feet.

The sheriff still wasn't moving. Jack squirmed inside his skin. But only for a moment. Experience had taught him to think before he acted. He wanted to make a place for himself in this town? Show them who wasn't to be messed with? Here was an opportunity. He'd ordered the third beer, knowing he wasn't going to drink it. It was all for show, to establish his reputation in Dahlia. A hard-drinking man didn't stop with two beers. And a hard-livin' man didn't walk away from a fight.

He rose from his seat, setting his beer bottle down with a thud as he stood. "The lady said, 'hands off.'"

"Lady?" Hank smirked as he turned to see who'd spoken. "All I see is Sandy Larabie standin' here."

"I don't know if you're too stupid or too drunk to understand." Jack moved out from behind his table. He twisted Hank's wrist, hitting a pressure point with his thumb and forcing the other man's grip to pop open. "Get your hands off her."

Jimbo pulled his arm from the brunette's shoulders, and slid a warning glance to the big guy. Artie snapped his phone shut. "Mister, what are you doin'?"

Hank's watery eyes blinked as though trying to bring Jack's face into focus. "Who the hell are you, stickin' your nose into my business?"

Jack released him and the drunk rubbed at what were most likely numb fingers. "Give them their check, Sandy. These boys are ready to go home."

Hank shot to his feet, rattling the mugs before he got his legs free of the picnic table. "I'll leave when I'm damn well good and ready to leave."

The waitress tugged at Jack's sleeve. "Mister, you don't have to stick up for me. I've dealt with him before."

"Well, apparently, he didn't get the message."

"You lousy son of a—"

It happened fast. A woman shrieked. There was a stream of curses. A plate shattered. Hank cocked his arm back and took a swing. The man was big and stocky enough that he could have done some damage, but Jack was sober. He ducked beneath the unsteady blow and came back up, clamping his fingers like a horseshoe around Hank's neck and driving him back against the wall.

"Mister—!" Sandy warned.

He knew Hank's buddies were back there, ready to pounce on him from behind. Jack was years past coming out on top in a four-on-one fight. Still, a cover was a cover—

"Now, now, boys. What's goin' on here?" a deep, slightly nasal voice drawled behind him.

"Hank's drunk and won't keep his hands to himself, Henry." Sandy was quick to position herself between Jack and the sheriff. "This gentleman stepped in to defend my honor."

With Hank thrashing harmlessly at arm's length like a fish on a hook, Jack looked back over his shoulder to meet the sheriff's dark eyes. With his napkin still tucked in at his neck, he didn't look like much of a threat. But the deputy standing behind him had his hand resting on his gun, ready to provide some serious backup if this little introduction to the fine folks of Dahlia got out of control.

Time to cement his role as the new bad boy in town and snag the attention of whomever the real bad boys might be. He gave Hank one more shake for good measure. "I was just clarifying a few things for Mr. Grabass, Sheriff. Since no one else here seemed to want to stop him."

The sheriff hooked his thumbs into his gun belt and assumed a smarter-than-you-think good ol' boy pose. "You let him go now, son." Son? Suspecting he was closer to the sheriff's age than to Hank's, Jack was amused enough to comply.

Hank dropped to his feet, rubbing his collarbone and nursing his pride. "Ain't you gonna arrest him for assaulting me?" He turned to his friends for help. "You saw. He started it."

The sheriff pulled his napkin from his shirt and dabbed at his lips. "Hank, you pay your bill and scoot along home with your buddies. Artie, you drive. I don't want no accidents."

"But Dad—"

*Dad?*

"Now, Hank. I'm not in the mood to argue with either one of you boys."

The young men grinched and grumbled, but with a pair of

"yes, sirs," they snatched up their money from the table and left. When Jack moved to do the same, the sheriff stepped into his path. "I don't know you, friend. You passing through?"

Yep, he was earning himself a reputation, all right.

"I'm here to race at the track," Jack answered. "I'm not looking for trouble. It just seems to find me sometimes."

"I see." The sheriff turned to the waitress and smiled. "You get on back to work now, Sandy. You okay?"

"Sure, Henry." She smiled up at Jack. "Thanks."

"No problem."

As Jack went back to his table to retrieve his cap, the sheriff turned to the curious onlookers who'd come out from the kitchen or were staring from tables across the restaurant and announced, "There's nothing to see here, folks. Eddie, you go on back to your grill. The rest of you enjoy your drinks and dinner."

Sandy was right behind Jack when he turned around. "Mister, uh—?"

"Riley. Black Jack Riley."

She reached out to shake his hand. "Well, Black Jack Riley. You always have a friend here." She gave Sheriff Pudge a less friendly look before smiling at Jack again. "Good luck at the races."

As she set about cleaning up the mess at Hank and Artie's table, Jack placed money on his table and turned to leave. But the sheriff blocked his path. "Mr. Riley? I'm Henry Buell, sheriff here in Dahlia." He gestured toward the front door. "Since you're going to be around for a while, we need to have a talk."

He headed back to his table where he dropped off his napkin and picked up his hat and a yellow rain slicker, expecting Jack to follow.

So Sheriff Buell wouldn't lift a finger to stop the sexual harassment of one of his citizens—or discipline his own sons—but he was ready to lay down the law to a complete stranger. That might explain a lot about the illegal drug trafficking going in and out of his county. Jack scratched nitwit off his list. Henry Buell's dark eyes were too sharp to miss much. That meant he was either a coward who turned the other way, or he was on the take.

Neither of those options gave Jack much comfort.

Jack wove his way through the tables and followed the sheriff out the door. The spring storm had ebbed into a steady rain that dripped from the brim of his cap and quickly soaked through the cotton of the black T-shirt he wore.

Though he was working his investigation in cooperation with the state police, they, along with NPD, had left it to his discretion as to when and how much information he would share with local authorities. Thus far, he wasn't inclined to talk about his suspicions with Buell, so the need to maintain his badass persona was more important than respecting the uniform at the moment.

In a subtle show of defiance, Jack ducked his head and jogged across the parking lot to his truck. After unlocking the cab, he pulled out his black leather jacket and shrugged into it. When Jack was good and ready, he shoved his hands into his pockets and faced off against the older man. "Like Sandy said, Sheriff, I was defending her honor. I wasn't looking to cause any trouble."

"It's not the first time my Hank couldn't hold his liquor. I imagine he'll go home and sleep it off." He strolled along the length of Jack's truck and charcoal-gray trailer. "I haven't seen you on the circuit. Where have you been racing?"

"I haven't for a while." Jack let Buell check out his license plate numbers before giving his well-rehearsed story. "I ran into some trouble a few years back and had to get out. Turned forty this year—decided I wanted to make one last run for a title before I give up the dream. I heard Dahlia was a good place to get my wheels back under me until I can hit the big-money races again."

The sheriff paused a few feet away, giving Jack the same careful once-over he'd given his rig. "Dahlia's starting to get some big money. The way we used to. Drew Fisk took over running the track from his daddy, and has really been turning the place around."

"Fisk? As in Fisk Racing?"

"Yep. The Fisks are selling it now. But to good people who know their stuff. You heard of Whip Davis? He used to be crew chief for Corley Motors."

"I've heard of Corley Motors." The track was changing hands? Transition and new ownership tended to make people with something to hide nervous. Maybe he'd better order a complete listing of track employees and investors, and see who was scrambling to save money or a job.

"Davis is settling down in Dahlia now. Hooked up with Cardin Worth, daughter of the folks who own this fine establishment." The sheriff thumbed over his shoulder at the restaurant behind him. "You mark my word. The speedway's making a comeback. I don't know what kind of trouble you're talking about, but as long as you keep your nose clean, you can make a comeback here, too."

"Thanks, Sheriff." Jack shifted his boots on the gravelly asphalt, giving the false impression that he was relaxing his guard now that Buell had given him permission to stay. "Say, you know a place where I can store my Chevy while I'm working on it? I can sleep in my truck, but I want my baby to stay someplace safe and dry."

Buell grinned and pointed down the highway. "Morgan's Garage. Out by the track. For a fair price, he rents out space where racers can work on their cars while they're in town. He's got a spare room out there you can sleep in for a few dollars more. They'll be up working late tonight."

"Sounds perfect. Thanks." Ready for the conversation to be over, Jack climbed in behind the wheel and started his truck.

When Buell tapped on Jack's door, he rolled down his window to hear what the older man had to say. "Mr. Riley? One more thing."

"Yeah?"

"I like to keep things peaceful in my town. I don't put up with troublemakers. You watch yourself. Because I'll be watching you." Buell tipped his hat, dripping water down the sleeve of his raincoat. "Evening, now."

Jack turned on his lights and the windshield wipers, clearing away the rain and his less-than-friendly first impression of Dahlia, Tennessee. He was definitely running this op without Henry Buell's help.

Jack pulled out of the Headlights parking lot and turned toward the speedway.

He pulled his cell phone from his belt and punched in a number, keeping his eye on the dark road out of town as the call picked up. "Daniel? I'm in. The local sheriff has already promised to keep an eye on me, so I think my cover is set. If there's any action in this town, the players will come looking for me to see what I'm about. I've even got a lead on a bunk right next to the speedway, so I'll be able to get in there and check it out after hours."

"Sounds good, Jack." Daniel Rutledge, his temporary boss at the state attorney general's office was younger than Jack, but the ambitious attorney seemed to have a good grasp of the details of the case, and had no problem keeping the joint operation between NPD and his organized crime investigation team running smoothly. He was probably gunning for a big promotion, or even a state office, once they solved this case and could make the news public. Rutledge could take the credit for it, as far as Jack was concerned—as long as this drug pipeline was shut down and Eric's killer was behind bars. "I'll report your progress to the task force at tomorrow's briefing."

"We're going to get these bastards. I promise."

"I believe you. Just keep your head down and don't blow your cover."

"I will."

"When you need backup, call. I know you think I'm nothing more than a paper pusher, but I know how to rally the troops. Keep me posted."

"I'll call in tomorrow at the regular time."

He heard an uncharacteristic hesitation in Rutledge's voice. "Jack? I know this is personal for you."

"Yeah?"

"Don't let anger over your partner's death keep you from thinking straight. I've already lost a good man trying to bring this crew down. I don't want to lose another."

"I'll get the job done."

A few minutes after disconnecting the call, Jack pulled into the parking lot at the track. Though the dashboard clock said it was half past nine, there was enough illumination from the security lights for him to see the three-story tall white skyboxes and viewing stands rising above the cracked brick walls that formed an entrance arch into the track. Driving past the main gate, Jack familiarized himself with the layout. Tomorrow, he'd get inside and start snooping around the offices, pits and control tower.

He pulled up to a steel-gray building adjoining the track. "Morgan and Son's Garage." He read the sign over what looked like an office entrance out loud. That part of the business was dark. But with eight garage doors—one standing open with light and the loud strains of Toby Keith pouring out—he knew he'd reached his destination. "Look out, Dahlia."

Big Black Jack Riley had come to town.

# 5
—————

"DAMN IT, PICK UP," Alex whispered into her cell phone, her free ear plugged with a finger to drown out the music from the garage.

*Give me a break, already.* She got up and closed her office door, pacing as she waited through a third and fourth ring.

Drew Fisk, Tater, Artie and a couple other friends from the racing crew Drew sponsored had the radio cranked up for their impromptu party to celebrate Drew's latest acquisition. Not only had Drew spent his paycheck to buy the new Corvette, but he'd plunked down a huge chunk of change on a Mustang that had been fitted with a nitrous comp engine and rigged to race at the Outlaw series time trials this weekend.

Drew's "quick ride" had lasted until Alex was obliged to let him drive through one of the local fast-food joints to buy her a burger and fries for dinner. Tater had covered her at work, finishing up Mrs. Stillwell's car, and her father had seemed pleased rather than irritated to hear she'd spent the afternoon with Drew—as though his rebelliously single daughter had gone on some kind of date.

*Dream on, Daddy.*

Even with the drone of the Corvette's powerful motor humming through her body, Alex had grown impatient as the minutes ticked on. Shirking her workload was the last thing she needed to do if she wanted to prove to her father that she could be a viable partner in the family business. And it had taken far too long to find the privacy she needed to return Daniel Rutledge's call.

"…leave your message at the sound of the beep."

"Great. Just great." Alex stopped in front of the desk, her eyes fixing on a family picture of her and her father with Nick at his law school graduation. She shouldn't really have expected any kind of breakthrough with her amateur investigation into Nick's death, should she? Still, she'd hoped. *Beep.* "Mr. Rutledge. It's Alex Morgan, Nick's sister, again. We seem to be playing phone tag." She left her number and a request he return her call. "I really hope you can help me find some answers. I just want to know why Nick went to see you that night. Thanks."

Alex snapped her cell phone shut. She squeezed it in her fist and tapped it to her lips, as if she could maintain some kind of connection to her brother if she just held on hard enough. She stared at the photograph until the image blurred behind a veil of tears. Nick had been a six-foot tall, golden-haired, handsome son of a gun. Valedictorian. Cum laude graduate. He'd had a successful practice in Dahlia, aspirations to work for the State in Nashville. Women wanted to be with him. Men wanted to *be* him.

And he'd been her big brother. Nick had been there through the fiascos in high school. The gossip. The shame. He'd defended her honor and boosted her morale. He'd made staying in Dahlia not only possible, but bearable. She'd lived in the shadow of his charmed life and felt blessed to do so because she'd loved him. She missed him.

It didn't get any simpler—or more painful—than that.

A stinging swat on her rump jerked her from her grief.

Alex whirled around to attack the offending hand. "Damn it, Drew!" Recognizing her friend didn't ease her irritation. She hadn't heard the door open, hadn't heard him sneak up behind her. And she sure as hell didn't want to hear whatever excuse he had for startling her like that. She shoved him out of her personal space and tucked her phone into the top pocket of her overalls. "Don't you know what a closed door means?"

"Come on, Shrimp. What are you doing in here, hiding away

from the party? I'm beginning to think you like my cars better than you like me." Right now, she did. "You all right? Hell. Did that phone call upset you? Are you missing Nick?"

"I always miss Nick." She swiped the tears from her eyes and sashayed past him, burying the hurt and frustration deep inside and assuming the perky, one-of-the-guys role the good folks of Dahlia allowed her to play. "Come on. Show me this guaranteed-to-win car of yours."

"Hey, now." Drew reached for her hand, his tone contrite. "If you need some time—"

"I want to look at the damn car." Pulling her hand from his grip, Alex marched down the hall.

The spurt of temper that had added kick to her stride sputtered out when she stepped into the garage and saw the circle of men with beers and flasks gathered around Drew's cherry-red Mustang. Unexpectedly, she flashed back to being a teenager again. Back to that awful night when she first discovered what kind of hero her brother had been.

But the cold chill of remembered humiliation lasted for only a moment. Alex breathed in deeply, taking in the smells of pit grease and new car and testosterone. These were grown men, not boys. Members of Drew's racing team—all friends of hers from the track. While it was never a thrill to run into Artie Buell after hours, she was relieved to see that his older brother knew better than to show his face around here. Seeing a couple of women she didn't recognize, Alex figured this was a party that had moved from someplace else. The only things these guys were interested in tonight were getting laid by one of those sexy women in their tight jeans, and revving up the Mustang's engine.

Pulling her hands from her baggy overall pockets, Alex headed straight for the middle of the pack. "You know you can't fire up that motor inside the garage, right? Dad frowns upon collecting fumes and starting fires."

Her teasing reprimand garnered a round of laughter and a

taunt from Tater Rawls. "We all know *you're* the one who really wants to see how fast this car can go."

"You better watch yourselves, ladies," she said to the brunette hanging on to Jim DiMarco's arm, and the redhead sitting on a workbench next to the tall guy she knew only as Crank. "All these bozos think about is *go* and *go fast*. I think like an architect. I want to see how this thing is put together." Alex gave as good as she got, absorbing the chest-thumping and ribbing and job-related chatter she usually enjoyed with the men who worked around the track. She nodded to Tater. "Come on, let's open it up and see what kind of horsepower this thing's packin'."

She detached the pins locking the fiberglass hood down on her side, while Tater opened his side. Together, they lifted the hood and handed it down the line to the other men who set it aside and quickly returned to gawk at the shiny new setup that included every bell and whistle that money could buy.

Lacking the height of her fellow car nuts, Alex boosted herself up onto the fender and leaned over the motor for a closer inspection. Not for the first time, she wondered just how much money the heir to a real-estate and bauxite mining fortune had in his bank account. Andrew Fisk III had spared no expense to make this Outlaw racer state-of-the-art. The insides were still shiny and sludge free—as perfectly preserved as a museum piece. Maybe even a tad boring because, while the potential power of the motor was obvious, there was nothing for Alex to tinker with.

She was almost afraid to touch anything for fear of mussing it with a fingerprint. Still, she knew that Drew had gathered them all together for some oohing and ahhing over his newest toy. "That carburetor looks hand-built."

Jimbo and the brunette moved aside so that Drew could lean over the car beside her. "It has an LS7 carbureted intake—guaranteed to give me 460 horsepower, minimum. Can't do that with a fuel-injected engine. Artie ordered it in from Nashville for me."

"Is Artie heading up your pit crew this weekend?"

"Unless I can sweet-talk someone else into doing it." Drew butted his hip against hers in a nudge-nudge offer that indicated the job was hers if she wanted it. "Interested?"

"Hey!" Artie protested. "I did all the work putting this baby together, I should get the glory of taking care of her."

Alex twisted her mouth in disappointment. Artie was welcome to it. There wouldn't be much to do on this motor except dust it.

"You gonna be driving it, Drew, now that you won't be managing the track anymore?" Tater asked. "Or is Jimbo still your man?"

Drew slid away, straightening to address the query head-on. "I'm still managing the track until the sale's complete and Whip Davis takes over full-time. I've got everything prepped for this weekend's races—the PR's out, the vendors are lined up, the prize money is ready for each class. I've been a busy man this week."

"So who's driving?" Tater was less interested in Drew's workload than in the details on the 'Stang.

He wasn't alone.

A flurry of arguments and bribes to get behind the wheel stopped abruptly when a dark, familiar voice interrupted them from the open garage door.

"Is this a party? Or are you boys still open for business?"

*OH. MY. GOD.* Every muscle inside Alex froze from her fingertips to her toes.

That voice wasn't just familiar. It was *his*.

Her knight in shining armor. Fantasy Man.

Tater introduced himself. Answered questions about storage facilities and a room to rent. Alex didn't hear many of the actual words, but she felt the timbre of that voice rolling across her skin. Deeply. Slightly husky. All sexy.

She'd been living with *"Milady"* and *"How may I seduce you this evening?"* for months now. He probably wouldn't even recognize her in her metamorphosis from hooker to tomboy. But

Alex would never forget Detective Opportunity from that night in Nashville.

She slid off the fender, nearly landing on her butt until she could will her legs to support her.

"Will it be available for a couple of weeks?" The sexy detective could read a muffler warranty with that voice and turn her knees to putty. "Sounds like a fair price. I'll take it. And call me Jack."

"Hey, I know you." Artie invited himself into the conversation. "You're that big guy from Headlights."

"That's right. You get your brother home all right?"

"No thanks to you."

"You work here?" the detective asked.

"I'm crew chief for this car."

Moving beyond the steadying grasp of Drew's hand, Alex pushed her way to the front of the crowd and stepped up beside Tater.

That voice was no figment of her imagination.

The smoky cast of his short, crisp hair was hidden beneath a black ball cap. But the eyes were the same—steel-gray, revealing only what he wanted. The curtain of rain falling outside the open garage door behind him had plastered his jacket to his shoulders and his black T-shirt to his chest. He stood with his hands at his hips, his jacket pulled back. She quickly looked for the badge and gun she remembered so vividly.

Though she didn't immediately see them, the rest was the same. The taut, muscled body she'd rubbed herself shamelessly against. The stern, handsome lips that she'd demanded kisses from.

Alex squeezed her hands into fists. She was shaking.

His eyes skimmed over her and past her in a guarded, all-seeing scan of each man and woman in the room. Then, boom. His gaze swung back to her. Locked on. Narrowed. So much for not remembering. "Trouble?"

She crooked her mouth into a wry frown. "What are you doing here?"

"What are *you* doing here?"

"I run this garage with my dad."

"Morgan and *Son?*"

"Um…"

Drew came up behind her. "You know this guy, Alex?"

She nodded.

"Is he a friend of your dad's?"

Detective Opportunity was drifting closer. She tried to read the hard look in his eyes, tried to communicate her own silent message. *Do* not *tell them about Nashville.* Mistaken for a hooker. First orgasm. Willing hand job. Any one of those would wreck her determined effort to blend in as one of the guys in Dahlia.

Maybe silent communication wasn't the best way to do this. Maybe turning him around and sending him back to the big city was the only way to keep the past buried.

Alex moved out to meet him halfway. "What can I do for you, D—"

"Shut up."

"What?" A knight in shining armor would never… "Look, just because you carry a—"

"Not another word." Advancing. Closing in.

Alex tilted her chin. "I beg your—"

"For old times' sake."

"What old time—?" He palmed the back of her head, leaned over her and stopped up her mouth with a kiss.

With her fists wedged between them, he looped an arm behind her back and dragged her against his chest. He straightened, lifting her feet off the floor without breaking the kiss.

Alex protested in her throat, pushed against him, twisted her hips—tried to reclaim some measure of dignity and control. But the big brute wouldn't budge.

The rain had warmed against his skin, intensifying the scents of leather and musk that clung to him—that clung to her now as her own clothes soaked up the dampness of his. Their noses butted as he shifted into a different position, driving his lips against hers, filling her mouth with the faint tang of alcohol and lust. Something inside Alex shifted, as well. Surrendering to the assault on her senses, she opened her fists to dig her fingertips into soft, damp leather and held on for the ride.

This was not some polite, pleased-to-see-you, namby-pamby kiss. It was a full-blown, tongue in her mouth, take-no-prisoners, stake-his-claim kind of kiss that shocked Alex to her core, then revived her with a liquid-hot desire that surged through her veins and throbbed in the crush of her breasts and at the juncture of her thighs. Every female cell inside her screamed for something more.

Drew's buddies were whistling behind her, laughing. Tater scratched his chin. Drew stood beside him, staring at the passionate greeting with a blend of curiosity and disdain shading his expression.

And Alex?

She wound her arms around his neck and kissed him back.

JACK HUSTLED TROUBLE DOWN the hallway, away from the hoots and questions and protective posturing of the men in the garage behind them.

*That* was the best plan he could come up with to keep his cover intact? Kiss the woman into silence before she blabbed his real identity and blew his investigation? The ploy had worked. But now he had a whole new truckload of problems to deal with.

He knew his grip on her arm was a little too tight, his stride a little too long for her short legs to comfortably keep up with him. But he was frustrated, damn it. Frustrated that one wrong word from this pint-sized stick of dynamite could destroy his investigation and let Eric Mesner's killer go free. Frustrated that when he knew he should be chewing her out about refusing to take a hint or obey a command, he instead wanted to ask her why she'd melted in his arms and turned that kiss into a wildly frenetic public display of affection. Why hadn't she slapped his face instead of firing his libido into overdrive?

And what was the deal with the Huck Finn look? In Nashville, she'd gone for too much makeup and too little dress. Now, she'd clamped down those honey-gold curls beneath a yellow do-rag, killed the makeup, and put on a pair of tank tops and men's overalls that were big enough to make her curvaceous figure look like a sack of potatoes. The woman definitely needed some fashion advice. Plus a good dose of common sense.

And, she needed to stop throwing herself, full throttle, into a kiss like that. Made a man think that he had nothing more important to do than to make love to a willing woman all night long.

Jack pushed open the door where she'd led him and released her inside the spare, functional office. He nudged her toward the desk and closed the door behind him, muttering a curse when he discovered that the lock on it was broken. Fine. He'd just keep his voice to a whisper and pray that she could do the same.

"So…" He spun around to face her. "Now that we're thoroughly acquainted—for the second time—are you going to tell me your name?"

Her cheeks were still adorably flushed, but with her fists propped on her hips and emerald darts shooting from her eyes, he didn't think he needed to worry about kissing her again. "The next time you want to stick your tongue down my throat, maybe you'd better give me a little heads-up first."

"A name, Trouble."

"Alex Morgan. Alexandra."

Jack whipped his cap off his head and raked his fingers through his damp hair. "Hell. That screws everything up."

"Gee, thanks, it's good to see you, too. Now that I've been found out, are you going to tell me your name?"

"Jack Riley. Look, it's nothing personal, but I'm working an investigation. Undercover." He paced off the room in three strides. Then paced back. "You cannot tell any of those people—anyone in Dahlia—that I'm a cop."

She knocked aside the finger he pointed at her. "I won't if you don't tell them Nashville thinks I'm a hooker."

"I'm serious."

"So am I."

"I'm talking about my job."

"I'm talking about my life. I'm trying to gain some respect here. I'd never live that down in a small town."

"I'm trying to live, period."

Damn it. He was leaning over her again, moving in closer with every degree that she tilted that defiant chin. Moving in close enough to realize she smelled a hell of a lot prettier than he'd ever imagined Huck Finn had. No amount of grease or working under a hood or hanging out with the local party boys back in the garage could completely mask that subtle fragrance of gardenias and woman.

Or lessen his instinctive male reaction to it.

But he needed to douse the sparks that flared between them and have a cool, reasonable conversation with Alexandra Morgan.

Releasing a deep breath, Jack tugged his cap back on top of his head and quickly surveyed the room. Even if that door locked, the privacy of this office wasn't good enough for him.

He nodded to the Tennessee Titans windbreaker hanging from the coatrack beside the door. "Is that yours?"

"Yes."

Jack plucked it off the rack, shook it open and held the jacket up for her to slip into. "Come on."

She stared at the jacket, then glanced up at him as though she didn't understand what he wanted.

"Put it on. It's raining outside." He flicked the jacket like a matador's cape, waiting impatiently. Finally, she turned and slid her arms into the sleeves. Jack pulled it up over her shoulders, then grabbed her hand and reached for the doorknob. "You and I need to go for a ride."

He shouldn't have been surprised to feel her plant her feet and tug against him. "I don't need to do anything but damage control.

There are already at least two men out there calling my father and ruining his night with questions about the stranger who just assaulted his daughter."

"Assaulted?" He pushed the door shut again. "I didn't want you to say *detective*. Or *badge* or *cop*, Miss Chattermouth. Besides, I wasn't the only one liplocked back there."

"I…" The tugging stopped. Her gaze dropped to the middle of his chest and her cheeks flamed with color. Ha! *So much for taking the high road, sweetheart.*

He took advantage of her embarrassed silence and opened the door, checking for company before leading her out into the hall. "Not one word to those men until you and I have a private chat. You're not supposed to be a part of this. But now that you are, there are things you should know about the plan and rules you have to follow. I will not let you blow this for me."

Adjusting his grip to lace their fingers together, rather than looking like a caveman dragging his woman back to his lair, Jack pushed open the door to the garage and nudged her out ahead of him. A flurry of conversations stopped abruptly.

The tall blond guy in the suit signed off on a phone call and snapped his cell shut, stuffing it into his pocket as his eyes darted from Jack to Alex to the clasp of their hands and back to Jack. He must have made one of those warning phone calls to Alex's father.

"Everything okay, Alex?" The shaggy-haired mechanic who'd introduced himself as Tater Rawls stepped forward to block their exit. He ducked his head to make eye contact with the woman at Jack's side. "I mean, you do know this guy, right?"

She nodded. "I met him in Nashville." She turned her head to Jack's chest and muttered out the side of her mouth. "I can tell him that much, right? It's what your cap says."

Jack tugged on her hand. "We need to go."

"He's a little old for you, isn't he?"

Alex jerked her head to the left. "Drew!"

Suit boy was on his feet now, his hands in the air in a pose of surrender—as if he hadn't intended the dig in his words. "I'm just saying—you're not trying to replace Nick, are you? Looking for someone older, wiser in your life?"

"Don't say that." She surged forward, her cheeks flushed, her teeth practically bared. "This has nothing to do with Nick. No one could replace him. I'm with…Jack…because…"

Jack pulled her back to his side. She'd said plenty enough already. He did not need her defending him. Once that mouth got going, there was no telling what might slip out.

"I don't believe we've met." He held out his hand. "Black Jack Riley."

"Drew Fisk. Andrew Fisk the Third." Fisk's mouth curved into a friendly enough grin as he shook Jack's hand, but the name and title were meant to remind Jack of his place. "I didn't mean any offense by the age crack. Alex's late brother and I were friends from way back. I'm just looking out for her."

"Well, Andrew Fisk the Third, let's just say I'm old enough to know a good thing when I see it." He looped his arm around Alex's shoulders. "And this little lady is old enough to know her own mind." He turned to make sure everyone in the garage understood they were a couple. "Excuse us for a while, ladies and gentlemen. I'll be back another time to get to know the rest of you. But Alex and I have some catching up to do and we thought this reunion might go a little more smoothly without an audience."

Her body stiffened against him. The angle of her chin dropped a good forty-five degrees.

A smattering of nervous laughter from around the garage was quickly stifled by an arch look from Drew Fisk. What the hell? First she went off at the mention of her brother and now she was burrowing into his side?

Tater nodded. "I can understand that." He moved aside, tucking his hands into the pockets of his coveralls. "I'll probably head over to Headlights to check in on Sandy before they close. But you've got my number if you need anything, Alex." He glanced out at the low-hanging clouds that were still dumping rain on the asphalt surface of the parking lot. "Don't stay out too late in this mess, or your dad will really worry."

When Alex didn't immediately respond, Jack pulled her forward, keeping her on her feet when she stumbled. "She won't."

It was just as well that she'd finally run out of words. Until he could brief her on his investigation and drive home how vital it was that she play along, he wanted to keep her away from any potential suspects who'd be keeping a close eye on him, already.

Faking a relationship with Alex would probably get him into the inner circle at the track sooner, but using Alex as a cover would be a definite risk. Jack had eighteen years of experience and a dead partner to prepare him for the dangers of infiltrating a drug-smuggling operation. He didn't need a civilian novice endangering herself—and him—by letting the wrong word slip to the wrong person at the wrong time.

"Let's move it, Trouble." The parking lot lights were dim moons in the night sky above them as Jack urged Alex into a jog and dashed toward his truck and trailer.

When Jack stopped to unlock the passenger-side door, she pulled her hood up over her head and hugged her arms around her middle. "What's he doing here?"

Following her gaze, Jack noticed the beat-up black truck parked just outside the closed garage door at the end of the building.

Son of a bitch. Hank—the sheriff's son who got away with shit Jack would have tossed him into jail for—was sitting inside the truck. Talking on his cell phone. Sipping from a silver flask. Staring at them.

"You know him?" Jack asked.

"Hank Buell." Compared to her usual fire, her voice sounded dead. "He's part of Drew's crew, too. I imagine he's here to check out the new car. Why is he just sitting there?"

Jack would like to say Hank was waiting for the weather to let up. But after putting him in his place at the restaurant earlier,

Jack imagined there was something more sinister than the elements keeping him in his pickup, watching them, in the dark.

He opened the door and reached for Alex's hand. "Get in the truck."

But she scooted away from his helpful grasp to check out his trailer. "No. I'm not going to let him intimidate me."

"He intimidates—?"

"Hank and I have history."

"Well, Buell and I now have history. We had a run-in at dinner. I guess it's your friend Tater's girlfriend that Buell was hitting on. Hank couldn't control his hands, so I helped him."

"You rescued Sandy Larabie?"

He'd done what any man should have done.

"I stood up to a bully. If Hank's looking for a rematch, I don't want you caught in the middle of it."

But the seconds he took to check on Buell were the seconds she needed to unlatch the back of his trailer. "What are you driving?"

"Crazy woman." Jack looped his arm around her waist and pulled her out of the way as the metal doors swung open.

Just as quickly as he'd moved her to a safe distance, she was pushing his arm away, wiping the rain from her face and climbing up inside. She slipped between the wall and the car, caressing the Camaro's smooth lines and fading paint as she inspected it from tail-light to grill. "I'd love to see this baby in the daylight. And look under the hood. Is it vintage?"

Ouch. Any pride at her interest in the car was short-lived. Jack climbed into the trailer and dragged her back outside with him. "It was my high school car."

"Oops. Sorry."

He appreciated her deference to his age about as much as he appreciated the slap of cold rain on his face. Keeping one hand on her arm, Jack closed the doors and latched them shut. "It's not as bad as it seems," he mocked. "I've been replacing parts and keeping her in shape over the years. She may be showing signs of wear on the outside, but she's in primo condition under the hood where it counts."

The double entendre wasn't lost on her. "I said I was sorry."

"Just do what I ask and get in the truck." The slamming of a vehicle door diverted his attention back to the garage. "Buell's on the move."

A tiny orange glow briefly illuminated Buell's watching eyes as he sucked the last drag of his cigarette and flicked it out into the parking lot, plunging his expression into darkness before he turned toward the party going on inside the garage. Right. Nothing suspicious about that.

"I wouldn't worry too much about Hank. I mean, it's cool that you rode in to Sandy's rescue and all." This time, Alex let Jack guide her to the open truck door. "Creep though he might be, he won't try anything on his own. He has to have his crew behind him before he'll sprout any balls."

Beyond the frank language, Jack was impressed by what he'd bet was an accurate assessment of Buell's character. But he was more impressed by the potential danger of their situation. He'd been outnumbered by Hank and his posse at the restaurant—he'd be more than outnumbered here if all those men in the garage turned out to be friends, as well.

"You mean *crew* as in a bunch of his buddies inside your garage drinking beer and 'looking out for you'?"

"You think they would…? Oh." Her face blanched beneath the orange-ish glare from the parking lot lights. The potential danger must have finally sunk in. "Maybe we should leave."

"Wish I'd thought of that." Jack reached around her to brush away the moisture hitting the bench seat of his truck. "What's going on with you? It happened back in the garage, too. Somebody says the wrong thing and you go quiet instead of mouthing off— which I'm guessing is your usual modus operandi."

"Modus operandi?" The sass was back. "First you tell me to keep my mouth shut, and when I do, you think something's wrong."

It wasn't hard to figure out that the tough talk and boyish exterior was a defensive armor for Alex. But what she was hiding, he had no clue. If she wasn't going to talk about it, he'd have to let the mystery slide. For now. Not knowing all the facts could come back to bite him in the ass if there was a problem, but right now his first priority was ensuring that his cover was safe and that she didn't blow this case for him. "I'm here to race. That's the plan. Black Jack Riley is making his comeback at the Dahlia Speedway. All you have to do is play along."

"Have you ever raced before?"

He wrapped his hand around her elbow to help her inside. "Don't worry, Trouble. I know how to drive."

"Is that a yes or a no?"

"Will you just get in?"

She spun around in the triangle formed by the seat, the door and his body, and tipped her face up to the rain. "Who are you investigating? Is it Hank? Someone else?"

To hell with this. Jack cinched his fingers at her waist, ignored her startled gasp, and lifted her onto the seat. "Do you argue every damn thing a man says to you?"

He looked straight into eyes that were deep green and dart free. She'd propped a hand at the center of his chest to balance herself. She curled up a palmful of leather before answering. "Only when I don't understand or trust what he's saying. Or I don't think he's listening."

Jack's fingers splayed out over her hips, finding the womanly curves he remembered masked beneath the butch outfit. His gaze locked on the delicate pout of lips that begged to be kissed. Not in haste. Not in a rough burst of passion. Not because of some damn charade. But gently. With reassurance. He wanted to kiss Alexandra Morgan. Taste the rare moment of vulnerability that softened the lush pink bow of her mouth. He wanted to press his lips against hers and take his own sweet time exploring this softer, more feminine side to the woman.

He bent his head, drifting closer.

The second he felt the whisper of her breath caress his cheek, Jack pulled back. What the hell was he doing? He was supposed to be laying down the rules here, driving home the danger of the situation, not succumbing to the need to drive himself deep inside her.

Removing his hands from the lure of her body, he pried her fingers from his jacket and stepped back to close the door. He circled around the front of the truck and climbed behind the wheel, starting the engine and pulling away from the curious onlookers inside the garage before speaking. "I've heard everything you've said. It's what you're *not* saying that has me worried. I may not be wearing it, but I still have a badge. You don't trust me?"

Alex pulled off the windbreaker's hood and wiped the dampness from those distracting lips. "I don't know you well enough to answer that yet. I never even thought I'd see you again."

"Likewise."

"That's a bad thing, isn't it. Seeing me again?"

"It sure as hell complicates things. I'd planned this as a solo operation." He glanced across the seat at her, wondering at the methodical way she rubbed her hands together in her lap. Damn, this woman was a puzzle. After ensuring the lane was clear, he pulled out onto the highway. "There's not a boyfriend or fiancé I need to worry about, is there?"

She snorted. Charming. "Are you kidding?"

"Why would I kid about that?"

"At any time during our brief acquaintance, have I struck you as a woman who gets a lot of action in this town?"

A remembered encounter, with her hand on his dick in this very same truck, leaped to mind.

*"There are ways, right? Safe ones?"*

*"Don't you know?"*

*"I'm learning."*

She hadn't known about hand jobs or oral sex. Her natural instincts had been right on the money, but even that night, he could tell she hadn't had much experience.

But with that figure of hers? The full-body kisses? Jack swallowed hard, shifting gears and picking up enough speed to divert his attention away from his crotch. Of course, she did have that whole Huck Finn thing going on—hiding her hair, hiding her curves, hiding any hint of weakness behind that mouth of hers. And there'd been obvious innuendoes about something bothering her.

Her world was obviously complicated. "Let's just drive. When I'm sure no one can overhear us, I'll fill you in on those rules."

"All right." She opened her jacket and pulled a cell phone from the top pocket of her overalls. "But I should call my dad—tell him I'm fine and that he doesn't need to wait up for me."

"Tell him you're taking a couple of hours to catch up with an old boyfriend."

"How about I tell him something he'll actually believe? Much to his chagrin, I don't date anyone here in Dahlia."

"Perfect. Tell him *I'm* the reason you haven't been seeing anyone here."

Honey-gold curls bobbed against her neck as she shook her head. "Look at me, Jack. I'm willing to help you, and keep your secret. But I'd rather we tell people that we're just friends."

He scoffed at that idea. "There are eight witnesses back in that garage who'd never believe that you and I are just friends."

"You don't know this town, Jack Riley. You don't know me."

"Trust me, Trouble. That's all about to change."

# 6

JACK STARED THROUGH the windshield at the still, utter darkness of the Tennessee countryside, so unlike the noise and neon of the nights in Nashville. The clouds overhead blotted out the moon and starlight, while the thickly forested hills and rain shut out everything else.

It was a perfect setting for illegal activity, especially if Sheriff Buell didn't keep a better eye on things out here than he did in town. A sizable group of men and an entire fleet of trucks loaded with East Coast drugs could cross state and county lines without ever being seen, unload and break down the shipments, smuggle them into cars or parts being shipped out of Dahlia to Nashville—and no one would be the wiser. Jack wouldn't have to work hard to figure out *how* the drugs were being shipped. Finding the men behind the smuggling network would be the real trick.

Only, Jack wasn't thinking about smugglers and drug busts right now. Not parked on a gravel road, with Alexandra "Trouble" Morgan sitting across the seat from him, filling up the cab of his truck with her unique scent. Too subtle to be perfume, the rich, evocative scent of fragrant flowers seemed to emanate from her very skin. His brain translated her scent as the essence of femininity. And every cell in his body remembered that scent, and responded to it with the same hunger they'd shared seven months ago in Nashville.

Kneading the steering wheel with both hands to keep from reaching for her, Jack glanced across the truck to find her sitting with her arms folded protectively across her chest, staring out into the same black nothingness he had. Though she wasn't a classic beauty, there was a porcelain-skinned freshness to her face without all that makeup she'd worn in Nashville. And that body…Jack breathed deeply to counteract the interest stirring south of his belt buckle. Petite and packed, and responsive to every touch of his hand and mouth, that body was a treasure, as hidden now beneath the man-sized overalls as it had been on display for him in her little black hooker dress.

He shifted in his seat to ease a bit more room into his jeans.

"So…Alex. How have you been?"

"You didn't drive me all the way out to Hickory Road to ask about my health."

Ah, yes. The mouth. He hadn't forgotten the sass hidden behind those full pink lips, either.

Something had changed from that night to this one, though. Was this guarded, older, almost disguised woman the real Alex? Was that curious, brave, bold woman in Nashville the real deal? Or was there another role he'd yet to discover that was closer to the truth? "Were there any…ill effects or repercussions after our close encounter in Nashville?"

"I'm fine." Not convincing, but he'd take it. "You?"

Seven months of misery every night, wishing he could reclaim the connection they'd shared, complete what they'd started. After Eric had died, the need to recapture the strength he'd felt that night, and the healing gifts of trust and surrender she'd given him had only intensified. But he could lie, too. "I'm fine."

She turned to face him. The lights from the dashboard offered enough illumination for him to see the turbulent emotions in her eyes before she looked down. When she looked back up at him, her eyes glistened with tears.

Hell. The instinct to hold her, to heal her, made the muscles of his stomach clench. He reached out to her. "Alex?"

But she swiped the tears aside and his hand fell to the seat between them. "My brother died in January. I think he was murdered. Is that what you're investigating?"

Double hell. Things *had* changed. But he was powerless to help her. "Sweetheart, I'm sorry. I'm so sorry. But I can't discuss my case, other than sharing a few basics you need to know so you don't blow my cover. It's safer that way—for both of us. If you don't know, then—"

"Nobody can get that information out of me. Logically, I understand that. But in here…" She pressed her hand to her heart. "I am damn tired of being out of the loop. Of officials not returning my calls, of Sheriff Buell patting me on the head and telling me that I'm trying to justify losing Nick."

"That was a cruel thing to say to you."

She inched closer, rising up on her knees. "I know Nick was in the middle of something that he couldn't talk about, either. He told me if the wrong people found out what he was up to that there'd be consequences. And there were. Damn serious ones. My brother's dead. Run off the road on his way to Nashville. His body burned…" Her voice caught on a tearless sob and Jack pulled her hand into his, holding on tight, silently offering his comfort and support. "If you know something about Nick's death, tell me. Please."

The plea in her eyes was hard to resist. So hard that Jack had to lower his gaze to the grip of her fingers around his. An attorney with a sharp eye, handling the right case, could conceivably have stumbled onto the same people Jack was looking for. Like Jack's partner, Alex's brother might be another casualty in the drug war Jack and Dan Rutledge and the Nashville task force were fighting. He'd be curious to know just what Nick Morgan had been working on. So yes, the drug smuggling and Nick Morgan's death could be related, and he intended to look into it.

But he couldn't tell Alex any of that. Instead, he lifted her hand to his mouth and kissed the back of her knuckles, apologizing for not being able to say what she wanted to hear. But he could honestly answer, "I'm not investigating your brother's murder."

She snatched her hand away. "Then, what?"

He needed to tell her something, or she'd keep asking questions he wasn't supposed to answer. And a man wasn't meant to look into eyes that held that much disappointment and accusation. Jack turned his gaze back to the night. "I'm investigating some activities at the Dahlia Speedway."

The energy flowing back into her expression was a tangible thing. He didn't even have to look to know he'd just given her hope. "Nick did work at the speedway. For Mr. Fisk. The blond guy you met—Drew. That's his grandfather. He owns the track. Well, he's selling it. He had Nick going through documents for him before he put it on the market. I've seen some of Nick's papers."

"Whoa, whoa, whoa." Jack faced her with a stern look. "You've been snooping through legal documents?"

"Not exactly. After Nick's death, I found some files in his things—tucked inside a box of books—paperwork from the Fisk offices. A lot of it is financial stuff that I recognize. But then, he's jotted notes, circled some things he questioned. I don't know if it's illegal, but it's certainly poor accounting." She had potential evidence? That'd go over real well with the thugs he was after. "I was going to give them to Drew. He manages the track. Well, he has for the past three years, and he's acting as interim manager until Whip Davis takes over. But then I thought there might be something in them to give me a clue about Nick."

Jack closed his fingers around her upper arm. "You still have these papers? Have you told anyone else about them?"

She shook her head. "They're in my desk at work. The rest of Nick's papers either burned in the car with him, were returned to his clients or were seized by the sheriff."

*Seized by the sheriff?* "I thought you said Buell ruled your brother's death an accident."

"He did. Even though there were two sets of skid marks on

the road that night. But only Nick's car was found in the gully. And Nick…he raced at the track. He wouldn't—"

"Uh-uh, sweetheart." He tightened his grip, giving her a little shake. She wasn't grasping the danger she'd be in if the wrong people suspected she was sitting on potentially incriminating information. And that jackass of a sheriff had just moved to the top of his suspect list. "There's no point in seizing legal evidence if Nick's death was an accident."

"That's what I thought. That it was some kind of cover-up. But I have history with Sheriff Buell. That's why I've kept the papers hidden and I'm trying to find answers on my own."

Jack pulled away, his eyes narrowing at her offhand comment. "You and the sheriff have history?"

Even in the shadows, he could see her face go pale. He didn't believe her when she tried to laugh it off. "I haven't been turning tricks in Dahlia if that's what you're worried about." He wasn't. The false smile disappeared. "It's personal."

"Something to do with Hank Buell?"

But he wasn't getting an answer. Instead, she tucked a loose golden curl back inside the controlling cap of her bandanna. Hiding herself again. Hiding the fact she was a pretty, vibrant woman. Hiding her emotions along with the truth.

Jack hated watching the transformation. He wanted to see the passion in her eyes again—for the truth, for success, for him. He wanted to see the confidence in the tilt of her chin.

Sliding over from behind the steering wheel, he draped his arm around her shoulders and tucked her to his side. She didn't mold herself to his body the way she had back at the garage, but she didn't push away, either.

"Hey." He tried to cajole a smile out of her.

"Hey, what?" *Wiseass.* A glimmer of spirit tried to show itself.

"If it means anything, I think it sounds as though you're on the right track."

"About what?"

"About your brother's death not being an accident."

She looked up at him. "You believe me? That Nick was murdered?"

He traced his forefinger around her jaw to the point of her chin. "I can't say for sure until I see those papers of yours. But I do know that the men I'm investigating are willing to kill to keep their secrets. If your brother stumbled on to something…"

"You really listened to me, didn't you."

"Why wouldn't I?"

She turned her whole body toward him, hooking one knee over his. The contact gave him a taste of what it would feel like to have her entire body sinking onto his lap. Suddenly, he wanted her there—on him, around him, crying out for him the way she had that night in Nashville. Her heady scent, eager touches and wanton responses had filled him with a renewed strength and virility.

But even though her fingertips lightly traced the zipper of his jacket from chest to stomach, Jack shifted the desire in his veins down to idle. A taut line had formed between her golden eyebrows. He dropped his hand to the small of her back, massaging gentle circles there. She was feeling the pain of her brother's death, but something was different.

"I'm still listening, Trouble," he coaxed. "Talk to me."

With a slight tug at the front of his jacket, she nodded, then raised her dark green eyes to his. "Just how dangerous is this investigation of yours? Would they kill you, too?"

There was no way to sugarcoat the truth. "They've already killed one cop. I'm dead if they find out I'm working with the state's DEA task force."

Her pretty eyes blurred out of focus as an all-too-familiar pain sank its claws into him. Eric had bled to death in his arms because they'd found out he was a cop.

"Jack?" Warm fingers brushed across his face, dragging him from the raging spiral of his thoughts. "Jack." He had both arms around Alex now, and he was squeezing her hard. Too hard. "They killed a cop? Who was he?"

He released her to run his palms up and down her arms in apology, willing his touch to be as gentle as he was ruthless about shoving the image and pain of Eric's death from his mind. But he didn't answer. He had secrets to keep, too.

Time to get down to the reason he'd brought her out here in the first place. He wasn't going to fail at this investigation. And nobody else was going to get hurt. Not on his watch. "This is a dangerous mess I've gotten you involved in, make no mistake. I'm sorry about that. I'll keep you out of the worst of it as best I can, but you're going to have to do your part."

"I want to help."

Jack stroked along the sleeve of her jacket one last time and then dropped his hand with a possessive weight over her knee, as if that small reassurance would make all of this craziness understandable. "There are three rules I need you to follow. If you want answers—if we want answers—this is what has to happen."

She nodded.

"Rule number one. You can't tell anyone I'm a cop—not your father, not anybody. As far as Dahlia knows, I'm Black Jack Riley and I'm here to race."

"That's easy. What else?"

He released a long breath into the quietness inside the truck. "I have a feeling this will be harder for you. Rule number two. Follow my orders. If I shush you, I don't want to hear another word. If I tell you to run, you book it." He squeezed her knee. "And if something goes south, you do exactly what I say. No heroics."

"But if I can help—"

"It's not open for discussion. You won't do your brother or me any good if you get hurt."

"What if you get hurt?"

Admirable to be concerned, but the rule didn't change. "Follow. My. Orders."

The green eyes flashed. Oh yeah, that one was grating on a nerve. "Fine. What else?"

Rule number three would be the tricky one. For him. Separating his emotions from the demands of the job had never been harder. He ran his hand up to Alex's hip and back down along the soft worn denim of her overalls, recalling how her skin was softer, warmer, underneath. He had to know she could play the undercover game. And he had to remember, despite the need sizzling from each and every pore of his body, that whatever he felt for this enigmatic woman had to take second place to accomplishing his mission.

"Number three? From this moment on, you and I are officially a couple. We've planted the idea, but we can't give anyone reason to doubt us or the wrong people will question my being here and I won't be able to do my job."

"I imagine people are gossiping about us already."

"If I could have come up with a different way to shut your mouth on such short notice, this scenario might have played out differently." He tucked his finger beneath her chin and tipped her face up to his. "But I need you to be convincing. We both know the seeds of attraction are there already." Her tongue darted out to lick her lips and parts of Jack clenched in response. Yeah. Attraction was definitely there. "But you closed up like a book a few minutes ago. You wouldn't let me touch you. You wouldn't talk to me."

"I was upset about my brother." She tried to withdraw even now, but he wouldn't have it.

"Be upset. Be pissed off. But don't avoid me." Jack reached for her right knee and turned her, pulling her right across his lap so that she straddled him. She pushed against his chest and tried to wiggle off him. Jack held on, forcing the kind of intimacy it would take to make them a convincing couple. "You can't be afraid to touch me or yell at me or interact with me, or no one will believe that we're an *us*. They'll start looking for other explanations that can get me—and now you—into trouble. Don't give them a reason to ask questions."

With a warm huff that caressed his face, she finally relaxed onto his lap. "I warn you, I'm not…" Her fingers curled beneath his leather collar. Only inches separated her flushed cheeks from his, but the uncertainty in her expression put her in some distant place. "I'm not very good at being with a man. I've never been anyone's girlfriend or gal pal or whatever you're going to call us. I don't know how convincing I'll be."

"Gal pal?" Jack frowned. "Sweetheart, you were golden that night in Nashville." He shrugged, trying to make Alex smile, trying to get her comfortable with the role he needed her to play. "I wouldn't recommend the hooker dress again, unless it's a private party just for me. But as far as I'm concerned, you had all the right moves. We can make this work."

"Right moves? Like what?"

Crap. Was she kidding him with this? No, the earnest, almost studious squint of her eyes told him she was looking for a serious answer.

"I'll admit we got off to a rocky start." He moved his hands to her back, sliding them beneath her jacket. When he found the nip of her waist beneath the layers of clothing she wore, he stopped, savoring the warmth of her body, treasuring the hesitant trust that kept her straddled across his lap, waiting for an answer. "Memories of the way you responded to every touch have kept me awake a lot of nights and sent me to a cold shower more often than I care to admit."

She arched an eyebrow. "You had to take a cold shower because of *me?*"

Jack pulled her closer, spread his thighs wider to let her feel the hardening evidence of her effect on him. Her soft gasp whispered across his ears like an erotic invitation. "You do this to me, Trouble. Nobody can argue that."

She trailed one hand down his chest toward the promised

land, following the bold curiosity of her eyes as she took in the unmistakable bulge filling the space between them. His skin remembered the last time she'd taken him in her hand and his muscles bunched and nudged with anticipation.

But her fingers stopped at his belt, and her eyes returned to his. "So, even though I look like one of the guys, it's convincing if I do this?"

Alex flattened both palms at the center of his chest, sliding them under his jacket to catch his flat nipples beneath the heels of her hands. The sensitive flesh instantly popped to attention through the damp cotton of his shirt, demanding more of her sensuous research.

"Works for me." Jack whispered his approval when she obliged, catching the nipples between her thumbs and hands and rolling them until he groaned at each zing of pleasure that shot from her touch to his swelling dick. He leaned forward, resting his forehead against hers, looking straight down into emerald-green eyes that darkened with her own blossoming desire. "You are so not one of the guys."

"I've never had the chance to explore a man's body before." He jerked when she pinched him. When she snatched her hand away, her mouth rounded with an apology, Jack pressed a quick kiss to her lips and guided her fingers back to continue their experimental touches.

"That was a very good move." His words were little more than a hoarse growl in his throat. After unhooking the straps of her overalls and letting the front fall away, Jack's own hands skimmed over the round weight of her breasts and squeezed, mimicking her exploration of his body, enjoying the answering gasps and moans he could solicit from her. "You touch me however you want. Wherever you want. I'm okay with that."

"Just okay?" This woman might look all tomboy on the outside, but her inner temptress had taken over. She was smiling now. Alex dipped her head, replacing her hand with her tongue, laving the hard bud through his shirt. "Is that any better?"

"Damn, sweetheart." His muscles quivered in response to each stroke. Groaning, needy, feverish with want, he moved his hands down to the firm curve of her butt and pulled her tighter into his lap, holding the apex of her open thighs against the helpless rotation of his body. Had he ever wanted anything as badly as he wanted to be free and thrusting up inside her right now?

*Patience.* Jack eased his grip, closed his eyes and tried counting to a hundred. *One. Two.* He had to get her comfortable with this, with him. He had to reassure her that she could play the part of his bedmate. He had no doubts about her abilities. But a partner who hesitated was a partner who made mistakes. And with two men already dead, mistakes were not an option.

*Three.* Ah, hell. He couldn't even make it to ten.

Somewhere between danger and isolation, this tutoring session had become a full-on seduction.

While her mouth wet him down to the skin, she tugged at the hem of his shirt. Her knuckles brushed across his stomach and Jack sucked in a sharp breath. His hands battled with hers to get his jacket off and his shirt untucked and get her hands on his feverish skin.

Every cell leaped beneath the brand of her touch. But the wicked vixen had something more in mind, and Jack's will was powerless to stop her. She pushed his shirt up beneath his armpits and closed her mouth, hot and wet, over his rock-hard nipple. She stroked the nub with her tongue, sucking the tingling skin. Jack's arms tightened convulsively around her back. He dipped his nose to the crown of her head and groaned.

"Good move." He stretched his jeans to an almost unbearable tightness as he imagined that wet, sassy tongue directly on his skin there.

She turned her attention to the other side of his chest. "So I'm doing it right?"

He was damn well going to burst into flame if this wasn't leading to the release he so desperately craved. Could she really not know the effect she had on him? He snatched the bandanna from atop her head and buried his nose in the fragrant curls of her hair. "You're a ringer, Alex. A sexy, irresistible natural talent." He slipped his hands beneath all the layers of clothing she wore to find warm, vibrant skin to hold on to. "Don't play with me. I don't feel like standing outside in the rain to make this go away. But I'll have to if you don't stop."

Her tongue left him as she straightened in his lap. "You want me to stop?"

"No." Feeling bereft of her touch, he brought his hands up to frame her face, to make her read the seriousness of his expression. "I never expected to find you again. But I never stopped wanting you. I've been dreaming about this since…" *Don't go there.* Jack squeezed his eyes shut. He couldn't think about Eric's death now. The guilt and anger and loneliness would destroy the mood. Get him to thinking. Turn this into something more than blind lust for a woman he needed to get out of his system. He opened his eyes and kissed her hard. Kissed away his own doubts when she eagerly responded. "I don't want you to stop."

She curled her fingers around his wrists. Her eyes were dark and drowsy with passion, her cheeks flamed with a rosy blush. "I've had a few fantasies about you, too, since Nashville."

Fantasies? Jack couldn't quite seem to catch his breath. His erection throbbed with anticipation. Just what kind of things had this woman been thinking about doing to a forty-year-old man who felt a decade younger just hearing her say that?

He made one last, valiant effort to remember that getting with Alex Morgan was supposed to be about the job. "So we can do this, right? You won't be afraid to touch me or flirt with me—"

"I don't know how to flirt."

Jack tunneled his fingers into her hair, stopping her from shaking her head, stirring up her scent, making himself crazy with the need to be inside her. "Telling a man you fantasize about him qualifies as a definite flirt."

She rose up on her knees and settled herself more purpose-fully on his lap. Every accidental brush of a hand or thigh coiled his body into an ever-tightening knot. He wanted her. Here. Now. As she talked she wound her arms lightly around his neck, sliding closer. The tips of her breasts were hard little spears that poked against his chest and reassured him that the desire simmering between them was mutual. "These are strange rules of yours, Jack Riley. You really think we can convince the people of this town that you want me?"

Jack pulled her in for a kiss. "Who's acting?"

And then there was little need for talking or coaching as Alex purred into his mouth and completed the kiss.

Snaps unsnapped. Hands explored. Mouths got greedy. There was a silent instruction to sit back on his knees while his jeans and shorts came down. Her overalls wound up around her ankles as neither of them remembered her boots. He pushed up the layered tops she wore, then pulled at the cotton and elastic of her bra. He suckled a proud breast as it spilled out, palmed the inside of her smooth, creamy thigh and traced the seam of her womanhood with his thumb until panties were soaked and she whimpered with need. She skidded her palms along the stubble on his jaw and tugged at the short strands of his hair. There was a twisting of bodies and bumping of hands when he pulled a condom from the glove compartment. There were no clever words, little finesse. This was about kissing and grabbing and sliding deep inside the warm folds of Alex's body. Again. And again.

This was about burying his nose in the perfumed valley between her generous breasts and holding on tight as he came up off the seat and exploded inside her. Every muscle in Jack's butt and thighs contracted as he pushed himself in as deep as she'd take him. She arched her back, tipped her head back and cried out as the tiny muscles inside her squeezed him and milked him and cascaded down all around him.

When she was spent, when he was empty, Alex collapsed

against his chest. Her breathing against his neck was as ragged and shallow as his own. Jack waited until their lungs had resumed a more normal rhythm and she was turning away to tuck her breasts back into her bra and shift her panties back into place before he lifted her onto the seat beside him and rolled down his window to dispose of the goods. The blast of cool air and cold rain provided the wake-up call he'd needed about thirty minutes ago.

*Smooth move, Detective.* He'd just broken one of his own rules.

He'd had sex with Alex. Hot, fast, mind-blowing sex. No matter how he tried to rationalize the loss of control—that it was part of Alex's basic training to get her used to the idea of playing the role of lover in his investigation, that she'd seemed to want it as badly as he had—he knew he'd just made a colossal strategic error. His judgment on this investigation was already impaired by losing one partner. Now he'd gone and involved himself with his new, unofficial, partner. *Involved* wasn't a good thing for a detective on a mission to find drug smugglers and killers.

Jack knew damn well that that had been more than sex. That had been something building up inside him for the past seven months. A need to connect. A want unlike anything he'd experienced with any other woman. But emotions were distracting. Need was distracting. Worrying about Alex on any level beyond strict professionalism was damned distracting.

Watching her sidle over to the opposite side of the truck to redress herself while he zipped and buckled everything back into place definitely worried him. Why was the mouth suddenly so quiet? Maybe she was just picking up on his moody second thoughts. *Jackass. Mr. Sensitivity.* "You okay, Trouble?"

She nodded without facing him. "That wasn't exactly how I'd pictured it would be." She wiped away the condensation from the inside of the window. Was she checking the sideview mirror?

Jack pulled down the visor in front of her and opened the lighted mirror. "How you pictured what?"

"Being with you. It's been...a while for me." Thank God she

hadn't said this had been her first time. No way was this sex kitten in disguise a virgin. But she did keep harping on her lack of experience with men. "I did okay, hmm?"

"Sweetheart, if that was your idea of *okay,* then I may not have the strength to survive you on a good day. You were…irresistible." He reached over to brush a honey-gold tendril off her cheek and tuck it behind her ear. Though she didn't exactly jerk from his touch, she did seem awfully busy tying her bandanna over the top of her head just so, checking in the mirror and then checking again. On the third take, he glanced behind them to see if she had spotted something moving outside. But the night was dark and muffled by the rain. "Did I hurt you?"

"No." She shot him a smile that was about as reassuring as the hasty way she turned off the lighted mirror. "You're good for my sex life. Hell, you *are* my sex life. That's the second time I've had an orgasm with you." She slapped her hand over her mouth. "Oh my God. Did I say that out loud?"

Jack swallowed the impulse to chuckle with relief. "Sweetheart, I know the setting and the circumstances aren't ideal, but that's just about the best compliment you can give a man."

He got a glimpse of eyes that were wide and dark and unreadable before she turned away to attack the buckles that fastened her overalls into place. "So what's our next step? I'm assuming you'll want me to take you to the track. Most of the regulars come into the garage at one time or another during the week, too. The next time we have—" she swallowed hard "—an audience, I assume you'll want me to kiss you? Or hold hands or whatever?"

"Just follow my rules, Trouble." He vowed to do the same. Jack started the engine, ending the discussion. "And don't worry. You're better at your part than you give yourself credit for. I guarantee you, within twenty-four hours, no one in Dahlia will have any doubts that you're my woman."

The only person who seemed to still need convincing was huddled in the far corner of his truck.

# 7

IT WAS WELL PAST MIDNIGHT when Alex sank into the fragrant hot water of her bath to ease the soreness from her muscles. She wasn't used to having sex like that—a frenzied mating that left her feeling powerful, sated, spent. She wasn't used to having sex, period.

Because she'd sworn off the men of Dahlia, sex had become an enigma to her. Orgasms from anything besides her own hand were an absolute mystery. It had been her very first time when she'd been taught that sex could be used as a weapon against her, when she'd learned that her needs and fragile hopes didn't matter.

But Jack Riley had made that awful night seem like little more than a bad dream. Despite the adult-like curves of her adolescent body, she'd been more child than woman then. Completely inexperienced. Tonight, Jack had made her feel like she was all woman. Like she mattered. Like the other women of Dahlia had nothing on her when it came to driving a man crazy with want.

Alex pulled a washcloth from the shelf beside the claw-footed tub. After soaking it in the water and oils she'd used, she rubbed the soft cloth over her skin, stretching out her legs and arms one at a time to leisurely cleanse and massage every inch of her skin—finding and remembering each place Jack had touched. Remembering how much she'd enjoyed it. She'd loved the power of it, the freedom from self-doubt as much as the rapidly building arousal and intense release it had given her.

Alexandra Morgan had had sex.

And the world hadn't ended.

It might not have been women's magazine style with tips and tricks and secret moves to increase his or her pleasure, and there'd been no courtly *milady* or background music. No gown. No gentle seduction like with the knight of her fantasies. Tonight in Jack's truck had been more like a souped-up motor revving on all cylinders and charging straight to the finish line.

She'd liked it. A lot. He hadn't joked at her inexperience or been impatient with her curiosity. He'd talked in plain terms and had used his hands and mouth to explain the rest. She could do this. She could get past her self-preserving inhibitions and fear of repercussions and make believers out of the men of Dahlia.

Alex breathed out a heavy sigh and relaxed against the pillow at the end of the tub. With a little more practice, she might even make a believer out of herself.

But how was she supposed to trust her feminine instincts when they'd failed her so miserably in the past? Blinking her eyes open, Alex retuned to the reality of her cooling bath water. Proving she could have sex once—albeit shake-her-world-down-to-the-core sex—didn't mean she was on the way to getting her love life in order.

She had to remember there were rules to this game. That this *was* a game. Any tenderness, any passion, was all part of the act. Part of the cover. Part of the job. Jack might fire her up like a combustion engine, but her dreams of a real relationship didn't figure into the equation.

Alex was still sitting there—wishing she had a mother to seek advice from, wishing she had some girlfriends she trusted to confide in, wishing she had Jack Riley here with her now—when her cell phone rang.

The soft whir of sound vibrating across her bathroom shelf startled her from her thoughts. It buzzed a third time, a fourth, before she could dry her hands and pick up the phone. *ID Restricted. 1:13 a.m.*

"ID Restricted? What does that mean?" Maybe it was Jack on some kind of untraceable line. Maybe there was a fourth rule he'd forgotten to dictate to her. Reluctantly, Alex answered the call. "Hello?"

Silence.

Her heart skipped a beat, then shifted into a higher gear. "Is someone there?"

"I saw you with him."

The voice was deep, muffled, unfamiliar.

"Excuse me?"

"You slut. You need to stop what you're doing. The outsider doesn't belong here."

Instinctively, Alex drew her legs up to her chest, hiding herself from unseen eyes. "Who is this?"

*Click.*

The disconnect jolted through her entire body.

*Not again.*

As soon as she could remember to breathe, Alex shut the phone and shoved it back onto the shelf. She pushed herself up out of the water on trembling legs.

"You son of a bitch."

This wasn't happening again. She wasn't going to let some dickless bully terrorize her the way the boys of this town had nearly a decade ago. She'd lived down that shameful night—sacrificed practically every feminine, sexual impulse inside her to do it—but she'd lived it down. She was a grown woman now. She had a college degree. A job. A cause for her brother that was far more important than any drunk, adolescent ego. She might hide her body from the lewd jokes and stinging gossips of this town, but she refused to be afraid.

With a few tendrils of righteous indignation giving her the courage to move, Alex stepped out onto the mat. Dripping across the cold tiles, she pulled her father's long flannel robe off the hook on the door. She tied it tight around her waist, overlapping the deep shawl collar at her neck, and opened the bathroom door. Nick and his buddy Drew had gotten her out of that high school nightmare.

Tonight, she was on her own.

After pausing at the foot of the stairs to listen for her father's reassuring snore, she tiptoed to the front door. Even in a small town, her dad was a fanatic about security, so the door was locked. But Alex checked it, anyway, opening and then refastening the dead bolt, making sure the knob didn't turn in her hand.

She parted the curtains that hung at the front window and peeked out. The storm had abated to a gentle, misty rain, but with the moon still hidden above the clouds, it was too dark to see much beyond the circles of light cast by the lamp posts at either end of the block. No one was moving along the sidewalks. Cars were parked on each side of the street. Houses were dark. Whoever had called wasn't watching her now.

Alex's racing heart finally calmed enough to hear above the frantic pulse that beat in her ears. The night wasn't so still as she'd first thought.

She leaned her cheek closer to the front window and heard the dapple of rain on the leaves in the trees outside. And another sound—this one lower, rumbling, mechanical.

Her trained ear recognized the sound. A powerful engine, idling in Park. The rhythmic spit of the motor told her it had been driven hard, and needed its oil and filters changed.

She peered into the darkness again, grateful for the shadows inside the house that would hide her from prying eyes. She scanned each car along the street and in her neighbors' driveways, looking for something to explain away that sound.

There. Alex squinted, thinking her eyes had played a trick on her. She pressed her forehead to the cool glass, stared harder. Across the street, beyond the glow of the street lamp, a chimera appeared. A ghost of movement among the rain and shadows.

But Alex didn't believe in ghosts. An idling car expelled exhaust from its tailpipe, exhaust that would be virtually invisible at night. But a tailpipe also gave off heat. That flux of movement was hot exhaust rising through the cool, damp air. That car was running.

"What are you doing out there?" she breathed against the glass. She skimmed her gaze along the car from tailpipe to headlight. Its body was like a giant black cat crouching in the darkness, its windows blank. The silhouettes of the seats inside blended into the shadows. "Who would leave their car—?"

A fiery speck of orange light suddenly burned inside the car's interior.

Alex jumped back from the window, quickly stilling the swaying curtains that might reveal her presence.

A man was sitting inside that rumbling car, smoking a cigarette.

Like Hank had smoked his cigarette and watched her leave the garage with Jack tonight.

Sitting and smoking and watching.

Watching *her.*

Dashing through the house as quickly as her heart was now pounding, Alex checked each window on the main floor, as well as the doors leading to the garage and backyard. Once she was certain she was locked in tight, she paused and took a deep, steadying breath. She was safe. She could relax.

But when she returned to the bathroom to clean up her mess, her phone was going off again.

She picked up the phone. *ID Restricted.*

"Stop it, you bastard. Just stop." When the phone went silent, Alex nearly dropped it.

Okay. So she was a little bit scared. She was definitely confused. She had no big brother this time who could make everything right, and she didn't want to burden her father with her paranoia over a couple of crank calls.

But there was another man she could turn to.

JACK EXHALED SLOWLY INTO the rain so that the fog of his warm breath wouldn't give away his position.

After steaming things up with Alex in his truck, the wet grass felt particularly cold as he lay on his belly in the shadows of Dahlia Speedway's infield. He'd give anything to be naked and snugged up to the warmth of her body, taking that get-acquainted session into round two. But when the track's outer gate had creaked open and a black pickup hauling a toter trailer had rolled in with its lights off, thoughts of tutoring Alex in the art of sex vanished and survival mode kicked in. Jack dove for the ground behind the infield's barrier wall, which was the only cover between the flat racing strip and the viewing stands where his visitors were headed.

He was lucky they hadn't shown up a minute sooner, when he was coming out of the track offices in the three-story tower that dominated the race grounds, relocking the door he'd picked open behind him. He was even luckier they hadn't arrived a minute later when he would have been snooping around the guest services and equipment storage area behind the metal viewing stands where they were pulling up and parking now.

His late-night search of the deserted race track hadn't turned up anything he didn't already know. Drew Fisk's office had been pretty well stripped of paperwork, in preparation for the pending sale, no doubt, or possibly because Sheriff Buell was trying to cover his tracks over something Nick Morgan had found. And the officials' offices held information on stats, records and regulations rather than the local connection he was investigating.

But his night at the track wasn't going to be a total bust. Ignoring the mud soaking his knees and elbows, he crawled to the opening between the concrete barriers that ran the length of the strip to protect onlookers from crashes, fires and other dangers that sometimes occurred. He squinted into the rain and spied on the after-hours rendezvous taking place beneath the stands some thirty yards away. Nothing like someone sneaking into a locked up facility after hours to make a cop suspicious.

From this distance, though, it was difficult to make out many details through the darkness. Once they killed the engine and turned off the wipers, a curtain of rain sluiced down the windshield, further blurring any chance at a positive ID. Without sound equipment, he could only imagine what the two men sitting inside the truck might be discussing. But whatever it was, the man in the passenger seat was giving the orders.

Jack trained his eyes on the driver's-side door as it opened, but the guy had his back to him as he headed around to the rear of the trailer. The best description he could come up with was medium build, dark hair. A few seconds later, the other man emerged, his face obscured by the cell phone at his ear before he, too, turned and walked to the back of the trailer.

Both men wore shapeless generic gray coveralls and dark ball caps. But he was guessing light-colored hair for the man on the phone, or maybe he had a shaved head like the guy he'd seen at Headlights and Morgan's Garage?

What activity there was to observe from his skewed vantage point didn't last long. The dark-haired man made most of the trips, unloading large boxes from the trailer and carrying them into the concrete-block building where track equipment was stored. Meanwhile, the guy on the phone pulled a pack of cigarettes from the glove compartment and lit one as he paced beneath the stands. Periodically, he'd look up, either cussing the rain or whoever was on the other end of the call.

Though he trained his ears to the man's voice, Jack could only make out a few phrases like "…product" and "…change everything" and finally a "You know damn well that money…" that sent the boss man off on a long stalking pace behind the storage building.

By the time he returned to Jack's line of sight, the call was done, the cigarette was out and his buddy was locking up the building.

"Damn." Jack mouthed his own curse, wiping the moisture

from his eyelashes, wishing the rain would stop and a full moon would light up the suspects so he could see their faces. But as the men climbed into the truck and pulled away, the best he could do was get a partial Tennessee plate.

He rolled over and sat up with his back against the concrete barrier wall. He was soaked to the skin from his knees to his chest, but the discomfort was nothing compared to the frustration of coming away with nothing more than half a license plate and truck make that he silently texted to Dan Rutledge's office in Nashville to run through the DMV system for him.

He gave the perps a solid two minutes after closing the gate behind them before he left his hiding place. *They* had used a key to get in to both the track and the storage building. That meant they had a legitimate reason to be here, along with the illegal reason that he suspected had brought them out tonight. Jack jogged across the asphalt track and made a quick search of the concrete beneath the stands until he picked up the lone cigarette butt that the man on the phone must have discarded. Now to find out just what was in those boxes they'd unloaded. Clamping his small flashlight between his teeth to light his work, he picked open the padlock on the storage building and stepped inside.

The place was jam-packed with rows of gray metal shelves forming aisles, while spare tires and anything else too big to fit on the shelves leaned up against the wall. Every flat place had something stacked on it, with everything from concession stand supplies to boxes of nuts and bolts. But Jack would bet his next paycheck that those boys hadn't been carrying in spare hardware.

"And we have a winner." Jack grinned as his search led him to the boxes he was looking for. Partially hidden behind a row of soda pop canisters. The only boxes that had been marked by the rain.

After a quick look out the door to make sure he had no more unexpected company, Jack pulled out his pocketknife and carefully sliced beneath the packing tape on the first box. Though it was labeled Fisk Aluminum & Fabrication on the outside, inside he found a steel air filter pan for a carburetor engine.

"No way." He couldn't be this lucky. His partner, Eric, had brought in something similar during his undercover investigation—various car parts with existing or built-in compartments where drugs could be stored and shipped. Jack quickly unscrewed the wing nut on top and opened the pan. "Damn."

It was shiny and new and empty.

No evidence tonight. Although…

Jack ran his fingers between the double interior walls of the filter pan. It could be a design modification to guide more cooling air in or out of a racing engine. Or… "Someone's built in a place to stash dime bags."

Nothing major, but if enough cut bags of dope were smuggled in enough cars and parts, he could still be looking at the pipeline that supplied dealers like Lorenzo Vaughn and the thugs fighting to replace him in Nashville. It was a start. Matching a name to the license plate and truck he'd seen or finding the actual drugs would be even better. Then he might start to feel some kind of vindication for Eric's murder. "I won't let you down, buddy," he vowed, just as he had the day Eric had died in his arms. Just as he had the day of Eric's funeral. And the day after that. "I won't let you down."

Moving swiftly and silently, Jack resealed the box and reached for the next one in the stack. He was in the middle of putting away a second modified filter pan when his cell phone vibrated in his pocket.

Rutledge couldn't have a plate match for him already, could he? He doubted the young attorney was even awake to get his message yet. It had to be one-thirty in the morning. Instantly on alert, Jack shoved the box back into place and pulled his phone from his belt. Only a handful of people had this number, and none of them would be calling at this hour for any good reason.

He pulled out his phone and checked the number. Hell. He couldn't get it answered fast enough. "Trouble?"

"Jack?" Alex's voice was soft, unsure.

"What's wrong?" Jack headed toward the open door, making sure no one was lurking about who might overhear his conversation. Or sense the protective fear that tensed every muscle of his body. "Did something happen after I took you home?"

He didn't like the sound of that pause.

"I think we already have someone's attention."

Jack pulled the door closed and secured the padlock. "What do you mean?"

"I just got a phone call."

At this time of night? "From?"

"I don't know. The voice was disguised. He said—well, I'm pretty sure it was a he—he said I should stop what I was doing. And I don't think he meant taking a bath."

She was naked? Jack braced his hand against the door, trying to catch a deep breath at the image of her lush, naked body rising up from the water, smooth and wet and... *Focus.* Curling his hand into a fist, Jack turned away and jogged toward the emergency exit gate where he'd snuck in two hours earlier. "Tell me exactly what the caller said."

"Not much. He said the outsider didn't belong here, and that I should stop what I was doing. I don't know if that means investigating Nick's murder, or making out in your truck or what. And I think someone's outside the house. I mean, Dad's upstairs and the doors are locked. But there's a car, and..." Bits of gravel crunched beneath his boots as he skidded to a stop, catching a quick, bracing breath right along with her. "In high school there was a prank, and this guy...well, these boys..."

"These boys what?" What was she trying to say? What the hell was wrong? Why hadn't that bastard threatened him instead of her? "Alex?"

She'd turned her mouth from the phone, cussing like a sailor. When she came back to speak, the vulnerability he'd heard in her voice a moment ago was gone. "I'm sorry. I'm babbling like a panicking idiot, and I've outgrown that. It's just another stupid prank. I'm sorry I woke you."

"You didn't. I—"

"I'll let you get back to sleep. Good night."

"No. You tell me exactly—" The disconnect echoed like a gunshot through his brain. "Trouble? Alexandra?"

Son of a bitch. Like he was getting any sleep tonight with a cryptic call like that. She'd sounded so afraid. He located her incoming number and rang her right back. Voice mail. Damn. She'd turned off her phone.

"I swear, woman, you're going to give me a heart attack one way or the other." Jack ran for the kudzu-covered brick wall framing the main gate. Not wasting the time it would take him to pick the emergency gate lock, he hoisted himself up over the wall and dropped down on the other side. Cursing the sticky friction of his wet jeans and jacket, he stretched his long legs into a run straight across the parking lot to Morgan's Garage where he'd parked his truck.

Eric Mesner would have had his hide if Jack's obsession with solving his murder had endangered an innocent civilian.

If he'd inadvertently done something to jeopardize Alex's safety, when he'd just been trying to cover his own ass with this fake affair… Jack climbed inside his truck, started the engine and squealed away over the wet pavement.

# 8

WITHIN TEN MINUTES of her call, Jack was picking the lock to the Morgans' back door and sneaking into a darkened house. Dark save for the light shining through a doorway at the end of the first-floor hall. The house was quiet except for some championship snoring coming from up the polished hickory staircase. Alex had indicated her father was asleep, that she was rattled and that calling him had been a mistake.

By damn, he was going to get some answers to something in this town. Moving toward the light without making a sound, Jack familiarized himself with the layout of Alex's house, and found himself standing in the doorway to her bedroom.

*"It was nothing," my ass.* Alex was pacing at the foot of an old-fashioned, white wrought-iron bed, wrapped up to her chin in a man's robe, her lips moving in some kind of *sotto voce* mantra or curse he couldn't understand.

Although he had no desire to frighten her further, it was even more important not to wake her father or alert the neighbors with a startled scream, so Jack crept up behind her and reached around to cover her mouth with his hand.

Her reaction was instantaneous. A shriek into his palm, an elbow to his gut, bare feet knocking against his shins. Damn, that woman packed a punch. He cinched his arm around her waist, pulling her off her feet and into his body, flashing back to that night in Nashville.

He pressed his lips against her ear, gentling her with a voice that was as reassuring as he knew how to make it. "Easy, sweet-heart. It's me. Shh. Don't cry out."

The fight ended as quickly as it had begun. When she gave an acknowledging nod, he eased his hold and lowered her to the floor.

"Jack?" As soon as he released her, she spun around. In the course of their struggle, the robe had gaped open, revealing one of the two most beautiful breasts he'd ever seen. But before he could note more than how the rosy circle of color at the tip stood out against her milky skin, she quickly covered herself, clutching the robe together at her neck and waist. "How did you get in here?"

He frowned. "I've been a cop for a lot of years. I've learned a few things. Now we need to have a conversation. Tell me about that call. And who's watching? You can't—"

"I'm just glad you're here."

She walked straight into his chest and the lecture died on his lips. As she wrapped her arms around his waist and nestled her cheek against him, the temper and fear that had carried Jack from the track to her bedroom dissipated. Her breasts pillowed against his stomach, the scent of flowery bath oils teased his nose. For one noble moment he tried to push her away. "Sweetheart, I'm a mess."

She didn't seem to care. "I've never had a man dash to my rescue before." Her lips moved against the cotton of his cold, damp T-shirt like a warm caress against his skin. "Except for my brother. And that hardly counts, does it."

With a dumbfounded sigh, Jack lowered his lips to the crown of her hair and folded her up in a snug, protective embrace. "I sure don't feel like your brother."

But this wasn't about riding in like some kind of hero. This wasn't about discovering tender, aching places inside him that had nothing to do with the need this woman stirred in him.

This was about understanding the rules. His rules.

"You and I have to get one thing straight, Trouble." Jack tugged the elastic band from the nape of her neck, hating the tight, sexless bun more than the bandanna that normally masked her hair. He sifted his fingers into the heavy golden curls, stirring up that sweet gardenia scent that was uniquely hers. "You *never* hang up on me in the middle of a conversation. Understand? Communication is everything in an undercover op. If you hang up on me, I don't know if you're in trouble or pissed off at me. And I guarantee you, if you hang up without explaining what's wrong, I will be on my way to finish that conversation in person and see with my own eyes that you're all right."

"Really?" She moved her arms beneath his jacket and snuggled close enough that he could feel every curve and muscle as if they were standing skin to skin. "That's so sweet."

*Sweet* wasn't what he was going for. Jack spread his legs slightly, adjusting his taller stance so that his thighs could more fully cradle the curve of her hips, lengthening the body-to-body contact that seemed to be calming her, soothing him, warming them both. If she didn't mind soaking up the mud and moisture from his clothes, he wasn't going to push her away. "That's team play, Alex, and we're a team now. We have to know what's going on with each other. Got it?"

"Yes. No more hanging up."

"Good." Reluctantly removing his hands from her hip and hair, Jack leaned back against her arms and tilted her face up to his. No signs of crying, but definitely paler than he'd like to see. He smoothed her hair from her face. "Now, tell me about this phone call. Why did it spook you?"

Her chin went down and her gaze landed at the center of his chest. "It's embarrassing."

He unhooked her arms from their death-grip around his waist. And though he could have enjoyed the view all night long, Jack folded the baggy plaid flannel over the deep vee of cleavage at the front of her robe and turned her toward the bed. "You were scared. You can't bluff your way through this one."

He pulled back the quilts and sheet and waited for her to

crawl beneath the covers. Alex rested back against the pillows, hugging her knees and the quilt up to her chest.

Jack sat on the edge of the bed, facing her. "Just talk to me."

Her eyes searched his for several seconds before she tucked her hair behind her ears and tried to shrug off the importance of this discussion with a laugh. "There was an incident when I was sixteen. Tonight's call was like the ones I used to get back then. I'm sure it doesn't have anything to do with Nick's death or your investigation."

"I don't care. I want to hear about it."

The false smile quickly disappeared. With the light from the bedside table illuminating her face, Jack could read all the nuances of emotion that crossed her unadorned features. He didn't like any of what he saw there—except the courage. "My mom died when I was a toddler. I barely remember her. So my dad and my big brother raised me."

"That explains your love for cars and the tomboy getup, not the phone call."

"I'm getting there. When I hit puberty, I was like any other girl. I wanted pretty clothes. I wanted a boy to like me. But I was different in one fairly significant way." She released the quilt long enough to gesture to her breasts. "I sprouted these when I was twelve. By fourteen, I was the talk of the locker room. By sixteen…"

Ah, hell. He caught her fingers on their way back to the quilt and laced them together with his own. He needed to hold on to something, too, because he had a feeling he wasn't going to like what she had to say. "What happened?"

"Well, there was a senior in school. Hank Buell—"

"The jackass from the restaurant?"

Alex looked down. "Hank was a real catch back in high school…"

"Tell me about Hank."

"I had a serious crush on him back then. He was an all-state wrestler. Raven-haired. Cute and funny. He was the first boy who talked to me about cars rather than asking my bra size." Her fingers jerked like a vise around Jack's, but he absorbed the pressure without complaint. "Hank asked me out and I was on cloud nine. We dated three or four times, kissed, petted a little."

A black hole of protective jealousy opened up inside Jack, but he quickly buried the reaction. "I'm guessing the next thing you'll tell me is how he urged you to go further? Maybe said all the girls were doing it, or if you really cared about him…?"

Alex nodded. "It was a beautiful warm spring night. He brought me flowers. Took me on a late-night picnic up in the hills north of town." Jack pulled both of her hands between his, massaging away the sudden chill he felt there. "The first time really wasn't very good. He said, maybe if I stripped for him… You know, touched myself, he could—"

"Alex…" That crackle in his voice warned Jack that he didn't have his emotions as fully in check as he'd like.

"In the middle of pretending I was enjoying myself, I heard applause. And laughter. Lights flashed. Hank had sold tickets, and I was the show. Somebody took my clothes and…ow!"

Jack popped his grip and immediately released her when he realized his anger wasn't in check at all. "I'm sorry." Playing that see-if-you-can-convincingly-seduce-me game with her on a secluded country road had probably been a painful reminder of that horrid night. "Did you report it? Him? Them?"

"Shh. It happened ages ago." Alex reached for his hands again, gently brushing her thumbs across his white knuckles.

Oh yeah, look at who was being the strong one and who wasn't getting his job done now. "Buell is still here in Dahlia. His father and brother, too, must be constant reminders. I suppose they turned it around and blamed you for it."

"It's okay, Jack. There was no real crime committed, just poor judgment on my part. I've learned to deal with it."

He wanted to punch something. "By hiding your gorgeous figure? Looking for dates in another town?"

The trace of a smile on her lips eased some of his anger at the torment she must have endured. "You're the only man I ever succeeded at picking up. And I had to nearly get arrested to do it."

Jack tipped his head to the ceiling, exhaling months of regret over that one. When he was sane enough to look at her again, he tried to think like a cop, listening to the account of a crime. But the man in him, who chomped at the bit to right a serious wrong for an innocent woman, added a sharp edge to his voice. "Did anyone do anything to help you?"

"Nick heard about what was going on. He drove into the middle of it and picked me up. Between him and Drew, they scattered the boys and got my clothes back—except for my bra. I guess somebody kept that as a souvenir. The next day, my dad tracked down Hank and beat the crap out of him."

"Good old Southern justice. I think I'm going to like meeting your father. Buell wasn't crass enough to press assault charges, was he?"

Alex shook her head. "But there's no love lost between our families. If Artie wasn't such a good mechanic, and we weren't so shorthanded come race time, Dad never would have hired him. I think Dad's the better man for moving on, but the Buells..." He followed her gaze to the cell phone beside her bed. "I thought I'd heard the last of it."

"You think it was Hank who called?"

"I couldn't recognize the voice. But it felt the same."

"You felt threatened." He couldn't seem to keep his fingers from the feminine cascade of her hair. He didn't like that his partner had paid the price he had, but he understood the logic. What he didn't understand was how a man—a boy—could take such pleasure in destroying a sweet, sexy woman like Alex. For what purpose? A few quick bucks? To show off his conquest to his buddies? The feeling of power over someone else? "You don't think the call was related to the investigation I dragged you into?"

She reached up to still the stroking of his fingers, and lean her cheek into his palm. "Once you finally allowed me to speak, I volunteered, remember?"

He nodded.

"I don't know who all the boys were, watching that night. But it didn't matter—even if they weren't there, they heard about it. For months afterward, I got phone calls at home and snide remarks at school, calling me a tramp or worse." The catch in her voice cut right to Jack's heart. "Someone must have seen us tonight. And whoever was in front of my house smoking his cigarette was hoping for a repeat performance, I guess. Sounds like I'm back to being Alex, the town slut."

"Shut up." He didn't want to hear her take any of the blame for that incident.

"What?" He could see that his harsh words stunned her.

"Just shut up." Not caring about mud or propriety or her father upstairs, Jack scooped her into his arms, quilts and all, and pulled her into his lap so he could hold her tight. So *he* could hold on to something warm and beautiful before the black hole where his soul belonged consumed him. He buried his lips against her hair and rocked her back and forth. "Don't say that word. Don't believe it."

There was a whole new slew of names he was putting on his shit list in this town. They'd pay for hurting the people he cared about.

Cared about? Hell. He'd only known Alex Morgan for what? Five hours? Five hours and seven torturous months of wishing she was in his bed and at his side during those awful days surrounding Eric's murder and funeral.

It had taken him months of running into Rosie every day in a coffee shop before he'd decided he wanted to ask her out. But he already felt more connected to this sweet, baffling bundle of trouble than he'd felt in a year-long relationship with the woman he'd lived with.

His partner would have loved to analyze that one. Something Freudian, Jack was sure. Something reckless that made no sense beyond the fact he'd wanted that mystery woman from the streets of Nashville so badly. Jack wasn't sure he wanted to take the time to figure it out himself. Mostly because he wasn't entirely comfortable with where he thought this insane relationship with Alexandra Morgan might take him.

He needed her arms looped around his neck, holding him tight, before the haze of vengeance that burned behind his eyes began to recede.

"Jack?" Her lips brushed against his jaw. He'd been quiet for too long. He'd gone to that dark, angry place inside him and had lost track of the time. "Are you okay? You're not having second thoughts about me helping you, are you? I can deal with this. I've dealt with it before."

He didn't have to find all the answers tonight. He just needed to be a cop. He needed to look out for Alex the way he would any partner he worked with.

She'd been scared. She'd been used and hurt in ways he couldn't fathom. But she had more strength and courage in the tip of her nose than the entire male population of Dahlia put together. She'd handle this undercover operation just fine.

"Not a one. Just as long as you remember my rules." He kissed the tip of that brave little nose and stood up with her in his arms. For a moment, he simply enjoyed the perfect weight of her, molding to his body. Something deep inside him lurched with the memory of how their bodies could meld together in other ways that were equally perfect. He longed to test the instincts that told him a relationship with Alex Morgan would hold as much pleasure as it would adventure. But was he really in a place where he could handle that kind of commitment?

More importantly, was Alex?

With every honorable instinct he could muster, Jack set her back on the bed, alone, keeping his feet firmly planted on the floor. He tucked her beneath the covers, robe and all. "If you get another call like that, or you think someone is following you I want to know about it ASAP. For now, leave your phone off and go to sleep. I'll be parked right outside, keeping an eye on things. No one is going to get to you tonight."

"*You* did."

"Only because you hung up on me. I can be a very determined man when I'm trying to find out the truth." She looked so young and vulnerable lying there that Jack felt every one of the fifteen years separating them. She needed someone closer to her own age to sweep her off her feet and rebuild her confidence as a desirable woman and make her world the fairy tale she deserved.

But she was stuck with him. At least until his investigation was complete.

Jack leaned over and kissed her forehead. "I'll lock the door behind me when I leave. You might want to, uh, check for muddy footprints before your dad wakes up in the morning."

Then, ah hell, he kissed her mouth. Kissed her again when she responded, parting her lips for him. He kissed her a third time because a taste of this woman never seemed to be quite enough. When he leaned in to kiss her a fourth time, common sense finally smacked him in the back of the head and he pulled away. He'd better leave before he climbed under those covers with her. His presence would be harder to explain away than the footprints.

"Sleep tight, Trouble. We have work to do in the morning."

"It is morning."

"Then I'm the one who needs some sleep. I'll be out in my truck. Good night."

"Good night, Jack."

THE STREET WAS DEAD. A thorough check of every parked car reassured Jack that he was the only nocturnal animal sitting inside a vehicle in front of Alex's house.

But he had no doubts that someone had been out here. The hilly street was full, nearly bumper-to-bumper, along each curb. Yet when Jack had arrived, there'd been one empty parking space—and a trio of cigarette butts out on the grass where he had pulled in. Putting faith in Alex's claim that someone had been watching her, Jack bagged the butts as evidence and tucked them inside his jacket next to the one he'd recovered from the track. He was miles away from a lab to get any DNA tests run, but he'd find an hour to take them into Nashville tomorrow, to see if they could put a name to the bastard who'd terrorized her. And if they matched the one from the track, then *he'd* be the one doing the terrorizing.

He pushed his seat back, giving his legs a little more room to stretch out beneath the steering wheel, wishing the upholstery didn't still carry enough of her scent to mess with his concentration when he needed to be rethinking his plan of action to include bodyguard duty. Jack reached for the cup of coffee he'd bought at the twenty-four hour truck stop out on the highway. He'd planned to be staking out after-hours activity down at the speedway, not here in town, parked across the street from the Morgans' house. He owed his dead partner and his boss in Nashville a speedy investigation, but somehow, protecting Alex from phone calls and past nightmares seemed a more pressing problem at the moment.

Especially since resurrecting that nightmare was probably his own damn fault.

Jack sipped from the plastic cup. Though the call and his investigation might not be related, he had a sneaking suspicion that there *was* a connection. Alex said she'd gone years without any harassment, and suddenly, now that he'd publicly announced them as a team, some prick wanted to torment her again?

More than likely, it was an attempt to scare her off. But off what? Interest in him? Something at Morgan's Garage? Her amateur investigation into her brother's death? Had his claim on Alex stirred up some vindictive nightmare from her past?

The coffee was too bitter to really enjoy, but Jack took another drink. It was still warm, and loaded with enough caffeine to keep him awake until sunrise. He could manage thirty-six hours without sleep, but he'd have to come up with yet another plan to keep an eye on Alex tonight because he suspected that by the end of the day he'd be ready to crash. In bed with him would be the safest place, if she'd go for it. Maybe he should approach Alex's father, or one of her friends, like Tater Rawls or Drew Fisk, for help in keeping an eye on Miss Trouble.

Then again, maybe he was selfish enough to not want any help. He glanced up the slope of Alex's yard to the curtains hanging at her bedroom window. Doing something positive for Alex would be a lot more beneficial for her than tracking down Hank Buell and finishing the beat-down George Morgan had started. She wanted to be a lady? A fair damsel who was treasured by men, not ridiculed by them? All she needed was a man with a little bit of patience to see the woman hiding behind the tough talk and overalls. Under the guise of maintaining their cover, he could teach her that sex was a beautiful thing, not just a bad memory.

Jack wasn't much for games, but he could play an undercover role with the best of them. He'd mull that one over a little bit— Alex Morgan's knight in shining armor. He had a lot more Terminator than Sir Galahad in him. But knew how to treat a lady like a lady. And he had a whole lot of ideas about how he could show Alex just how sexy and desirable she was. Of course every last one ended up with her in his bed. Or his lap. Or…

A bright pair of headlights bounced off his rearview mirror, interrupting his planning and momentarily blinding him. Jack shaded his eyes and turned to the side mirror.

Seems he wasn't the only one keeping watch in Dahlia tonight.

The white Suburban pulling up behind him didn't need its lights flashing for him to recognize an official vehicle. Jack set his coffee in its holder and straightened, ready to do battle if need be. He made sure his jacket covered the gun tucked into the waistband at his back and waited. The man behind the wheel put on his flat-brimmed hat before climbing out. His good buddy, Henry Buell. Watching the sheriff waddle up beside his truck soured Jack's mood and put him on guard.

Neither man bothered with greetings as Buell braced his hand on the edge of Jack's open window. "My deputy said he'd spotted an unfamiliar vehicle parked outside the Morgans' house." The sheriff casually adjusted his belt and turned to spit into the grass. "I got another call saying someone saw a man breaking into the back of the Morgans' house around two this morning. You wouldn't know anything about that, Mr. Riley, would you?"

Jack waited for those beady dark eyes to face him again. "You wouldn't know anything about who'd be keeping that close an eye on Alex and her back door, would you?"

Buell smiled. "The free parking ordinance is just for night time on the residential streets. Come eight o'clock, when folks are off to work, you'll need to move, son."

Jack wondered if Buell had ever enforced the rules so vigilantly with his own sons. "I'll be finished with my coffee right about then, sheriff. Driving Alex to work. Appreciate you lookin' out for me. I'd hate to get a ticket."

Jack's sarcasm wasn't lost on Buell, and Buell's warning wasn't lost on Jack. Alex Morgan wasn't the only one being closely scrutinized in Dahlia. But was it just the good ol' boys being suspicious of a newcomer? A father making sure his boys didn't find more trouble than he could get them out of? Or was Buell guarding something else, altogether?

With a tip of his hat, the sheriff walked back to his Jeep. As soon as he disappeared around the corner, Jack was on the phone to Daniel Rutledge, his liaison in Nashville.

The phone rang twice, then tumbled off its receiver before anyone spoke. "Yeah? This is Rutledge."

"Sorry about the early hour, but I'm discovering it's hard for a stranger to get much privacy here in Dahlia. Did you get the plate number I texted you?"

"Riley?" The grogginess disappeared from the attorney's voice. Jack imagined him pushing back covers, sitting up, going on alert. "You already stirring up the locals?"

"And then some. Grab a pen. I need you to run a few names for me."

"What have you found?"

"I spotted a couple of guys unloading car parts at the track. No drugs, but the parts were fitted to conceal a shipment if they wanted."

"Get me a description. I'll match it up against the parts we have in evidence here." The kid *was* ready to work. "What are the names?"

"Henry Buell—he's the sheriff here in town—"

"The sheriff?"

"And his sons, Hank and Artie Buell. I want to know if any complaints have been filed against them. Ever. DUIs. Restraining orders. Harassment. Criminal mischief."

"Criminal mischief? Are we talking the same case?"

Jack checked the rearview mirror to make sure Buell hadn't circled around to eavesdrop on his conversation. "The Buells act like they're running the show in this town. That kind of power makes me suspicious. There are too many secrets here. And apparently, there's some bad blood between the Buells and another family—the Morgans."

"As in Nick Morgan?"

"His father and younger sister. You know them?"

He heard the pen go down. A drawer opened and shut. Dan Rutledge was getting an early start to his day. "Nick and I went to law school together. He's the one who brought me evidence of the track's illegal activities in the first place. He died in a car wreck before we could get any names. The papers he had burned with him. My office's investigation stalled out after that, until you and your partner uncovered the operation in Nashville."

"Alex Morgan doesn't believe her brother's death was an accident."

The movement on the other end of the line stopped. "That woman is a thorn in my side. Her relentless curiosity is making it difficult to keep our investigation hush-hush."

Though the insult set Jack's teeth on edge, he kept the emotion out of his voice. "I think she can help us."

"As methodical and discreet as Nick was, everything I hear about Alex is that she's loudmouthed and impulsive. Hardly someone I want to trust with the kind of information we've been collecting."

"I need you to return her call."

"Why?"

"Because I think she's right."

"About Nick's death being murder?"

"She's got an inside track on who the players are in Dahlia and at the speedway. She helped establish my cover and is giving me suspect insights you can't get off any report."

He heard the disdain in Rutledge's tone. "Has she been talking to you? She claims she's got some of her brother's notes and wants to know if they're evidence that can prove someone had the motive to run his car off the road."

Jack sat bolt upright, glancing up at Alex's window again. "You knew she had evidence and didn't ask to see it?"

"If it was something useful, Nick would have had it with him when he crashed into that canyon. At best, she's a biased source—at worst, she's a flake. She's looking for a reason to justify a cruel twist of fate, and I feel for her pain. But I can't make it go away. The sheriff there ruled Nick's death an accident."

"The sheriff here is a pile of horse crap." Jack knew the young attorney was his boss on this particular investigation, but he needed to set the record straight. "He's hiding something. I trust Alex's instincts more than I trust his word."

"So it's 'Alex' already, huh?" A long pause punctuated by a heavy sigh indicated Rutledge was reluctantly conceding. "Fine. I'll run a check on Buell and his sons, I'll get you an owner for that plate number and I'll take a closer look at Nick's accident report. If I find any anomalies, I'll give you a call." The shuffling noises at the other end of the line told Jack that Rutledge had resumed his morning routine. "But I'm not trusting Alex Morgan with information that our task force has been keeping under wraps for months now."

"You should. I've already told her most of what I know."

"Are you crazy, Riley?"

"Talk to her, Daniel. We owe her that much."

## 9

THE BANDANNA WAS BLUE TODAY.

The overalls and the attitude were the same.

"Those are the papers Mr. Rutledge said to give you—the ones
I've been trying to get him to look at. He's finally taking me seriously." Jack obeyed the tug on his arm and circled around Alex's
desk to sit. She tested the door to make sure it was closed, then
pulled a chair over and propped it beneath the knob before
turning to face him.

"Expecting company?" he asked.

"No. But I'm not taking any chances if someone *is* watching
us." She waved his attention back to the folder on her desk.
"That's why I wanted to come in early, before everyone else
reports for work. I don't want Dad to know I have that file. If he
finds out I've been snooping around on my own, he'll go into
overprotective-marine mode. And if it's nothing more than a pile
of papers Nick fished out of the trash, I don't want to get his
hopes up. Just read them, okay?"

Her office chair creaked as it took his weight. "Yes, ma'am."

And then the pacing started. Her chin was tilted, the fists
were on her hips. Jack had to look hard to find any trace of the
vulnerable woman who'd phoned him in the middle of the night,
terrified. "I can't believe I've called him twice a day for two
weeks with no answer, and you dial him once and snap—he's
suddenly interested in what I have to say." She groaned. "He still
doesn't believe I know anything, does he? You twisted his arm."

"I told him he was being foolish to overlook any possible clues." Jack wouldn't be so arrogant. "Let's see what you found."

With a closed door and a good forty-five minutes of privacy before anyone else reported for work, Jack opened the binder marked "March–October '07." It looked like a haphazard collection of business papers—purchase orders, receipts, computer printouts, ledger sheets.

While Jack turned pages, Alex walked circles around the room. "So Nick was working on the same case you are?"

"I didn't know until Rutledge confirmed it this morning. Your brother's instincts were good enough to alert the state attorney general's office. Rutledge made the connection to our end of things in Nashville." He stopped at a receipt stapled to a spreadsheet with two different totals circled in red. Jack was no forensic accountant, but even he could see the discrepancies in income, payouts and profit margins. Somebody was hiding some money somewhere. "Any idea whose papers these are?"

Alex shrugged. "Nick wrote 'Andrew Fisk' on the folder. But that's probably just because Mr. Fisk hired him to go through things. I found several different signatures when I looked at the files. Drew, who is still managing the track until Whip Davis takes over. But that won't be until he and his fiancée, Cardin Worth, return from their honeymoon."

"Here's your buddy, Hank." After Alex's suspicions regarding last night's phone call, even seeing his signature dashed across the bottom of a delivery receipt turned Jack's stomach. "He works at the track? You run into this guy every weekend?"

"It's a small town, Jack. It's hard to escape your past." He hated the way she shrugged off the pain and anger that having Buell around all the time must cause her. "Hank makes a lot of deliveries for the Fisks' aluminum plant. They built the stands at the track, and sometimes fabricate replacement parts for cars that race in Dahlia."

Hank Buell delivered fabricated car parts? Jack filed away that nugget of information. He already knew the rat smoked. That gave him two strikes in Jack's book.

"Even my dad's name is in there," Alex continued. "I don't even know if the papers came from one office. Maybe it's just some work Nick discarded and I'm the only one hoping it's important."

This *was* important, especially if the bulk of Nick Morgan's evidence had been destroyed in his accident. "We're only talking a few hundred dollars," Jack cautioned, "but there's enough funny accounting to indicate a much bigger problem. I definitely want Rutledge and his experts to look at this."

Jack closed the file and smiled at Alex. But it faded quickly. Funny, he'd thought she'd be more excited to find out she'd uncovered a trail of criminal activity with this information. But she was still circling the office, staring into some other place and time. "Someone in that file killed Nick over funny accounting? Couldn't they just pay back the difference if he reported them?"

"Alex, sweetheart…" The grim truth would be more of a comfort to this woman than a useless platitude. "It's a way to hide money. These are small amounts—maybe someone's early efforts to hide the fact they stole from petty cash."

"My brother was not killed over petty cash."

"Neither was my partner."

"Your partner?" The pacing stopped. "You said a cop was killed—"

"Forget about it." Shit. How had that slipped out? What was it about this woman that made him drop his guard and forget his common sense?

She circled around the desk. "Jack… You lost someone you were close to?"

He couldn't stand to see those deep green eyes narrowed with pity. Ignoring the question, he stood suddenly, sending her desk chair rolling back until it hit the shelves behind him. "I'd better check the garage to make sure it's clear before I move this file to my room."

He needed to talk about work, focus on the investigation. He did not need to deal with this woman's curiosity or concern.

But she wouldn't let it rest. "What was your partner's name?"

No. He couldn't do this. Instead of talking about Eric, Jack retrieved her chair and placed it between him and Alex, who was resting her hips against the desk. "Before a perp starts hiding a big influx or payouts from drug money, they practice padding smaller bills and receipts. Small successes give them the cajones to go after the big money."

She crossed her arms in front of her, the tilt of her eyes warning him that she understood exactly what kind of diversionary tactic he was using. But, for the moment, she gave the personal questions a rest. "Why would Nick suspect someone at the track was selling drugs in the first place? We know all the people there. They're our friends."

"Friends change if they get into money trouble, get greedy, develop a habit. Drugs are big bucks. The bastards who traffic them are dangerous. Whether you're taking them or selling them, drugs change people. Period."

"Thanks for the public service announcement, Officer Riley." There was no humor to the bite of her sarcasm. "I still can't believe anyone in Dahlia would hurt someone as good and kind as Nick."

Jack met her eyes. "You can't?"

He almost came around the chair at the shiver that rippled through her body. "That was nine years ago, Jack. They were just boys playing a stupid prank."

"Did that phone call last night feel *stupid* to you?" When she conceded the truth with a shake of her head and the resumption of her pacing, Jack felt only marginally victorious about changing the subject and making his point. "Don't you dare defend what they did to you, or think for one minute that you deserved that. I don't know if that event is related to what's going on now, but trust me, kids who can come up with sick tricks like that grow up into the kind of men I'm looking for."

*Way to go, Riley. Those are some real words of comfort.*

He shoved his fingers through his hair, trying to shove some compassion into his brain, as well. "Look, Alex, I'm not trying to be a bastard here."

"Yes, you are." She whirled around. Walked right up to him. "You don't want to talk about your partner and you're trying to shut me up."

"Is it working?"

"If you're grieving for a friend, you can't keep it bottled up inside."

"Didn't think so." When she threw up her hands and turned to walk away, something inside Jack leaped to have her back at his side. He grabbed her arm, swung the chair around and pulled her into his lap. Despite the stiffness of her arms braced between them, he felt instantly better with the warmth of her bottom resting atop his thighs. He stroked a loose curl free from the grip of her bandanna. "Eric Mesner was more like a brother than a friend. Doesn't mean I want to talk about him."

"Was he killed in the line of duty?"

Jack simply nodded. "By the same people I'm after now." He spread his fingers with a gently protective grasp around her hips, determined not to inflict any more of his pain on her. "I need you to understand just how serious, how dangerous these people can be. It galls me to think about anybody hurting you. Ever."

Instead of "Thanks, Jack" or even "You're a pig," she mimicked his actions and smoothed the spikes of hair off his forehead. "You look like crap today."

Jack fell back in the chair, laughing. Great. No damage done if she could still dish it out. "That's it. Shred the old fart's ego. That'll shut him up."

"There's nothing old about you, Jack, except maybe that old soul inside you that sees everything in black-and-white or doom and gloom."

As much comfort as he found in touching Alex, there was

something even more soothing about her laying her hands on him without any kind of hesitation. She framed the sides of his face, dragging her thumb across the stubborn line of his bottom lip. "You're not exactly how I imagined you were all these months. You're rougher around the edges. There's a whole lot less sweet talk. But you're a good man, Jack. I'm glad we're in this together."

"You're not exactly what I imagined, either." She pulled her hands away self-consciously. Jack caught them and put them right back. "Touch me, Alex—I want you to. I…need you to."

Her cheeks blossomed with color. "You *need* me?"

"Yeah." Hell of an admission from big Black Jack Riley. But he was tired. His emotions were raw. And this woman brought an amazing light into his dark, isolated world. A little mutual petting might be a good thing for that "old soul" of his. Lifting her bottom, he adjusted Alex more snugly in his lap and invited her to do what she would to him. "Hell, yeah."

Her soft, tentative touches grew bolder the longer he sat there without responding. Outwardly, perhaps. But his eyes weren't missing a thing, and every cell inside him was reviving, volunteering to be the next one graced with Alex's touch.

Guileless in some ways, a sensual delight in others, Alex Morgan was completely irresistible in everything she did. He watched her fascination with his responses to each tender caress, darting his tongue out to catch her thumb when it passed by a second time. Seeing the pleasure she took in exploring his face was an unexpected turn-on. Watching the self-assurance grow in her expression as she saw the pleasure even these simple touches gave him aroused something potent and male deep inside him.

With his upside down schedule, he probably needed a shave. But she seemed to like scraping her palms over the prickly stubble almost as much as she enjoyed toying with his hair. Would her hands be so bold, so thorough, if they were exploring the eager flesh behind his zipper?

"Didn't you get any sleep last night?" she asked, tracing the shadows under his eyes.

He leaned his forehead against hers and groaned his misery, deciding that was a safer move than grabbing her wandering hand and placing it right where he wanted it most. "I'm okay, Trouble."

Misreading his guttural response, Alex cupped his jaw again and pushed him back far enough to search his eyes. "You have enough on your plate without worrying about me, don't you? Praying the bad guys don't find out what you're really up to before you catch them. Pretending you aren't missing your partner—your friend?" Her eyes darkened with the bitter sorrow she must be reading in his face. "I'm right, aren't I?"

His head jerked with a nod.

She pressed a gentle kiss to the corner of his mouth, another to the opposite side. Caught off guard by her insight into Eric's death and the way the pain of losing his friend tore him up inside, something salty and hot burned beneath Jack's eyelids. Her soft, cooling kisses were suddenly there, as well. "You're hurting already, and I only add more stress. I swear I don't mean to. Tell me about your partner."

"Eric Mesner," he stated matter-of-factly. "They shot him up." Those words were harder to squeeze past the tension knotting his throat. Oh man, he did not want to cry. Gettin' busy with Alex, yes. Crying? Hell no.

"I'm so sorry. Shh." Alex pressed her lips against his. "It's okay."

"How is Eric being dead ever going to be okay?" That better not be a tear she was kissing from his cheek. He slipped his hands inside the loose gape of her overalls and hugged his arms tight around her back, crushing her against his chest. He wanted to feel *her,* not the pain. His lips found the velvety arc of her bottom lip, but words tumbled out, getting in the way of sealing the kiss. "Eric was smarter than me. Saner. Patient. Loving. He had a family. He made *me* family. He had everything to lose."

Alex wound her arms around his neck and rubbed her soft

cheek against his coarser one. "You lost, too. When you love someone that much, you lose, too. I know."

He tugged at the double-layered tank tops she wore, needing the contact with the warm, soft skin underneath to distract his shaking hands. "I just need to find the bastards who shot him and let him bleed out in the street. That's all I need."

"Oh my God. How awful." She squirmed, trying to pull back far enough to read his expression, look into his eyes. "You were there when he died? He suffered?"

"Long and slow before I got there."

With a hot, angry breath, Jack buried his face against the juncture of her neck and shoulder and squeezed her until the images of blood and shock and his own angry screams could be pushed aside. He had soft woman against his mouth to muffle the urge to release those screams. And soon he was tonguing, tasting, suckling her delicate skin. "He was barely alive when I got to him. He…" A hot tear, not his own, dripped onto his ear and trailed along his neck. "He…" No. Jack jerked against images of his partner's lifeless body lying heavy in his arms, of an empty street, mocking the brave man who'd fallen there ignored and alone. "Oh, God." His teeth nipped down a little too hard and Alex grunted at the unintended pain. Jack immediately pulled away. But he couldn't release her entirely. He couldn't make himself let go. "I'm sorry, babe. I'm sorry." He couldn't do this. "Let's not talk about it, okay?"

Her fingers cupped the back of his head and neck, pulling him back to her embrace. "Jack, you need to talk."

"I just need you." He dragged the straps of her overalls off her shoulders, kissed the swell of her cleavage, followed her erotic scent down to the cleft between her breasts. He moved his hands to lift the heavy globes, knead them through her clothes, push them up to bury his nose between them. "I don't want to talk."

Her fingertips clawed at his shoulders, stretching the cotton of his T-shirt, trying to hold on to that hug. "You're just like my father. You don't want the world to see any kind of weakness, so the grief festers away inside you and goes on and on—"

"Don't lecture me." He found the hooks cinching her bra together and released all four of them, freeing her bounty to his eyes and lips. He greedily went straight for a pebbly tip and pulled it into his mouth. Her skin was fiery and responsive beneath the pull of his tongue. He ignored her strangled gasp and her fingers digging into his shoulders. He squeezed the pale globe's heavy weight up against his tongue. "Don't tell me what to feel."

"I'm not." Her voice jerked in time with the needy impulses of his hands and mouth. "You're…hurting. I'm only…trying…to help."

"Enough!" Jack shot to his feet, sending the chair spinning as he dropped Alex onto the top of the desk. But the call of her body couldn't be denied. When she tried to jump down, Jack spread her knees open and moved between her legs. He pulled her to the edge, aligning her hottest feminine softness against his own hardening need. "I'm here to work, not sit through some down-home, Dahlia-style psychoanalysis. I don't need that kind of help."

"You need something." She braced her hands against his chest, squeezed her knees around his hips, squirmed right against his arousal. "Jack!"

He pinned her thighs open as he rubbed himself shamelessly against her. "Yes, I miss Eric. It pisses me off that he's gone and I haven't found justice for him yet. But I will deal with whatever I'm feeling later. I have to do my job first. I have to finish the damn job!" He finally paused when he heard the roaring in his own ears, saw the faint pink mark he'd left on her shoulder, saw the mixture of shock and pity on Alex's pale face. He made a valiant effort to rein it all in, to ease his hold on her, to back away. But he was failing miserably. "I am not going to break. Believe me. I'm as tough as I look."

Damn, if she didn't look as though she saw right through that lie.

"You have to grieve." Her fingers crept up to frame his jaw again, to feather against his hair, to draw his mouth down for a gentling, healing kiss. But the instant he hardened his mouth over hers, she pulled away, sprinkling kisses along his jaw and neck, whispering wise words for her limited years and tormenting him with what he couldn't have. "I know what it's like to be the one left behind. The guilt you feel. Nick had so much more to offer the world than I ever will."

He plucked a metal button loose at her waist. "That's not true. Don't say that."

She skimmed her hands down over his arms, making every muscle quake beneath her touch. "Some days, the only way to get through the grief is to promise myself that I'm going to do more with my life—care deeper, be stronger than I thought I could be. I want to make a difference in the world. I may never measure up—"

"Don't say that." He tipped her chin up to kiss away her doubt. *He* was the one who'd never measure up. He'd never have half of what Eric had lost. "Don't ever say that."

"But I have to try. I have to honor Nick's memory and try." Another button went by the wayside. Now she was kissing the center of his chest, moving over a muscle, touching his heart. "I want him to look down from heaven and be proud of me. Just like I know your partner is so proud of you."

"No." He tried to set her away, but wound up pulling her overalls taut at her crotch, thinning the barrier that separated the helpless push of his hips from the heat and temptation of her feminine center.

Alex gasped at the contact. Her fingertips clutched his chest. She pressed her face against his neck, moaning as his thumb followed the seam of her pants down between her legs.

"Jack." The more she tried to squeeze her legs together to relieve the torment, the more Jack rubbed. And still she tried to reason with him. "You have to…let it go." Every gasping breath was a hot, moist caress against his skin. "You...have to let yourself...feel."

"I don't want to feel." The denim was damp now, fragrant with her alluring scent. "Don't make me feel anything but this."

A profound need to bend Alex over that desk and take back the emotions she'd stolen from him, to lose his pain buried deep inside her blossoming heat spasmed through Jack. No, no, no! Damn it. He wasn't going to hurt. He wasn't going to feel. He had to keep his wits about him, stay in control and get the job done. Alex was his cover, his source for information—a freaking tempting lay—but not his salvation.

She was clinging to his shoulders now, panting, reaching for something he couldn't quite give her. She pressed a kiss to his neck. Another to his chest. In between gasps, she found his nipple through his shirt and tongued it until it stood as erect as his aching dick. But he didn't need gentleness. He didn't need patience or understanding. His body was screaming for release. Raw. Mindless. Fast. Hard. He wouldn't cry. He couldn't grieve. He needed...

"Let go, Jack," she whispered against him. "You don't have to be patient or teach me anything this time. Let me help."

"Damn it, Trouble—Alex." He kissed her mouth. Kissed her cheek. Kissed that damn bandanna. "I need... Do you know what I'm asking?" He thrust his thumb deliberately against her swollen heat and she whimpered. "I need you. Everything." Last night in his truck had been good, but he'd needed this, wanted this, forever, it seemed. "Please let me..." Jack pulled away, barely able to stand. He held his shaking hands up, surrendering himself to her will. "Or say no. There's a crappy cold shower in a room not twenty yards from here."

He held every screaming cell inside his body in check until she answered.

"Yes, Jack." With those deep green eyes holding his gaze, she reached down to her waist and pulled her tank tops up and off over her head. The bra tumbled down her arms and quickly followed. She knocked aside items on top of the desk before setting the wad of tops behind her. Then, like the helpless man he was, he watched her lie down on top of the clothes and vee her legs open, offering her body, herself—her healing mercy—to him. "Yes."

With a hell of a lot more urgency than finesse, Jack untied his boots, unhooked his belt. He retrieved a condom from his wallet before shoes and pants disappeared. Alex slithered out of her plain white panties while he sheathed himself.

When she sat up to reach for him, Jack pushed her back down onto the desk. "Don't I need to help?" she asked.

"No." Her pale skin stretched taut across her weepy mound, and Jack breathed deeply the heady fragrance that was this woman's alone. She lay there before him, a naked, willing sacrifice spread-eagled on an altar, just for him. Ready to be taken. Ready to be his. Ready to give him what he'd needed for so long. "Just be there for me. Let me look. Let me touch. Let me take."

With his left palm holding her writhing hips flat on the desk top, he slipped two fingers inside her, testing her readiness. Her body jerked against his palm. Clenched around his fingers. Her fist pounded the desk and she moaned. She was slick and tight and gasping for a deep breath as desperately as he was. Her breasts bounced up and down in erotic display, beckoning him as she twisted helplessly against his probing hand. Her eyes locked on to his, telling him in yet another way how primed and ready she was for this.

He pulled his fingers out of her and slicked her own moisture around her clit and thighs, trailed it around the rosy areola of each proud, perfect breast, making her whimper and pulse with every stroke. "You're a beautiful woman, Alex. Never doubt that." For a moment, he considered stooping down and taking her with his mouth, making her come again and again. But he hadn't even taken the time to remove his shirt. His dick was hard and swollen and butting against her thigh, telling her exactly what he needed. "Never doubt how much I want you."

Alex propped herself up on one elbow and touched herself, wetting her fingers before reaching for his straining cock. When she wrapped her hand around it and squeezed, Jack cried out, lurching against her grip. The innocent little vixen smiled. "I want you, too, Jack." Her breathless command was a pure carnal invitation. "Don't make me wait any longer."

Jack removed her hand and pushed her back onto the desk. She was as golden and perfect down below as she was on top, but Jack spared little time to admire the view. Unwilling to wait a second longer, he pushed open her thighs, pulled her right to the edge of the desk and buried himself inside her. Buried himself to the hilt. Pushed down into her and ground himself against her, gritting his teeth against the promise of release, even as she cried out and arched her back. She was tight, damn tight, and little ripples of muscles were grabbing him like tiny hands inside her.

He meant to go in slowly, pull out, enter her again—ease her into growing accustomed to the size and shape of him. But he needed her. Damn, how he needed her.

"Are you all right?" He moved one hand to brace himself against the solid oak of the desk. He could barely breathe, barely see around the haze of need swirling behind his eyes. "Damn it, Alex, are you all right?"

Her back relaxed against the desktop, yet she was breathing so hard he could scarcely hear her. "I didn't know...you could come in just...one...time."

"Oh, hell, baby." He would have laughed if he had the strength in him. But Jack Riley was a driven man. He was already moving inside her. "Let's go, baby. Let's do it."

She snatched at his wrist, moved his hand back down to the thatch of hair where he was pumping into her again and again. "Take me, Jack. Take me. Take me."

Even with the fever building inside him, he understood her

request. While he rammed himself deep into her welcoming heat, he sought out the responsive nub between her nether lips and pressed his thumb against it. Alex bucked on the table. Papers flew. He pulled his other hand from the desk and ran it along her abdomen and stomach, easing her back into position. He retreated a fraction of an inch and plunged in as deeply as he could again.

Thoughts of lonely nights and solo showers and mindless grief tried to sneak into the mix of rocket fuel charging through his system, filling his groin with a powerful surge not unlike an engine running at smooth top speed. He moved his hand to a straining breast and anchored himself to the decadent pleasure this woman gave him.

"Jack…it's okay." He closed his ears against the tender voice and focused on the hard nipple and swollen nub beneath his hands. "Jack…"

He rocked against the desk, thrust into her body. Squeezed. Rubbed. The need in his body shifted to a higher gear, erupted through his pores, demanded satisfaction.

The desk moved across the floor with a grinding screech and he felt the finish line slipping away from him. "Stay with me." He pulled her body partway off the desk to sheathe himself again. She wrapped her legs around him, hooked her heels behind his thighs, opened wide and gave him everything he wanted. Unable to make sense of her urgent words, he felt the traces of her second orgasm begin to squeeze him, urging him on. But he wasn't there yet. He wanted something more.

"I need…" No. A powerful emotion latched on to the desire screaming through his veins. He felt strongly about this woman, about this joining. But he didn't want to feel…"Oh, God, sweetheart, I need…"

Jack looped his arms beneath Alex and scooped her up against his chest. As though he was behind the wheel of a speeding car that threatened to spin out of control, Jack felt things inside him buffeting him from every direction. Three long strides carried them across the room. And then he had her up against the wall, her arms and legs wrapped tightly around his body, her breasts crushed against his chest, his mouth covering hers in a fierce kiss as he drove himself home.

Jack roared as his release overtook him. The explosion deep inside her was the most powerful, most humbling, most freeing moment of his entire forty years. He was dizzy with the force of it. Drained.

"Oh, Jack…Jack…Jack." Alex's gasps of weary satisfaction matched his own. She continued to pulse around him as their ragged breathing pushed their sweaty chests and sticky stomachs against each other. She had her fingers in his hair, whispering sweet little somethings into his ear as Jack buried his face against her breast.

Dots of hot moisture hit his cheek and trailed rivulets down through his beard. "Sweetheart, don't. Don't."

Jack pulled her away from the wall, snugged her in his arms and held her close as Alex wept the tears he couldn't shed.

"ARE YOU GOING TO TALK TO ME?" A leather office chair wasn't the most comfortable place for a man to sit when he was naked. But bare skin on warm leather wasn't the discomfort that concerned him. He felt even more exposed inside—all because of the woman in his lap.

Alex sat with her knees curled up, her head tucked beneath his chin, while one hand rested almost protectively over his heart. He wasn't the only one exhausted by that out-of-control desktop session. As their bodies cooled, Jack trailed his fingers in a long line up and down her bare back, lifting her hair to cup her nape, sliding down to the flare of her hip. "I'm not used to you being this quiet for this long. I'm not sure what to think when you're not arguing with me."

"I'm just…tired."

Understandable. He was physically and emotionally spent.

But he was also the one with the experience. She was the one who'd been used and terrorized by a lover before. They both needed a gut check.

"Come on, Trouble," Jack coaxed. How terrifying must it be to have a man of his size and life experience come unglued like that? "Are you hurt? Did I scare you? Unless you have a camera hidden somewhere inside your office, you don't have to worry about anyone seeing us."

"It's none of that. I pushed you too hard to let your real feelings out. I thought I could help, but it's like opening a wound. I only made things worse for you, didn't I?" She stirred restlessly, pulling her arms down to hug them around her knees. She was being self-conscious now? After what they'd just done? After all he'd revealed? "I warned you I wasn't very good at this relationship stuff."

Jack's eyes were gritty with the emotions he'd buried for far too long. The grief and rage that had been trapped inside him had found an outlet that no police psychiatrist, no clergyman, no well-meaning friend had been able to tap into until this tough-talking tomboy-goddess had simply held him, welcomed him, dared him to open up and give himself—all of himself—to her. "You're far better at it than I am. You've got a big heart. I hope I didn't take advantage of that."

"You didn't." She inched a little more space between them, but Jack's hand on her hip asked her to stay with him a while longer. "I'm still having a hard time resolving Fantasy Jack with what it's really like with you."

"Fantasy Jack?"

She sat straight up now, dropping her feet to the floor. The heat he felt warming his cheeks was nothing compared to the deep blush on hers. "I shouldn't have said that out loud. Since we met last October, you kind of, um…" she gestured meaningless circles in the air, "when I imagine…"

"I think I can fill in the blanks." He hoped Fantasy Jack had done a better job of seeing to her needs than he had. He grimaced at how this morning's encounter must compare to her knight in shining armor dreams. "You know, it's hard for a man to live up to the heroes in fairy tales and fantasies."

"I know." Was that disappointment? But then she turned and looked at him with a wry smile. "It has been different, but I like the real thing better than…oh." She pressed her fingers to her lips to hide her embarrassment.

"Than what?"

"My washcloth."

"Ah, hell." Jack wrapped his arms around her and pulled her back to his chest. As much as she knew about the darker side of human nature, she was still so damn young and naive about the craziest things in this world. "It can be better for you, babe. It *should* be better. Next time I'll make sure of it."

"Next time? We could do this again?"

Jack nodded at her curious, hopeful expression. He didn't deserve the rush she was giving his ego. "I'm not a cop 24/7, Alex. I won't be on this case forever. If you let there be a next time for us, I promise it won't be the quickie like last night in my truck, or the catharsis that this was. There's a way a man's supposed to treat a lady. Slow, gentle—"

"But exciting, right? I…" Her eyes dropped for a moment before looking back up into his, exacting a promise he intended to deliver. "I'm learning a lot from you, Jack. I'm learning that sex can be a wonderful thing. That it's more than hormones and hot spots. It's kind of…empowering, isn't it? I love how it makes me feel…with the right man."

Exciting? Empowering? Exactly. "I'll make sure it happens that way for you."

"Next time," she murmured, snuggling back against his chest. "You know, I've never done it in a bed. I know that's the usual place, but…"

Laughter rumbled deep in his chest as Alex chattered on about some interesting possibilities for more sex. This woman had the resiliency of…Alexandra Morgan. There was no one else like her in the world—at least not his world. She'd endured cruelty and grief and still came out swinging. She had self-doubts, but an instinct about people far wiser than his own at times.

Something deeper than the sex, more profound than the physical release, had bonded them in a way that left Jack feeling closer to this woman than he'd felt to anyone in his entire life. Closer than Rosie. Closer than Eric, even. He'd let Alex Morgan into a place where she alone knew his deepest, darkest secrets. He felt raw. Beholden. Like she already owned half his heart.

He wasn't exactly comfortable with that kind of closeness. It was as if she'd gotten inside his most personal undercover role and could expose him if she was so inclined. How was he supposed to trust someone else with that kind of power over him?

The solace he'd found in Alex's willing body made him feel at once lighter, calmer, and yet, somehow more burdened than he'd been an hour ago. She'd unleashed a dam of emotions inside him. And, until he sorted them all out, he needed to be careful or he'd wind up giving his whole heart to another woman who didn't want it.

# 10

not be to her. Third, he would have to marry. There will be no ... to fill.
A lthough ... but when she made to move, she had not said no. She hadn't ...

THE SOUND OF MALE VOICES in the hallway startled Jack from his drowsy speculation. By the time a key scraped into a lock across the hall, he was wide awake. Alex jumped off his lap, dove beneath her desk and crawled across the floor to retrieve their clothes.

Apparently, the time for cuddling and reflection was over.

She jerked her panties up over her hips and tossed Jack his jeans. "Come on. Dad will come looking for me any minute. We always start our work day with a cup of coffee and discuss our schedules and plans."

Carefully peeling himself off the chair, Jack picked up a sock and began to dress. "Alex..." She hooked, buttoned, gathered papers, straightened a picture frame—moving too fast to get a touch or word in. "This doesn't change anything."

"I know." She pulled on her yellow tank top, and then the blue one.

Jack slid into his shorts and jeans. "We still have to work at the track today, still have to get those papers to Rutledge."

"I know."

"And I still think you're the classiest lady I've ever known."

"Lady?" She paused in the middle of tying a boot. "I don't think so."

When she straightened, Jack grabbed the strap of her overalls and fastened the last hook for her. "*These* don't keep you from being a lady." He leaned in and kissed her pale mouth, bringing back its warm, rosy color. Everything was still a mess inside him, and he didn't know where to begin or where he needed to end up. He just knew… "Thank you."

"Jack, I…" A rap at the door silenced whatever she'd meant to say.

"Alexandra? You in? I didn't see your car out front."

Her father? Great. How teenagery was this scenario?

Alex squeezed his forearm, trying to reassure *him*. Hell.

"We can't talk about this right now." She turned and shouted toward the door. "Good morning, Dad. I'm just finishing up some paperwork. I'll be right out."

"What paperwork? Honey, you're not spending my money to sponsor another driver, are you?"

Alex hurried over to the door to push the chair aside, but stopped and popped up mid-slide. Uh, oh. What was she thinking now?

"Trouble?" Jack scooted the desk back into place, waiting for an answer.

"Alexandra?" Her father knocked again. "Is someone in there with you?" The knob rattled and turned. "Alexandra?"

With one quick shove of the chair and a pat to make sure her bandanna was on straight, she opened the door. "Morning, Daddy." Alex stretched up on tiptoe to kiss her father's cheek and trade a hug. But *Daddy* was looking over her shoulder, straight at Jack. Uh, oh. Jack was too old for the lecture he saw brewing. Could Daddy tell Jack had just had sex with his daughter?

"Dad, this is Jack Riley, the driver who's renting our back room. Jack, my father, George Morgan."

The two men shook hands. "Mr. Morgan."

"Jack. Word's already out about you down at the coffee shop." George's suspicious green eyes traveled from Jack back down to his daughter. "This isn't the back room."

"We were having a meeting." Alex jumped back into the conversation. "I have a plan, a way to boost promotion for the garage and bring in new business."

Was that the brainstorm that had struck moments ago?

George splayed his hands at his hips. "Funny how my daughter's never mentioned you before."

"Dad—"

"Long-distance relationships are hard to maintain. We've kept ours very low-key, in case it didn't work out." Jack dared to drape a possessive arm over Alex's shoulders and pull her to his side. If they were playing the roles, they needed to play them for her father, too. "She's told me about how the gossip works in this town."

The stern suspicion turned to surprise. "She told you?"

"Yes, sir. I'm very aware of protecting Alex's reputation."

Surprise became a glimmer of acceptance, if not necessarily approval. "Not to be rude, but how old are you?"

"We're both legal age, Dad."

"Yeah, but he looks a little more legal than you are."

"Dad." Alex nudged Jack aside. "I want to tell you about my idea."

She'd played along with everything he'd asked of her thus far. A business meeting, eh? Jack could play along, as well. "Yeah, I'm anxious to hear you explain the plan, too."

"This one's always getting ideas in her head," George groused with a mixture of love and trepidation in his voice.

Alex rolled her eyes at them both. "Come on in and have a seat, Dad." She took one look at the desk, then turned and pushed her father back into the hallway. "Better yet, let's talk in your office." They were all settled with chairs and coffee before Alex continued. "My promo idea is a good one, and it won't cost you a thing."

"Sounds too good to be true. How do you figure that?"

As Alex and Jack sat side by side on her father's couch, she reached over to squeeze Jack's knee. "We're going to sponsor Black Jack at this weekend's races."

"I told you not to be buying anything but car parts."

"I won't, Dad." Jack imagined that smile could convince Daddy to agree to just about anything. He knew *he* found it hard to resist. She set down her coffee and crossed to her father's desk.

"I've decided to donate my time and expertise to prep Jack's car for the race."

"*You're* going to soup up his car?"

"I'll be a one-woman pit crew. We'll put a *Morgan & Son's* logo on Jack's racing suit and decal it on his car. All I need from you is the space to work. And a couple of days off to get it all done."

George took Alex's hands in his. "You're serious about getting into this business, aren't you."

"Yes. Sorry, Dad, but you're never going to make a Southern belle out of me."

He gently tweaked his daughter's chin and smiled. With a sage nod of acceptance, George leaned around her to address Jack. "And you're okay with this arrangement? We wouldn't be paying you anything." He glanced up at Alex. "We're not paying him *anything,* right?"

Jack unfolded himself from the couch and joined them. "I've been out of racing for a while, sir. Believe me, I'm glad to have the help to…" A startling realization put the charade on hold for a fraction of a second, and turned Jack's entire plan to get into Dahlia, get the truth and get back out, sideways. "She's helping me get back to where I want to be. Your daughter seems to have a real gift for fixing things."

And he wasn't talking about cars.

THIS WASN'T RIGHT. The wires weren't original and the engine block looked a couple of micrometers short of being properly aligned inside the chassis. And what was that extra seam of solder inside the wheel well for?

Alex's heart skipped a beat, then pumped a little faster.

Someone had tampered with this car.

She guessed that shouting for Jack to come and look at her discovery while the garage was busy with mechanics and customers wouldn't fit his rules for undercover work. So she took a deep breath and pretended her heart wasn't racing with excitement as she scooted off the fender of Drew Fisk's Corvette and pulled the shop rag out of her back pocket to wipe her hands. "I'd definitely say it's your alternator, Drew. It just doesn't seem to want to hold a charge."

Her friend muttered a much more civilized curse than the gasket she would have blown at learning his sixty-grand investment was a piece of recycled junk inside. Drew closed the hood. "I just spent a fortune on these two cars. I can't afford to add repair bills on top of that."

Alex tried to offer a bright side to having a new sports car die after three days. "Well, the 'Vette is this year's model, so it has to be under warranty. Why don't you just take it back to the dealer?"

Drew skimmed a hand over the top of his trim blond hair. His face had gone pale beneath his tan. "I didn't go through a dealership. The guy I bought the Mustang from threw in the Corvette to make it a real sweet deal."

"Too good to be true, hmm?" Alex squinched up her face in sympathy. When Drew had come into the garage this morning, asking for a favor, she'd been willing enough to help. But this was one she couldn't fix. It was, however, something she really needed to show Jack. Wasn't that how he'd said the drugs were being smuggled into Nashville? Through modified cars and parts? Hello! She'd just seen the evidence that one of her friends had possibly been duped by the very men Jack was looking for. Maybe they could find out where the car had come from. "Will you be sending this back to Nashville for repairs, then?"

"That's a hell of an expensive mistake to make." Drew turned nearly 360 degrees, perhaps checking to make certain no one was eavesdropping on his misfortune—or maybe just looking for an empty place where he could throw something without hitting anyone. "Are you sure it can't be fixed here? Grandfather will freeze my trust fund again if he finds out I've been taken on a stupid deal like that. First, he sells the track out from under me, and now he'll start checking every business deal I make."

"We'd have to order in the parts, but I suppose we could do it." Wait a minute. "What do you mean, sell the track out from under you?" She pulled a boxed set of socket wrenches from her tool chest and dropped them into her portable tool box for the trip she and Jack were taking to the track this afternoon. She used the task of packing the rest of her tools to scan the garage for a sign of where Jack might have gone. She spotted him having a conversation with her father near the office exit—hopefully about cars, and not her. Or Jack's investigation. "I thought the Fisks selling the speedway to Whip Davis was a group decision, that you had some big job lined up somewhere else in the family business."

"Are you kidding? I have no desire to end up like my father—tied to his work twelve months a year, living every day trapped in his corner office or on an airplane." Drew circled around his car to take Alex's arm and turn her full attention back to him. "You understand what it's like. I love the excitement of the track, getting my hands dirty down in the pits, the thrill of finding that next great car and driver who are going to make the Fisk name famous. I want to create my own fortune so that I don't have to follow Grandfather's boring old code of Fisk family behavior and expectations."

Startled by his touch, but not afraid, Alex patted his hand and smiled. She could understand the drive to be his own man. After all, she was desperately trying to be her own woman, and make her father as proud of her as he'd been of Nick. But Drew Fisk getting his manicured nails dirty down in the racing pits? She doubted she'd ever see that day. "I never knew you had goals like that, Drew. I thought you were all about Fisk family traditions. Trophy wife. Plantation life. Running empires."

"Very funny. I'm serious. That track was my baby."

She smiled at the rare glimpse of real passion etched beside his eyes. "So you want to discover that next great car and driver?"

"Did I hear someone mention my name?" The shift in Drew's gaze warned her a split-second before Jack walked up behind her.

Drew released her and retreated a step as Jack rested his hands at either side of her waist. She felt a kiss at the crown of her hair before he stepped around her to shake Drew's hand. "Fisk. Good to see you again."

"Jack."

Jack nodded toward the Corvette. "Problem with your ride?"

"She died on me this morning. I thought maybe it was all that rain we had the past few days getting up under the engine, but Alex says it's the alternator." Whatever warmth and camaraderie had been in Drew's voice a moment ago had cooled now that the conversation included Jack. No doubt, like her father, he was reserving judgment on the stranger who'd allegedly laid claim to her heart—or at least her bed.

Either Jack didn't sense the change, or he didn't care. He flattened his palm at the small of Alex's back. "Are you sure your dad doesn't mind you taking the day off to put my car through its paces?"

Drew's frown filled his voice. "Aren't you going to order the parts for my Corvette? I want to get it fixed as soon as possible."

"Sorry, she's spoken for." Jack pinched the back of her overalls and tugged her toward the next garage bay. "Come on. I want to hit the track while the sun's still shining and the asphalt's dry."

"I'm coming. Here, make yourself useful." She picked up her tools and pushed the heavy box into his hands. Turning back, she gave Drew an encouraging smile. "Don't worry. Ask Artie to call in the order. He maintains your drag racers. I imagine he can take care of your street car, too."

"Artie?" Drew grimaced.

Alex laughed. "Go talk to him. He's downstairs in the lube pit."

Leaving Drew behind to dig through the Corvette's glove compartment and whine to himself about his own foolishness, Alex looped her arm through Jack's and whispered. "You and I need to talk. But not here."

Jack was pulling her along as much as she was pushing him. "No. You and I need to talk."

"About what? Oh, wait." Alex snapped her fingers and pulled away. She'd nearly forgotten. "Hey, Drew?"

Apparently not finding what he'd been looking for, he slammed the car door shut and straightened his jacket. "Decided to take pity on me, after all?"

"I tell you what, if Artie gets the parts, I'll make the repairs on your car first thing next week. After the races."

"Promise?"

"Only if you do me a favor."

The frustration lining his face eased. "Anything for you, Shrimp."

"Could we borrow your keys to the track so we can open it up and do a couple of test runs on Jack's car?"

"So that's whose engine you'll be tuning this weekend."

If there was anything suggestive in Drew's comment, Alex overlooked it. She knew people were talking about her and Jack. She supposed that was the point, really, to get people used to him as a fixture around the track and town so that he wouldn't attract so much attention. They'd gossip about that new driver in Dahlia and what he was up to with Alex Morgan. Hopefully that would distract them from the fact that he was asking lots of questions and poking his nose around in track business. "Thanks, Drew. I appreciate it."

"Just make sure you lock the gate when you're through. There'll be a couple of deliveries from Jim DiMarco in concessions and a replacement awning from Dad's plant later this afternoon. Other than that, you should have the track to yourselves."

On impulse, she stretched up on tiptoe and kissed his cheek. "You're the best. We'll try not to beat your car too badly come Saturday."

He dropped the ring of keys into her hand. "You care to make a small wager on that?"

Large hands closed around Alex's shoulders and steered her

back toward the Camaro in the next bay. "I'm the man to make a bet with if you're talking cars," Jack challenged. "You think your Ford can beat my Chevy?"

"A hundred dollars says yes."

Alex realized a hundred bucks was a drop in the bucket to a Fisk, but what happened to Drew just blowing sixty grand on a lemon of a car and getting called on the carpet by his grandfather for throwing his money away?

"Make it five hundred and you've got a deal."

"Jack!"

Drew nodded and extended his hand. "You're on."

With the two big men done trading testosterone, Jack turned to catch up as Alex stalked away.

"What was that about?" she asked. "We haven't even towed your car out of the garage yet and you're betting you'll win?"

"Testing a theory. Is Fisk always that anxious to make a wager?"

"I suppose. I mean, the man comes from money. If he wants to play…" Alex stopped, sending Jack colliding into her backside. She was already turning before he could ask if she was all right. "I get it. The numbers in that file of Nick's. If Drew is losing money gambling…"

Jack dipped his face close to hers, keeping his voice at a whisper and urging her to do the same. "There were plenty of padded numbers in those papers to cover a few five-hundred dollar bets. And your father just told me the last person your brother talked to before he left for Nashville that night was Andrew Fisk. They'd set up a meeting for when he got back to town. That'd throw up a red flag to anybody who didn't want your brother talking about his suspicions."

Alex thumbed over her shoulder. "Drew's grandfather, Andrew Fisk?" A shocked *O* rounded her mouth. "The man is pushing eighty. You don't think a sweet old gentleman like Mr. Fisk is running dope through his own racetrack, do you?"

Jack pressed a finger to his lips, reminding her to keep her voice down. "What I'm thinking is that a lawyer spending that much time at the track offices is likely to run across more than doctored books. Whatever he planned to tell Fisk's grandfather probably set off the chain of events that led to his…accident."

"Wait a minute. You talked to my father about your investigation? I don't want you to upset him."

"I just asked him about Nick. Offered my condolences. He's the one who started talking about your brother's work. Let's get out of here before someone overhears us."

He stepped around her to the four-wheeler they'd already tethered to Jack's Camaro and set her tool box in the rear basket. Rather than waste a drop of the expensive fuel used to run the drag racers, or risk any kind of damage to the delicate motor inside, it was customary to tow the car onto the track instead of driving it across the parking lot.

Once he'd strapped her tools in safely, Jack straddled the ATV and patted the seat behind him. "Let's move it, Trouble."

Alex was slower to climb on. She wondered how a man could be overwhelmed by deep emotions in the throes of passion, and then turn it all off and become this calculating investigator again, trusting no one and sharing none of the need or even concern he'd shown for her in the privacy of her office that morning. She hugged him tight with her knees and arms, missing the private Jack more than she cared to admit.

The mild warmth of the midday sun was a welcome comfort to the lonesome chill working its way through Alex's body. As they rode the four-wheeler across the lot to the track's brick arch entrance, Alex tried to take a lesson from the master. Turn down her emotions. Think like a cop.

She leaned into his back, hoping that he could hear her above the vibrations of the four-wheeler's motor. "Do you really think of Drew as a suspect? He was a friend of my brother's from as far back as I can remember."

Jack slowed as they approached the Dahlia Speedway's white

metal entrance gate before looking over his shoulder to answer her. "Every crime needs three things, Trouble. Motive, means and opportunity. I've got nothing to prove your pal Fisk is covering debts by moving drugs through his business." He stopped and idled the four-wheeler, putting out a hand for her to hold on to so she could climb off and unlock the gate. He held on, waiting for her to face him before finishing his answer. "If Fisk has problems with money, that's motive. He comes from a family of business entrepreneurs, so I'm guessing he has the means to travel and meet these people. And if he's running the place, he's got all the opportunity in the world to manage the cars and cash and goods that come in and out of this speedway."

"Drew would never be a part of killing Nick or your partner. His financial problems don't make him a criminal."

Those steel-gray eyes didn't flinch. "No. But they make him a suspect. You watch out for him. Even if he's not a part of this, he's not above taking advantage of you."

"I watch out for every man in this town." Alex pulled her hand away. The dart of her eyes let Jack know he was currently included on that list.

"How much did you plan to charge him for working on his car?"

"Just for parts."

"And which one of you is the millionaire who can afford to pay for the work?"

"Doing a favor for a friend isn't the same as letting someone take advantage of me." She fished Drew's keys out of her pocket, reminding Jack that Drew was doing them this favor. "In fact, I believe someone might be taking advantage of his gambling and investment problems. If the clues all point to him, as you suggest, he'd make a perfect fall guy for someone working behind the scenes, right?"

"I suppose." Jack followed behind her, pushing open the gate once she'd unlocked the chain. "What's your theory, Detective?"

"Very funny. Remember, back at the garage, I said I needed to tell you something?"

"Yeah?" He towed the Camaro through the gate, then waited for her to climb on before heading over to the staging area.

"Drew's Corvette—the one he bought in Nashville a few days ago." They drove onto the 1/8 mile strip of asphalt and lined the Camaro up in the staging lane beside the starting tower. "I didn't have time to get a really thorough look at it, but someone had modified it under the hood."

"Modified the motor?"

"No." Alex got off and unhooked the tether from Jack's car. "To me, it looked as though someone had removed the engine so they could reshape the interior wheel well."

Jack rode the four-wheeler over to the nearest pit and jogged back to pull his fireproof racing suit from the driver's seat of the Camaro. "You think there was a hidden compartment built into the car?"

"Things are tight inside a Corvette. Whoever did the work didn't put it back together very well. I think that's why it stopped running. Drew said he bought both the Corvette and his racing car from the same guy in Nashville. Maybe both cars have been modified to transport drugs." She unstrapped Jack's helmet while he pulled his black racing pants on over his jeans. "Tonight, after the garage is closed, I can get back in there for a better look."

"*We* will go back in for a closer look. You're not doing anything on your own in this town. There are too many people I don't trust."

"I can tell my dad that you and I have a date."

Jack shrugged into the matching fireproof jacket. "Your dad suspects that you and I have done a little more than date."

Alex busied her hands with zipping up Jack's jacket, ignoring the familiar sting of disappointment in herself. "He was so hoping to have Suzy Homemaker for a daughter. Instead he got stuck with Alex the tomboy who sleeps with mystery men before he even gets a chance to meet them. No wonder the slut rumors have started again."

"Don't say that. From everything I've seen, George is very

proud of you." The flinty hardness of his eyes softened, giving Alex a glimpse of the man who could show he cared. "What he got stuck with was a loyal, talented daughter whose heart is big enough to carry both of you through these tough times. He loves you, Alex. He's a lucky dad. And for the record, you've slept with one *man.*" His voice deepened. "Anyone who tries to say you're anything but a lovely, loving woman will answer to me," he growled.

Alex tilted her chin to read the powerful flux of emotions that darkened Jack's features. A smile blossomed across her mouth and deep inside her heart. "Who needs a knight in shining armor when I have a fierce warrior like you on my side?"

Jack laughed. Sort of. "You know, the sage old warriors usually don't make it to the end of the movie. We teach what we know to the young bucks, and then they wind up with the girl."

With his helmet hugged between them, Jack was too far away. His joking doubts about a lasting relationship with her put even more distance between them. But Alex was a woman with an idea on how to fix problems like that. She grabbed the collar of his black jacket. "I have a feeling that you're one old warrior who's going to make it all the way to the end of the flick."

Alex tugged on his collar and pulled him down for a kiss. She held on tight and kissed him hard, kissed him deep.

In a matter of seconds, the helmet was gone, and so was the cop. The Jack that wrapped his arms around her and lifted her onto the hood of the Camaro was the lover who held her tight and took his own sweet time kissing her.

Alex was breathless and dazed and a little less afraid of giving her heart to this man when he tore his mouth from hers with a groan and rested his forehead against hers.

Smiling, he pressed a kiss to the tip of her nose. "Does this mean I get the girl?"

"You'll get her tonight," Alex promised. "Our date at the garage, remember?"

"That's work. I'm interested in play."

"Wasn't that one of your rules, Jack? Pretend that we're lovers?"

"Screw pretend. I want to screw you."

It was no *milady,* but in that deeply pitched husky voice, the honest request was more of a turn-on than anything her imagination could devise.

Alex gave him a quick kiss and then pushed him away. She jumped to the ground and retrieved his helmet, planting it in his gut and earning an "oof" and a smile. "We'll talk about that later. But first, let's see if this car has as much fire in it as the man who's driving it."

# *11*

"YOU LET ME DOWN, BABY."

Jack pulled off his helmet, tossing it out the window before attacking the harness that strapped him into the Camaro's safety cage. The vibrations from the Outlaw class engine were still shaking through his body. He didn't need to see Alex's honey-blond head shaking back and forth over on the sidelines to know that hadn't been a good run.

His line hadn't been straight and he'd hesitated a fraction of a second too long before shifting the car from third to fourth, missing out on the maximum power boost it should have given him. If there had been a car in the opposing lane, Black Jack Riley would have been left in his competition's fumes and dust. A few things had changed since his glory days of drag racing back in high school. Namely, the driver. He was rusty.

Seeing Alex grab her toolbox from the four-wheeler and jog toward him, with those delectable bouncing Bettys leading the way, Jack grabbed on to the roof and hauled himself out of the car. He'd better stand up for what was coming. His disappointing run was bound to earn a pointed debate with the sexy ace mechanic.

He unzipped his jacket and flung it onto the Chevy's roof, feeling the cool spring breeze on his hot skin like a steadying breath. Instead of moaning about what hadn't worked, he'd better look for the positives. But the list was short as he circled the car. He grunted a laugh. At least the chute had deployed to let the air resistance help drag him to a safe stop. Alex reached the hood of his car and set down her tool box. Jack met her halfway as she pulled her earplugs out and let them dangle around her neck. "All right, Trouble, let's hear it."

He gave her points for pausing a moment to at least pretend she was thinking through her response. "People are going to laugh you off the track." She pulled her stopwatch from her pocket and showed him the time. "Yes, you shaved a half second off your first run. But at 8.1 seconds, you won't even clear the prelims to make it to the weekend races when the big crowds are here. This bad-boy comeback you're trying to intimidate people with won't be very impressive if you're sitting in the stands."

Jack propped his hands at his hips and tipped his head up toward the clear blue sky. "You know, I'm all for honesty in a relationship, but if you want to shred my ego why don't you just say I'm too old to play at this game anymore."

Four fingers latched on to the waist of his pants and pulled his attention and body to the front of the car. "You'll be too old the day I'm too girly. Quit feeling sorry for yourself, Stud Man, and help me get the hood off."

"Stud Man?" Jack arched an eyebrow. "What—"

But she'd already run to the other side of the car to unscrew the hood clamps. "I'll see what I can do. If I can get the parts, I can make this thing go." Jack unfastened his side and lifted off the hood, leaning it against the car while Alex pulled out a flashlight and shimmied up onto the fender. The motor itself was probably still too hot to touch, but she was already checking wires, shining the light down into the bowels of the engine. "Yeah. I can get some more horsepower out of this baby. I'd have to add another coolant tank, but it looks like there's room to rig that up under the seat. I'll add an air spacer, too, to keep the carburetor cooler and increase the torque. Don't worry. I'll get you down under six seconds, maybe even five. If you stay on the track and drive a straight line, we could win. Or at least keep you around till Sunday."

Jack wasn't sure how long he stood there, mostly enjoying the view of her ass as she started adjusting things in the engine. Even without the fireproof jacket, he was making himself sweat imagining all the things he could do with Alex bent over a car like that. Then his eighteen years of investigative experience finally kicked in. The reminder hit him like a slap in the face. This week wasn't really about him and Alex, or even about racing. He had a prime opportunity here with no one on site except for the two of them. What was he doing just standing there? Justice for his partner—and now Alex's brother—was waiting.

"Hey, Trouble." He announced himself before he palmed her butt to warn her of his intentions, and stuck his hand inside her right pocket to pull out the ring of keys she'd used to open the gate. "Hearing you talk cars gets me about as excited as hearing you talk dirty."

"Do you want me to talk dirty to you?"

He leaned over her and kissed the blush warming her cheek. "Desperately. But I have some work I need to do first. Will you be okay here for a few minutes? I want to take a look through the supply room. Follow up on something I found earlier this week."

Alex glanced over her shoulder. "It'll be locked up."

He jangled Drew's keys. "Not for long."

She slid back to the ground, tucking a loose curl beneath her bandanna and leaving a cute little smudge next to the worried frown on her forehead. "What if someone finds you snooping around? Do you need me to be your lookout?"

"I need you to stay right here with the car and provide anyone who shows up a plausible reason for me being here. See if you can get this baby into racing shape again. I'd like to run another eighth-mile before we take her back to the garage." He pressed a quick kiss to the smudge and turned toward the viewing stands. "I'll be back in fifteen minutes."

ALEX WAVED TO JIM DIMARCO as the bald man drove his unmarked truck through the track gate—waved as though he was a long lost friend she hadn't seen in years. She waved and gestured, desperately hoping he'd drive over and talk to her. She wanted his attention right here at the drag strip with her instead of at the guest services area where Jack was still looking for evidence.

When Jim pulled up and shifted into neutral, Alex wiped her hands and strolled over for a chat. "Hey, Jimbo. Hey, Crank."

As usual, Jim's partner in the food delivery business was sitting beside him, waiting to provide the muscle to unload the supplies from the back of the truck. He glanced her way. "Miss Alex."

Jimbo, on the other hand, made up for his short stature with a friendly, good-ol'-boy charm that always made her smile. He hitched up the sleeve of his Fisk Aluminum racing team jacket and leaned out the window, nodding toward the Camaro. "So what's goin' on here, little darlin'? Did you get yourself a new toy?"

She tilted her head up to the truck cab. "It's my boyfriend's car." Though there was nothing boyish about Jack, it sounded like a reasonable response. "Pretty sweet, isn't it? I'm fixing it up for him."

"Would that be Black Jack Riley?" Jimbo seemed inclined to chat. Good. Hopefully, Jack would have heard the truck and would be locking up by now.

"You've heard of him?"

"Down at Pammy's over morning coffee with the guys. Word is he's been paying you surprise visits." Jimbo scanned the empty stands and track buildings. "Is he here?"

*Keep your attention right here, buddy.*

Alex walked up to Jimbo's door. Making up stuff outside her bathtub fantasies wasn't as easy as she'd hoped. She avoided his question and jumped on the first thing that came to mind. "Have you heard good things about him? I mean, what are people saying?"

Jimbo chuckled as he faced her again. "It depends on who's talking," Jimbo answered. "Pammy and the ladies were throwing out words like 'tall, rugged mystery man.'" Crank snorted.

Alex winced. Folks in Dahlia really were talking about her again. "But the men are more interested in what he's driving and what his stats are." He nodded over her head toward the car. "What's she running?"

8.1 seconds wouldn't impress anybody around here. Counting on her expertise and Jack's determination, Alex lied. "About 5.2. I'm hoping to get it down a few more tenths of a second."

Jimbo nodded. "Nice. That should give him a shot at the money. How'd you two meet?"

"Yeah." Crank was joining the conversation? The bearded man leaned forward. "Seems he showed up out of nowhere."

The question caught her off guard, changed the topic and rattled her composure. "How did we meet?"

Jimbo shrugged his shoulders. "Don't take this the wrong way, but we kind of thought you didn't like guys."

"Really?"

"The word I heard was that you didn't want to have anything to do with men, you know, in that way. I knew Hank Buell always had a thing for you, so I figured that's why you two only hooked up that one time."

Hank was still talking about that night? Figures he'd turn it around and make that humiliating virgin sacrifice for the boys her fault. "I guess I'm a one-man kind of a woman. And Hank wasn't it."

Jimbo ran his fingertips over his smooth, shaved head. "That's good to know. I mean, when Drew Fisk steered me away from asking you out, I just always figured it was because you didn't like men."

Like there was no other reason to turn away from a bastard like Hank or the disturbing innuendoes of how the men in town were still talking about her sex life. A fuse of anger lit and simmered through her veins, giving Alex the courage to move her hands to her hips and tilt her chin higher. "You can lay those rumors to rest, Jimbo. I think Jack Riley is hot. Hank Buell doesn't know the first thing about making a woman feel like a woman. But Jack does. As soon as I met him in Nashville, I knew he was the man I wanted."

Jimbo raised his hand in surrender to her vehement defense of her relationship with Jack. "Down, darlin'. I believe you. Of course, with a car that runs the eighth in five seconds, even I'd be interested. Hell, if I'd have known that a fast car was all it took to get you hot and bothered, I'd have—"

"Jimbo." Crank's stern warning put the kibosh on the conversation. "We've got a schedule to keep."

"No." Where was Jack? Alex grabbed the door of the truck as Jimbo shifted it into gear. "Can't you stay and chat?"

"Sorry, darlin'. But we're on the clock. I'm guessing you are, too." He winked. "Have fun with that Chevy."

Alex stepped aside and Jimbo drove the delivery truck over to the concrete-block buildings behind the stands. She wondered at the double entendre of his last comment, suspecting that was how a lot of the locker-room talk about her in town was going.

But gossip she could survive. She was an old pro at that. Worrying that she hadn't bought the tall, fierce warrior she was falling in love with enough time to get himself someplace safe, however, was a whole new experience.

*NICE WORK, SWEETHEART.*

Jack had long suspected that Alex Morgan's mouth could be a potent weapon. He was just glad she was using it for the forces of good.

He'd heard the delivery truck driving through the gate, but she'd distracted its occupants and given him plenty of time to lock the door and hide out inside the darkened men's room while the two men unloaded enough boxes of cotton candy and funnel cake mix to give a small army a sugar high. He'd have to find an appropriate way to thank Alex for giving him ten uninterrupted

minutes to conduct his search. A half dozen long, leisurely ways
to advance the sexual education she craved sprang to mind.

Jack waited until the truck was heading toward the main
entrance before he risked leaving his hiding place. After trading
a reassuring wave with Alex, he pulled out Drew Fisk's key ring.
Having the keys instead of his lock-pick tools made getting in
and out of the track buildings easy. Searching through all the
boxes Crank and Jimbo had unloaded would be a more time-
consuming task. But if even one box held the drugs he'd been
looking for, then Jack had himself a case.

The grinding rumble of a diesel engine stopped Jack with his
pocketknife poised over the box in his hand. What was this?
Grand Central Station?

Instinctively changing his grip on the knife to a defensive
position, he crept out of the storage unit and peeked through the
bleachers. Instant recognition charged his pulse and sharpened
his senses.

A black pickup truck and toter trailer were pulling into the
speedway arena. Jack ducked behind a support post. The truck
was the same make and model as the one he'd seen the other
night. In the light of a clear spring day, he could read the Fisk
Aluminum logo on the side of the truck. A second delivery, like
Drew had said. Would this one be just as suspicious?

Today, the truck and trailer were heading straight over to the
edge of the infield grass near the drag strip where Alex was
draped over the fender of his Camaro again. Unless there was a
car inside that trailer, the driver had no business being there. As
muddy as it was, a truck that size could easily damage the grass
around the asphalt staging area.

But it wasn't concern for Dahlia's newly remodeled strip that
kept Jack from retreating inside to search for drugs.

It was the black-haired man who climbed out of the truck.

The hairs on the back of Jack's neck stood up in warning as
the man approached Alex. He must have startled her, judging by

the way she scrambled off the car. Even then, Jack knew Alex's mouth could keep a man at bay for the few minutes it would take him to find out whether there were any drugs hidden inside those boxes. For one moment, the cop in him who wanted justice for a murdered partner turned to the potential evidence just beyond his reach. A split-second later, cursing his own conscience, he pulled the door shut and locked it behind him.

There were different types of threats a man had to answer to in the world.

And right now, the one that made Alex Morgan turn pale and shrink against his car was the only one that mattered.

JACK SLOWED TO A STROLL and fixed a casual smile on his mouth as he came up behind Hank Buell. The slow-rolling drawl unmistakable.

"I have a right to be here, sugar."

"Fine. Be here. Just quit spreading lies about me and go do your job. And leave me to do mine." Alex's tone was tough enough, but there was a pinched look about her mouth that told him she was getting through this encounter on sheer guts.

Hank pulled the stub of a cigarette from between his lips and flicked it to the ground. "What job's that, sugar? Waitin' on your man?"

"I hope so." Jack announced himself, circling around the black-haired man. Oh, yeah. This ought to be fun. "Hank."

Jack draped an arm around Alex. She tensed for a moment, then leaned into him, clenching a fistful of cotton shirt at his back.

"Riley." Hank Buell's shoulders straightened and his stance widened a fraction. He was on guard. Must have felt some kind of threat from Jack.

Good.

"Is this him?" Jack didn't have to specify "the bastard who sold tickets." Alex knew what he was asking.

"Yes."

Keeping one eye on Buell, Jack tucked a couple of fingers beneath Alex's chin and tilted her mouth so he could kiss her hard, publicly claiming her in no uncertain terms. When he felt the tremor of her response softening her lips beneath his, Jack pulled back an inch, stole one more kiss, then tucked her possessively to his side.

She looked calm, but Jack could feel her hand trembling at his back. Knowing this man could make her afraid pissed Jack off.

But he knew how to hide what he was feeling, too. "Have you learned any better manners about how to treat a lady?"

"Look at you buttin' into my business again." Buell tucked his thumbs in the back pockets of his khaki work pants and laughed. "Seems you have a knack for causing trouble wherever you go, Riley. We were having a polite conversation, weren't we Al?"

His dark eyes sought out Alex's for confirmation.

"He didn't hurt me or anything." To her credit, Alex didn't shy away from Buell's gaze. "But I did ask him to leave."

"'Nuf said." Jack pointed to the cab of Hank's truck. "Goodbye."

Buell's skin flushed beneath his tan. "I am not watching my step just to please you, pal. We live in the same town, work around the same track. Alex and I are bound to run into each other. I've moved on from our past relationship."

"What you did to her had nothing to do with relationships."

"You still on about that?" Hank shifted his glare from Alex up to Jack. "We were kids then. Stupid kids. It's time she got over it and grew up."

Jack pulled his arm from Alex's shoulders and stepped forward. The need to protect her, to right the awful wrong this town had done to her, thundered in his ears so loudly that the crunch of gravel at the front entrance barely registered. "You're telling her to grow up?"

"Jack…"

He shoved Hank up against the truck. "You apologize to this lady right now, you jackass."

"Apologize?" Buell shoved Jack's arm away. He was just as mean sober as he'd been drunk. "I'm the one who got blackballed by her brother and daddy. You think I could get a job in this town when I graduated from high school? I had to call in a favor from Drew Fisk just to get the crap factory job I started with."

"Pity you didn't take the hint and move on."

"This is my town, Riley. Not yours."

"Jack, let it go." He felt a tug at his back.

He ignored it. "This woman is under my protection. You stay away from her, understand?"

Maybe if Buell hadn't grinned, maybe if he'd just kept his mouth shut, Jack would have let him walk away.

"Don't know what you see in her. I never did like used cars, myself."

With that crack, Jack grabbed Buell by the shoulder and spun him around to meet his fist. The satisfying crunch against Buell's cheek laid him flat on the ground.

"Jack, stop!"

But he was already advancing as Buell scrambled to his feet.

"Not now!" Alex latched on to his right arm with both hands, pulling him far enough off balance to give Hank the chance to land a punch to the left side of his ribcage.

Jack swore as pain bloomed in his side. He dodged a second blow and jerked free of Alex's grip. He bent low and charged forward, catching Buell in the gut with his shoulder and driving him to the ground. The two men rolled across the grass and dirt. Buell kicked. Jack punched.

The blip of a siren finally registered. Then there were hands pulling Jack off Buell. Another pair of arms helped Hank to his feet. When his opponent lunged forward, Jack squared off to meet him.

"Jack, please."

The small hand at the center of his chest calmed Jack's need to mete out punishment more quickly than the arms that bound his shoulders or the tan uniform that blocked his path to Hank. Jack nodded at the worried look on Alex's pale face, indicating he was in full control of his fists and temper now. He nodded again at Drew Fisk, the man who'd tied his shoulder up in a wrestling hold.

"I'm done," he assured them both. "I'm good."

He even retreated a step when Fisk decided it was okay to release him. Jack saw the black-and-white with the spinning lights on top now. He saw the dark gray clouds gathering in the sky to match his mood. He saw Sheriff Buell chuff his son on the shoulder and hustle him back to his truck. "You get on over there now," he ordered.

"Ow!" Hank protested. "What are ya gettin' on me for? He took the first swing."

Short on breath after dealing with the tussle, Sheriff Buell panted when he turned and advanced on Jack. "That right, Mr. Riley? You started this? I knew you were gonna be trouble."

"Back off, you tin-plated—"

"Shut up, Jack." Alex pushed him away another step, wedging herself between Jack and sheriff. She backed her shoulders into his chest, blocking him, protecting him. "Hank insulted me. Jack was defending my honor."

Hank snickered from the truck. "Honor?"

"You son of a…" Jack pulled Alex aside and surged forward.

"Stop right there, Riley."

"Look out!"

Her shove against his bruised ribs didn't stop him. Henry Buell's gun, pointed right at her head when she jumped between them again, did.

Shit. Jack picked her up and moved her aside, putting his shoulder between her and the barrel of that gun. "This is getting out of hand, Sheriff."

Drew positioned himself in front of Alex, too. "Buell. Put that damn thing away. You know your son. I'm sure Hank was out of line."

"Listen, Fisk, your granddaddy may own half the county, but he doesn't own me." Buell sucked in his gut to holster the gun, but his beady black eyes made it clear he didn't appreciate the interference. "And a young pup like you never will."

"Maybe not, but the Fisks do influence votes." Drew's tone was devoid of his usual cultured Southern charm. "And if you still want your job come November…"

"Are you threatening me? Fine. Get out of here, Hank. Go on about your business." He tipped his hat to Drew with mock deference. "Mr. Fisk here insists."

"But Dad, I have a delivery to—"

"Git! Do your job." The sheriff waited while Hank groused all the way into the cab of the truck and started the engine. Then Sheriff Buell walked up to Jack, pointing a pudgy finger a little too close to Jack's chin. "I'm issuing you a warning, Riley. You keep your hands off my boys." The point of the finger shifted over to Drew. "Or not even Fisk here will stop me from throwing your butt in jail."

It was a good thing Alex had such an tight grip on Jack's hand, or he'd be tempted to add assaulting what passed for a fellow officer in this town to his list of infractions for the day.

As it was, he shifted to lace his fingers with hers and hold on to the calming strength and emotional stability he seemed to have lost since coming to Dahlia. "I'm okay, Trouble." After the sheriff turned off his lights and sped away through the track's front gate, Jack raised Alex's hand to his lips and pressed a grateful kiss to her knuckles, ignoring the bruises and scrapes that now dotted his own. "I'm sorry I lost it, but I'm okay."

Drew straightened the sleeves and lapels of his jacket as he turned to apologize. "He's pretty sensitive where his sons are concerned. Probably because they've given him so much grief over the years."

Jack didn't want to hear excuses. "There's something he can do about that. It's called parenting."

Drew shrugged. "Too late for that, don't you think? At any rate, I wouldn't have brought him over here if I'd known what was going down between you and Hank. The sheriff was at the garage to meet up with Artie, and when he left, I hitched a ride." He held out his hand. "I need my keys. Grandfather summoned me out to the house for a family meeting. That's never a good thing. Especially with my new car in the shop. I'm sure I'll have to explain that one." Jack pulled the keys out of his pocket and dropped them into Drew's open palm, clasping his hand over them to shake the other man's hand and thank him for his help. Drew nodded, then winked at Alex. "Y'all take your time and finish up. I'll be back later to lock everything up."

Alex released Jack to wrap a hug around her friend's neck. "Thanks, Drew. For everything."

"No problem, Shrimp." He squeezed her right back, holding on until Alex pulled away. Then he walked to the door of Hank's truck and knocked to get his attention over the grind of the engine. "I'll help you unload whatever's in the back if you'll give me a ride out to Grandfather's."

As Drew walked around to climb into the passenger seat, Hank leaned out the window. His cheek was already red and puffy from Jack's fist. "I'll be beatin' your ass on the track this weekend."

Jack hugged Alex to his side. As long as Hank kept his distance from her, he was welcome to try.

ALEX TWIRLED AROUND IN the dressing room of Beverly's Closet, admiring the deep blue-green silk and ivory lace of the robe and nightgown she wore. Who knew such a pretty thing existed in her size?

Beverly Stillwell, the boutique's owner, was a successful businesswoman for a reason. Alex had ventured into the alien territory of ladies' shops off the courthouse square of downtown Dahlia in order to find a tailor who could sew a couple of *Morgan*

*& Son's Garage* logos onto Jack's insulated racing jacket. But the stylish older woman with the platinum hair and bejeweled wrists and fingers had seen the way Alex was drawn to the rainbow of colors in her lingerie display. Pale blues and sunny yellows. Rich reds and a sleek steel-gray that reminded her of how Jack's eyes darkened when a need or emotion that was too powerful to control got hold of him.

Despite Alex's protests that none of the beautiful skimpy things would fit her short and busty dimensions, Mrs. Stillwell had tutted her into silence, taken a few quick measurements, and brought her a tray full of beautiful things to try on. And there wasn't one plain white cotton and elastic over-the-shoulder-boulder-holder in the bunch.

Sure, this particular gown had a wider strap than the one displayed on the mannequin out front, and an underwire helped support and contain the twin curses. But it was a damn sight more feminine than her father's plaid robe.

Alex smoothed her hands along the silk at her hips, wondering if Jack would even recognize her in something this feminine. She almost looked like the princess of her fantasies. The deep color flattered her pale skin. The lace tickled her nipples, making her feel unexpectedly sexy. All she needed was a tall man in black—her warrior knight—standing behind her in the mirror for the fantasy to be complete.

"Come on out here and let me see you," Mrs. Stillwell urged.

After one more twirl, Alex obliged. The shop owner's approving nod triggered an unexpectedly confident smile. "It looks good, doesn't it, Mrs. Stillwell?"

"Sugar, you call me Miz Beverly, like everyone else does. 'Mrs. Stillwell' reminds me of my mother-in-law." She winked. "Bless her heart, I never did like her and she couldn't stand me."

Alex snorted a laugh through her nose. She quickly covered her mouth, finding nothing feminine or princesslike about the horrible noise she made when something amused her. "Sorry."

She imagined the embarrassment that bubbled up had stained her cheeks as rosy a pink as the silk blouse Miz Beverly wore.

But Beverly Stillwell was the class of Dahlia's grande dames, and her smile never wavered. "I knew that color would be wonderful on you. You don't need this, though." She pulled the bandanna from Alex's hair and encouraged her to shake out the strands that were curling with the rain and humidity. "Lovely. Looks as though it might need a bit of a hem—unless you have some heels to wear with it."

"I don't have any high heels." Not since the silver mistakes she'd trashed in Nashville.

"Hemming it is, then. I can send it to Mrs. Spooner along with the jacket if you like."

Alex was tempted, but asked, "Where would I wear something like this?"

Miz Beverly laughed. "Well, now, that part's up to you. But a man almost always likes to see something pretty on his girl." She dropped her voice to a whisper, and Alex leaned in, absorbing every word of advice. "Though, to tell you the truth, they generally prefer to see you naked. But I think he'll appreciate a woman who makes an effort to wear something like this for him. And he'd certainly be proud to see just how beautiful the woman he loves can be."

Alex pulled back, her smile fading. The woman he loves? Lusty impulses aside, there was no way the big-city cop with the emotional baggage was ever going to love a country tomboy car geek like her. Especially when Jack seemed so hung up on the age difference between them. His maturity was a part of what attracted her to him, but it was by no means the only thing.

Broad shoulders, strong arms and gorgeous eyes didn't hurt. And those kisses—in every way she could imagine, he'd taken her mouth in a kiss. Savagely. Gently. In laughter. In tears. He'd kissed her to keep her quiet and because he just couldn't resist. And, she imagined there were even more ways he could seduce her mouth.

How could all of those kisses possibly be an act?

The turmoil inside must have reflected on her face because she felt the older woman's hand gently squeezing her shoulder. "Alexandra?"

The bell over the shop's front door jingled, saving Alex from having to analyze or explain what she was feeling.

"Miz Beverly?" A familiar man's voice hit her like a punch to the stomach, robbing Alex of the confidence and hope that her time with Beverly Stillwell had given her. Sheriff Buell. Alex snatched back her bandanna and turned toward the dressing room.

But he moved surprisingly fast, despite his rotund belly. He suddenly appeared in the doorway to the dressing rooms. "Ma'am." Though he tipped his plastic-wrapped hat to Beverly, his gaze had settled on Alex. More specifically, on Alex's breasts. "My God, Alex Morgan in a nightdress. What are you doin' in here, girl?"

She instinctively hugged her arms in front of her, feeling his damning scrutiny as much as she had back at the track. "I had business. I needed a tailor."

His gaze finally wandered back up to her eyes. "Riley's a lucky man."

"Now, Henry," Beverly pushed against the sheriff's chest and turned him around, "you're going to scare off my best customer of the day. Everyone else must be staying home because of the rain." She scooted him out to the main floor. "You come and tell me your business at the counter."

Appreciating the escape, Alex ducked into the dressing room and threw on her clothes. With one last regretful stroke across the silk, she left the nightgown on the tray with the bras and panties. She grabbed her jacket and hurried on out, barely slowing as she interrupted what sounded like a man and a woman changing plans. "Thank you for everything, Miz Beverly." *From making me feel welcome and feminine right down to your advice about men.* "I have to get back to work. Dad needs me at the garage today and I've already taken too long a break."

Beverly came around the counter, her expression baffled as she tried and failed to catch her. "Is there anything—?"

"Will Mrs. Spooner be able to finish the jacket by the qualifying prelims tomorrow night?" Alex paused after opening the door, hoping the kind, intuitive woman could read the apology in her eyes. "Please tell her I'll pay extra for a rush job like this."

Beverly nodded. "I'll call you when it's ready."

"Thank you, ma'am."

If Alex had spared a glance for the sheriff, she might have seen him excusing himself and catching the door before it closed behind her.

"Hold it right there." His meaty fingers closed around her arm, stopping her. Alex swung around, but the badge on his chest kept her fist at her side. The forecaster's prediction of another evening of rain had been accurate. The cold drops hit her face as she tilted her chin to meet the warning in Buell's dark eyes. "You tell your man Riley that if he comes after either of my boys again, not even Drew Fisk is going to be able to talk me out of pressing charges against him."

Alex twisted her arm from his grasp. "My *man* doesn't start the fights he's gotten into with your boys. He just finishes them."

The sheriff dipped his head, spilling water off the brim of his hat onto Alex's shoulder. She twisted away as if the cool water had singed her. "Don't you get sassy with me, girl. I'm the law in this town."

"Henry Buell." Beverly Stillwell had come out beneath her awning, her tone as protective a rebuke as Alex imagined any mother might give. "You let that girl go. She has a job to get back to."

He touched the brim of his hat, his expression a friendly good-ol'-boy smile now. "Don't rush off on my account. But if you are headin' back to your daddy's, you tell Artie I need to speak to him, all right? He must have turned off his phone."

So why didn't he just call the garage? They'd still be open for another half hour. But she wanted this conversation to be done. "I'll tell him."

Leaving Buell and his warnings and her hopeless dreams behind, Alex booked it back to her car. She'd unlocked the door and tossed her bandanna across the seat before she saw the brown envelope tucked beneath her windshield wiper.

Alex reached between the car's frame and door and pulled the soggy paper free. The rain soaked through her hair and trickled down her scalp as she looked all around the square for some sign of who had placed it there. Though only a few cars were still parked along the sidewalks, it seemed that she was alone on the street. And yet…

Feeling more spooked than she cared to admit, Alex climbed inside her car and locked the doors. She wiped the rain from her face and tucked her hair behind her ears before opening the envelope.

She pulled out the contents. "Oh, God."

The rain had made spots on the old instant photograph's finish. But the image was clear. It was from that night. She looked so young and helpless, her arms uselessly trying to hide her naked body, her eyes red and swollen with tears. Hank Buell, belting up his pants, and another boy, little more than a blur of blond hair, were fuzzy images laughing in the background.

Anger surged through her, blotting out shame and fear. She was about to crush the image in her fist when she saw the message, typed on a sticker and glued to the back of the photo.

*It'll be worse than this if you don't send your boyfriend back where he came from.*

"You son of a bitch." Tossing aside the crude picture, she pulled out her phone and dialed Jack's number.

"Riley," he answered on the second ring.

"Jack?" Damn. She hated when her breath caught like that. It revealed far more than she ever intended.

"Trouble? What's wrong?" She heard a stern man's voice in the background, warning Jack back to some meeting. Jack ignored him. "Is it Buell again?"

"Which one?" But sarcasm didn't help. The anger seeped out of her, leaving her helpless. "I got another message. On my car. With a picture this time."

"Shit. I'm still in Nashville at Rutledge's office, arranging for backup at the track this weekend."

"Oh." That explained the voices in the background. Jack had said he was taking in some evidence he'd found and reporting to his task force team leader. "Okay." She nodded, discarding the belief that she just might be more important than the job he had to do. "I'll deal with it."

"Don't you dare hang up on me. What did it say?"

She didn't need to see the photo again to recall the threat. "It says I should get rid of you. Or…" *Just say it.* "Or they'll hurt me worse than they did that night in high school."

Alex had heard Jack cuss up a blue streak and talk his way in and out of whatever lie he needed to maintain his cover. She'd been soothed and seduced by the deep timbre of his voice and had heard him cry out his physical satisfaction against her naked skin. But she'd never heard him this quiet. Not for this long.

The silence worried her. She finally understood the "talk to me" rule. "Jack?"

And then she heard a rush of sound. The screech of a chair, voices protesting his hasty departure, a door opening. "We'll finish this later," he said to the men in the room with him. "You get anything on the DNA or car parts I brought in, you call me." Then he was back on the phone with her. "Trouble? You still there?"

"I'm here."

"Are you anywhere near a fax machine?"

"Dad has one at work."

"Is he still there?"

"Yeah."

"Good. I want you to send me a copy of that note and anything else that came with it." She wrote down the number he gave her. "You go to the garage and stay with George until I can get there."

"But I don't want my dad in any danger—"

"*He* won't want you in any danger, either." A door slammed. "Fax me the note. As soon as I get it into forensics, I'm leaving. You don't have to tell George anything. Just stay with him until I get there. Okay?"

Alex nodded. "I'll see you at the garage."

# *12*

ALEX GRITTED HER TEETH and pushed with all her strength against a stubborn nut that wouldn't turn. Jack's rebuilt motor had been going together nicely with her design modifications and a few purchases from the local parts store. Until now.

Because of shipping delays, she'd been forced to cannibalize a couple of key components from an old GM motor of her dad's. But even with some reshaping on the sander, the spacing was off, and the bolt refused to tighten. With the motor secured on a chain and steel sawhorses, she should have been able to get the leverage she needed. But the stubborn thing just…wouldn't… turn.

The wrench bit cracked, slipped.

"Ow!" Her knuckles scraped across the iron block and the tension of the day blew up in her face. "Stupid, stupid, stupid!"

She slung the broken wrench into her tool box, thinking the crumpled up photo and vile message made a better target for her wrath. Where the hell was Jack? He'd promised he was on his way an hour ago. She'd locked up the garage and had kept her hands busy out in the shop while her father finished up some paperwork in his office. She hadn't told him about Jack or the message yet. And she was hoping she wouldn't have to say anything to worry him until she had the proof in her hands to show him who was responsible for Nick's death.

She'd wanted Jack to tell her the threat meant nothing, that she should throw the photo away and pretend the jerk-ass Buells couldn't harm her or make her feel afraid the way she'd pretended for nine long years. But she *was* afraid. Afraid of Jack's long, cold silence. Afraid that calling him back to Dahlia would put him in danger. Afraid that locked doors, her father and the marine-issue pistol he kept in his office weren't enough to stop the dangerous men who'd already killed her brother and Jack's partner in order to keep their secrets.

Being afraid was getting mighty damn old.

Alex picked up the wrench and pulled off the broken socket head. She didn't know if she was pining away for a man who was only hers for the duration of their undercover charade, or if the fear she felt for Jack's safety meant their relationship had never been a charade for her at all.

She hurled the broken socket across the concrete floor. "Stupid, stupid, stupid!"

Her heart nearly stopped as a familiar friend materialized from the shadows where she'd cast the offending part. "I'll hold it down for you if you want to kick it a couple of times." Tater raked his fingers through his shaggy blond hair, grinning from ear to ear.

Once she could breathe again, Alex answered. "Go on, let it out."

By the time Tater had had his laugh and retrieved the broken piece for her, Alex was smiling, too. "What are you doing, all spiffed up in clean jeans and a dress shirt? Got a hot date?"

"I might."

"With Sandy Larabie?"

Tater winked. "I might."

Good. Alex was pleased to see a guy she liked as well as Tater find someone special. "You two have a good time."

"No Jack yet, eh?" he teased, misinterpreting the cause for her mood. He thumbed over his shoulder to the empty bays in the garage behind him. "Looks like your dad has another couple hours of payroll work ahead of him. You want me to wait until Artie or someone else gets back to keep you company? He's over at the track setting up the Fisk team's trailer and tent for the races tomorrow."

Artie keep her company? No thanks. Alone was definitely preferable to one-on-one time with him. "Nah. Like you said, Dad's here. You go on. Don't keep Sandy waiting."

"You're sure there's nothin' else I can do to help?"

Alex held up her broken wrench. "Not unless you've got a rachet bit I can borrow."

"Help yourself to my tool chest. And if you can't find what you need in there, check Artie's locker downstairs. He's been braggin' about that European alloy set he bought with his winnings from the Moonshine Run. To hear him tell it, if he doesn't have the tool you need, then it doesn't exist."

"I'll keep that in mind. Thanks, Tater." She locked the main door behind him and sent him on his way with a wave.

Short of pestering Jack with another phone call or raising her dad's suspicions by hanging out with him in his office, Alex had nothing to do but continue her work. Besides, if she wanted to get Jack's Camaro in shape for the races tomorrow, she didn't have time to sit around and worry about Jack's safety—or her own.

A quick scan of Tater's tool chest revealed it was as neat and tidy as his hair was a rumpled mess. So it was easy to see that he didn't have the odd-sized part she was looking for.

With a sigh of resignation, Alex walked to the lube pit and turned on all the lights. She peered over the steel railing, working up her nerve to climb down the ladder attached to the wall. As much as she loved working on motors, she hated going down into the concrete vault where Artie drained the oil and worked beneath cars. Sounds always seemed muffled down there, and the lights, especially after dark like now, never seemed bright enough to illuminate the deepest corners. The mice and spiders she knew scurried around down there didn't help. And years ago, before she'd been old enough to work at the garage, a man had fallen into the pit and died. Maybe it was a little girl's imagination about ghosts that made the pit such an uncomfortable place, or maybe it was the very real scents of stale cigarettes and Artie Buell that made the pit so loathsome.

However, the lure of Artie's state-of-the-art ratchet set meant she was climbing down that ladder. The Moonshine Run trophy displayed for all to see easily identified Artie's locker. Since he was the only one to work down here, nothing was terribly neat. Though she felt a little awkward about getting into Artie's things, she rationalized opening his locker by remembering that she and the other mechanics often shared and traded tools as needed. Besides, Tater had given her permission.

By the time she'd jimmied the handle open and pushed aside an illicit whiskey bottle to reach the metal box that housed his swanky European ratchet set, Alex wondered if sorting through the mess inside was worth the trouble. When she pulled the box forward on the eye-level shelf, two cigarette cartons came with it. She caught the cartons in her arms, along with the Fisk Racing cap that had hooked on the box and was dragging the contents of the entire shelf out with it.

"Good grief," she fussed, juggling everything to keep it from hitting the floor. Sneaking booze into the workplace against her father's rules was bad enough—she'd have to report him for that. But Alex's distaste for the man and his habits grew with the discovery of something much more sinister. A dozen tiny plastic bags spilled out with the rest of the junk. "What's this?"

After stuffing everything back onto the shelf as haphazardly as she'd found it, Alex carried the bags to Artie's work table and turned on a work light to study the tiny crystals sealed inside. She had no firsthand experience, but she'd taken enough health education classes through school to suspect that she was looking at crack or crystallized heroin, bagged and ready for sale on the streets. Stretching up on tiptoe, she counted the loose bags on the shelf. A search through the rest of his things uncovered three larger bundles, wrapped in enough plastic to mask the contents inside—or protect them from bursting open within the hidden compartment of a modified race car.

She didn't know whether to feel victorious or scared spitless.

Was this what Jack's fast-paced life was always like? Walking that fine line between acceptable risk and certain danger? It was like being behind the wheel of a powerful engine, gunning it at the starting line. Sometimes, you won the big prize. Sometimes, you crashed and burned. What a rush. What a scary, satisfying, she'd-better-call-someone-who-knew-what-he-was-doing rush.

Alex pulled out her phone again and called him. "Jack?" Damn. Voice mail. He was either on the road or back in his meeting. Alex left a brief message. "I found them. I found the drugs. In Artie Buell's locker. Call me when you can so I know what to do. I…I really wish you were here."

How did a himbo like Artie come up with the brains to organize a drug smuggling operation? Of course, hiding the goods in an unlocked locker wasn't the smartest move a criminal could make. That kind of arrogance and stupidity sounded more like the Artie she knew. But he'd certainly have the means and opportunity Jack had mentioned to alter the race cars and stash the drugs inside. As long as someone told him what to do, he'd be a good worker bee. And Alex had a short list of suspects to share with Jack as to who might be giving the orders.

Tucking the bags deep into her pockets, Alex closed the locker door so quietly that even the mice couldn't hear it. Just in time. The jangle of keys from the garage above her warned to run for the ladder before the footsteps she heard reached her. Too late.

"Well, isn't this a surprise?" Alex looked up beyond the rungs of the ladder to see Artie standing at the top. Grinning. Leering. Had he seen anything? He pocketed the keys that had gotten him inside the locked garage. "What are you doing down there, sugar?"

*Don't panic. He hasn't caught you at anything. Yet. Act the part you're supposed to play.* She had to clear her throat before the words would come. "I needed to borrow one of your tools. Tater said you had a new socket set."

"'Zat so." She backed away as he turned and gripped the sides of the ladder with his hands and feet, sliding straight down, blocking her escape. She jammed her hands into her pockets to mask the bulk of the drugs she'd confiscated, but Artie didn't seem to notice, his eyes lingering on her chest as he strolled toward her. "You ever want something from me, all you have to do is ask."

About the time the stench of his coveralls reached her, Alex's brain and her bravado finally kicked in. "What are you doing here? I thought you were at the track, setting up Drew's pit area for tomorrow."

"I was." Alex retreated when he kept advancing, kept smiling, as though finding her in his work space was the sweetest surprise of his night. "But I finished. It's still muddy at the track, so me and the boys thought we'd come back here and do a little partying."

*Me and the boys?*

Alex jerked her chin to find they had an audience. The overhead lights reflected off Jimbo DiMarco's shiny shaved head. He grinned. "Evening, Alex."

"Hey, Jimbo." He was wearing his Fisk Racing jacket. So was the bearded hulk standing at the railing beside him. As usual, Crank had little to say. He didn't even respond to her acknowledging nod. Drew Fisk's crew for the races, they had every logical—legal—reason to be here. But they were one man short. Alex prayed the fourth member of their team wasn't with them.

"Hey, sugar."

So much for praying. She turned toward the voice. "Hank."

The elder Buell brother braced his hands against the railing and looked down at her. Looked inside her. Licked his bruised and swollen lip and smiled. A remembered dread spread like ants crawling across her skin. She was surrounded. Just like that night. The setting was different. She wore clothes four layers deep. But the feeling was the same. All eyes were on her. She felt exposed, outnumbered, afraid.

Alex's breath caught in her chest, grew shallow. Every muscle in her tensed with the urge to bolt. But backed against Artie's work table, with her path to the ladder blocked and three men waiting like vultures at the railing above her, where did she think she could run?

"Well?" Artie prompted, sliding a toothpick from one side of his mouth to the other. If the smell of his breath was any indication, the party had already started. "Tell me what you need."

Why hadn't she heard them sooner? Had she been too focused on breaking a lead on Jack's case? Were they sneaking in so her father wouldn't know they were here after hours with alcohol on the premises? Were they here for the drugs?

What was she doing, just standing here, trembling as though the past was repeating itself? She was a smart, college-educated woman who'd returned to Dahlia because her father needed her. She wasn't the girl Hank had terrorized nine years ago. She wasn't even the same inexperienced woman who'd left seven months earlier to find a man who could see her as more than a mechanic or pair of boobs. This was no role she was playing. She was Jack Riley's woman. Down in her heart, she was beginning to understand that loving a man—loving the right man—made her strong. These jackasses better start realizing that she wasn't an easy victim anymore.

"I'm here to work, Artie. Not play." She shoved him back a step and pulled out the broken socket piece. She studiously kept her gaze from lighting anywhere near Artie's locker and asked, "Do you have one of these? It's an odd size I need for a custom job."

"You're in luck, sweet thing." Artie grabbed the bit along with her hand and pulled her with him to his locker.

She held her breath as he pounded the lock with his fist and swung open the door. What if he saw something out of place? What if he suspected she'd already sorted through the contents inside?

"Artie." Hank chided his younger brother from above. "Leave it." Did Hank know what was in that locker, as well? Now there was a man she could believe had the will and know-how to organize an operation like this. He shifted his dark eyes to Alex. "You get on up here, girl."

"I don't answer to you, Hank."

"Pretty bold words for a little lady all by herself. Where's that badass boyfriend of yours?"

Jimbo circled the railing to thump Hank on the arm. "What are you doin', Hank? I thought we were here to get the car."

"I'm having a conversation with the lady, so you back off." His eyes hadn't gotten any friendlier when they returned to her. "Come on up here and talk to me, Al. I'm not gonna hurt you."

Right. And all this rain wasn't going to make the track slick. Her heart didn't know whether to race or stop cold.

Artie nudged her toward the ladder. "You better git."

Resisting the urge to adjust the extra lumps in her clothes, Alex grabbed the first metal rung and climbed upward. She got the crazy notion in her head that if she delayed long enough, Jack would come storming to her rescue. Not that she wanted to think she was in any real danger from Hank with the other men around, but then, she hadn't suspected she was in any danger that night in the tenth grade, either.

But she didn't even get the chance to dream. Artie's palm was on her bottom, pushing her to climb faster. "Move it."

"Keep your paws to yourself." She smacked his hand away and hurried up, stepping between Jimbo and Hank on the garage deck, finding herself boxed into a triangle when Artie scrambled out behind her. With no place to go and no chance to shove all three men out of her way, Alex turned to the one weapon she had left in her arsenal. She tilted her chin to the most dangerous of the three. "Get out of my way, Hank. I have work to do."

"Now, now, sugar." His once-handsome smile, now bruised by Jack's fist and tarnished by her own memories, was as menacing as the hand that cupped the side of her neck and pulled her closer. "All work and no play for all these years?" She twisted out of his grasp, but that only made him reach for her with both hands, holding her face still as he moved closer. "Here I thought you'd sworn off sex. If I'd known you were lookin' to get some more experience, I'd have helped you out." His eyes hooded in some drowsy representation of passion. "You didn't have to go all the way to Nashville to find a man."

Alex seethed beneath his touch. "I don't see one here."

Hank's fingers tightened like vises against her jaw and scalp. He brushed his lips across hers in a mockery of a kiss. "You aren't woman enough to know what a real man is."

"You bastard." Alex squirmed. His grip tightened painfully and she clawed at his hands to free herself. "Damn it, Hank."

Jimbo closed in behind her and she jerked, knowing a moment of terror. "Hey, pal, I didn't sign on for this."

"Nobody's askin' you to stay." Hank released her face to wrap his arms around her. "You owe me an apology for what your boy-friend did to me."

Alex shoved at Hank's chest before he got too close. Why didn't anyone do something to help? "Jack will be here. We have a date." She punched his mouth with her fist, aiming straight for the imprint Jack had left behind. "Let go!"

"You bitch." Hank grabbed her arm and twisted it behind her. She cursed the sharp pain that shot through her shoulder and Hank laughed, rubbing his body shamelessly against hers. The blood from the cracked lip she'd reopened dripped onto her shirt. "Jimbo, didn't you tell me you saw Riley headin' down the highway out of town?"

"A couple hours ago."

These men were watching Jack? Taking note of when and where he went? Alex tried to get her footing, tried to kick. She had to find him, had to warn him. Had to get Hank off her before he discovered the bags she'd stolen.

"He's coming back," she insisted.

Hank leaned in. His hot breath whispered against her ear. "He's gonna be late."

She raised her knee, fighting in earnest. "What did you do? Get your hands off me." With every kick, every protest, Hank's grip tightened. His black eyes turned cold and mean.

Artie was laughing now. He had his phone out. Oh, God. Was he taking a picture? Texting the image to someone? "She's a handful, big brother. Need some help?"

But Hank lifted her off the floor and reached into the pocket of his jeans. "Get out of here." He tossed a ring of keys to Artie even as he shoved her up against Tater's tool chest and knocked a couple of drawers open. She was in trouble. "Take Drew's car. Open her up and get her ready for tomorrow."

Crank uttered a foul word and pulled Jimbo and Artie away. "Let's get out of here."

"No!" Hank squeezed her breast and Alex screamed. "Don't leave me with him!"

"Hey, man. Shouldn't we—?"

"Get out of here," Hank ordered. "And you?" He slid his tongue against her neck and groped her again. "You need to stop fightin' me. How many layers of clothes you wearin', girl?"

The packages inside her pockets shifted, squeezed upward. Oh, no. No, no. He couldn't find the drugs on her. "Get off me!"

A gunshot rang out through the garage, pinging off metal and thunking off concrete and plunging the entire building into a taut, dangerous silence.

Hank released her and Alex's feet sank to the floor as her father reached around him and pulled her to his side. "What the hell is going on out here?" George Morgan looked more elite force than motor pool as he leveled his service pistol at Hank. Alex held on tight to the back of his shirt, trying hard to breathe, trying harder not to curse or cry. "Keep your hands off my daughter," he barked, "and get the hell out of my garage."

Holding his hands up in surrender, Hank tried to reason with a father guarding his daughter's life. "Now, George—"

"Now, nothing. Get out." George used the barrel of the gun

to back Hank up beside his brother. "And you. Pack your stuff and go with him. You're fired."

Artie's mouth dropped open. "What? Why?"

"Because you're a son of a bitch, Buell, and I'm tired of making nice while you refuse to grow up or even say you're sorry for what your family did to my girl."

"You don't think I've been payin' for that night—"

"Did I hear a gunshot?" The outside door opened and Drew Fisk came charging in. Alex finally took a normal breath as the odds against her and her father changed. Drew slowed to a stop beside Hank and Artie, eyeing each one with first concern and then disdain. "What the hell is going on?"

George hugged Alex to his side. But the gun never wavered. "There's been a change of plan, son. If you're going to have the Buells working for you, then you're going to have to store your car somewhere else."

Drew's wide, stunned eyes swept over Alex. Her arm and jaw ached. She probably had marks on her. "Hank, did you—"

"Shut up. We can take him."

"He has a gun, you idiot." There was more ruthless business mogul than playboy best friend in the look Drew gave Hank. "George Morgan is a reputable businessman in Dahlia, a man to respect. Until you outgrow your vindictive need to own this town and the people in it, you'll never know what that feels like."

For a moment, Hank glared right back, exchanging a silent message that Alex couldn't understand. When Hank dropped his gaze, then turned to look straight at her, she pressed her hand to her chest, hiding both the drug package and the fear he burned into her heart. "I guess you'll never know the real truth about the good men of this town, either."

"What?" Alex frowned. What kind of spiteful remark was that?

It didn't matter. Drew was already herding Hank and his buddies toward the unlocked door where they'd come in. He pushed a button to open the garage door in front of his Mustang.

"I'll grab what's mine out of my locker," said Artie in a voice that was far too agreeable to be trusted.

Wait! How did she stop Artie from moving the rest of the drugs without endangering herself or Drew or her father? How did she get Jack or anyone else here in time to arrest him? It was pretty obvious that calling the sheriff wouldn't be an option.

Perhaps sensing her need to end this nightmare, George pointed his gun at Artie and shooed him toward the others. "Just get out. You can come back in the morning for your tools."

"Okay, old man." Artie held his hands up in surrender. "Just don't shoot that thing."

Alex watched from behind her father's strong, protective shoulder as Artie, Jimbo and Crank loaded the car onto Hank's toter trailer to drive it over to the track. She hugged her arms around herself and shivered. She felt dirty and helpless and frustrated that these men were going to get away with hurting her and her family all over again.

She wanted Jack. Needed him desperately. And not because he was a cop.

*"He'll be late."*

Had Hank done something to Jack? Had the four of them ganged up on him? Had they tampered with Jack's truck or run him off the road?

Maybe her father understood her a little better than she gave him credit for. Maybe he could even read her spinning thoughts. Letting Drew take over watching the Buells and their buddies leave the garage, George Morgan hugged her close and pressed a kiss to her temple. "Call him, honey. Tell Jack I'm taking you home."

ALEX WAS NECK DEEP IN A hot sudsy bath, soaking the aches of her body and washing the feel of Hank Buell off her skin, when she heard the door knob turn.

She recognized Jack by scent alone. "You're late."

The dampness of the night outside clung to his jacket as he

shrugged out of it and set both his holster and badge on the vanity across from the tub. "I like not having to break in to come see you. Your father had his chat with me and went upstairs." Jack untied his boots and tossed them in a corner. Then he was kneeling down beside the tub—like the knight of her fantasies, only stronger, tougher, sexier. Real. His fingers trembled as he touched each bruise dotting her jaw and neck. A tight muscle beside his mouth flinched. He brushed a wet curl off her cheek and leaned over to press the gentlest of kisses there. "He said if I wanted to stay the night it was my choice. I say it's yours."

Alex laid her soapy fingers over his stubbled cheek and soothed the tension stamped there. "Stay, Jack. Please? I'll be through here in just a minute."

When she fished her washcloth from the water to resume her bath, he plucked the soft terry from her fingers and took over the duties for her. "George said you just got in here."

"You'll get your clothes wet."

"Yeah?" He squeezed out the excess water and tenderly wiped it over the line of bruises left by another man's hand. Alex closed her eyes beneath his gentle ministrations, feeling every stroke along her shoulders and arms, down her legs and between her toes. Once he started, he never broke contact with her body, not once. His touch was soothing but sure. He eased away the hurts and left something much more pleasurable in his wake. "Sit up."

He broke the seductive spell only long enough to catch Alex around the waist to give her something to lean against as he reached behind her to wash her back all the way down to her bottom. "I told George everything," he confessed in a soft rumble against her hair. His hand moved the cloth over her hips now, seeking out places much more private to bathe. "That I'm a cop. What I'm investigating. How I got you involved. Facing a father with a gun in his lap isn't the easiest thing. I hope I never have daughters."

Alex hugged the strong arm that crossed between her breasts and blinked her eyes open. "Did you tell him about Nick?"

"That I suspect he was murdered?" Alex hugged him tighter. She was beginning to see that there was much more to being treated like a lady than simply holding coats and opening doors. A gentleman protected a lady. Listened to her. Made her feel like she was worth the effort of being with her. Jack had done all those things and more. "Is he mad at me for not telling him?"

"No, sweetheart. He's proud of you. He's in this fight with us. Something about not losing another child to the secrets of this town." Stroke. Caress. Alex's eyes drifted shut again. "I did get the paternal lecture about not keeping my eye on you 24/7, though. He said that's always been a challenge for him, too."

Alex smiled against the wet sleeve of his shirt. "Are you saying I'm a handful?"

"Oh, yeah. But I like a challenge." He eased her back against the pillow and paused to peel off his soggy T-shirt and toss it after his boots. Then his hand and the cloth were back beneath the water, sliding along the inside of her leg. Alex gasped at the deliberate boldness of his touch, coming so close to her most intimate self, then pulling away, leaving a tightening knot of need hungry for the pressure of his hand at the juncture of her thighs. "Easy, Trouble." He must have felt her flinch. "Just try to relax."

Alex closed her eyes again and tried to do just that. Only Jack's hands sliding over her legs and belly and up beneath her breasts, creating a soft friction even warmer than the bath water, made it difficult to do much more than remember to breathe.

"You were right, Detective Trouble." She tried to concentrate on his soothing voice, though the seductive tones were sinking deep inside her, waking other things beyond her sensitized skin. "I don't condone you taking the risk you did, but the crystallized heroin you took from Artie's locker matches the product Eric was buying from the distributor in Nashville, right down to the make of the plastic bags. I took a detour up by the track to make sure the Buells and their buds were all accounted for, and then I went back through the garage. As I suspected, Artie's locker had been cleaned out and there was no trace of any drugs." His hand was moving gently over the swell of her breasts now. "I'd love to have a drug dog go over Fisk's car that Artie was working on to see if he can hit on where the drugs were moved to. I asked Rutledge to secure a warrant for that."

Alex could barely speak when he swirled the washcloth around the tip of her breast. "You did...all that in the two hours you were gone?"

He moved on to the other breast. "I also got the preliminary report on the cigarette butts I found. The DNA doesn't match up to either of the Buell boys."

Her eyes snapped open. Despite the temperature of the water and the heat generated by Jack's hands, Alex felt chilled. "You mean someone else is watching me? Leaving those messages?"

Jack's eyes were dark and bleak. "You told me Artie wasn't smart enough to run an operation like this. And in my book, Hank's too hotheaded to be in charge. Can you remember anyone else who was there that night? Maybe the blond bastard in the background of that photo?"

There'd been plenty of boys, with every hair color, that night. Alex drew her knees up to her chest and tried to hug the delicious warmth back into her body. "I didn't see Drew until he came later with Nick. Tater's blond. But I don't remember seeing him there. Of course, they didn't have to be there to see the pictures or hear the gossip."

He reached around her to wrap her folded-up body into a hug, lifting her partway up out of the water. "It's okay, sweetheart. We don't have to figure it all out right—" He swore under his breath and pulled back. His splayed fingers hovered above the five bruises on her left breast, bruises that perfectly matched the span of a man's rough hand, bruises left by Hank's vile touch.

For a moment, shame twisted in Alex's stomach. Jack touched

his fingers so lightly to the deep purple and red marks that goose bumps popped up across her skin. Alex looked up and the shame went away. Something strong, needy, more compassionate, flowed into her veins as Jack's eyes narrowed. *Now* he was going to cry? "Jack…"

"I'm sorry I couldn't get to you sooner." He stroked each wound with shaky fingers.

"Shh." She reached over to cup the clenched line of his jaw.

"How can I make it up to you?"

"I'm just glad you're here with me now."

"Don't argue with me on this one. What can I do to make things right?"

She didn't have to think for long. She was transforming into a woman who understood what they both needed. "Be my knight in shining armor. Help me forget what it feels like to be used. It's always good with you, Jack. I'm never afraid when I'm with you."

"Then I'm not going anywhere."

In a feat of strength and determination that made her feel as feminine and cherished as any fairy-tale princess, Jack scooped her up out of the water and carried her down the hallway to her bed. After putting his gun and a condom on the bedside table, he stripped down naked and crawled beneath the covers to gather her up in his arms.

He took his time, kissing her deeply, thoroughly, completely. On her mouth, her breasts, the aching mound between her legs. His hands wandered where they would, gentle one moment, more urgent the next—retracing every inch of her that he'd washed earlier, replacing the memory of any other man's touch with the brand of his own. By the time her skin had cooled from the bath, the delicious weight of his body was covering hers, sliding inside her, setting her on fire from the inside out.

Stretching her body taut, he guided her hands up to hold on to one of the wrought-iron curlicues of her headboard. He withdrew, then entered her again, teasing her a little more deeply with each

slow, delicious foray and retreat. Anything softer than iron would
have bent in her hands, she wanted him so badly. He pulled out
one last time, tormenting her when she was so ready for all of him.
"Jack," she whispered, writhing beneath him, wanting.

And then they found a rhythm that taught her there was still
more pleasure to be had. Everything inside her was building,
reaching, needing, loving.

"Now," was all he said.

He slid his thumb down between them, pressing the switch
that made her come unglued as he emptied himself inside her.

Jack swallowed up her blissful cry with a kiss.

# *13*

"WHERE THE HELL IS ALEX?" Jack shouted the question above the roaring engines of the two cars gunning their motors at the starting line. The telltale beeps and flash of red, yellow and green lights indicated a heat was about to start. "She should have been back by now. The stores don't stay open past five on a Friday night here in Dahlia."

Daniel Rutledge stopped snapping pictures of the suspects they were surveilling and pulled off his ball cap with the press card ID pinned to it. He combed his fingers through his short blond hair, using the offhand movement to glance around at the other teams prepping cars and lining up in the staging lanes. "I told my man to stay with her. You want me to give him a call?"

"Yes!" Jack pulled out his own phone, checking to see if he'd missed a call from her, explaining why her trip into town was taking more than an hour. He wasn't worried about the Camaro's motor or where he placed in the rankings or the surprise gift Alex had been so excited to go pick up from a shop called Beverly's Closet. He was worried that neither her father nor the undercover agent Rutledge had assigned to her could stay ahead of the trouble that woman seemed to get herself into.

No message. "Anything?" he asked Rutledge.

Daniel pocketed his phone. "My man's still parked in front of the shop. Says she hasn't come out yet."

"Send him in to look."

Jack would have gone with Alex himself if Rutledge and the

ten other task force operatives blending into the crowd at the track hadn't decided that tonight was the night they were going to shut down the Dahlia drug smuggling operation once and for all. Against Jack's knee-jerk reaction to want to punish the man who'd assaulted Alex in her father's garage, Rutledge had decided to let Hank Buell and his entourage work the speedway the way they'd planned. Artie was the only one they could conclusively link to the drugs. Crank and Jimbo had delivered the modified car parts, but that didn't make them killers. Hank had the balls to run a man off the road, but even Jack couldn't yet book him for anything more than assault. They might have the players in their sights, but a lack of brainpower and a bunch of cigarette butts with a stranger's DNA told Jack they hadn't found the man in charge of this operation yet.

Along with the evidence he and Alex had already gathered and turned in, the idea was to catch the men, the modified vehicles and the drugs all in one location, giving them a dead-bang case to take to court. According to Rutledge's legal machinations, such a certain conviction should convince the Buells and their buddies to turn on whoever was running the show. So Jack had agreed to follow the plan.

Jack owed Eric Mesner, he owed Nick Morgan—he owed Alex—the permanent shutdown of the drug pipeline. Eric deserved the justice Jack had promised. Nick's family and this town deserved to know that he had died a hero. And Alex deserved to be safe.

She'd been coping with the constant reminders of the cruel prank that had forced her to rev up her tomboy attitude and shut down her natural feminine instincts and desires for too long. She'd found a way to survive in Dahlia. But it was no way for a woman of her spirit and talents to live. Even when Jack's work here was done, he wasn't going to let her face any more past or current demons on her own. He might even decide that watching over her was a full-time job that demanded his attention here instead of in Nashville.

But that was a decision for later. Right now, he had to get the damn job done. Putting these bastards away—all of them—was the best way he knew to keep her safe.

So what the hell was taking her so long? He was due at the starting line in less than thirty minutes. And while he had no doubts that his car was ready to run, he wanted his crew chief with him. He wanted Alex on the sidelines to fix anything that went wrong. He wanted her close by to make him feel like he was a young man in his prime with just a word or a kiss or a smile.

A sense of foreboding crept up the back of his neck. Jack scanned the ebb and flow of fans and locals, in and beneath the stands. They sported bright team colors and carried armloads of snacks and souvenirs as they found their seats. He spotted Henry Buell moseying through the front gate, chatting folks up more like a welcoming host rather than working any kind of security that Jack could see. Maybe the sheriff was studying the crowd himself, serving as a lookout until his boys could get clear of the track with their car and drugs.

But there was no yellow bandanna anywhere to be seen. No honey-blond curls he recognized. No denim overalls stuffed with courage and curves and heart.

A loud horn and the clamor of the fans blended into the explosive roar of the two cars speeding down the strip. Jack tuned out the din and vibrations and focused his gaze on the drivers and their teams in the speedway's infield. He paid particular attention to the purple-and-silver awning that marked the Fisk Racing team's trailer and pit area.

His blood boiled beneath his skin as he caught sight of Hank Buell and his buddies, Crank and Jimbo, who'd stood by and done nothing to help Alex when Hank had turned abusive. Hank stood at the hood of Fisk's Mustang and shouted orders to his brother, Artie, who was leaning over his cell phone, texting a message. He smacked his brother in the back of the head, demanding his attention. But Artie made some kind of protest, pointing to the leader board and list of names for the upcoming time trial match-ups posted on the viewing tower. Then Hank was reading the phone, scanning the crowd, looking straight at Jack.

Suddenly, Hank and his crew were moving around their car as if they'd just been called to the starting gate. Nothing suspicious about that. Hell.

"I think we've been made."

"What?" Rutledge shouted over the cheers and boos of the crowd as the eighth-mile times were posted.

Enough of this. Something was wrong. Jack tossed his helmet inside the Camaro and pulled out his phone. He jogged toward the front gate and Morgan's Garage, where he'd find his truck and enough quiet to make a phone call. "Round up Buell and his crew," he told Rutledge. He nodded toward the Fisk tent. "They know something's going down. Seize the car and the trailer now. Have the sheriff help you so we don't lose track of him, either. And get ahold of Artie Buell's phone and find out who the hell just gave him the heads-up."

"Wait a minute," Rutledge snapped. "I give the orders here. We have a plan."

Screw the plan. "Has your man found Alex yet?"

"No."

"Then I will."

"PICK UP, SWEETHEART." Jack tucked his gun into the back of his jeans and pocketed his badge as he bypassed the line of cars waiting for a parking space and jumped the curb. He spun onto the highway and raced his truck toward downtown Dahlia. He pressed on the accelerator and jammed on the horn to warn oncoming traffic that he was flying in their direction. "Come on, Trouble, answer your damn phone!"

Fourth ring. Fifth ring. *Do not go to voice mail!*

"Hello?"

Thank God. "Trouble? The Buells just got an alert that we're on to them. They're scrambling, but Rutledge and his men will round them up. I need you to stay with—"

"Yes, this is Alexandra."

What the hell? Jack ratcheted down his relief at hearing Alex's voice and tried to think like a cop. Tried to think like a record-holding driver who was hitting curves on the road about fifty miles above the posted speed limits. "Are you still at Mrs. Stillwell's store? Is your dad with you? Did Rutledge's man find you?"

"Miz Beverly's just fine."

She was freaking him out. Something was way wrong with the dulcet tones and screwy answers to his questions. "Are you still at the shop?"

"I'm fine, too. Why don't I meet up with you after your run?"

*Answer the damn question, woman!* "Are you at the shop?"

"Good luck racing tonight. I know you'll win that bet."

Bet? What bet? The only wager he'd made was that theory he'd tested with… "Are you with Drew?"

"I have to go. I'll catch up with you later."

"Are you in his car? Where's he taking you? Whatever you do, leave your phone on. I can track you. Talk to me, Alex. What's going—?"

She disconnected the call without answering any of his questions.

She hung up on him.

Jack lost his focus for a split-second and nearly blew off the road. Now he knew she was in trouble. Finding the truck's balance again, he decelerated onto the brick streets of downtown Dahlia.

He stopped long enough to find an agent nursing a concussion behind the counter at Beverly's Closet. He found Beverly Stillwell and George Morgan tied up and gagged in one of the dressing rooms. He called Daniel Rutledge and told him to track down the signal on Alex's cell and put an APB out on Andrew Fisk III.

Then he followed a vague hunch about deep hidden gullies and roads to Nashville.

"Come on, baby," he urged, climbing into the hills outside Dahlia, coaxing a few extra mph out of his truck.

Losing Eric had gutted him. But he was healing. With Alex's help, he was finally healing.

If he lost the woman who'd jumpstarted his heart he'd never recover.

"WHERE ARE THE DRUGS?"

Running into Drew at Miz Beverly's shop had been a pleasant surprise. It had seemed odd, though, that he wasn't at the races to watch his new car run. It had been odder still to note the sheen of sweat beading his upper lip. The oddest part had been her father disappearing when he and Drew had gone into the back room to find out why Beverly was taking so long to retrieve Jack's jacket. She'd suspected the truth when Drew came back out by himself. Showing her the gun hidden beneath his suit coat, and inviting her to join him for another ride in his Corvette, confirmed it.

Alex looked straight into the wavering barrel of Drew's gun as they veered off the main road and headed up into the hills along the same road where her brother had died. She bit her tongue and refused to answer.

"The people I work for don't take kindly to someone stealing their merchandise. They'll want money or some kind of payment that isn't pleasant. And it's not coming out of my hide."

The hand on the wheel clutched the last, flaking embers of the cigarette he'd pulled from the glove compartment. That explained the expensive cologne. He was covering up an old habit that he couldn't quite shake.

Apparently Drew had been covering up a lot of things.

"Is that where you're taking me? To your so-called friends? I thought *I* was your friend, Drew."

"It's business, Alex. I have a delivery to make or I don't get paid."

Alex gripped the armrest and dashboard and rode every bump

and curve as night descended around them on the remote county highway. She prayed Drew wouldn't remember her phone was on after hanging up. If he did, she hoped that she'd wedged it far enough between the seat and door so that Jack and anybody but the Buells would arrive before Drew could get around her to dig it out. Even as she mourned the loss of a friendship that she'd known almost from the day she'd moved to Dahlia as a child, Alex was trying to get her head around the facts. "You ran my brother off the road, murdered him—murdered your best friend—to cover up your drug smuggling operation?"

"Ten thousand dollars or the drugs, Alex. Or you'll have to find some other way to pay," he warned. "Artie said you were in his locker. I don't know how you got so many bags out, but you were the only one who could have taken them."

"What if Artie took the drugs?" she challenged. "After all these years, you're saying you trust him more than you do me?"

Muttering a curse, he cracked open his window and flicked the cigarette butt outside. For one crazy moment, Alex considered grabbing the gun or the steering wheel and fighting her way free. But she wasn't that crazy. Shooting the driver or losing control of the Corvette at these speeds would probably ensure her own death, as well.

"Artie may not be the brightest bulb on the tree, but he knows how to fix cars the way I want them. And he knows where his paycheck comes from. He's not so stupid that he'd cross me."

"Oh, but I am?"

He slid her a patronizing glance. "You're not exactly in a position to be mouthing off to me, Shrimp."

"Don't call me that." Her stomach turned from more than the hills and valleys of the road. "That's what my brother called me."

Drew shook his head. "Nick went all good guy on me. He was going to my grandfather with printouts that showed where I'd laundered the money from our Nashville sales. I would have paid him off if he'd given me the chance."

"Nick would have expected better from you."

"Don't get all righteous with me. You're nothing in this town. But folks would listen to Nick. I'd be disinherited and out of a job."

"Not to mention in prison." The crest of the hill where Alex had seen two sets of skid marks was just beyond the next ridge. She dug her fingers in tighter. *Where are you, Jack? Find me.* She hoped he'd understood the message she'd been trying to give him.

"When he wouldn't listen to reason, Hank and I followed him to Nashville. We had to stop him."

Drew Fisk had stood there at her brother's funeral, holding her hand. All these months since, he'd hugged her and advised her and tried to fill the shoes of the very man he'd taken from her life. "You're a third generation millionaire, Drew. You've got a degree from Princeton and opportunities the rest of the world doesn't usually have. Why drugs?"

"I needed the money. I may be the heir to millions, but Grandfather's such a penny pincher that he rations out the money with an eye dropper. That's why he's selling the track. He says I'm squandering his fortune, tarnishing the family name with my lack of success. I got in too deep with my gambling debts, and the mob offered me a way out. Get their drugs to Nashville—get their money back out. Hank owed me for landing him a job and covering his ass in this town. And Artie does whatever Hank tells him. He was a natural at refitting the cars to hide the drugs, and Hank…"

"He's the muscle? Your thug? Your connection to all things evil?" Tears of anger burned behind her eyes. "You killed Nick!"

"I didn't want to."

"Do you expect sympathy from me?"

"I tried to scare you away from this business. All your poking around into Nick's things. The phone calls. The questions I couldn't answer. Hell, I even hoped you'd turn to me for protection. Then I could explain everything away nice and neatly. But no, you had to go find that old man to warm your bed."

"Scare me away?" The cigarette fit. The watching was possible.

Wait a minute. Her grip went slack as her body chilled. "You're the blond boy in the background of that picture from that night. You didn't rescue me—you were a part of it."

Drew laughed, but there was no humor in it. "You honestly think Hank is smart enough to see an opportunity and turn a profit? He isn't now and he wasn't then. He just wanted to get laid and have Artie take a few pictures to prove he'd had you."

"*You* sold the tickets to all those boys."

The smug bastard actually seemed proud of the fact as he shifted into a lower gear to climb the next hill. "And my grandfather says I'm not a motivated businessman."

Alex wanted to reach across the seat and slap the grin off his face. "Is Hank and Artie's father part of this, too?"

"Not at first. But Henry knew his boys were up to something. At first he just looked the other way. Pretty soon, for a cut of the money, he was running interference for us."

"Saying Nick's death was an accident so there'd be no investigation."

"Who knew you were so smart about anything except cars?" Were they actually slowing down? Did he think stopping at the scene of Nick's death would make her break down and tell him what he wanted to know? "I already sent a message to the others and told them to meet us here. Look familiar? Will you listen to reason any better than Nick? Tell me where my drugs are, Alex, and I might let you live."

As the engine gradually powered down, Alex became aware of another sound. Low and growling. Powerful and smooth. There was another finely tuned engine out on the road tonight. Her pulse beat with anticipation. Her heart hoped.

And then she saw the headlights, piercing the darkness through her side-view mirror. Her knight in shining armor drove a big black truck instead of riding a white horse. She wouldn't have it any other way.

"Did you kill that cop in Nashville, too? Eric Mesner?"

"How did you know…?" Gravel crunched beneath Drew's tires as he pulled onto the shoulder of the road. "My associates in Nashville took care of him once we found out he was a cop. Let me guess, Jack Riley is more than a fast driver."

"He's a very fast driver. And he's right on your ass." The car had slowed enough that Alex figured she wouldn't break her neck. She opened the door and tumbled out.

"Get back here, you crazy bitch!"

The next few seconds were a blur of noise and fear and adrenaline. Alex rolled over rocks and grass and slammed into the trunk of a tree. Brakes squealed. Drew cursed as he leaped from the car. A zillion pinpricks of pain burned across her scalp as he grabbed a handful of hair and jerked her to her feet.

"No!" Alex screamed.

Drew's gun dug into her temple. "Get up!"

Lights flashed. Drew spun around. Alex twisted away from him, her bandanna ripping from the top of her head as she fell to her scraped knees. He snatched at the strap of her overalls.

And then she heard the most beautiful voice in the world. Jack's.

"Try it, Fisk. Give me a reason to blow your sorry hide away."

Drew dropped his gun and raised his hands in surrender. "You're Nashville PD?"

Jack's gun never moved from the target between Drew's eyes. "That's right. And you're under arrest. We'll start with kidnapping and assault and work our way up to murder. You okay, Trouble?"

Alex scrambled to her feet. "I am now."

"Then get over here." He held out his arm and tucked her to his side. "And you?" With his gun, he motioned Drew to the ground. "Get down in the dirt where you belong."

# 14

*Three weeks later*

"THANK YOU, DAD. It means a lot to me." Alex didn't try to hold her tears in check as the painters on the scaffolding over the first garage door pulled away the tarp to reveal their handiwork.

*Morgan Family Garage*

The bold red letters said much more than the fact that her father had made her an equal partner in the family business. It honored her brother's name, yet made her feel included, as well. He believed in her abilities in the office and under the hood of a car, even though she wore overalls to work instead of a business suit. He trusted her instincts about money and people, even though she'd have to hire a new mechanic now that Artie was in jail awaiting trial with his brother, Hank, Jim DiMarco, Oswald "Crank" Peterson and Drew Fisk.

He accepted her as she was. Not a poor replacement for Nick, nor a pale shadow of her mother, but a unique woman who calibrated engine blocks better than she cooked a casserole. He finally saw that she was a woman of skill, determination and strength. Her ideas might be a little outside his traditional box, but her heart was always in the right place. She could help take down the bad guys and share the truth about her brother's murder.

He loved her. Unconditionally. And he was making sure the world—or at least Dahlia, Tennessee—knew it.

A girl could get used to that. She might start thinking she

deserved the same kind of respect and acceptance from all the
men in her life.

"Now, now." George Morgan pulled a handkerchief from his
pocket and dabbed at her eyes. But Alex brushed aside the tender
gesture and wrapped her arms around his waist, loving when he
folded her in a hug. She let the tears flow until she felt his skin
warming her cheek through his damp shirt. "Good grief, honey,
you're going on the way your mother used to whenever I brought
her flowers or something."

Reluctantly, Alex pulled away. But the unexpected compari-
son made her smile. "So you think I have a little bit of Mom in
me, after all?"

He chucked her gently on the tip of her chin and grinned. "I
see more of her in you every day. She'd be proud of the young
woman you've grown into. I know I am." Her eyes stung and
filled up again. "Now stop that. I can't have my director of re-
sources and development tearing up every time someone pays her
a compliment."

"Right." Alex sniffed. Loudly. "Oops." The noisy pronouncement warmed her cheeks and earned a smile from her father.

He winked. "Good to know some things never change." He
pointed across the crowded parking lot to the speedway and the
sound of the loudspeaker announcing the Outlaw Modified Street
Car Division time trials that were about to start. "You'd better get
going. Last I saw, Jack was still on the phone in your office. If I'm
paying money to sponsor him, I want him at the track racing."

Alex swiped the last of the tears from her eyes and grinned.
"Yes, sir. I'll get our driver up to the track ASAP. Tater's still with
the Camaro, right?"

"As far as I know. I'll head on over to help him get the car to
the staging lanes. Just make sure you lock up before you come
over, okay?"

Alex stretched up on tiptoe and kissed his cheek before
dashing inside to her office.

"That's right, Daniel. Yeah, I'll tell my captain." Alex quietly closed the door, smiling at the sound of Jack's voice, and how even disguised in those clipped, professional tones, it danced across her ears and made her heart beat a little faster. "I just wanted to let you know that I'll be around to supply whatever assistance you need on the case." After tapping her watch to point out the time, she unfolded the racing jacket with the new red-and-white logo from the box from Beverly's Closet. Updated racing gear wasn't the only thing she'd picked up from Miz Beverly this morning. But Alex was saving that surprise for later. She lifted Jack's helmet from the corner of the desk and waited for him to finish his conversation. "I will. Thanks, Daniel."

"Well?"

Jack shut off his phone and dropped it into his weekend bag along with his badge and gun. "It's official." As he changed his clothes from city cop to weekend drag racer in the middle of a very successful comeback, Jack explained the phone call to Daniel Rutledge. "I applied for the job. With Sheriff Buell's hasty retirement, Dahlia will be needing a new sheriff. It'll take me a couple of months to get everything off my desk in Nashville, but…" He paused, tucking his black T-shirt into his racing pants and circled around the desk to take the helmet and jacket from her hands. He set them down on top of the desk and reached for her. "If you think there's enough reason for me to move to Dahlia…?"

Alex smiled, tilting her chin to lock on to those steel-gray eyes as she aligned her hips against his. She reached up to brush a silvering spike of hair off his forehead. "Let's see. You cleaned up the drug smuggling ring in town. You made friends with my dad and Tater and Sandy Larabie. You're making more than respectable progress in your runs at the track—"

He pressed a finger against her lips and shushed her. "I was hoping for a more personal answer to my question. I don't like this weekend relationship of ours. Don't get me wrong, I love our weekends, but Monday through Thursday gets mighty lonely without you. Would it freak you out if I was around all the time?"

Losing two people they loved had brought Jack and Alex together. Finding love in each other would keep them together.

"Remember that night when Hank…" She dropped her gaze to where her plain, strong hands rested against Jack's chest. "That night when I found the drugs, I asked you to stay."

"And I did. I'd have been camped out on your doorstep even if you hadn't invited me into your bed that night." He tipped her chin back up, asking her to have the confidence to look him in the eye and speak her heart. "Talk to me, Trouble. What are you saying?"

"Stay, Jack. I want you to stay."

A slow smile spread across his face. "So the sage old warrior *does* get the girl in the end, hmm?"

Alex nodded. She rose up on tiptoe, wound her arms around his neck and welcomed his kiss. Welcomed him into her life and into her heart.

He traced the seam of her lips with his tongue and Alex willingly opened for him. He claimed her mouth, driving his tongue inside to slide along hers. Alex suckled the strong line of his bottom lip, scraping her palms against the masculine prickle of his evening stubble. He shucked off her bandanna and tunneled his fingers into her hair, turning her head to give him access to the soft skin beneath her ear and the sensitive column of her neck. Jack nibbled his way down to her collarbone, sending warm ribbons of desire curling into the tips of her breasts and down low into her feminine center.

When he suddenly stopped and lifted his head, Alex blinked, momentarily disoriented by the haze of pleasure still swirling through her head. "Jack?"

He hooked a finger beneath the collar of her T-shirt and pulled it across her shoulder to expose the emerald-green strap of satiny material that held up her bra. "What's this?"

Alex brushed his hand away, remembering the plans she'd

made for tonight after the races were done. "It's for the fashion show later."

"Fashion show?"

"We have work to do first. Then we can try my little project." She turned to grab his jacket and helmet off the desk.

He moved in right behind her, setting his racing gear back down and trapping her against the solid oak with his body. "I seem to recall your *projects* getting me into a whole lot of trouble."

"I think you like having a little trouble in your life, Jack Riley." He wrapped his arms around her waist and Alex shivered at the chest to bulge-behind-his-zipper contact. "Miz Beverly found me a whole bunch of pretty things in my size. And I intend to model them for you and let you take every last one of them off me."

"Who knew I could be such a slave to fashion?" He dipped his head and pressed a hot, wet kiss to that sensitive bundle of nerves at her nape. Her knees turned to jelly. "Do you still have that little black hooker dress? I'd love to take that off you, too."

Alex turned in his arms. One of them had to be strong here. "Later, Jack. Right now you've got a time trial to run at the speedway. I want to see if my Alex Morgan–special engine can take the competition."

"I'll take the Alex Morgan special anytime. Day or night." Jack picked her up and set her on the edge of the desk. He pulled her knees apart and moved between her legs. He reached for the strap on her shoulder and Alex surrendered to what they both wanted. "Now let's see what girly thing you have on under these overalls."

They finished just in time to make the starting line for the race.

\* \* \* \* \*

# HOT UNDER PRESSURE

BY

KATHLEEN O'REILLY

First published in 2001, **Kathleen O'Reilly** is an award-winning author of more than twenty romances, with more books on the way. Reviewers have been lavish in their praise, applauding her "biting humour," "amazing storytelling" and "sparkling characters." She lives in New York with her husband, two children and one indestructible goldfish. Please contact the author at kathleenoreilly@earthlink.net or by mail at PO Box 312, Nyack, NY 10960, USA.

For booksellers everywhere.
Stacey, Anne, Elsie,
I'm looking at you.

# *1*

---

ASHLEY LARSEN climbed over the family of three, mumbling "excuse me," but honestly, in the wide-bodied jet, there was no elegant way to get to her seat with her dignity intact—especially since darling little Junior kept poking her in the rear and laughing maniacally. All the while Mom tried to pretend that nothing was amiss.

*Little booger.*

With a tight smile plastered on her face, Ashley climbed over the skanky-handed hellion, and then plopped into her seat with a relieved sigh. She hated the five seats in the center aisle. What designer thought *that* was a good idea? Especially on a day like today, when the direct route to her seat was blocked by the sweet little old lady who wanted to stuff the three-foot antique lamp into the overhead compartment. Patiently, the flight attendant was explaining how honestly, truly, cross her heart, the baggage handlers would treat the fragile piece with care. Stubbornly, the little old lady wasn't buying it for a minute, and Ashley wished her all the luck in the world. Thank God that was over; now on to the real death-defying feat—preparing for takeoff. After a slow count to three hundred—twice—she pulled the plastic bag from her carry-on and then pushed the suitcase back under the seat in front of her. Furiously she kicked off her travel shoes with some previously unleashed aggression, and then donned fluffy pink bunny slippers. If she was going to die in the air, she wanted to be with at least one thing close to her heart.

Ashley hated flying. Her sister Valerie called it her Erica
Jong moment, but it wasn't sex that Ashley was afraid of, only
moving through the skies at supersonic speeds, a gazillion feet
off the ground. Physics had never been her best subject, and
besides, she knew there was something seriously wrong with
the concept. However, she hated the idea of being a slave to her
fears, so, as a survival mechanism she had created her flying
ritual. Every month, when she took off from O'Hare airport on
her latest buying trip, she meticulously followed the same
pattern to maintain sanity. Whatever worked.

Soon everyone was seated, the antique lamp was stored
below and the flight attendant droned the standard disclaimers
about pulling away from the gate in ten minutes. Just as Ashley
had properly prepared herself for takeoff, another passenger
made his way down the aisle, claiming the one remaining empty
seat in the airplane. The one between Ashley and Mr. and Mrs.
American Family, who were futilely trying to keep Junior
amused. *Now* they decided to resume their parental responsibility. Couldn't they have done it earlier, when he was playing
pin-the-sippy-cup on Ashley's butt? *No.*

Pointedly, Ashley stared out the window because she wasn't
normally a rude person, but air travel brought out one hundred
and one demons in her, none of them Emily Post-like. Valerie
said that the buying trips were good for her. That the only way
to conquer a fear was to tackle it head-on. Valerie could be a
total pain, and one day Ashley was going to stop listening to
her sister's advice. But not today. Today she needed the ritual.

A hard thigh brushed against hers, and she jumped.

"Sorry." The voice was deep, husky and appropriately apologetic. Okay, there was another reasonable, sane human being
on this flight. Ashley turned and the polite smile froze.

*Hello, hot man.*

His trousers were an off-the-shelf-khaki, his shirt, a nicely
mussed crisp white, which, on most men would scream copier
repairman, but here…it was like newsprint veiling a diamond.

Yes, sometimes clothes made the man, but sometimes, the man made the clothes.

After logging thousands of air miles, she'd traveled next to perfumed matrons decked in crystal-encrusted fleece, overly large seat huggers, squeegee businessmen who thought she looked lonely and, yes, a veritable cornucopia of families from hell, but never, *never,* had she actually sat next to a man with a nice smile, wonderfully wicked hazel eyes and a lovely, lovely body that begged to be unwrapped.

Ashley swallowed.

"Not a problem," she said, and then promptly looked away.

*Come on, Ashley. Flirt a little. Pep up your game. Give him the goofy smile. Guys like that.*

It was Valerie's voice. The first time in three years that Ashley had felt heat between her legs and she was listening to an imaginary lecture from her younger sister. *Not anymore, no way, no how.*

"I didn't think I was going to make it," said hot man, continuing to converse with her.

Ashley was torn between wanting to converse with hot man and sinking farther down into her seat and hiding her bunny slippers, but alas, it was impossible in the sardine-like conditions. "And you made it," she said, giving him the goofy smile until she realized what she was doing and promptly stopped.

"After running the four-forty through Terminal two. The next flight to L.A. isn't until tomorrow at six, and I just want to get this over with. You ever feel like that?"

"Always."

He smiled, then immediately frowned, the wicked hazel eyes glancing politely to the aisle.

Married. Must be. Or attached.

Subtly—unconsciously—Ashley's eyes drifted, which she hated, to his left hand. She wasn't on the make, she wasn't interested, she didn't need a man. She wasn't even thinking about being on the make, no matter how much Valerie nagged her.

But that didn't explain the little heart-thud when she noticed there was no ring.

*You're a wimp, Ashley.*

As she contemplated her own human needfulness, the stewardess pulled out the life vest to demonstrate the life-saving effects of the floatation device. Ashley imagined the floatation device bobbling alone in the ocean, her hands aching with cold from the water of the Great Lakes, her face dimming to a pale blue, her lungs weakening ever so slightly. Her hand locked onto the armrest because she knew that Lake Michigan had an ambient temperature of fifty-nine degrees Fahrenheit in April, which didn't sound too bad, but she'd seen that damn Titanic movie. She didn't want to live it.

"First flight?" asked hot man, the nice smile returning, which did have the unexpected effect of calming her fears…somewhat.

"No, sadly, I became a platinum passenger last year. I'm merely a coward at heart."

"I'm sorry," he said, the hazel eyes flickering more toward green—a warm, earthy green that did more to distract her than a muscle relaxant ever could, and reminded her that she hadn't had sex in a long time.

"Don't be. It's a family trait. Yellow-bellied, lily-livered Larsens, that's us."

He smiled again, and she felt the tell-tale heart-thud again. She unlocked her gaze from the captivating green of his eyes, and drifted to where Junior was most likely planning his latest nihilistic techniques.

*Ask his name.*

*No.*

*It's only a name, a polite introduction. Not an invitation to the mile-high club.*

*I don't care. Shut up, Valerie.*

*I'm not even here.*

*I know. I swear when I get back on land, I'm going to see a therapist. It's the only answer.*

*Don't be a wimp, Ashley.*

*I'm very self-aware. I'm a wimp.*

*Why do I even try?*

*Because you're sadistic, and you revel in my pain. It makes you feel superior.*

*I'm not even here.*

"Don't talk to me," muttered Ashley, wondering if hearing her sister's nagging meant that she was a woman on the verge of a nervous breakdown. The wind was certainly blowing in that direction.

"I'm sorry?" asked hot-guy.

"Oh, not you. I hear voices."

His brows rose—charmingly, of course. He really had a great smile. It wasn't a full-bodied smile, just a quick rise on the right side of his mouth where his mouth smashed headlong into a tiny dimple. "Part of the phobia?"

"No, my psychotic sister. Do you have a psychotic sister?" she asked, firmly believing that everyone should have a psychotic sister.

"No."

"You are *so* lucky. I always thought a brother would be cool. As long as he doesn't nag."

"Your sister nags?"

Ashley nodded. "Like a mother."

"I'm sorry," he said, apologizing again, and she noted how rare it was to hear a man apologize. Jacob had never apologized. Not once.

Right at that precise moment, Junior stabbed hot man in the hand with a particularly lethal twisty straw, and he yelped, his hand diving toward the armrest, trapping hers in a death grip of pain.

Ashley yelped, too, Junior laughed hysterically and Mom politely looked in the opposite direction, as if all were right with her world. Muscle relaxants could do that to a person.

Hot man's hand lifted from hers, and Ashley's normal blood flow resumed. He looked at her, the hazel eyes no longer wicked—now they showed true fear. About time he appreciated the seriousness of their situation. Four hours next to the toddling terror of the skies, who was now demanding macaroni and cheese, obviously oblivious to the plebian limitations of airplane food.

"He just broke out from the pen," Ashley whispered confidentially. "Wanted in four states. I saw his mug on the post office wall."

Hot man leaned in close and she could feel the whisper of his breath.

*Ah, yearning loins, aching to be filled. Thy name is lust.*

*Shut up, Valerie.*

"Stabbed you, too?" he asked.

"Nope. Butt-fondling in the third degree."

"Really?" He grinned. "A mastermind of crime with discriminating taste."

*He's flirting with you, Ashley. That's definitely flirting.*

*Shut up, Valerie.*

"So, why're you going to L.A.?" asked Ashley, flirting in return. "Vacation. Business. The fresh air?"

"Business," he answered, kicking his feet toward the computer case in front of him. "I'm a business analyst. You?"

"Buying trip. Clothes."

His eyes raked over her, noting the bunny slippers, and she felt the twinge again. The loins were definitely starting to yearn. "You like to shop that much?"

"I own some boutiques," she spoke, the words stumbling out of her mouth like pebbles. She'd bought the stores as a post-divorce present to herself, but what had been an impulsive plan to reinvent her life, hadn't quite blossomed as she'd hoped. As a kid, she loved to shop for clothes, loved to put together outfits that seemingly didn't belong, but then somehow worked. Unfortunately owning four disjointed clothing boutiques required more than stylish élan. Ashley's business sense hadn't magically appeared as Valerie had believed, and a good eye for color and style couldn't compete with designing ads and balancing the budget. In fact, in the past few months, usually when she was paying the bills, she thought about selling the stores, worried that she couldn't cut it. It was when the rent got raised for the second time in as many years that she worried she was like some people on those television reality shows. Thinking they could sing, but when their mouths opened the world's worst sounds emerged, and the home audience is sitting there wondering why the heck these types ever, *ever* had the wonky idea that they belonged in the limelight.

There were certain similarities.

Ashley's smile fell, the plane moved slowly back from the gate and she felt the familiar lurch in her stomach.

"Scared?"

"I'll be fine," replied Ashley, and she would. Business problems, personal problems, fashion problems, in the big scheme of things, they didn't amount to much that couldn't be overcome. In the end, Ashley was a survivor. When she was working on a new store window—surrounded by encouraging mannequins draped in subtly fitted, beautifully crafted, casual couture—the dream returned. She could do it. All she needed was to keep the faith.

She gave hot man a weak smile, and he covered her hand, a grip that was supposed to be comforting.

*If you'd only twitch the thumb, a tiny caress….*

*Shut up, Valerie.*

He had large hands, warm hands, with long, long fingers that looked so full of possibilities.

"Everything all right?"

"Peachy." The engines start to roar.

Quickly she took out the air-sickness bag.

Just in case.

DAVID MCLEAN hadn't been excited about a side-trip through Chicago to see his brother. Ex-brother. Chris had lost any claim to family bonding after he'd slept with David's wife. Yeah, nothing like a little wife-sharing between brothers. Four years, and it still pissed him off.

Still, in the face of pink bunny slippers and shoved in close quarters with a young psycho in training, David felt something unfamiliar tug at his face. A grin. Yes, that was definitely a grin.

The woman was just nervous enough to be unthreatening. He liked her. Her hair was dark, nearly black, and she had soft brown eyes and a nose that was too big to be called pert. But it gave her a little something extra—character. And she had a nice mouth, plump lips that were always held slightly parted, like a kid viewing the world for the first time, or a woman in the beginning throes of climax.

There was something stirring in his khakis—trouble. Sex held the whip hand, and turned men into stupid dogs. Like, for instance, Chris. And Christine. When he first introduced his future wife to his brother, all three of them had laughed about their matching names. The day he had found them in bed together, the laughter had stopped.

He shot a furtive look at the bunny slippers.

"I'm David," he said, carefully displacing thoughts of Chris and Christine.

"Ashley."

"Are you from Chicago?"

"Born, bred and will most likely die here as well."

"Cubbies fan, aren't you?" It was there in her eyes, that sort of lost hope, winning seasons long denied. Idealistic dreamers—a rarely seen species that was going to naturally select itself into extinction.

She winced. "I know, it's pathetic, isn't it? Are you from Chicago?"

"New York."

"Ah, home of the Yankees."

"What can I say? I live in New York. We always back the money team."

"Sad to be bought so easily."

He shrugged, and looked out the window. The plane had stopped moving toward the runway. They were returning to the gate.

Immediately Ashley noticed. "Something's wrong, isn't it?" Her finger jammed at the call button, just as the captain came on the speaker, his voice Prozac calm and soothing, which only made her more nervous.

"Ladies and gentlemen, we've had a slight mechanical issue. Nothing to worry about. I'm going to pull us back to the gate and have the mechanics check things out. We'll have a short stop where you can disembark, if you choose. However, you will need your boarding pass to reboard."

"We're not flying?" she said, and he noticed the relief in her voice.

"We're going to fly," answered David, wanting to reassure her, but more importantly, he needed to get to L.A. The sooner he left Chicago the better.

"I'm not taking off my slippers," she answered. "They can't do that to me."

"It's okay, I'm sure it won't be long," he told her, not his usual brutal honestly, but he suspected there was normally more color in her face, and if bunny slippers made her happy, who was he to take them away?

"What sort of mechanical problems do you think we're stuck with? I was on a flight to Miami when they thought the landing gear was hosed, but it turned out fine."

"Let me tell you about the time that I was flying to Houston. The engine blew…." Her eyes shot up four sizes, the pale color bleached to a ghostly hue, and he clamped down on his tongue. Hard. *Okay, David, great going here.* "Sorry. We landed fine. They have back-up engines, so if anything fails…" He realized he wasn't helping, so wisely he decided to shut up.

*Damn.* He liked talking to her. Normally he pulled out his computer and worked through flights, but this afternoon had left him feeling unsettled. Two weeks ago he had told his ex-wife that he would be in Chicago for a meeting. He would finally see them. But then he'd arrived at O'Hare and the city of big shoulders closed in on him.

He shouldn't have called them. Christine had said she was pregnant—*oh, joy!*—but in the end, David lied, leaving a message saying that his meeting had been canceled and he wouldn't be stopping in Chicago after all.

David didn't like being a coward. He never did—except for this.

The pregnancy had stung. Not that he wanted Christine back, but it irked him that she preferred his brother, that fidelity wasn't part of her vocabulary, and that he, a man who evaluated million-dollar business opportunities on a daily basis, could do so poorly when picking out wife material.

"I know of a little knockwurst place in Terminal One," he blurted out, because he didn't want to sit here sulking over the social implications of having a nephew birthed by his ex-wife. Bratwurst and sausage were so much more appealing. Then he glanced down at her feet. "Oops. Never mind."

"Down by Gate B12, between the ATM and the security check?"

"Yeah, you know the place?"

"Heh. I eat there all the time." Her mouth parted even more, drawing his eyes. Trouble stirred once more. "There are few things to get me out of my bunny slippers, but knockwurst and blown engines will do it. Let's go before junior scarfs down another chocolate bar."

# 2

---

HIS NAME WAS David McLean. His hair was a rich brown, cut conservatively short, but it suited him, suited the all-American, man-most-likely-to-know-how-to-fix-a-car-engine allure. Yes, he'd never model like one of those designer-wearing scruffy-jawed man-boys, but there was something about him that fascinated her. He was curious and intelligent, asking questions about everything, yet not so willing to talk about himself. Eventually she discovered why.

He was divorced and his jaw clenched like a vise when he'd mentioned it, so it wasn't one of those "parting as good friends" situations.

The restaurant was quiet and dark, the wait staff moving efficiently and effortless, and the large, overstuffed booths were conducive to divulging confidences to perfect strangers.

"It's not easy, is it?" she asked, thinking of her own divorce. Two weeks of wounded pride, several weeks of sorting out the finances and understanding what was whose and five months of awkward questions and well-meaning advice from friends. But then Ashley woke up one cold December morning and she knew she would be okay. Not fine, not great, but she was going to live. It was while in that fragile state that Valerie convinced her that she should do something radical with her life, live out her dream and buy a chain of four small Chicago boutiques. Start fresh.

"Not going that well?" asked David, when she told him what she did.

"Why would you think that?"

"I don't know. You don't have the joie de vivre that a lot of small business owners get when things are breezing along."

"You see a lot of small business owners?"

"Oh, yeah. From Omaha to Oahu. Kalamazoo to Klondike. I've seen a lot."

"Oh."

"Owning your own business is a lot of work. I sit on the sidelines and tell people how much their business is worth, how much it's not worth, what they are doing wrong, and recommend whether our investors should go all in or not. My job is the easy part. After I look over the operation, talk to a few customers and suppliers, I go plug some numbers into a spreadsheet, and then I'm on to the next business, the next opportunity."

"I used to be an insurance claims appraiser."

His mouth quirked, amused, and she cut in.

"Don't say it. I know. I have the insurance adjuster look."

"Nah, not an insurance adjuster. Maybe bookstore owner or candy maker. Something more personal."

"I think that's a compliment."

"It is. You're too cute for the insurance business. So why fashion?"

*Cute. He thinks you're cute.*

*He's from New York.*

*Who cares? Take a chance, Ash.*

For a second she met his eyes—a little more bold than usual. "I want to prove something. I want to take a plant and nurture it, care for it, water it and watch it bloom."

He snapped his fingers. "Florist. I can definitely see that in you."

She began to laugh because if he ever saw her plant shelf, he would be rolling on the floor, too. "No florist, sorry. I wanted to do something that I could master. Something challenging. I was stuck, and I needed to prove that I could do something different." It was nearly Valerie's post-divorce speech verbatim, but Val had been right. Ashley had just neglected to tell her sister that last key point.

"And fashion is challenging?"

Ashley nodded. Men really had no idea. It had taken her two hours to decide on the yellow gypsy skirt, the perfect pale green cotton T-shirt and a kaleidoscopic glass-bead necklace. The outfit had vague Easter-egg overtones, but worked nicely with her hair, and best of all…no wrinkles when traveling.

"Good luck."

"Thanks."

He sat back from the table, his eyes tracking to the bank of departure monitors nearby. "We better go back to the tarmac of terror."

"You're anxious to get out of here?" she asked, noticing the slight jaw-clench again. That, and the disappearing smile.

"No. It's fine."

Yeah, she'd seen that movie, too. Knew the ending. "Denial, much? Don't worry. It'll get better."

His gaze met hers, and the warm green was analytical hazel once again. "Has yours?"

"Oh, yeah," she lied. It hadn't gotten worse, but it hadn't gotten better. Instead she was stuck in this post-divorce limbo where she had no knowledge of how to proceed, and no inclination to leave the comfort of her own solitude.

"So when's the last time you went out?"

"Not too long ago."

"How long?" he probed, and she didn't like the awareness in his eyes. It was that same probing look that her sister got before she would launch into a lecture. Ashley shifted in her seat.

"I don't know," she answered vaguely. The divorce had been three years and eight months ago, but she didn't like the idea of dating again. It felt too wrong. She was a thirty-two-year-old woman, not a twentysomething college kid. She couldn't go sit in a bar. If she signed up for a matchmaking service, she was afraid no one would pick her. And most of the blind dates she'd had had been with total losers. People had good intentions, but their judgment left a lot to be desired.

"Has it been longer than a year?"

"Maybe. But I've been busy," she said, dodging the question.

He stayed silent for a second before nodding. "Understand that. I'm not one of those men who has to be married. I cook. I do my own laundry. There's a whole group of guys who get together to watch the games in a bar. I'm independent. I like my independence." It was the battle cry for the walking wounded. Ashley knew it well.

"Then it sounds like you're in a good place." She gave him the fake smile. The one that says, "whatever you say is fine."

"I think I am. You?"

"Oh, yeah." Abruptly, she decided to stop the charade. Here was a comrade in arms. Someone who knew exactly how it felt. Why not tell the truth? She missed cooking for two. She missed waking up on a Sunday morning and not having to plan out the day. She missed being able to come home from work and laugh about her coworkers—not all of them, but there were a few who were laugh-worthy. Ashley and Jacob had been married for seven years, and it was never the world's greatest marriage, but still… "Sometimes it is, but sometimes it's not. Well, you know, there are things I miss."

"Gawd, yes."

"At night. It's lonely."

"Exactly."

"I mean, I know I can get Valerie to watch…." He shot her a shocked look and then recovered quickly, but not before she noticed. Oh, man, he thought she was talking about sex, which she wasn't, but now, okay, her mind was going there, she was thinking the sex thoughts… *No, don't think about it, Ash.* Quickly she fumbled back into the conversation. "I like watching horror movies at night and my sister is a total wimp. All we get are historical dramas. Television is something best done with another person." *Okay, Ashley, got over that one.* Not too shabby.

David, however, still looked mildly shell-shocked. "Totally," he answered in a tight voice.

"You like horror movies, too?" she asked, getting a little cocky and daring to tease.

"We should get back to the plane," he answered, not taking the whole teasing thing well. She knew that men got a lot more wired than women about sex, but he seemed more laid-back than that. Wrong, Ashley. Quickly she changed to a safer topic.

"Get back to Junior? You're as sadistic as Valerie."

"Maybe he's asleep."

THEY HAD NO SUCH luck once they got back on board. Junior was riding a sugar high, judging by the chocolate smeared across his face and the way he kept bouncing on his seat. But at least all weapons were out of his possession.

David watched as Ashley changed shoes again, noticing how nice her feet were. Smooth, compact, lots of well-turned curves. His cock stirred and he turned away. Turned on by a foot? Weak…very, very weak. It'd been a long time since he had spent several confined hours in the company of a single woman. After the divorce, he'd thrown himself into work, mainly because he liked it, he was good at it, and if he couldn't have a family life, at least he could build up his retirement account. Today had been like a cold dunk in a deep ocean, the familiar patterns coming back to him, the jittery nerves coming back to him, and the hard-on coming back to him as well.

It was because there wasn't anything they could do about it. That's what this was. Economics. Supply and demand. Decrease the availability of supply, and boom, demand shoots out from every pore, zipping in his brain. Ergo, the hard-on.

*If she hadn't mentioned sex.* Well, honestly, she hadn't mentioned sex, she just mentioned the word *night* and his imagination took off from there, wishing they weren't at an airport, wondering if that skirt was as easy to slip off as it looked so he could feel her skin under his hands. Tawny skin, creamy skin, soft, touchable skin rubbing up against him…

David studiously avoided looking at her skin, his eyes moving upward, touching on her chest. Lots of well-turned curves there, too. After that, he looked away, met Junior's knowing eyes and glared. Heading to an altitude of thirty thousand feet, it wasn't going to get any easier, so better to concentrate on other, less arousing things. Junior launched a Lego piece in his direction.

Like survival.

TWO HOURS LATER they were still at the gate. They were waiting on either a part, or a new plane, the pilots weren't sure which would arrive first, but they had high—ludicrously delusional— hopes for getting away tonight. In the face of such facts, Ashley had long abandoned her fear of flying. It was obvious they weren't going anywhere anytime soon.

Instead she was thigh-locked with David, who had very nice thighs, too. Hard. His arms were fab as well. Thirty minutes ago, he'd pushed up his sleeves, and her gaze kept stalling out on the biceps, which were bigger than most, an odd incongruity for khakis and a button-down, and she wondered why. He wasn't bulky enough to be a weight lifter, but his arms were too big for a swimmer or a runner, and definitely too big for a tiny airplane seat. They kept brushing against hers, casually, which didn't explain the electric shock to her system.

Not that he was making it any easier. Conversation had ceased about half an hour ago when she caught him staring at her chest, and they both looked politely away.

Damn.

She crossed her legs, uncrossed her legs, and had a hare-brained urge to ask him to join her in the bathroom. She'd pulled out *Vogue* and *Harper's* and *Lucky,* but even the lure of the sloe-eyed models in their daring designs hadn't dimmed the awareness that simmered in the air.

The bright spot in the tension was Junior, which said a lot about her feelings of desperation. Junior wrote on David's hand with a pen, and David laughed, sounding more relieved than amused. Junior ran up and down the aisle, and Ashley counted the number of times, choosing note to fixate on the discreetly covered ridge in David's khaki slacks.

*Do not go there.*

*Go there, Ashley.*

*Oh, yeah, good of you to talk. You can't have sex on a plane, Valerie.*

*People do.*

*Not me.*

There was a momentary pause in her thoughts, because right now, given readily available options, she could *so* have sex on this plane.

Another thirty minutes passed, and the flight attendants were passing out drinks. Yes, alcohol, the world's most potent aphrodisiac. When the flight attendant stopped at their row, David shook his head, Ashley shook her head, and Junior's mother and father opted for double vodka tonics.

Outside the window, the lights of the airport started to dim. If she lowered her hand one inch, just one tiny inch, she would be touching his thigh. If she were careful, it would look like an accident.

Junior spilled a glass of orange juice on those khakis that she was not looking at, and David shot sideways, and there was a momentary barrage of touches. His hand, her breast. Her hand, his thigh. She jumped back, arching toward the window, and he moved away, hugging his seat. Junior's mother apologized, and Ashley's nipples were powered by a thousand jet engines, ready for takeoff.

It was shortly after her breasts had recovered from the shock that the captain came on the speaker and announced that moment they all had been expecting.

"Ladies and gentleman, we tried. But there's bad weather

in New York, and we couldn't get the plane that we were hoping for, and they can't get the part here until the morning. So I'm sorry to say, we won't be going anywhere. If any of you need hotel accommodations at the airport, there's a flight attendant waiting to give you the details."

*A hotel.* Suddenly the word took on new connotations and images. A hotel implied a bed, privacy, something much more comfortable than a tiny bathroom designed by Boeing. A hotel implied *sex.*

The cabin lights went on, and people around them began to move. Everyone was moaning and complaining, and, in general, not in a very happy place. However, Ashley's happy place was getting happier by the second. She didn't want to look at him, didn't want to assume, most of all she didn't want to act as if she didn't know what she was doing. After all, she was mature, she was an adult, and after eight hours of sitting thigh-to-thigh with this man, she was primed to explode with only a touch.

He turned, a slight inclination of his head, and she met his eyes. It was ESP of the most carnal kind. She licked her lips, his gaze tracked her tongue and she knew that he knew.

He leaned down, his mouth near her ear. "You should know that right now, I'm a very happy man." Ashley felt the touch in her ear, down to the soles of her feet, and every single inch in between, especially the happy place. She tried to smile, but that involved mind-body cooperation, and right now there was none. Slowly she regained the capability to speak and she did manage to smile, although she wasn't sure how it looked.

"Happy is good," she told him.

She was going to have sex with David. She was going to peel off his shirt, feel the muscles of his bare chest crushing her breasts. She would rip off his briefs, since she instinctively knew he wore briefs—tight, white briefs, with his sex jutting out from the band—and then finally, finally, he would push up inside her, filling her…

She felt her muscles contract once, contract twice.

Her mouth tightened and her eyes opened and spied David, who was watching her with eyes that were nearly black.

Ashley nodded once. "I think we need to go. Now." He grabbed the carry-ons and then they both took off running through the airport, Ashley's bunny slippers cooperating nicely.

# 3

THE FIRST STOP was at the newsstand for condoms.

Condoms!

*I can't believe you're sitting here watching a man buy condoms. I mean, I'm glad and all, but Ash, he's not a serial killer, is he? This is not smart. How much do you know about this man?*

*I know enough that I want to sleep with him. No, not sleep. I want to have sex. I want to kiss him, I like watching his eyes get all dark and sexy. You'd be surprised what you get to know about a guy when you're trapped on a grounded plane for eight hours. He's not a serial killer.*

*It's your funeral.*

*Shut up, Val. You're not here, and he is.*

She pulled out her flats from the carry-on and switched out of the bunny slippers. Not going to need those until tomorrow.

After an eternal four minutes, David walked back from the newsstand wearing a slight flush, his eyes dodgy, not like a guy who was an old hand at buying condoms at the airport—and not like a serial killer, either.

"I don't carry them," he apologized.

"I understand," she said, and decided it was best not to talk about this anymore.

The shuttle to the hotel was fast and silent, and it glided through the darkness, getting them there way too fast. David didn't touch her. He didn't need to. She could feel him, feel his eyes, feel his thoughts.

When the shuttle arrived at the hotel, David took her bag,

his arm brushing against hers, and she jumped. It was like a scene in some of her favorite horror movies, but not in the "someone's going to get hacked up" sort of way, but more "someone's going to get laid," and it was going to be good. Really, really good. Her loins started to ache, her blood pounding.

At the front desk was a seventeen-year-old who didn't need to be up this late. As David handled the registration, Ashley held back because she didn't know hotel registration protocol for this arrangement. Did they need two names? If so, should she use her real name? It was a whole new world, and honestly, she didn't need to know about it. There were much more important things to think about, so she and her aching loins were going to hang back and wait it out.

Three seconds later, and then David was back. It was time. *It wasn't enough time.*

"You don't look so good. You need a drink? We can chat more," he told her, because obviously eight hours stranded on a plane wasn't enough for Ashley. Oh, no, she needed more chat time.

"We should get a drink," she said, her brain furiously stalling for chat time, while her other parts were yelling at her to get the heck upstairs.

To the right of the front desk was the hotel bar. It was dark, sleek, a place with low lights, big comfortable chairs, and an IMAX-sized mirror on the wall. Ashley leaned up to the bar. "I'll take a double shot of tequila," she told the bartender.

"Make it two," added David.

While he waited for the drinks, she picked out two chairs, far from the bartender, but not far from the mirror. David set the shot glasses on the low table and settled in the chair next to her. "You should know that I have taken defensive driving, been married only once, have no contagious, nor sexually transmitted diseases and I never pick up strange women in airports."

For some reason, that made her feel a lot better. "Me, neither.

I mean, men. I never pick up strange men." And after that mangled confession, she licked the salt from the rim of her glass.

David leaned over, and kissed the corner of her mouth.

"Salt," he murmured.

"Mouth," she responded automatically, staring at his mouth. It was a good mouth. It was hard, stubborn and looked liked it knew what it was doing.

"Tongue," he replied.

"Oh, God," she whispered, and then poured a sharp splash of tequila down her throat. "You would tell me if you think this is slutty, right?"

*Ash, that's a stupid question. He's not going to tell you that. Men like slutty. When it comes to sex, men have no scruples, no morals, no ethics.*

"Absolutely," he lied.

"Okay. That was stupid."

"We can get two rooms," he told here, doing a great impersonation of an ethical man who still wanted sex.

*Is this what you want, Ash? If it's really and truly what you want, then Do It.*

She looked at David McLean, the once-divorced, defensive driver with eyes currently tending to brown rather than green. Eyes that said he wanted her. And Ashley made up her mind. It was no contest. Not even a minor dilemma.

"I want to have sex with you. I want to do something new and exciting, at least once before I die, most likely in a plane crash. Stranger sex is exciting." As she said the words, she caught her reflection in the mirror. Her eyes were the same, yet different. She was...glowing, which could have been the warm-toned lighting, but she didn't think so.

"Stranger sex?" he asked, his mouth quirking up at one side. She liked that about him, the way he didn't fully smile, but only partly committed to it. Like a man who wants to laugh, but isn't quite sure it's the correct thing to do.

"Yeah, you know, stranger sex. The unknown, the forbidden, the lady and the tiger."

Now she was fully staring at the mirror in front of her. Her, the wild-eyed seductress—slight overstatement—with him, the harried businessman, which was probably true.

*Kiss him, Ash. Plant a big smoochie right there.*

Throwing caution to the wind, Ashley leaned over and kissed him. Once, on the side of the mouth.

"Salt," she murmured.

Then she boldly moved her mouth to his.

"Mouth," he whispered against her lips.

It was nearly a kiss. A press of skin, an exchanging of breaths. It wasn't enough.

"Tongue," she said, and magically, it was a kiss. Mouth, tongues, and oh, yes, that was passion. David McLean was a most excellent kisser. He was earnest, sincere, unafraid. Best of all, he made Ashley feel earnest, sincere and unafraid. She forgot about the mirror, and the hotel room, and only focused on one thing— his mouth. The way his tongue mated perfectly with hers.

He tasted like lime and salt and hot, sweaty, body-smashing sex. Maybe that was only her subconscious talking or the humming moisture between her legs, but she didn't think so. Ashley moved closer, wild-eyed seductress that she was, and then his hand was at her jaw, holding her while that magic tongue moved in and out, intensifying the hum between her legs.

When he lifted his head, those hazel eyes were dark, sleepy and irresistible. Ashley could only stare.

"Two rooms?" he asked.

She shook her head, not wavering or worrying even once.

They walked to the bank of elevators without touching, because Ashley didn't want to touch him at the moment. Touching implied combustion, and neither a hotel hallway nor a hotel elevator was the place for combustion.

Not for Ashley, and apparently not for David.

*This is it, Ash. We're sure he's not a serial killer, right? What if you get strangled or something?*

David looked at her, his hungry gaze falling to her mouth.

Ashley told the voices to shut up.

DAVID'S HAND SHOOK as he inserted the keycard in the lock, but honestly, he was too primed to try and be smooth about this. He opened the door, told himself to go slow, then immediately ignored all his normally responsible, conventional wisdom and grabbed Ashley, kicking the door shut behind them.

Her arms curled into his hair, pulling him closer, and they stumbled toward the bed. He wasn't like this. He wasn't ever like this, so who was that man fumbling her shirt over her head, lifting her skirts, or dive-bombing for her mouth?

That mouth.

She kissed like she dressed. Not completely stylish, but there was an understated flashiness, and a zing. Definitely a zing.

David heard a moan. Hers. Oh, definitely a zing. Now he was moaning, too.

He tumbled on top of her, completely without finesse, but thankfully, she didn't seem to mind. Her legs wrapped about him, pelvis surging toward him, and his hands went to his fly. Her breasts pressed against him, soft peaks in white cotton. If his zipper would ever get unstuck, he'd shove the bra aside, because he wanted to see…

The room began to shake. What was that? He could hear the roar of a jet engine. The airport. They were at the airport. That wasn't his cock. Calm. Remain calm.

Condom. Oh, shit. He needed a condom.

"Wait," he nearly yelled. He needed to get control. He needed to breathe. In the dim light of the single bedside lamp, she looked up at him, clothes ransacked into parts, exposing more skin than covering. Great skin. Gold and rose mixed together like mother-of-pearl. She wore white cotton panties. With a sun-yellow gypsy skirt, she wore white cotton panties, and did she even *know* he had a thing for white cotton? He definitely had a thing for white cotton. It was sexy as hell. She was sexy as hell.

His hands were still shaking as he shoved her bra aside. Like a total amateur.

*Dude, get a hold of yourself. She's going to think you haven't done this in like, months.*

She'd be right, but he didn't want to advertise the fact.

The foil packet tore exactly as it was supposed to, and then…

"Let me," she whispered in a husky voice that sent every drop of his blood out of his head. Into his head. There was courage in her eyes. The bunny-slipper woman, who was a trembling coward at ten thousand feet, now seemed mightier than any warrior queen with her clothes askew.

Oh, no. Her capable hands got busy on his cock, sending ten thousand volts to his system. *Concentrate on something else. The breasts, for instance.*

Didn't work.

David wasn't going to last, he was going to explode and this was going to be over. No way.

He pushed her into the bank of pillows, roughly, again with the no-finesse thing, and then…

Then…

Yes.

She was tight, perfectly tight, and wet.

He opened his eyes, looked down at those dark, dancing eyes and swallowed.

*Had he truly forgotten that sex could be this awesome? Yes, yes, he had.*

"Oh," he managed to say.

Ashley smiled at him, and it was a marvelous smile. A smile for a hot summer's day, and he was so glad the airplane had had a mechanical failure. He was even glad for Hellboy Junior. Being like this, surrounded by her, was worth it, so worth it. He rocked his hips, going deeper inside her, and her smile turned serious. Again he thrust, just to see if it was as good as the first.

Yes, yes, it was.

Then his mind began to shut down, and biology, desire and sex took over.

Greedily he drove inside her, plunging into that moist heat. Her pupils were wide, dilated, and her mouth…it was exactly as he'd imagined. No, it was better than he'd imagined. This was so much better than he imagined. Ashley tried to talk. Couldn't. Her nails scraped down his back, down his butt, and it was the best pain ever. *Ever.*

He should be doing more for her, pushing buttons somewhere, but his body was running on autopilot, pumping hard and fast, and she didn't seem to mind. Her hands locked on his shoulders, pulling him, pushing him, and there was no finesse there, either. And he'd never had such great, mindless sex in his entire life.

Another plane took off, and the bed shook, only this time it wasn't a plane, it was David and Ashley. It was nearly an hour later, after all the planes had been grounded for the night that the room stopped spinning, the bed stopped moving, and David's heart landed back on the ground.

Stranger sex? Is that what that meant? Shit. They were going to have to do that again.

ASHLEY SLID OVER to the far side of the bed. You didn't cuddle with a man you'd known less than one day. Actually, you normally didn't share a hotel room with a man you'd known less than one day, but in this case, after the last two hours, her standards could be relaxed. There was a moment as she listened to the ever-efficient sounds of used condom removal. Too much information, oh, man, she was not cut out for this.

"Are you okay?" he asked, rolling over, and they were so close, so naked, actually not completely naked, there were clothes still attached to both of them…barely.

"I'm good," she answered, a total understatement if there ever was one, and Ashley didn't usually understate. Honestly, she had to say that David McLean had the best bed head ever. Brown strands falling into his eyes, a cowlick in the back, and she wanted to reach over, smooth it back into place. She kept her hands still. They were strangers. You couldn't go around fixing a stranger's hair. Sex? Yes. Hair-fixing? No. Again with the rigid standards.

"How good?" he asked, not seeming to be needy, but still curious.

"Really good."

"Oh, good," he sighed, and fell back on his back. "That was freaking nuts. You were right."

"I was?"

*And what did "nuts" mean? He sounded happy, beyond happy even, but nuts? What sort of word was that? No, she was getting all paranoid again. She would not get paranoid. This had been awesome, and she had been an active part of that awesomeness.*

He cleared his throat. "I've never done something like this before, and it's…I don't know, it's just…great."

*Now, see, "great" is so much better than "nuts."*

"It was, wasn't it?" she said, sounding like she did this all the time.

He nodded, and she grinned, completely ruining the confident, sophisticated image.

"Why isn't it always like that?" she asked, studying her past sexual behavior pattern to figure out why this was different. Why here, why him, why now? She hadn't had sex in a year…two? Maybe it was the long dry spell that made things so…stimulating?

"It isn't always like that because not every man is me," he answered, sounding exactly like every man. He started to laugh. "Whatever it is, it's not ambience, that's for sure." He cast a long look around the all-American airport hotel decor.

She followed his gaze. He was right. A single torchère light stood in the corner, the bedcovers were orange—*orange!*—but the drapes were a nice touch. A garden green with large tropical flowers. Cheery.

Ashley pulled up the sheet and blanket to cover her chest discreetly. David McLean, on the other hand, was certainly not shy. His legs, half in half out of bed, exposed lean thighs. The legs were tan, with an indentation where his ass joined the thighs. It was a fine ass, smooth, firm…exactly like his… *No, Ashley focus on the conversation.*

What were they talking about? Oh, yeah. "That…bam," she began, searching for a better word, failing, and no, it wasn't because of his fine ass. "I mean, what's that about? If I knew you better, would it disappear?" Her eyes kept stealing lower. Conversation with a naked hot man was harder than it looked.

"The zing? That never lasts. I've had some great first dates before, and then, you get to the third date, and you're thinking, who is this person?"

"Exactly," she said, curling up next to hot man with the fine ass, because miracles did not happen often. "Familiarity. And then it all goes down the drain."

"Too bad they can't market that. That bam, that zing. Advertisers would go crazy."

"I know absolutely nothing about advertising, but you're right."

"Thank you," he told her.

"For what?" she asked, because honestly it was no big deal to agree with him. He was right. She knew he was right.

He cocked his head toward the bed. "For doing this. For staying with me tonight. I feel good. Normal. Better than normal. Like I could run a marathon. Alive. Not so dead."

*Don't look, Ash.*

Not looking, not looking, not…looking. Nope, she looked. Not dead yet. Getting livelier by the second.

He turned, studying her. "I didn't know I could have sex with a stranger in a hotel without guilt. Without trying to analyze everything."

"You're analyzing everything."

"Occupational hazard." He leaned back into the pillows and sighed. Not a restful man, David McLean. "It shouldn't be so hard to start over. Just a date. That's the Holy Grail for me. I want to find a woman to go out with, and have a nice evening. A good conversation, a little fun."

"There would be tons of women wanting to go out with you," Ashley told him.

*Good God, what was wrong with the women in New York?*

*Nothing wrong with him. He's a serial killer.*

*Right, Val.*

"It seems like all the women I meet are weird, neurotic, or needy. Or eighteen. I have standards."

Speaking as a weird, neurotic woman, neither needy, nor eighteen, Ashley knew he was doomed and felt it her duty to speak the truth. "Sorry, you're out of luck. All that comes with the estrogen…except the eighteen part." His eyes looked nervous and she laughed. "Have you tried online services? A friend of mine met her husband online."

"Normal people don't do that, do they? It doesn't seem like, I don't know, there's something wrong with me?"

Ashley waved a hand. "Not anymore. Everybody's too busy to go and hang out somewhere on the off chance they'll meet—" she held up quote fingers "—the One."

David still didn't look convinced. "A dating service. It sounds painful."

For women, yes, for men, ha. "Go for it. Women would jump all over you."

*Like you did, Ash.*

"You really think it'd be okay?"

Ashley nodded.

"And you swear that normal people sign up?"

"On my honor as a fashion professional."

"I don't know."

"Try it," she urged, because he needed to find that perfect

petite blond, black-dressed New Yorker who would appreciate a man who was simply…nice. That, and a pile driver in bed, which made for a nifty combination.

After a moment of consideration, he sighed, but then nodded. "I'll do it. Just a test. You've given me courage."

That out of the way, his eyes skimmed over her, and she felt the tingles again. That wasn't courage. No siree, that was lust. She gave him courage. He gave her lust. There was something wrong with that equation. "You should do it, too," he added.

"Oh, no. It's not for me."

Ashley didn't want to date. She didn't need the hassles, the aggravation, or the neurosis. Nope. Everything she longed for was right there. Long, lean, stranger man, naked in her bed. She hadn't known she could do this. "I don't want a date. I want an affair. An exotic, femme-fatalish affair. Doesn't that sound perfect?"

"You should live in New York," he said, possibly reading her mind. "If you lived in New York, I'd give you an affair."

"No, thank you, Yankee man. I'm staying right here in the Windy City. Well, actually, I'm leaving in the morning for L.A., but I'm coming home here. To Chicago."

There was a momentary silence as she contemplated that statement. They were complete strangers, didn't even share the same state. One more plane ride to L.A., and then she'd never see him again. It made the night seem…alluring, adventurous. The lady and the tiger, and tonight she wasn't the lady.

*Become the tiger, Ash.*

David propped up on one elbow. "You want to get dinner in L.A.?"

"Aren't you tempting fate?" she asked, tempted to tempt fate herself.

"By eating?"

"By having a date. What if that destroys the bam, the zing? What if the only way we can have this is by meeting in hotel rooms and losing our exterior selves in a moment of wild abandonment?"

David looked at her, slightly awed. "You came up with all this from one shot of tequila and sex?"

"No. I've been thinking."

"You could think?" he asked, his eyes narrowed. "I couldn't think. Why could you think?"

"Not then. Now."

He rapped a hand against his heart. "Good." Then he looked at her in that way she was learning to recognize. "Do you honestly believe all that?" he asked seriously. There were two David McLeans. One, resident goofball, but the other was hardcore analyst. He was probably excellent at his job.

"I think it deserves some consideration," she replied, but honestly, she did believe it. It explained everything.

And he didn't look at her like a crazy person, which made her like him more. "Okay, meet me in L.A. In a hotel room. Chateau Marmont. We can be Mr. and Mrs. Jones. We'll test your theory."

"We'd just…exchange a room number and then I knock three times on the door, and…?"

"Yeah, or we could just meet up in the lobby," he explained in a practical voice.

Ashley sighed. "It's easy to tell you're Mr. Bottom Line. No sense of adventure at all."

"This from a woman in bunny slippers?"

She held up a naked foot. "Not a pink floppy ear in sight."

His eyes crinkled. "Bare flesh. Seductress."

"You think?" She held up her foot again, watching one of his long, lean thighs dig itself into the covers until it was buried completely. She was going to miss that naked thigh, that firm flank, *that stellar ass.*

"You have very sexy feet. I was watching them on the plane."

*Feet? No. It would have been better if he were a serial killer.*

"You think my feet are sexy? You're not gonna get weird and suck toes, are you?"

He must have some flaw. This one would explain it.

Thankfully, he looked horrified. "No. But I could, you

know, start at the arch, work my way up, see where I land…"
And she could see the gears turning in his head…all because
of a foot. Her foot.

Ashley stared at the appendage of interest, considering the
possibilities. "That sounds…decadent."

"Bam?" he asked, raising a brow.

"Definitely."

"Good. I didn't push any buttons before, and I'm sorry about
that, but you felt so good. I got carried away, and I feel like I
have shirked my manly duties."

She wiggled her toes. "Go forth, and unshirk, my devoted
slave of pleasure."

He pushed down her body, and his mouth pressed against
her arch, and the first time it tickled, causing her to giggle. But
then he moved up her calf, and it still tickled, but a different
tickle. A warm tickle, a tickle between her thighs.

"Oh," murmured Ashley, then she shot upright, horrified by
a new thought. "You have more condoms?"

"A whole box. Now let me get back to my unshirking."

Ashley fell back against the pillows, and his mouth touched
the inside of her thigh, and there were no more giggles. Only
the sighs and ragged breathing of a woman having her buttons
pushed. Every single one of them. Sometimes twice.

"I'm very glad you went for the box, rather than the travel
size," she told him.

"Bam?" he whispered, his mouth unshirking behind her knee,
and moving north at a steady, yet wholly orgasm-inducing speed.

*Ash, you're way too easy.*

*Shut up, Val.*

# 4

THEY HAD GONE through four more condoms, and the 5:00 a.m. wake-up call hadn't even been necessary.

Ashley was dog tired. She hadn't been this tired in years. Thirty-two-year-old women did not stay up all night having sex with strange men in airport hotel rooms.

Or at least not every day of the year.

"We can't do this again," she told him, her face buried in the pillow.

He chuckled, an exhausted chuckle, but a chuckle nonetheless. "Eighteen was a long time ago. You can sleep on the plane. I can sleep on the plane. I need to sleep on the plane."

She lifted her head from the pillow. "We shouldn't do this again."

Comprehension dawned. "Oh." He waited for more of an explanation. Ashley gathered her meager, yet dog-tired courage.

"Tonight was fun. Like being somebody whose life I've secretly always envied. But if we go out to dinner, or meet in a hotel, I'm afraid I'll lose this fantasy, get embroiled in the completely weary minutia of my life, and I'd rather end on the high note."

"That's a very defeatist attitude."

"No, sometimes things are just too good to take a chance and possibly ruin," she told him bluntly.

"Do you ever get to New York?" he asked, a totally unfair question, because fashion, New York? *Hello?* Did he honestly think she was *that* bad at what she did?

"Sometimes. A bit. You ever come to Chicago?"

"Not if I can help it," he answered, a defeatist attitude if she ever heard one.

"This was fun," she repeated, rising from the ashes of the bed. Outside, the windows started to rattle again. The airport was waking up. She walked to the shower, femme fatale of the friendly skies, and she felt muscles that she didn't know she had.

He watched her closely, and she gave her hips an extra wiggle.

"I could help you," he offered gallantly.

"In the shower?"

He lay there naked, on his back, head pillowed on his hands. Long, lean, and ready to go. Dog tired? Who said she was dog tired?

*You did.*

"Come on, Yankee-man," she ordered in a husky voice she didn't even know she possessed.

And she didn't have to ask twice.

LATER ON, they didn't talk to each other on the plane. The 6:00 a.m. flight to L.A. was crowded, but thankfully, Junior and the doting parents from hell were absent. Ashley was stuffed next to a plumbing salesman from Portland who wanted to chat. She pulled out her magazines and pretended to be interested in the latest fall forecast, but instead, her sandpaper eyes kept tracking to the front of the plane. Seat 16A to be exact, where she could see the back of his head. A perfect bed-head, neatly combed into place.

It had taken her two hours to dare to stroke his hair, smooth it the way it longed to be smoothed, and she could still feel it, the fine strands tickling her fingers, still smell the shampoo and soap. Still smell the sex.

*Don't get there, Ash. Not with you-know-who sitting next to you.*

Ashley stopped gawking at Seat 16A and instead focused on the magazine spreads in front of her, but her eyelids drifted shut.

She woke up three hours later, having slept through the flight. In her lap was a small white piece of paper. A business card.

*David McLean.*

*Brooks Capital.*

*Analyst.*

On the back, in firm, decisive, indelible black ink was scrawled a cell number and one word.

*Anytime.*

It was enough to make her not-quite-jaded-enough divorcée's heart sigh.

Carefully she put the card in her wallet, hidden right behind her driver's license. It was her memento, a souvenir she would never forget. Some moments were best not to be repeated… except while dreaming.

CHICAGO WAS WARM, windy, and loud. Ashley took a cab back to the Larsen house in Naperville, which was equally warm, not so windy and not nearly so loud. Their street was lined with towering elm trees, hand-painted mailboxes and well-used bicycles. It wasn't New York, certainly not Los Angeles, but it was home.

Already Ashley began to feel revived.

After the divorce, she'd moved in with Val, their mother, Joyce, and Val's daughter, Brianna. Three generations of Larsen women sharing one roof. A scary thought, all those hormonal fluctuations duking it out with the inherent uncertainty of the family genes. Frank Larsen, the ne'er-do-well who had sired Ashley and Valerie, was now on his fourth marriage, electing to spend his golden years with his twentysomething secretary in Malibu.

Ashley threw her carry-on in the general direction of the couch, and walked into the kitchen. Val was talking on the phone, stirring dinner over the stove and watching the news. Multitasking, thy name is Valerie.

Val punched a button on the phone, and waved a wet spoon as a way of greeting. "How was the trip?"

"Productive. Very productive," Ashley answered, focusing

on the business aspects of the trip rather than the pleasure aspects, because Val might be her sister, but there were secrets that would never be divulged. Doing David McLean in the O'Hare airport hotel was one.

"Can you watch the monster while I go to a meeting?"

"Mom not home from work yet?"

"No. Inventory."

"I can watch her. You don't need to ask." Val was thirty, a single mom with a fondness for things that weren't good for her and a hard line in her eyes that Ashley didn't think would ever disappear. Ashley liked to blame it on Marcus, the drummer who'd dropped into Val's life, left her pregnant and alone, and then moved on to a bigger gig in St. Paul, never to be heard from again.

Sensing her guilt, Val gave her a long, searching look. "Why are you so jumpy?"

"I'm always jumpy. Flying. Slays me every time." To further illustrate her point, she held up a suitably unsteady hand.

"Ash, you are one weird sis, but you're the only one I've got."

A small tornado ran into the room before skidding to a halt. "Ashley, Washly, Bo Bashley, Me Mi Mo Mashly. Ashley." At eight, Brianna Larsen possessed the trademark Larsen nose, which all plastic surgeons yearned to compress, and more energy than Val and Ash combined.

Brianna shook back her hair in a completely eight-year-old diva manner. "I learned a new word from *South Park*. Douche bag. As in, Kenny is a world-class douche bag."

Ashley looked at Val, fascinated yet delighted by the sparkle of humanity in her sister's too-hard, too-black eyes. "And did your mommy tell you what douche bag meant?"

Brianna nodded. "It's a soap bottle filled with water and it gets you springtime fresh."

Ashley knocked fists with her sis. "Creative and honest. Excellent, my friend. Her vocabulary is improving by leaps and bounds. Her teacher will love you."

At that simple yet comforting discourse, Val's eyes narrowed, and Ashley realized her mistake. Ashley was acting too relaxed, too confident, too pleased for a woman with a deathly fear of flying and a business that wasn't getting off the ground. Immediately she wiped the satisfied smile off her face.

"You sure you're okay?" Val asked, because she was the blustering bull. Ashley was the worrier. After living together for four years, everyone had their assigned roles. Ashley knew hers, Val knew hers, their mother knew hers, and even Brianna was very aware.

"I'm fine," replied Ashley, giving her voice an extra quiver. "Go on. I'll take over the supper. What's on the menu tonight?"

All doubts appeased, the world back in order, Val continued to stir, her eyes focused on the stove, rather than her sister. "My specialty."

"Mac and cheese it is."

Val glared. "With spinach, darling child, because we all love green food."

Brianna, being one-hundred-percent Larsen and knowing a con job when she heard it, promptly rolled her eyes. "Douche bag."

Val ruffled her daughter's hair. "Brat. Listen to Aunt Ash. I'll be back in a couple of hours, and Ash, do not forget the green food."

Brianna fought with every inch of her small being, but in the end, responsible parenting prevailed, and Ashley shamed her niece into eating an extra helping of green food. Val came home from her meeting, Mom came home from work and four Larsen women sat on the couch watching *Pride and Prejudice*—the Colin Firth version.

Truly, there was no place like home.

Every time there was a crisis, home was always there. Every time she felt alone, home was always there. No, they weren't the typical American family, but in a lot of ways, the typical American family had nothing on the Larsen women of Chicago.

Ashley had never imagined herself divorced. She thought her marriage to Jacob would be forever. He was comfortable. They were comfortable. Why would anyone want to leave that? But Jacob had, and Ashley had no place to go but home. Home was good.

By the time the grandfather clock struck eleven, Mom was sacked out in the recliner and Brianna was curled up with her head in Ashley's lap, fast asleep.

Val picked up her daughter in her arms, sagging a little from the weight. "I think you're overdoing the mac and cheese."

"She's only eight once. It's too early for her to start dieting," Ashley replied, as would any overindulgent aunt who thought her niece was perfect.

"You're not her mother, only the auntie." Val looked down at her daughter and shook her head. "How did I get this kid?"

"The old-fashioned way."

Val's laugh was harsh and self-directed. "What if you screw her up with all your spoilage and worrying?"

"I won't," assured Ashley automatically, not insulted at all. It was a conversation they'd had many times, and usually late at night, when doubts were prone to wander in on creeping shadows. They weren't talking about Ashley. Deep down, Val had the same paranoid Larsen heart they all did, certain that when anything good happened in her life, it was going to disappear, just like the mac and cheese. Golden and gooey and warm, and then poof, you look down and the pot is empty, and your stomach curdles with an angry hunger.

"Swear you won't screw her up?" Val asked.

"Swear."

Val looked at Ashley, still doubting, but hopefully not quite so much. "Okay, but I only believe you because secretly we know you're the smart one. And because you're here."

"You're smarter than you think, Val," said Ash softly.

Accustomed to performing feats of unimaginable flexibility, Val used one knee to power off the television remote. "A 'searching and fearless moral inventory' Ash. That means you don't lie to yourself. You don't tell yourself you're smart when you're on your third job in five months. You don't tell yourself you're smart when your bank account is DOA."

As it always did when the doubts grew larger, Val's voice also got louder, a little bit brassier. Brianna stirred in her mother's arms. "Hey, loud people, I'm trying to sleep here."

Val swore, completely unacceptable to eight-year-old ears. Nobody minded. "Wake Mom, will you?" she asked Ashley.

Ashley fought back a yawn, uncurled from the couch and rubbed her mother on her shoulder. "Mom. You need to get to bed. You have to work in the morning."

Joyce Larsen blinked her eyes and came awake abruptly. "Did I miss the news?"

"Yes, Mom, you slept through the news."

"Darn. I wanted to hear the weather. I bet it rains tomorrow. You should have woke me up."

"I'm waking you up now. Go to bed, Mom."

"I'm glad you're back, Ashley. I always worry about you flying. You're going to crash someday and die."

"I know, Mom. Get some sleep."

And people wondered where she got it from.

Thirty minutes later, Val dragged herself into the kitchen, obviously knowing where Ashley would be. When faced with the complications of life, some people turned to the church, others turned to sports. Ashley turned to the kitchen. To be more precise—cheese. "What should I do?" she asked, slicing up a wedge of swiss into small bite-sized nibbles.

"About what?" Val asked. "Your pathetic excuse for a love life?"

At that, Ashley almost told her. The words nearly slipped from her lips, but even with Val, she couldn't share. How could she talk about something she didn't even understand, and still didn't quite believe? "I'm talking about the stores."

"You're going to figure out what's wrong and fix it."

Fix it. *Yeah, just fix it, Ash.*

It sounded so easy, so completely staring-her-in-the-face easy. So why couldn't she figure it out? Forcefully Ashley hacked off another square before handing the cheese to her sister. "Why don't the women of Chicago realize that not only am I providing non-cookie-cutter clothes at a decent price, but by shopping at Ashley's Closet, they are contributing to the livelihood of struggling fashion designers everywhere?"

Val shrugged. "You could have a sale. A big sample sale thing."

"Sales, schmales," mocked Ashley, sawing furiously again. "Tell me how you really feel."

"I need something pizzazzy, jazzy."

"You'll find it. You've got jazz."

*I need jazz.*

Ashley watched as Val popped a cube of swiss into her mouth, glad to see her sister's confidence level back to normal.

Val was a fast-spinning top that could fall off with only a word, a look, or a doubt. Unlike most people, when Val tipped over, it wasn't minutes or hours before she got up, it was weeks and months. It was Ashley's job to make sure she didn't tip.

"What's your schedule tomorrow?" Ashley asked.

"Seven to three. Why?"

"I've got a lot of catch-up to do at the stores. The Lakeview manager isn't returning messages, so God only knows what disaster will befall when I walk in the door. You won't see much of me. You and Mom have Brianna covered?"

"Yeah. We're good."

"Night, sis," said Ashley.

"Night." Quietly she took the last bit of cheese, then flicked off the light. Ashley could hear the soft sounds of Val padding down the carpeted hall behind her, and she ended the night the same way she always did.

"Val, I'm proud of you."

"As you should be."

Ashley smiled.

ONCE IN BED, Ashley pulled out The Card. She should have slipped him hers as well. But no, she didn't, she'd been cowardly, and because of that, if she wanted to ever see him again, it was all up to her

*Ash, you go to Manhattan lots of times. Go see that new designer on the Lower East Side. You've been dying to see his work. This is your chance.*

And what was the polite time frame to call up a man, whom you expressly told that it would be a mistake to see again?

There was no statute of limitations on a booty call.

*He truly did have a fine booty.*

Her hands curled and uncurled like a happy kitten because she could remember the feel of that firm piece of flesh under her fingertips, remembered the pleasuring fill of his thick sex. Now that was jazz. And no, she wasn't completely cheap and shallow. She liked him. He made her comfortable with herself. With everything, really.

That was the pull of one David McLean. He wasn't exotic, or vain, or some slutty billionaire.

He was, quite simply, the man she wanted.

Ashley stared at the card, recalling how his voice whispered against her ear, and she knew. That was it. Decision made. She'd set up an appointment in New York. Then she would call him, and if things were meant to proceed, he'd be ready, willing and available.

A long-distance affair.

Decadent.

Her mouth curved up at the corner, and all that night she dreamed of David.

THE LAKEVIEW STORE was a wreck. Her manager had quit, one salesgirl was late and the strapless smocked sundresses were priced twenty percent lower than what she paid for them. It was enough to make a weaker woman cry. But not

Ashley, not this time. She was still flying high on the after-shocks of great sex.

For the next week, Ashley worked eighteen-hour days to get the store back in order. Her first instinct was to promote the lead sales associate to manager, but honestly, that wasn't smart and she knew it, so she caved and put a Help Wanted sign in the window. Forty-eight hours later, she'd hired a new manager, a gum-popping twentysomething named Sophie, who didn't meet her eyes all the time, but her resumé was good, and she wore a great vintage Halston to the interview. That alone was enough to get her the job.

By the middle of the week, the Lakeview store was in better shape, and the Naperville, State Street and Wicker Park stores were holding their own. She was ready to make the call. It was late on a Wednesday that she decided to do it because she worried about whether he'd be alone on a Friday, or whether a Monday morning call seemed too needy. And what if he slept in late on Sundays?

Thankfully, he picked up on the first ring.

"Hello."

"David? It's Ashley," she told him, praying that he wouldn't ask, "Ashley-who?"

"Hi," he said, completely the perfect response.

"I'm going to be in New York."

"When?"

"Two weeks. If you're not busy…"

*Don't be busy. If you're busy, I'm never going to call a man again in my life. Ever.*

*Don't be dramatic, Ash.*

*Shut up, Val.*

"Not busy. We'll get dinner. Or a show. Or does that sound too normal? We don't have to do normal. You can stay here if you want. I've got space."

"No. I'm booking a room," she answered firmly, not the frugal answer, which was part of her problem, but hotels were dim, mysterious, sinful. Apartments were warm, homey and mundane. And if she found herself settling into his warm, homey and mundane, what would happen to all that smoking-hot passion? Would it disappear, as if it had never existed?

Not going to happen. She liked this smoking-hot passion. She was going to keep it.

"Is your hotel near the airport?"

Ashley tried not to laugh, but failed. "No."

"Good. How's work?"

"Not so good. But I'm optimistic."

"Much better than defeatist."

"Probably."

She thought about all the other things she could say, but they sounded neither exciting, nor affairish, so she elected to hold her tongue. "I should go now," she told him.

"Call me when you get in. Have a good flight, don't forget to pack your bunny slippers, and Ashley—"

"Yeah?"

"Thanks for calling."

"Anytime," she answered, before quickly hanging up.

# 5

THE FRIENDLY SKIES were extinct, along with dinosaurs, cheap interest rates and the commitment to customer service. The next week David flew fifteen thousand pain-filled miles to Portland, Houston, Seattle and two trips to DC. In the process, he discovered that the plastics company in Portland was running dangerously low on working capital, the oil services company in Houston was ripe for a friendly buyout and the people who worked in government had zero people skills. As he was waiting on the tarmac to head back to New York, Christine called.

"I'm sorry about your meeting. I debated a long time to call, kept hoping that you would call, but you didn't, so I decided I should. It would mean a lot to me, and Chris, too, if you could come and visit."

David eyed the air-sickness bag, felt the aftertaste of hard feelings rise in his throat and in the end politely opted to spare his fellow passengers excessive hurling noises. He was thirty-four, not four. "I'll try," he lied.

"Maybe you can reschedule the meeting. He misses you. He's your only brother."

*Sucks, dude. I feel your pain.*

"They're telling us to shut off all electronic devices, Christine. I need to hang up."

"David, you don't have to be like this."

Because he was exactly like that, David hung up.

IT WAS A WEDNESDAY afternoon at the start of earnings season, and the offices of Brooks Capital were humming with closing-bell guesses and bets and gossip and shadow numbers that were most likely pulled from someone's ass. David's office was on the forty-seventh floor, one below the executive floor, but he wasn't worried. His boss liked him. He liked his boss. Things were proceeding nicely. And nowhere else but Brooks Capital could he learn from the best of the best, Andrew and Jamie Brooks.

There were three monitors on his desk, one green screen to monitor the markets, one open to e-mail and the last was his latest work in progress, Portland Plastics. Market recommendation: Hold.

The door opened, and his boss, Jamie Brooks, walked in, perching herself on the desk, high heels swinging to an unknown beat.

"You have the latest on Houston Field Works?" she asked coolly.

Without missing a step, David handed over the folder. It was a test. She liked to test him, see if he was ever at a loss. He hadn't failed yet. "Anything else?" he asked confidently.

Jamie opened it, skimming over the introductory fluff, jumping right to the bottom line. "You're going to Omaha on Friday?" she asked, not looking up from the words, her expression an unreadable blank. David still wasn't worried.

"I'll be there." Nebraska was the home to an alternative energy company that was close to going public. On paper, they looked good. But David's job was to visit, kick the tires, peek under the hood and in general, see if the hype was worth it.

"Good," she said, and then closed the folder with a snap. "You're in for the pool on the Mercantile Financials report?"

David pulled a crisp c-note from his pocket. "Down ten-point-one percent."

She stared at him with appraising eyes. "Gutsy."

He shrugged modestly.

"Andrew says up three-point-four," she remarked. Andrew was Jamie's husband. The Man. Capital *T,* capital *M.*

In the last seven years, David had followed Andrew's every

move. When Andrew opened his own fund, David jumped at the chance to follow. When the market had put most hedge fund managers out on the street dancing for nickels, Brooks Capital had not only survived, but they were also still turning the same solid returns year after year. Andrew was as thorough and methodical as David, and he was usually right. Andrew Brooks made his reputation on being right. This time, however, Andrew Brooks was wrong.

"He's too high," David told her, perhaps more confidently than he should, but he'd done his homework, and he had a feeling. You always did your research, always gleaned over every piece of data available, but when push came to shove, bet on your instincts.

Not taking her eyes off David, Jamie slid the bill back and forth through her fingertips, thinking, considering, wondering if David could beat the master. Eventually she broke down and laughed. "Breaking from the crowd. I like it."

During his first days on the job at Brooks Capital, Jamie had intimidated David, but then one afternoon he had brought her a report on a waste management company in Dallas, and she'd pointed out the one tiny, yet deal-breaking detail that he'd missed. At first, he'd been all pissed and thought there was no way that she could be right, until that night, when his cooler head prevailed, and he went over his numbers, and holy shit, she was correct. Since then, she'd earned his respect in spades.

"We'll see who knows better," she said, still doubting him, but he didn't mind. Jamie provided a novel perspective in the male-dominated world of finance. And currently, that was exactly what he needed. A novel female perspective.

"Can I ask you something?"

"Shoot."

"Do you know fashion, you know, the business side—what makes a company work, what makes it not work, what women like in clothes?"

The swinging high heel froze. "Broadening your horizons

into fashion?" she asked, coughing discreetly. "Brave and not afraid of the stereotypes. Definitely gutsy."

"What do you know?" he asked, battling forward, even though he was deathly afraid of stereotypes.

"Driven by trends at the high end. At the mid-level, it's more about the classics and originality, and at the low end of the spectrum, it's nothing but trendy knockoffs and bargain-basement prices. What are you interested in?"

David thought over Ashley's travel attire and took a guess. "Mid-level. So, classics and originality are the drivers?"

Jamie nodded. "It's the *America's Next Top Designer* mentality. Women don't like to wear something that someone else is wearing. We're very territorial about fashion."

*"America's Next Top Designer?"*

"Television show. Ratings up ten percent on an annual basis, three years running. They've launched four successful designers, one not-so-successful designer, but I think that's because of his crappy designs. The guy was a certified disaster area."

His face assumed the requisite manly look of horror. "A show about sewing?"

"You have to watch. It's a train wreck, but a fun one. Why the interest?" she asked.

"It's for a friend. She's got these clothing boutiques, and is having some issues. I thought I could give her some advice. Try and figure out what's going wrong." Next week Ashley would be in New York, and he wanted to understand the fashion industry, help her determine what problems could be fixed, and also have his wicked way with her eight ways to Sunday. It was a big assignment, but not impossible. It might mean watching reality TV. It might mean learning what was hot on the female clothing market. He would survive. Probably. Hopefully.

"This is all for a *she?*" asked Jamie, quirking one perfectly arched brow, just as David's e-mail window popped into sight, indicating an unread e-mail had arrived.

David, I would *love* to meet you. I'm nineteen, which is
younger than what you requested in your profile, but it's
a mature nineteen...

He inched his shoulders forward, blocking the view,
blocking the view...not quite blocking the view from his boss.

Jamie glanced at the now-fading window, then glanced
pointedly at David. He elected to stay silent. It seemed the
prudent thing to do.

"Dating again?"

He shrugged in a completely noncommittal, I-don't-want-
to-talk-about-my-private-life manner.

She didn't take the hint. "I think it's a good thing. You should
have done this a long time ago. I have some friends—"

"No," he answered quickly.

His boss shook her head, then smiled. "All right. Have it
your way. But if you change your mind, I swear, they're all
nice women."

David pulled another hundred out of his pocket, mainly to
divert her. "Give me another hundred on Mercantile Financial."

She took the bill, clearly not fooled by the diversionary
tactic, but gave him a pass, because Jamie was nice like that.
"More courage, sport. And Andrew's going to kick your ass,
but you're brave. I like it."

Once Jamie left, David wiped the wayward sweat from his
brow and opened the offending e-mail.

*Dating.* He could feel the perspiration pooling at his neck.
After the night with Ashley, he'd thought he was ready for this,
she'd told him he was ready for this, but...this was wrong. It
felt wrong. It felt...idiotic. David never liked feeling like an
idiot, but after he saw the picture, the idiot feelings got worse.

Oh, yes, there was a picture. It was a picture that men—
cheap, goaty bastards that they all were—would jump all over.
Totally not safe for work. She was pert, all right. Too pert. There

was no meat in those breasts. No experience, no… Stop, he thought, stop now. He minimized the window, opting for a safer, more calming spreadsheet.

Right then, his cell phone rang, saving his cheap and goaty ass. Was it boneheaded to stare at a topless picture of a willing nineteen-year-old from Brooklyn while wishing his caller ID said Chicago? Probably.

"Yeah," he answered.

"David?"

"That's me."

"It's Martina. From I-Heart-You.com. They said you okayed the call."

David closed his eyes. Courage. He only needed courage. He could do this. "Yeah, I remember you," he mumbled, trying to remember. "Female…twenty-seven."

"Twenty-four."

"And a…lawyer?" he guessed.

"Editor."

"Oh, sure. Only a second ago I got off the phone with a lawyer. My mind can be like a black hole sometimes. Too many late nights," he rambled on, wincing.

"I wanted to call and chat. See what you sound like."

*What he sounded like?* What was that about? He had a voice. An average voice. And now what was he supposed to say? "Yeah. This is what I sound like."

*And who was this Martina anyway?*

"You work on Wall Street?"

"Yeah," he repeated, exactly as an idiot would.

"I like that. It must be very exciting."

David glanced at the green screen, then at his report, and frowned. "Thrilling." After a long, panicked moment, he realized he was supposed to add to the conversation. "So, why a dating service? Do you meet any…good guys this way?"

"They're all better than my ex. The man was a pig. Cheated on me once, but I stayed strong. Kicked him right out of my life."

And what could he say to that? His panicked eyes shot to the Dow, searching for some constant, some bit of normalcy.

The market was down three hundred for the day. It seemed only fitting. "Sorry. Want to have lunch?"

"Love to. I'm in midtown. Tomorrow?"

"Can't." David checked his calendar, looked at the open day next week and frowned. He didn't want to do this, he really didn't want to do this. But it was time to man up, move forward and get back on track. "Next Wednesday? April twenty-second. Noon?"

"Love to," she told him.

Good God. He had a date.

IN ALL THERE WERE four mindless dates. One Kim, one Pam and two Ashleys, who sadly, were nothing like the original. Oh, the women were all nice enough, hot enough, but there was no zing, no bam. Just a feeling that he was reading a magazine, looking at pretty pictures, and there were no articles with the pictures. Ashley had been wrong, telling him to try a dating service. He'd known she'd been wrong, but he felt a strong urge to go through with her suggestion, if for the sole purpose of being able to tell her she was wrong when he saw her again.

The only slightly enjoyable date was with Martina, who was nice, blond, the type who wore a lot of black. Not in the goth sense, but in the twiglike New York female sense who only know one color. Black.

They met at an outdoor café on 52nd, crowded with spring-time traffic, and for forty-five minutes he listened to her talk about Barney, the ex, until David felt solely responsible for the sins of the entire male gender.

"You must hate listening to me like this," she told him over dessert.

"I don't mind. Honest," he said, because as long as she monopolized the chatter, he didn't have to say a word.

"Sometimes I think I still love him. He liked to flirt, and some-times he carried it too far. That makes me stupid, doesn't it?"

David's first instincts were to agree, that infidelity could never be forgotten, but that wasn't the way to carry on normal human relations. Besides, he knew what love could do to people. "Not stupid. Love isn't easy. You think it should be perfect. That if two people are together, they stay loyal, they stay together. If you can't do that, is it really love?"

"I think it could be."

"Your ex was weak."

"Not true. He was very strong, but sometimes Barney…" Martina's voice trailed off with a sigh and David understood that an argument over her ex's flaws was pointless. She had her heart set to stupid and he wasn't going to talk her out of it.

"He works on Wall Street, too. Chase, in investment banking. I shouldn't have called you. I should be out looking at cops, or firemen, or cabbies. Some other type. Instead all I want to do is call him back, say I want to try again."

"Don't do that."

She looked at him confused, not getting the big picture. "Why not?"

"'Cause he's a pig. You told me he was a pig. You don't want to be in love with a pig."

"You're right."

"I know I'm right." When people got soft, they got stupid. Here was Martina, proving his theory and he'd only known her for an hour.

She twirled her fork on her plate, making circles in the raspberry sauce. "Do you know any guys from Chase?"

"You're thinking of hooking up with one of his colleagues? That's pretty cold. Clever, but still cold."

"And betray him? God, no. I wanted to see how he was doing."

David felt like banging his head on the table. She was turning soft. Martina would call this prick, take him back and get screwed all over again. Sad story. Why did people do this to themselves?

But who was he to judge? "If I hear anything, I'll let you know," he promised. Inside he told himself that she should be

running from this clown, far and fast. She was a nice kid. Too
bad he couldn't help her.

Hmm, maybe he could.

FOR DAVID, Ashley couldn't get to New York fast enough.
Three days and counting, and already his nights were getting
better. Two nights before, he'd dreamed about her e-mailing
him a photo, not safe for work. And then last night, she'd been
there in his private Lear jet, dressed in a flight attendant's
uniform. She came toward him, then sat on his lap in the best
sort of way. In between triple-X fantasies, he'd been research-
ing the fashion biz, even reading the top magazines, not that it
helped. David still hadn't developed a clear understanding of
the business side of the industry, but he had developed a clear
understanding that he didn't know shit about fashion.

Women were odd.

His ex had understood fashion. Christine was always meticulously dressed, down to the perfectly matching shoes and
earrings, and David hadn't bothered with the details of what
women wore. There were two states. Clothed and unclothed,
and honestly, as a man, he preferred the latter.

But this time, he perused the pages of *Vogue* as a man on a
mission. He could help Ashley. He didn't know how, but he
knew he could, and he knew he would. He was an analyst. It
was in his blood.

Eventually, Tuesday arrived. David told himself it was no
big deal. Of course, he did so *after* he dug out a tie that he hadn't
worn in seven years—not since his first lunch at Brooks Capital.
In the back of his mind, after two weeks of dealing with samples
of New York's single women—strange e-mails, stranger propo-
sitions, and more personal questions than he'd ever known
existed—he'd been worried about seeing Ashley in person
again. Wondering if the reality lived up to the Ashley-memory
hype in his brain. After Brittany, Pam, Ashley and Ashley, he
was now a lot more doubtful about his own judgment.

He was supposed to meet Ashley after she finished her meeting at a small studio in Brooklyn, because to pick her up at the airport would seem *ordinary*—her word, not his. However, a cab ride across the Brooklyn Bridge was no big deal, and with the late afternoon sun at his back, he now found himself on an artsy street that looked like Soho-cum-late '80s. Up and coming, trendy, yet not quite brain-exploding expensive.

The front of the building was a large plate-glass window with sleek black mannequins in the window. Some were dressed, some undressed, and he suspected that was intentional, although it did defeat the primary purpose of a large display window, which was to advertise one's wares. David wasn't interested in mannequins though, dressed or otherwise, instead his hungry gaze sought out Ashley, nearly buried beneath a rack of dresses.

She didn't see him; she was too engrossed in the clothes to notice. For a second, one greedy second, he stopped to stare, comparing reality to the hype. Three weeks vanished into nothing. His mouth grew dry.

He shook his head, his brain, lungs and libido all running amok.

Why her? What was it about her that drew his eye? Her hair? It wasn't long; it wasn't short. It hung right at her shoulders, curving under on the ends. She wore what seemed to be the requisite Ashley Larsen skirt and tank. Her curves weren't model-thin, nor Playboy-lush, just neat and cushiony, and exactly right for his hands…for his cock.

David told himself not to go there because he was *not* a randy dog. They had several hours of polite conversation before he could go there. No point in killing his self-control before he even started.

Then she pushed back the dark of her hair, starting a conversation with the designer, and he could feel that hair, remembered that hair brushing against his chest, and oh, yeah…

Hell.

There he was, killing his self-control, and there wasn't a damned thing he could do about it.

She turned, met his eyes. He couldn't look away. He wanted to take her right there. His cock pressed forward, exactly as if that was the plan. It wasn't memory or hype.

Sex. The great decider.

He focused on the concrete sidewalk, shaking off the lust that he knew was in his eyes, and when he walked through the door, he was completely in control once again.

# 6

CONTROL LASTED about seven minutes because it took David seven minutes to decide he hated Enrique's guts. The man-boy was stab-you-in-the-back ambitious, with a Latin glo-tan, and the biggest sin of all, he kept dismissing Ashley with his eyes, as if she were intruding on his personal space at this tiny, most probably rat-infested workshop.

"I like what you're doing with prints," she gushed, while David stood there, silently seething.

The little twit swept toward the green flower print in the window, his arms wide, as if he were about to burst into song. "People shy away from big, but if it wraps the body, captures the spirit in a sensual embrace of fabric, it's fantabulous. There is no other word."

"I'd like to sell some of your designs in Chicago," Ashley told him, nodding politely.

"My work belongs here in New York. Next to the latest Polly Sue's Fashions, my clothes cannot breathe." He took a deep breath, drawing circles of air with his hand. "They need to breathe."

"Ashley…" David started, but then she flashed him a nervous smile. No, he was not here to interfere, he was not here to smash a fist in Enrique's smarmy little face.

"Give me a second here," she told him, completely not understanding the dynamics of the room. People got one shot, and if they weren't in one hundred percent, you walked away, no mess, no fuss.

Ashley turned back to Enrique. "It's a very good opportunity. I don't carry a lot of stock. I'm more interested in quality than quantity. Ashley's Closet—the unique, exclusive, shopping experience."

Enrique smiled tightly. "No, Enrique does not think so."

David didn't think so, either. He stepped beside Ashley because now it was time to interfere. "If Enrique doesn't see the opportunity, he's not the visionary you want. You need designs that cry out above the masses." David looked around the store, hiding his anger, his eyes carefully bored. "This isn't it."

Enrique turned four shades of red, and Ashley punched him in the arm.

"My designs are miles above the masses," the designer snapped. "Who are you?"

Now, there were certain times when Wall Street had a cachet, when David knew he'd picked a job in high finance for a reason. This was one of those times. He pulled out his card and handed it to Enrique. "We're backing Miss Larsen on this. A retail play on *America's Next Top Designer.* Finding only the best designs, letting judges and her clientele see who is most deserving of Chicago's Next Big Look."

Ashley's mouth gaped, only slightly. David kept his features carefully schooled in arrogant boredom.

"You're going to create a reality show?" asked Enrique, his eyes now resting on Ashley with the appropriate amount of respect. *Yeah, buddy, don't mess with my girl.*

*No.* Ashley mouthed the word to David. He ignored her, and waved what he hoped was an artistic hand. Now that the words were out of his mouth, honestly, it was a brilliant idea.

"Oh, no," he said. "Not at all. We're going to create exclusivity. As you said, above the masses, not mingling with the masses. There will be exposure, of course. The press, possibly some morning-show type coverage, but we want the experience to focus on the designs themselves, rather than a three-ring circus surrounding the designers."

Ashley only stared.

"Why not New York?" Enrique asked, dollar signs now reflected in his eyes.

"Why not New York?" repeated Ashley, and there were no dollar signs in her eyes, but now she was curious, and he could see her working through the details.

David nearly smiled.

"New York has been done. L.A. has been done. This is a very boutique experience, not something for the tabloids. We felt Ashley's Closet had the right mix of both fresh and élan. Image is all."

"Can I think about it?" asked Enrique, and Ashley nodded her head.

David clenched his hands, not happy to be working with Enrique. The dimwit would have to learn to treat Ashley with respect, but that would come eventually. "You have twelve hours to decide. We have other designers to look at. There is no time to waste."

Enrique looked at the clock on the wall. "I'll do it," he said.

David nodded once. He'd never had a doubt. "We'll messenger the contracts."

Ashley turned to David, her smile nervous. "Contracts? What contracts?"

DAVID SLUNG HER carry-on over his shoulder and Ashley scurried out the door after him onto the busy Brooklyn sidewalk.

"You are in so much trouble," she started, as soon as Enrique was out of visual range. "I can't believe you just made all that up."

He stopped, and looked at her with complete seriousness, no twinkle of mischief at all. "No. I think you can do it. Do you?"

He'd been serious? *Seriously serious?*

"Of course I think I can do it," she lied. Her mind flipped through all the pros, and the cons, and then more cons, and then the biggest con of all, that she could actually get anyone in the fashion universe to care.

"You shouldn't doubt yourself, Ashley," he told her, because she'd never been a good liar. A double-barreled baby carriage zoomed past, and Ashley moved aside, only after the mother glared meaningfully.

Hesitantly she took a step closer to the safety of the brick wall behind her. "David, I was looking to get some interesting designs in the stores, to sell more stock, not make the evening news."

The light turned, cars began to move and David moved dangerously close to the curb, signaling for a cab, handling her luggage and still managing to carry on a conversation at the same time.

"You won't make the evening news. It's the morning show circuit you're after. *Good Morning, Chicago.* Maybe Oprah. Nothing too much because you want people to come into the stores to see the designs. Just a taste. That's all you need."

Oprah—oh, God, he was tossing out Oprah like they were discussing last season's overstocks. Ashley watched as the line of cabs moved past, and there was no one stopping. "Are there no empty cabs in Brooklyn?"

"It's a bad time of day. Everybody is leaving Manhattan, not going in," he explained, his arm still patiently outstretched.

"How long are we going to have to wait?"

"Not that long."

Ashley took a hard look at the line of unlighted cabs, took a harder look at the weight of her carry-on and then took a hard, hard, hard look at the bridge. The choices were narrowing exponentially. Again, she glanced toward David, so capable, so confident, so sure.

He actually thought she could do this. He actually thought that she could bribe/blackmail/arm-twist almost-famous designers to bring their newest and best looks into her boutiques.

Maybe she could. Maybe it wasn't a big deal. So why did it feel like a big, big deal? She looked at the bridge, looked at her heels.

*No, Ash, don't be a fruitcake. You'll only embarrass yourself.*

*David doesn't think I'll be embarrassed.*

*He doesn't know you're thinking of hoofing it across a huge-ass bridge in heels. Do you know what those little rebars do to heels?*

*I can do this.*

*Go ahead, don't listen to me. But if you get stuck...I'll be laughing.*

Ashley lifted her chin, grabbed her carry-on from David. "Let's walk."

"There will be cabs, Ashley. We can wait."

He didn't think she could do it.

"No," she said, taking off for the span as if it were Everest.

She was about to walk to Manhattan. Frankly, it didn't seem that far. And they had a nice walkway specifically for pedestrians to walk safely across, high above the traffic. Of course, the walkway was very high. Very, very high. Very, very above-the-clouds high.

*Okay, Ash. One step at a time. Not hard at all.*

"Ashley!"

She turned and looked, hefted her bag an inch higher. "Are you going to come, or not?"

"This is not a good idea," he told her, but he was walking. Progress.

"And yours is?" she drawled with more than a little sarcasm. Yes, it was sarcasm because he was probably right, and she didn't want to admit it; however, he didn't think she could do this, she didn't think she could do this, but the only way to overcome a fear was to do it. So, while there might not be intelligence in this decision, there was value, and sometimes that made it smart.

David tugged the carry-on from her hand and continued onward. She didn't fight much. Any. "The show is a great idea."

Sadly, he was right, and she took two steps to catch up. "Are you actually considering backing this?"

David shook his head—that was a big no—and she was

both relieved and disappointed. Relieved because with money came lots of responsibility. Disappointed because, well, it would have been heady to know that David was behind her, and with money, she could do wondrous things.

"You don't need any capital, Ashley. That's the beauty of the idea. Maybe a few ads if you want. You should have some receptions for the showings, but mainly, it's the idea. Do you like the idea?"

"Maybe," she replied, trying to keep pace with him. He was fast, his legs a mile longer than hers, but she managed and now they were up on the span, climbing higher and higher in the center lane, the going-home pedestrian traffic flowing against them. Still David kept on walking, not looking in her direction. On the level below them, the cars zoomed back and forth, and below that—far, far below that—lurked the black waters of the East River. She didn't know how cold the East River was in May, probably not as cold as Lake Michigan, but it looked dangerous nonetheless. Ashley looked down, slowed down.

"If you don't like it, don't do it," he stated, his voice laced with frustration.

"It's brilliant," she admitted. "What if no one cares?"

"Of course they'll care," he answered, starting up again, over-taking her, passing her, until she was nearly running to keep up.

"Can you stop for a minute?" she yelled, causing a biker to nearly tip over. She didn't even care. Damn Yankees. Thought they owned everything.

"What?" He stopped and turned. His dark eyes focused on her, without a trace of comfortable green. His face looked pinched, flushed, and not from the heat. At ten thousand feet in the air, there was no heat, or at least, not that sort of heat.

He was aroused.

Oh. My. God.

Well, maybe mad and aroused, a strange combination that piqued both her curiosity and her nipples. Why was he mad?

She was the one who should be mad. What right did he have to steal her hard-earned anger?

"I'm talking here," she said, determined not to be intimidated—or seduced—out of her own self-righteous indignation. "Couldn't you have discussed this with me first, instead of throwing it out there?"

"It just came to me, Ashley. If I had thought of it earlier, I would have discussed it with you, but honestly, it's the perfect solution, and you got Enrique—the prick—but okay, you got him locked in, so what's the problem?"

It would have helped if they weren't standing on a bridge with a gazillion New Yorkers walking home from work. It would have helped if there wasn't a large body of water way too close beneath her. It would help if he didn't look so Davidly. He stood there, feet wide, her carry-on slung on his shoulder, letting the sea of people wash around him, ignoring the cabbies a thousand miles below them, cars honking, bikes whizzing past, the barges schlubbing through the water, all the noises, the bigness of the city, and simply stood there, staring at *her.*

*And your boutiques, Ash. Let's not lose sight of the boutiques.*

Some of the hardness, some of that arrogance, left his eyes, and immediately she felt her body release the tension, and her breathing return to normal.

"If you don't want to do it, you don't have to," he offered again, watching her carefully. "I'll go back, tell Enrique that the whole thing is a sham, give him an earnest and sincere apology. Then you can get back on your trail of finding more clothes for the store. Is that what you want?"

Oh, undermining her own undermining. Sneaky. Very, very sneaky.

She peered out across the bridge, through the webbing of steel cables toward the booming skyline of Manhattan. Why the hell not?

"I'm going to make this work," she announced, completely

without fear, or mostly without fear. There wasn't a lot of fear. Honestly. "Do you think I can pull this off?"

He nodded once.

"Really?" she probed, looking carefully to see if there was even a speck of doubt in his eyes.

He nodded again. No doubts.

"Thank you," she said, smiling. A man who evaluated million-dollar deals for a living believed she could pull off the most out-of-left-field idea she'd ever heard.

Whoa. Awesome stuff.

David started walking again. "And it's about time you thanked me. Now, tell me where we're going. I have no idea where we're going."

"Hotel Wilde. I thought it was unboring."

"You're not boring."

"I could be more exotic though, more flashy, more élan-ful." She checked her skirt, and immediately thought she should have accessorized better. Maybe a clunky bracelet…or gold. Gold was good.

He stopped, put down the carry-on and leaned against the metal railing. Then he took her hand, laid it hard against the thick ridge behind his fly.

*The man has no need for accessories.*

*Do not say another word, Val.*

*S'all right. I like him.*

"You don't need more élan. Trust me."

The oxygen was getting thin up here, causing a throbbing void between her thighs. It had been three weeks since she had felt—or filled—that void. In Chicago, Ashley had tried not to dwell on the void because it seemed pointless and unsatisfying. Although in that moment, with the feel of all that, Davidness still hot in her hand, Ashley realized the void was about to get filled.

*Hello, New York.*

With the breeze whipping through the steel girders and deadly water a meager thousand miles below, Ashley tugged at his tie, drew David close and touched his mouth with hers. It was intended to be a hello kiss, a thank-you kiss, but it wasn't any of those. Instead, it was two very overheated people exploding. In less than a heartbeat, she was locked to him, his hands knotted in her shirt, pulling and twisting. His hard mouth worked over hers, and she could feel the anger firing under the surface, his heart pounding against her breasts. Mad…and aroused.

*Bliss.*

She dug her hands in his hair, his hard ridge firmly pressing between her thighs, and her wanton thighs quivered again.

Below them came the sound of a siren winding down, and then a bullhorn. "I know it's a tourist thing, but you guys really need to get a room."

David lifted his head, his breathing labored, and Ashley felt the sea of traffic wash over her, and it didn't seem scary. It felt exciting. Her gaze met his eyes, and she could read his mind. They were going to have sex again…soon. And it was going to be even better. She was going to be naked. He was going to be naked.

Eighteen naked hours before her flight home.

Eighteen hours wasn't going to be enough.

The siren wound up again. "Hello! Earth to Romeo and Juliet. Get a room, will ya?"

Ashley smiled, as any good tourist would. "That's where we're headed."

THE HOTEL ROOM had red walls. Scarlet walls that were the color of hell. Behind the bed hung a modern painting of a woman's open mouth, or at least David hoped that was a mouth. Red, wet. He twisted his head.

No, that wasn't a mouth.

Whoa.

Ashley was in the bathroom freshening up. He shouldn't have walked her across the bridge, but he needed to work off some of his excess energy. He hadn't been ready to sit in a cab with her, not without mauling her. David wasn't a mauler. He was an analyst.

The extra poundage in his shorts seemed to dispute that fact.

"The bathroom is great. You should see this," Ashley yelled, and then she emerged from the bathroom, wearing a blue striped tank, blue skirt and sandals, and it was sexier than black lace. There were no buttons, no hooks, no zippers, nothing but easy-access cloth.

"Are you still mad?" she asked, and it took him a second to realize she meant emotionally, not mentally. Madness. In a lot of ways, that's what it felt like. He was fevered and incoherent. It couldn't be healthy.

"I was never mad," he answered, fighting for what was left of his self-control.

She walked toward him, and then he could smell her—smell the quiet intensity that always hung in the air around her. He closed his eyes, absorbing her smell. For the past hour, all he could think about was touching her, burying himself inside her.

Nearly three weeks since he'd seen her; three weeks was a long time. A man could want a lot in three weeks. A man could hunger a lot in three weeks. It was the most logical explanation.

Except he had no logic. It was as if she twisted the wires until logic was impossible.

The madness started all over again. His eyes opened, and she was still there. Waiting for him to do something.

"David," she whispered urgently. Her eyes flared, and he snapped.

They fell to the bed, and he offed her skirt in mid-fall. The panties were not removed, merely pushed aside. Condom was hastily installed, this time his fly was thankfully unstuck, and then David was buried deep inside Ashley. It took a second to restart his lungs, restart his heart, but his cock needed no re-starting. No, it had found heaven all on its own.

Once again, there was no finesse. Actually, after three weeks of waiting, it was more frenzied than before. He prayed she didn't mind. The blind hunger in her eyes said she didn't.

It was fast, it was furious. Way too fast and way too furious, and she came with a long, low moan that ripped through him. This was more death than sex. His orgasm nearly killed him. After he came, David collapsed against the pillows.

Once again, Ashley scooted over to the far side of the bed. Considering the size of this bed, that was halfway to Jersey. His arm raised toward her, his fingers stretched, but her back had that turtle-shell look going, and David admitted that he didn't know what to do.

They had a relationship defined by sex, hijacked by sex, and anything outside of sex—friendship, romance, business—now felt strained.

Was that really a bad thing?

He considered the smooth bare back in front of him, the golden rose hue of her skin, the sleek curve of her spine and decided that yes, yes, it was.

This was going to have to stop. He was going to have to make it stop.

He liked Ashley, he liked talking to her, he liked the almost-not-quite confidence in her. As a divorced man getting e-mails that flipped his stomach, he understood it.

The first time they'd had awesome sex, they had talked about it, laughed about it, because it was so extraordinary, a once-in-a-lifetime deal. But the second time? What do you say when you realize it's not once-in-a-lifetime, but every time?

No, he wasn't going to analyze this. Not now.

"Ashley," he said, and the turtle-shell relaxed…a little. She turned, and her hair brushed across her eyes. He wanted to see her eyes, but she kept them hidden.

"Are you okay?" he asked.

She nodded quickly.

"Are you mad?" he asked.

She shook her head.

"Are you ever going to talk to me again?"

She giggled. The face lifted, and he saw the spark back in her eyes. Something lifted in his chest.

"Are you hungry?" he asked, because he thought he should feed her. It seemed polite.

"No, thank you."

"How was the flight?" he asked, and she inched closer. That was good.

"Uneventful."

"Takeoff?"

"I took four Dramamine," she admitted.

"Landing?"

"I slept through it."

He gave her an attagirl smile. "Excellent."

"I think it was the medicine and the two glasses of wine that did it."

"I think it was you."

Divorce had done a number on him, but he could look at his career and feel good about his decisions. Ashley didn't have that luxury. Divorce and career were going after her, double-barreled. It didn't seem fair. He wanted to pull her to him, and hold her, but lying in a black-sheeted bed with a woman's sexual organs artistically laid out on the wall was not the place to hold someone in comfort.

His fingers opened and closed, and if a man wasn't an analyst, he wouldn't have noticed.

She sighed, and rolled onto her back, staring up at the red ceiling. David eyed the shadowy curves where the covers barely hid her nipples, and his cock pushed against the sheet. Oh, jeez, he was such a goat.

"I'm going to have to find more designers," she stated, her voice a little firmer now.

"You will."

"Can you help?"

It was a tempting idea, part of the reason—a lot of the

reason—he blurted everything out to Enrique like he did, and didn't give her a chance to say no. So, she was in Chicago, and he was in New York. It was the best of both worlds. All the excitement. None of the commitment. No worries.

"Is that what you want?" he asked.

Her worried gaze met his eyes. "It's what I want." After a minute she spoke again, not so worried this time. "Why the argument on the bridge?"

"Because the *USS Intrepid* was booked."

She didn't laugh.

He met her eyes again, and this time, he knew he was the worried one. "I thought you'd like it," he offered.

"No, you didn't," she told him, completely unfooled.

David sighed. "Okay, I didn't think you'd like it. You needed the distraction. You needed to walk across to know you could do anything you wanted."

"Like stranger sex?" she asked, an innocent question. The look on her face wasn't so innocent.

"Not exactly," he told her. Honestly, he didn't know why he kept pushing her like some cheese-dick asshole. It wasn't who he was. He was laid-back, carefree, except when consumed by raging lust. But when he'd watched her with that jerk of a designer, when he saw the beaten look in Ashley's eyes, it ate at his gut and pissed him off. Probably because it reminded him of a lot of things about his own life that pissed him off, too.

And wasn't that too much self-analysis for the day? His analytical eyes wandered back to the covers where he could ogle Ashley and analyze her naked flesh to his heart's content. No worries.

"I liked being on the bridge," she told him, and then she smiled.

"I did, too."

"Do you like the hotel?" she asked, and her voice was so full of enthusiasm, he wasn't heartless enough to tell the truth.

"Love it," he said, punching a pillow in a golly-gee sort of way. Frankly, it wasn't so bad. Actually, it was growing on him.

The red walls were growing on him. The sleek black sheets were growing on him. Nah, that was all bullshit. It was the idea of Ashley underneath him that was growing on him.

Perhaps sensing the direction of his thoughts, she sat upright, covers falling away, and she grinned. "It's sorta goth-vampire falls in love with George O'Keefe and they have a love child. It's very now."

He liked seeing her unassuming grin, seeing the way it belonged on her face. This was Ashley Larsen the way God had intended. "Yeah."

"And you should see the shower." She stood up, all bare and curves, and David felt his control slipping away. "It's delicious. You can fit like fourteen people in there."

All David needed was two.

# 7

AN HOUR HAD PASSED, her skin slightly pruned. Ashley stepped away from the three walls of jets and wrapped a toasty towel around her body.

David was otherwise occupied, studying the brass pipes and hardware that trailed down the tiled walls like a half-filled Scrabble board.

His hands were gentle, yet firm on the metal. "I like it. Brass Fittings. I'm going to have to remember that name. Easily customized, yet still well made."

Honestly, he was well made. Very subtle, very lean. Wide shoulders that would be best displayed in a straight-cut European style. Long legs that could wear white, a pant color that few men could carry off well, and then there was the derriere...

Ashley sighed.

He looked back at her. "I don't think they're public. Have you heard of them?"

She shook her head, totally bemused. "I don't think I ever have."

"I'm going to look it up."

He was so curious, so intent, so completely content with himself, whether he was sexy, jerky, analytical, or nice. She didn't understand him, didn't quite understand what they were doing, and she didn't think he did, either.

*You're having great sex. Go with it, Ash. It's nothing more than that.*

*And what happens when it goes bad, or even worse, fizzles?*
*What happens if it doesn't?*
*Can you just relax and enjoy the moment?*
*No. Moments don't last, that's why they call them moments.*
Right then, her cell rang, and Ashley ran to get it.

It was Val.

"Hey, what's up?" Ashley asked in a brisk, businessy, not-having-fun, not-getting-laid tone.

"I can't find the school form from Brianna's doctor. I looked everywhere, Ash. Where'd you hide it?"

A family crisis. They occurred often, usually on a daily basis. Ashley tucked the towel securely in place. "I didn't hide it anywhere, Val. Did you look in the desk?"

"I looked there. Mom took apart the kitchen. They need it tomorrow. You won't be back tomorrow. I need to find the form."

"Don't panic," Ashley told her in a calm, soothing voice.

"That's easy for you to say, she's not your kid."

"That's not fair."

"You're right. I'm panicked. I'm in bad-mother mode. I don't like bad-mother mode. It makes me surly. Tell me where the form is and I'll get off the phone and leave you to your clothes calls."

David padded into the room, completely naked, completely not shy, and her eyes were drawn…drawn…

Ashley swallowed, not used to overt male nudity. Jacob had been shy, never wandering around naked, never making her tongue grow too big for her mouth.

"Ash?"

She jumped and shifted her eyes away from the light. "Did you check the coffee table in the living room?"

"I did."

"Did you move Brianna's books out of the way? Things get hidden under there."

"I didn't move the books, but wait a minute, we're moving the books now, still moving, still moving, and yes, thank you, Jesus, that *is* a doctor's form. You are a lifesaver."

"I know," she said, feeling the bed shift under added weight. Ashley kept her eyes averted until she couldn't help herself and the eyes turned back to the light.

David was sacked out next to her on the bed, and was studying her with his analyst's look. Curious, assessing, trying to figure out the conversation from the one side that he was hearing.

"I should go, Val." And she should because she wasn't going to tell David about Val, and she wasn't going to tell Val about David.

"Why are you trying to brush me off here?" asked Val.

"Work to do," she lied, not liking the lie to Val, but it made things easier. There were dishonest lies, and then there were lies for the betterment of mankind. This was definitely the latter kind.

"Brianna wants to say hello. Say hello to Aunt Ash, will you?"

"Hi, Ashley, Bashley."

"Hi," whispered Ashley.

"We miss you, Ash. Valerie said that when you got back you'd take me shopping."

"I don't think she said that."

"She didn't, but she thought it."

"I don't think she thought it."

An impudent hand was tugging at her towel, threatening to remove it, and she clapped strong—pit-bull strong—fingers over the hand. She would not have this conversation with her niece without the sanctity of a towel. It seemed…well, way too debauched for her.

"I have to get back to work," Ashley said, since she sensed the towel would not be around for long.

"I love you, Aunt Ash. We all do. See you tomorrow. And don't be too scared on the flight."

"You're an angel," Ashley told her, then hung up the phone.

"Who was that?" asked David.

"My niece and sister. I told you."

"Oh, yeah, the bossy one."

"We should get dressed and go eat," she said, feeling intensely naked under his gaze even though she was still wearing a towel.

"Okay." So with an easy shrug, he got dressed just like that. As if everything was no big deal. For Ashley, everything was a big deal, worthy of consideration and internal debate because her first instincts usually weren't good.

She liked analyst-David. He was harmless, sometimes goofy and didn't make her think about things she didn't want to think about, and when he was like that, the David need wasn't so overwhelming. It felt warm and comfortable, like homemade chicken soup.

It was when he was hard and moody and decisive that she got nervous. Ashley was, or had been, a firm believer in considering all your options, make a plan—i.e., buy four boutiques—stick to the plan, and with enough hard work and perseverance, the plan paid off, or you hoped it would. But sometimes it didn't—i.e., expenses for said plan boutiques outweighed income—and you had to readjust. It was the readjustment that gave her grief because Ashley wasn't a good readjuster. She needed consistency. She needed routine. She needed time for the internal debate—in order to plan, of course.

Ashley took her clothes from the bed and got dressed, as if everything was no big deal. He watched her though, and the air started to heat up again. She kept her eyes on the mirror, but in some ways that was worse. She could see his eyes watching her, and feel the automatic pull in her body. She wondered if he could see what was happening to her—see the damp clench between her thighs, see the heavy swell in her breasts.

She thought he could because his eyes were hooded and shadowed, and there was a dark flush to his face.

Quickly she pulled on her skirt, tugged that tank over her head, and this time when she looked at him in the mirror, his eyes had returned to the same no-big-deal hazel, and the heat was nothing more than the lack of an open window.

Her smile was mostly relieved.

"Ready to go?" she asked.

"Anytime," he answered in a warm, comfortable voice, exactly like chicken soup.

That, she could handle.

DAVID TOOK HER to eat at a barbecue place on 125th street. It was a hole-in-the-wall with great ribs and fried green tomatoes. Over dinner they argued about baseball, politics and the irrational idiosyncrasies of the female fashion style. Actually, David threw Ashley that last one because he liked to hear her argue, liked to watch her cheeks smolder and her shoulders jerk when she got particularly fired up. It took a lot to fire up Ashley Larson, but when she was sparked, the whole world burned brighter. David liked the burn.

"Tell me about your family," he asked after their plates had been cleared from the table. He felt like he should know more about her. He knew the big stuff. Knew she was afraid of flying, knew she wanted to make her stores a success, but he didn't know all of the little stuff. Like her family, and why she didn't say much about her marriage. He wanted to understand how a female came by a fascination for horror films, and whether her ex-husband was somehow responsible. David made his name, and most of his decisions, by thorough research, and reviewing a problem from all angles, and although he'd reviewed Ashley from many physical angles, it was the stuff inside her head that made him curious.

"You don't want to know about my family," she commented, dodging his question, which of course, made him more curious.

"I do."

"I have a sister, a mother, and a niece."

"What was the call about?"

"Val lost a form. She needed help finding it."

At one time, David might have called Chris for exactly that, called him to talk about the hell that was now airline travel, might have even called him to bitch about the dating service.

It was one of the reasons that Chris' betrayal hurt. He wanted to cut his brother out of his heart, out of his life, but Chris was there, they shared DNA, they shared memories. For nearly ten hellish years, they'd shared a room. Amputating your brother wasn't as easy as someone might think.

"And they called you on a business trip to help find it?" he asked, watching her push back her hair, part avoidance, part nervousness, a lot sexy.

Quickly she shook her head, sending her hair back in her face. "My family's boring. Let's not talk about my family. Let's talk about exciting things. Like how you're going to revitalize Ashley's Closet." She propped her chin in her palm, waiting for David to spout forth some powerful bits of sage business acumen.

He shifted uncomfortably in the old wooden bench of a seat. "Not only me. We. You're a part of this team. You can do it. I have faith."

It wasn't that he was worried about his part. He'd given insightful advice to corporations valued in the billions, and he was always on target. Her four measly boutiques would be a walk in the park. However, if he went in, turned around her business and left, what would she do without him?

That question echoed over and over in his head like an annoying commercial.

Somewhere, buried beneath the sizeable ego—earned, not exaggerated—below the male pride, which wasn't his fault, beneath the canniness of his brain, David knew that Ashley Larson was a helluva lot braver than he was, and that she kept her wings clipped for some reason he didn't understand. He wasn't convinced it was the divorce, although that seemed the most likely culprit. It was important to him that she succeeded— even without him, especially without him, because David McLean was only a temporary fixture in Ashley Larson's life.

One of them would move on, settling into a permanent relationship first. Maybe David, maybe Ashley.

David frowned.

Ashley laughed at his face. "You don't need to look so worried. I'll help. These are my stores. My dream. What kind of slug would let somebody take over their dream? Stop looking so miserable, you're making me nervous. What are you thinking?"

David was still caught back at "temporary fixture." "Thinking about what?"

"How many designers do we need? It should be small enough to be manageable, but big enough to rate on the event-o-meter."

"Three," he answered without hesitation.

"Three is great. I thought about four, but that's a strange number, and there could be a tie. Seven's too many, and five feels too big. I couldn't handle five."

"You could handle five."

Ashley frowned, a long wrinkle of forehead and nose. "Do you think I should do five?"

"Yeah," he told her, just to see what she'd say.

She met his eyes, shook her head. "Nah. Too many."

"I think you're right."

"Me, too," she agreed. "We'll have Enrique, there's a girl in Miami who's great. Mariah D'Angelo. I saw her work online, and I'd love to see it in person."

"So you should go."

"I'll go." Then she paused to consider. "You'll meet me there, right? I mean, would you want to come—no, no." Finally she sighed, and there was that sad look of resigned self-awareness in her face, like when you overslept and you knew you shouldn't because there were eighty thousand things to get done. David never overslept, but sometimes he thought about it.

"I wasn't always like this," she told him.

"Like what?" he asked, knowing exactly what *this* was.

"I've never been the most decisive person. Actually, *thoughtful* is the word I like best. But after Jacob, I don't want to commit to anything. Do you have that problem?"

Of course not. David was decisive, able to leap tall judgments in a single bound, and once the decision was made he didn't look back and never had any regrets. "Not a problem for me."

"Then what happened to you? Because everybody knows, when you get divorced, you're marked for life. What's your mark?"

David bore the mark of Cain, or in this case, Chris. But that hadn't *marked* him. He wasn't indecisive or lacking in self-confidence as a result. No, compared to Ashley, David had come through his divorce fairly unscathed. "I don't think I have one."

She held up a hand to her ear. "Can you repeat that please? I missed it against all those throbbing molto-basso sounds of male denial."

"I'm not in denial."

"Lie, much?"

"Honestly, I'm fine."

She laid her chin on her palm. "Then why don't you talk about your marriage at all? Huh? Riddle me that one, Mr. I'm-So-Well-Adjusted."

That small puff of air was the sound of male ego being deflated by a woman who wears bunny slippers on a plane.

David gathered his courage, met her eyes and almost lied, but eventually the truth made its sorry way out of his mouth.

"My wife had an affair," he confessed.

Okay, it was a half-truth, and he hadn't even told her the worst part, but some things were not meant to be shared.

Instantly her face was awash with concern. "I'm sorry. You must have really loved her. You look like it still hurts."

He schooled his features, removing all looks of hurt. Hurt was not to be shown. Showing hurt belonged to the female of the species, not to men. "Wounded pride," he answered crisply, schooling his voice to remove all sounds of hurt as well.

Ashley still didn't look convinced. "I'm sorry, even if it is merely wounded pride."

"Thanks," he said, and quickly changed the subject from the details of his divorce. "I'll meet you in Miami."

She brushed one thoughtful finger over her lips. Lucky finger. "Why are you doing this? For the sex?"

David was frustrated. It wasn't the way she said it, she was thoughtful, strike that, pondering, and didn't seem insulted at all. No, it was what she said because it sounded so…wrong. David thought about defending himself, since it wasn't like that, he wasn't like that. Not completely.

"I signed up for an online dating service. It was miserable, thumb-screws, drawn-and-quartered sort of torture. I can't do that. This, I can do."

"This?"

"This." He pointed an accusing finger at her because he didn't like the snickering twinkle that was fast appearing in her eye. "And don't make it out to be sleazy. It's not. Not completely. If you lived in New York, it wouldn't even sound remotely sleazy. It'd be completely normal. But noooo, you don't, so if it's quasi-sleazy, it might sound that way, but it's not. I travel a lot. It's not a big deal to synchronize my schedule to match yours." David sighed. It still felt sleazy. Possibly because he wasn't an affair type of guy. He and Chris were raised to respect women, value honesty, work hard, and stand when "The Star Spangled Banner" was played. Apparently, David had been listening to their parents harder than Chris when the whole "value honesty" lectures were covered. No, not going there. This time he concentrated on Ashley, met her eyes squarely.

After a moment, a smile bloomed slowly. "Okay," she said.

He peered closer, checking to see if Inquisition Ashley was really finished. "Really?" It seemed too easy. "Okay? Just like that?"

"Yeah. Just like that."

David heaved a glorious sigh of relief. "I like you, Ashley Larsen."

*I like you lots.*

"I'm glad." She shot him a curious look. "You really signed up for an online dating service?"

"You said I should. I thought, it's time, I should, and then I did." He shook his head. "I knew I shouldn't have."

"What happened?"

"So, first there was Kim, then Pam and then…" Abruptly he stopped, frowning.

"And who was next?" she prodded.

"Jane." It sounded oddball to tell Ashley that he'd been out with another girl named Ashley. Actually two other girls named Ashley. The world was full of Ashleys, and it wasn't his fault. Now it sounded a little obsessed, and he wasn't. There was just a hell of a lot of Ashleys. Statistically, that did not make him obsessed.

Ashley leaned across the table. "Why does Jane make you guilty? I see guilt on your face. You slept with her, didn't you?"

"After one date? Do I look like a man whore?"

Her eyes said yes, thankfully her mouth stayed shut.

And now he was blushing. A thirty-four-year-old divorced man who'd been cuckolded by his brother did not deserve to be labeled a man whore. He shouldn't have to stoop so low as to blush. He told himself to stop, but she started laughing. The damned blush remained. "Only for you," he defended. "And that's only because I don't see you enough. I think you're right. It's the distance thing. It's like Spanish Fly."

"It's a good thing I don't live in New York," she told him, and he nearly disagreed with her, clamping down on his tongue just in time. That would be twice that he brought up her living in New York, which would suggest a pattern, a train of thought, a need, and that's not what their relationship was. It was not how they defined it. It was not what they both wanted.

"I think we're moving on," he said. "You know, getting past the whole black plague of divorceness." There. That sounded correctly ambivalent.

"I should sign up for a dating service, too," she said.

Instantly he knew that was a bad idea. An idea of disastrous proportions. She was vulnerable, easily swayed, ready to leap into bed with every Dick, Dick and Harry Dick that was out there.

"After all the horror I've endured, now you want to endure it, too?" he asked. It sounded logical, completely unlike the throbbing molto-basso sounds of male denial.

"It sounds interesting. I should broaden my horizons, don't you think?" There was a glint in her eyes, a spark of mischief and things that he knew were cock-twistingly bad.

"I think an intracontinental affair could broaden horizons," he told her, not wanting to think about his cock. Not thinking about his cock. Not thinking about his cock. "Jet-setting around the country, a hotel room in every port, a glass of champagne under every beach umbrella. That could seriously broaden your horizons."

And if that didn't work, there were some other positions they could think about. Light bondage, for instance. David had been a one-hundred-percent homogenized sex participant before, but scarlet nether lips for hotel wall art made a guy think about nether lips, and how his cock fit into said wall art.

Ashley lifted her hands, feigning innocence. "But that's only once a month."

"We could go bi-weekly. I'm not averse to the idea," he offered, a total understatement.

"But you thought that would get boring."

"No, you thought it would get boring," he corrected. "I never thought boring. Not once."

"But what about all that variety that I'll be missing out on…" Her voice trailed off wistfully.

"If you want variety…" And his voice trailed off wistfully, too.

"With other men," she finished.

David narrowed his eyes, sensing mischief afoot. "Are you toying with me? Me, Mr. Not-So-Well-Adjusted? Me, Mr. I'm-Heartbroken-After-the-Divorce? Me, Mr. Downtrodden-and-Depressed? Are you that cold?"

She nodded once, a smile playing on her face. "Miami."

"Miami in June. And now that that's decided, can I escort you back to your hotel room? You could toy with me some more," he coaxed in a low voice that was carefully designed not to sound carnally obsessed. But to be fair to himself, they didn't have a lot of time, and it'd be another month before he saw her again. Miami in June.

"It would be my pleasure."

"Yes, I think it will," he promised, and when David made a promise, he kept it.

IT WAS LUNCHTIME on Friday when he took her to JFK, and there was a particular moment when she was about to go through security. He was all charm and old-school proper, but the hazel eyes were darker than before. His hand stayed firm at her back, a polite touch, yet a little more. Around them, a thousand air travelers rushed through the terminal. Posted signs were explaining what the FAA allowed, what the TSA permitted, the proper procedure for taking off your shoes, but there was no protocol posted for saying goodbye to David.

He confused her, he fascinated her, he wanted her…yeah, she knew all that. Their relationship was all flash in the pan, big fireworks, little common sense. It was the leaving that made this relationship work. Instinctively she knew it, and she wasn't going to give him any more. Because that would be stupid.

Ashley put a hand on his arm, pulling him closer, ostensibly to be heard above the madding crowd, but actually because she needed to be closer, needed to share his personal space for just a bit longer. She liked it there with him. They fit.

David looked at her. Frustration clouded his eyes, which were even darker now, and a particularly vile suitcase jammed into her side.

He swore, pulled her against the wall and kissed her.

It was a lot more flash in the pan, big fireworks, and she lifted up on tiptoes because she loved the flashing lights behind her eyes, loved the way he kissed with such desperation.

He lifted his head, gave her a last glance and then walked away without looking back. Not once did he look back. It was a tiny thing, but it hurt. She watched him leave, wondering if he would turn around, but he didn't. Casual white shirt, well-worn blue jeans, but no regretful look back. Eventually he disappeared into the crowd, and the businessman behind Ashley prodded her. "You in line?"

She nodded once, went through the motions of pulling off her shoes and wondered why David hadn't looked, and why it should bug her. A no-look was better. It illustrated the casualness of their relationship, their twin desire to have a fling. Besides, airports were busy places, everyone fast and ready to go about their business. It wasn't the place for look-backs. It was the place to be processed and pressed forward.

After she handed her boarding pass to security, she passed through the metal detector. She was flying eight hundred miles back home, back to her family, back to her stores. Back where she belonged.

If this intensity didn't fade though, if this fling turned into something more, David would want her to move to New York. He even brought it up, and she had seen the worry in his eyes. David was the one who would demand things of her, doing a mock TV show with three up-and-coming designers was the least of what he'd expect her to do. He'd want her to leave Chicago, leave her stores, leave Val.

Ashley wasn't a leaver. Jacob might have left her, but Ashley was the port in the storm, the parked car, the unbudgeable rock. That was what her family needed, and that was who she was. Then she laughed at herself. She and David had seen each other twice. Three nights of great sex didn't a relationship make. No, relationships were built on things more solid and reliable.

Her bunny slippers came out of the bag and she rubbed the pink fur affectionately.

"Looks like it's just you and me, kid," she said to her good-luck charm, but she did look back, just once, and frowned.

# 8

DAVID DIDN'T STOP until he climbed inside the cab, and then he was forced to sit, forced to think. It wasn't supposed to be difficult to say goodbye when you're having a jet-setting intracontinental affair. It was supposed to be easy. The brain of a man last screwed by the female sex did not filter through a hundred excuses to get her to stay. The brain of said man, who really didn't need to be thinking like this right now, should not want to pull her close and whisper promises— unless they were promises of the sexual kind. David whapped his forehead with his palm, telling his half-wit brain to get it in gear.

And then came calm, rational reasoning to explain said half-wit thinking. Ashley was right. It was the distance. It made things seem better, more mysterious, more erotic. He kept telling himself in the cab all the way to his financial district apartment, skipping the afternoon at the office. When he got home, he sorted the mail, paid the bills, ordered groceries for the next week, skimmed through all the shows on TiVo, but by the time eight o'clock came around, he was still restless, still itchy in his own skin. So, ignoring the actually functioning part of his brain that said he was making a mistake, he called her.

"It's David," he said stupidly, racking his brain for something mundane to talk about that wasn't boring, and on the other hand, didn't indicate he was calling simply to hear her voice. Because he wasn't. He wasn't.

"Hey," she told him.

"Any problems on the plane?"

*Scintillating, dude. Late night snooze-a-polooza.*

"Miraculously, not a one."

"You're a regular Captain Kirk now, aren't you?"

"You watch *Star Trek?*" she asked, her voice dripping with amused scorn.

"Never," he defended.

"Liar," she told him softly, and the word wrapped around him, nearly as soft as her. Nearly as warm as her.

"Maybe," he answered truthfully because a weakness for *Star Trek* and the accompanying jokes was much safer than explaining a month was a really long time to wait. A freaking long time, and she'd been in Chicago for less than thirty minutes, and his apartment was way too lonely, and she'd never even been there. And why hadn't she been there? Was there something taboo about his apartment?

"What did you say those Miami dates are?" he asked

"I didn't. I've got to check in with Jenna, the designer, and then my store managers will have a collective hissy fit if I'm not around to hold their hands, and then there's Val…"

Ashley had responsibilities. She had ties. She had things that occupied her time, rather than sitting in an empty apartment with a great view of the South Street Seaport. When had his apartment gotten so empty? "Oh, yeah. Stupid me."

"You're not stupid. Why did you call?"

"It was good to see you," he started to say, but then switched channels before he could freeze up. "I wanted to make sure the plane didn't crash."

"No crashes."

"No crashes are good."

There was a long pause when he knew it was time to say goodbye and hang up, but he didn't. He sat there listening to her breathe.

"You could come to New York next weekend. I'd spring for the ticket. I know things are tight for you."

*You're being stupid, you shouldn't say this. You really shouldn't say this.*

"I can't do that. Work. I've been playing hooky too much already. Weekends are the busy times." She didn't even have to think about it. Not a second of hesitation.

"You're right. It was an idea. A stupid idea."

"You're not stupid."

"No, I guess not. Ashley…" David forcibly restrained himself from talking. He was a smart guy, but something about this whole situation was turning him stupid. He liked to think it was his Boy Scout personal ethics and sense of nobility—the idea that he wasn't a guy who would do anything for a quick lay. But it wasn't a sense of honor that had him pushing her for more. It was the simple fact that he couldn't stop thinking about her.

"Listen, I have to go," she told him, stopping him before he could get really carried away, which was only a good thing, and he should be grateful that one of them was seeing sense.

"I should go, too," he said, lying back on his pillow, wondering if he'd ever see her in his bed. On his pillow. Stupid.

"'Bye."

"'Bye."

"David?"

"Yeah."

"Thanks for calling," she whispered, and the hesitancy didn't sound as if she were being polite, didn't sound as if she were lying, and he told himself that maybe he wasn't being so stupid after all.

WHEN ALL ELSE FAILED to occupy his time, David threw himself into work. Every night, he was haunting the downtown offices of Brooks Capital, pouring over 10Ks and 10Qs and building models of company financials. If his instincts were starting to go on the fritz, there was always the hard truth of numbers. Numbers didn't lie, numbers didn't sleep with your brother and numbers were not afraid of flying.

It was the middle of a bustling Wednesday afternoon, and

he'd just spent two hours on a conference call with an adhesive supplier to a vinyl-composition-floor-covering manufacturer. By the end of the call, he was propping his eyes open with paper clips. Retail, yes, biomedical, yes, technology, yes, energy, not great, but okay, but vinyl flooring? God deliver him from vinyl flooring. He had just switched over to the warm comfort of his spreadsheets, when his cell rang. David checked the caller ID. New York. It was safe.

"David McLean."

"This is Robert Golden from Goldstein, Goldstein and Lowe. I'm calling to discuss the property at 357 East 39th Street."

His mother's old apartment. "Yeah?"

"I'm sorry to interrupt your workday, but I think you'll find this good news. The building's going condo. You've been making some tiny rental income up to now, but with a sale we believe we can make you and Christopher McLean a nice chunk of change. Is Christopher your father?"

"Brother. Mom gave the apartment to both of us before she passed away." Their mother had thought two names on a deed would mend fences. Their mother had been wrong. David managed the rental, and every month he wrote out a nice check to Chris. Look, Ma, no talking necessary.

The lawyer named a figure that caused David's blood pressure to spike. "That much?"

Money was a tricky thing in the McLean family. Pete McLean, David's father, had been raised on a cotton farm in Arkansas before moving to New York to make his mark as an electrician. Pete McLean hadn't trusted money or flash, he valued hard work and honesty. David valued hard work and honesty, too, but he knew what money meant. He knew what a college education meant—choosing a different path from Chris, who was now a practicing electrician in Illinois. Chris would never make the money that David had already made, but he had a three-bedroom house in the burbs and an SUV in the garage. Like his father before him, Chris never wanted to be anything more than solid middle-class. In a family of sturdy everymen, David was the ambitious outsider.

The lawyer droned on, explaining all the benefits of selling the apartment. "You'd be foolish to turn it down. We want the transition to be a win-win for everyone."

"And if we're not interested in selling?"

"That's what the court system is for."

Spoken like a true shyster. David interrupted him before he got too deep into his spiel. "Let me talk to Chris," David said and then hung up.

For the next seven hours David went through spreadsheet after spreadsheet, studying the numbers until everything ran together in a big blot of red.

It was ten at night before he decided to call his brother. It was late. He hoped they were in bed. He hoped he was interrupting. Unfortunately, Chris sounded wide-awake.

After David finished explaining the apartment situation, he added the single cherry to the top of what felt like a melted ice cream sundae.

"You take the proceeds, Chris. I'm good."

"I don't want your money," his brother explained, while David took his desk magnet and trailed paper clips around in circles.

"Stop being a proud idiot," David told him.

"I'm not saying this because I'm a proud idiot. It's because I won't give you the satisfaction of showing Christine how much money you have and exactly how much money we don't."

"It's the right thing to do," David said, not denying the other remark. It was probably true. Okay, it was true.

"No. We split it up even. Half to you, half to me," Chris insisted.

David set his mouth in a hard line. Chris couldn't see it, but he could sure as hell hear it. "No. I don't need it."

"David, this is insane."

"There're a lot of things that are insane, Chris."

"You're not going to get over this, are you?"

That was the heart of the matter. Exactly the reason he now

hated talking to his brother. "Would you get over this? Would anybody? I'm the guy who's been screwed, Chris. Screwed in the ass. Don't be all martyr because your brother is pissed that you slept with his wife."

Chris was quiet for a long, guilty minute. "I love her."

Like that absolved him of sin. Not in David's world. Not even close. "I loved her, too, asshole."

And of course, Chris picked up on the least important part. "But you don't, anymore?" he asked, and David heard the hope in his voice. Yeah, betraying your own brother did that to you.

"You don't get a free pass because my feelings change. Love can be killed, Chris. Spousal love, brotherly love."

"I miss you, David."

David stopped pushing paper clips around his desk. He didn't want those words to hurt, didn't want his brother to have the luxury of opening one of David's veins and letting the blood flow. It had been four years. David hardened his heart because only a stupid man would get sucker-punched twice.

"Screw you, Chris."

After he hung up, David threw his cell phone across the room. A second later he listened to the tinny ring, ignored it and ran a muddled hand through his hair. He wasn't a phone-thrower. He was an analyst who watched *Star Trek* and read to feel better about his own life. It used to be easy to look around and know his life was the best. Arrogant? Yes. True? Yes. But now…something had changed inside him. His balance was off, the arrogance felt gratuitous, thrown in without anything to back it up. As if he didn't deserve it anymore, and David didn't like it.

Right then his boss stepped into his office. Not Jamie, Andrew. "Bad time?"

"No." David frowned at the phone in the corner. BlackBerry on Berber. Classy. "Sorry."

"I wanted to talk to you about Mercantile Financials."

*The bet.* "The earnings report came in today. I forgot to look."

"You blew the call."

David stared into Andrew's impassive gaze. Always cool. Not a phone-thrower. "They're up?"

His boss nodded.

A thousand questions sped through his brain like a CNBC crawl. He had been sure about this. Seven down quarters, and then oops. You're back in the black. The numbers had to be wrong.

"The euro's up. They made a killing overseas."

David wanted to stick to his guns, but it was really late on a Friday night. His brother was snug in bed with David's wife. The only woman David wanted to be snug with was eight hundred miles away in Chicago, and he'd blown a call because he'd assumed that nobody could have an up-year in this financial environment. There were no guns in his holsters to stick to.

Yet still he couldn't stop. "Their model's off."

"Sometimes it doesn't have to make sense. It just is."

David's phone began ringing again. Andrew looked in the direction of the BlackBerry. Looked at David.

David stared at his boss impassively. Always Be Cool was a good motto to follow. "I was so sure they were overshooting their projections."

"I was probably just lucky," Andrew said, showing humility for absolutely no good reason except to protect David's ego. David didn't reply.

"You okay?"

"I'm good."

"Jamie said—"

"I'm good," David interrupted because he didn't need sympathy. He didn't want pity. He was fine. He'd be fine.

Andrew looked at him, nodded. "Okay. You're in L.A. on Thursday? McKinsey Partners?"

David checked his desk calendar. "L.A. Then Phoenix. Sigeros Labs."

"You've been logging a lot of miles. Maybe you should take a break."

Which was a nice way of saying his judgment was starting to blow.

David shrugged, choosing to ignore the unspoken directive. "You can take time off. I won't stop you."

"I've got a long weekend scheduled in a couple of weeks, but I can double up the week before."

"You don't have to clear your schedule with me."

"I thought I should say something."

"She's nice?"

"Who?"

"Long-weekend she."

David nodded.

"Good. Not the reason you're throwing the phone?" Andrew picked up the BlackBerry and tossed it back to David.

David stuffed it into the desk drawer. He didn't want to hear the ring if it began again. "No, she's easy, low-maintenance. It's nice." Out of everything, Ashley was the one thing that made him smile.

"Nice is nice."

"Yeah, thanks."

FIVE DAYS LATER, Ashley broke down and called David. She wasn't supposed to, had convinced herself that she was throwing gasoline on an emotional bonfire, which really didn't need to be stoked, but she had thought David would call again. There had been that last conversation when she'd tried to put some much-needed distance between them because apparently eight hundred miles wasn't enough. Silly man, he had listened.

That same silly man sounded stressed when he picked up.

"Is something wrong?"

"No, why?"

"You sound mad. I'm not making you mad, am I? I shouldn't have called, should I?"

"Nah. It's stuff with my ex."

Ashley heaved a long sigh of relief. "Sorry." She didn't want to pry. She was dying to pry, but this was a closed subject. Pandora's box.

"You ever talk to Jacob?" he asked, and she was surprised he remembered the name. She didn't know the name of his ex-wife. Ashley thought about lying about her relationship with Jacob, and pretend that she was one of the mature adults who could be close friends with their ex. But David didn't need her to be a mature adult now. He needed a soft shoulder that he could lean on.

"No. It's like it's all an embarrassment to him now. You know, as if we'd both like to forget about it."

"You think that way, too, or is that just him?"

"It used to be just him. But now it's me, too. Marriage is hard. I didn't used to think that. You really have to love somebody—really have to like somebody—to want to invest so much work in it."

Over the line, she heard him quietly swear, and she hated that he still hurt. For now, she'd just call his ex-wife "bitch." It made her feel smugly superior. "David? What's wrong? With your ex, I mean. Do you still love her?"

"No." His voice was flat, emotionless, and she wished he trusted her. "It's nothing."

"I'm sorry. I wish I was there."

"Me, too."

Ashley bit her tongue because she wanted to get on a plane, which was a damned fool idea any way she sliced it.

"If I did, you know, it'd be better than Spanish Fly."

"Are you teasing me, Ashley Larsen?"

"Does it help?"

"Yes."

"Then I'm teasing."

"And if it didn't help, what would you be doing then?"

"Embarrassing myself."

He laughed, just as she intended.

"I wish you were here, Ash."

"Ditto." In the back of the house, she could hear Val's restless padding. Never a good sign. "I should go."

"Miami."

"Yeah, Miami."

# 9

---

DAVID'S GYM downtown was a beaten brick warehouse that looked more like an automotive garage than a health club. But this was no ordinary health club. It was a place where the white-collar types fled their desks, pulled on the gloves and proceeded to beat the crap out of each other. And it was all sanctioned by the New York State Sports Authority. White-collar boxing. Yahoo.

The newfound desire for bloodshed had started shortly after the divorce. He was spending too much time alone, too much time wondering how he'd screwed up, and a guy from work had invited him here. David had taped up his hands, pulled on the gloves and ended up with a full set of blisters, a serious dent to his confidence and a walloping punch to the gut. He'd had the time of his life.

Today was no picnic. A few rounds with the heavy bag, and then sparring with Tony DiNapoli, a trader from Goldman still who had a house in the Hamptons and a Lamborghini in his garage that cost more than David's monthly rent.

David narrowly dodged two jabs in the general direction of his chin, and Tony landed a lucky slug to his chest, but in the end, the bout was never in doubt. After they climbed out of the ring, David pulled off his gloves and flexed his fingers. He shouldn't brag. It was a sign of poor moral character.

So, he was a scumbag. He grinned happily. "Money does not buy happiness, nor does it buy stamina and the ability to whip my ass."

Tony was still hunched over, breathing heavily. "Some day, McLean."

"In your dreams," he quipped, pulling the tape off his hands.

"Trish wants you to meet her cousin."

David dumped the tape in the trash and grabbed a towel, heading for the locker room. "No."

"I'm going to tell her you're gay."

"Eat shit, Tony."

"Don't you miss it?" Tony asked, pulling his bag from the locker. "Don't you miss the siren's call of the pudendum? I bet you do. It's why you're walking around all tight-assed all the time. You're just remembering what it was like."

David merely stared blandly. "Why should I miss what I still have?"

"You're seeing somebody?"

Was he seeing Ashley? Did once a month in a hotel room somewhere across the United States count as seeing her? Slowly he smiled. "Yes. Yes, I am."

Tony swore, flipping his towel against the bench. "It's Elena, isn't it? She sits there, watching you in the ring with those exotic eyes, drooling all over herself. You should be ashamed, my friend, taking advantage of a young, nubile twenty-one-year-old with a body that could stop a rocket. I would beat you myself, if only because I am beside myself with jealousy."

"She's only twenty-one, Tony. That's not my speed."

"That's every man's speed."

"Not mine."

"You really got somebody? You're not lying to me?"

"I got somebody." I *think*.

"Now you've got me tied up in knots thinking of Elena. I'm heading to the showers, and if you hear ragged moans of pleasure, leave a man to his privacy. Next time, McLean. This time, I'm going to pummel you into a thousand tiny pieces."

"Save your bull for your customers, Tony."

"Do you know Transatlantic Pipe? The board's about to kick out the CEO, and bring in a new one. A good one. A very, very good one. I'm telling you, it's a buying opportunity."

"Really? What do you know?"

"Enough. And my friend, only for you."

At Tony's devious smile, David got an idea. "Say, do you know a guy at Chase Investments? Barney something?"

"Barney Thompson or Barney Burdetti?"

"He's probably young. Jerky. Full of himself and likes the ladies."

"That's Burdetti. Definitely Burdetti. You wouldn't believe—"

"Can you invite him for lunch?"

"Got a man crush, David?"

"Nah, doing a favor for a friend."

"The 'somebody' friend?"

"Another friend."

"And suddenly, you got a lot of friends. Do I need to hate you? Are you suddenly having more sex than me?"

This time, David swore. "Sadly, probably not."

"Okay, I won't hate you then. Give me a couple of weeks, and I'll see if I can't wangle him for lunch. I'll tell him your firm is still running double-digit gains. After the big meltdown, everybody's nervous."

"I'll be nice," David offered, lying through his teeth.

MIAMI IN JUNE was golden sunlight, pastel-painted stucco and ocean beaches so white it hurt your eyes.

Or so she'd been told.

Ashley had been in Miami for nearly three hours and all she'd seen was a muddled airport under renovations, the inside of a cab, the luxurious oceanfront room at the Setai hotel and the naked body of one finely made man.

Yes, Miami was a town of many, many things to see and do,

but currently, she was only interested in one, and that was what made her nervous.

She fell back against the plush pillows, this time too tired to roll away from the warm invitation of his body—until her hand reached out and found an answering set of fingers that clasped around hers. Ashley's heart squeezed in a manner that had nothing to do with the sex. She broke free and rolled away before the heart-squeezing got worse.

The room was intensely quiet. Too quiet despite the low thrum of the air conditioning, the rhythmic rush of the ocean lapping on the beach and the silent scream of a woman getting in over her head.

His breathing was slow and steady, in and out, then over again, and she noticed how quickly her lungs matched his in time. Her gaze held fast to the wall, desperately clinging there.

Damn.

He didn't try and touch her, nor speak to her, and she was grateful for that simple courtesy. Yes, David was a perceptive man, and he could tell she was a woman teetering on the edge.

The worst thing was that it had been different this time. Frantic coupling? Check. Heart-ripping pleasure? Check. Exploding orgasm? Check. Check. Check. So what was new?

The way she needed to lock eyes when he was filling her. The way her fingers buried in the thick hair as if they belonged there. The way his body felt covering hers.

This wasn't stranger sex anymore. The excitement and sense of the forbidden was gone, but what it left behind was something more disturbing.

*So, what's the big deal? Hop a flight to New York every now and again. You know this affair is nothing but compatible sex and working off a little stress.*

*You don't know anything, Val.*

*I know more than you.*

The hotel walls were dark brown, the color of the earth, the color of his eyes when he was spilling himself inside her.

Ashley buried herself farther under the sheets. Unfortunately, they smelled like her, like him…like them, but still her nose stayed there, her mind memorizing the scent.

His finger stroked down her back, following the arc of her spine. Ashley smiled at the wall, but kept firmly to her side of the bed.

"You make me feel cheap," he finally said, no trace of hurt in his voice, and she was grateful for that small courtesy as well.

David continued to talk, one benign finger coaxing her closer and closer.

"I know you're only here to use and abuse me, but I have needs, too."

At that, Ashley rolled over and stared at him suspiciously, but his face was as benign as that single finger that was tracking her skin.

"You think of me as just a fast-action pump and drill, variable speed settings and excellent torque, but I have feelings and when you turn away from me…" He looked at her, hazel eyes dancing, and sniffed.

All completely benign.

"What do you want?" she asked cautiously.

He shrugged. "I don't know. But I need to feel you respect me."

Ashley scooched closer. "I respect you."

He sniffed again. "I need you to like me for my mind, not just the awesome sex."

His eyes were still dancing, a smile playing on his mouth. As long as everything was casual, Ashley could play, too.

She scooched even closer, and curled into the safe crook of his arm, ignoring the warning voices in her head.

"You have a very nice mind. Sharp. Almost—dare I say—quick, for such a brawny stud such as yourself."

Slowly his hand slid over her shoulder, not nearly as casual as the smile on his face, or the easy look in his eyes.

"Thank you for noticing."

Content at last, Ashley smiled. For the first time she took a good look at their surroundings, at the steely gray ocean rushing back and forth outside the wall of windows.

He had picked the hotel this time because "the color red gave him a headache." Ashley was curious to see what he would do. It wasn't the stiff elegance of the Ritz, nor the lust tropics of the Biltmore, instead it was understated beauty.

"Nice room," she said. "I approve."

Beyond the windows, ominous afternoon clouds started to draw down on the Atlantic and announced the late-day storm you could set a clock by. Ashley watched as the clouds grew darker.

"The view's great," she added. He was so quiet that she turned her head, daring to look, but there was nothing to be afraid of.

"So, who's our target this time?" he asked.

Ah, business. That was safe.

"Mariah D'Angelo. Twenty-seven. Got written up in *WWD,* and she's starting to attract the attention of some of the big guns."

He quirked a brow. "Big guns of the fashion industry?"

"You know—the usual suspects in trendy poof."

"Trendy poof? You're going to have to tutor me on the fashion lingo."

She gave him a studious look. "I think you'll do fine."

The rain began, a quiet patter, starting slow, then quickly growing in intensity.

"You like the rain?" she asked him, enjoying this easy camaraderie. It was like being friends, with benefits.

"Rain in New York is a bitch. Streets flood, subways are late, cabs are scarce and there's always an umbrella to jam you up."

"Sounds charming."

"However…when I'm not outside…for example, if I'm sleeping late or watching TV, or reading, I don't mind it. I like it then."

Her cheek rubbed against his chest, ostensibly because she felt restless and needed to move. This wasn't easy camaraderie. This was "I miss you and I want to lay with you."

*And what's wrong with that?*

*I can't go to New York.*

*Okay, you win with that one.*

*No, I lose.*

"You actually read?" she asked, back to snarky-snark because mundane chatter wasn't mundane enough anymore.

"Shocking, I know."

"I bet you read work stuff." She needed it to be work stuff because any other answer indicated depth of character, and a seriousness that she didn't want to think about. He was already too close to ideal. She needed to find flaws. Serious character flaws that she could sink her teeth into.

"Some of it's for work," he answered, so she hedged her bets.

"Comic books the rest of the time, right? Sci-fi, big trolls eating up Hobbit civilizations?"

"Comics, Steinbeck, Tolkien, Harlan Coben and Edgar Allan Poe. A veritable smorgasbord of literary taste."

Ashley looked at him, shocked. "Poe? Nobody does that."

"I do," he protested, looking slightly hurt. "I'm very cerebral."

She studied the hard swell of his arms, biceps that had never hefted the pages of Poe. No, David McLean just knew how to play a good game of mind-screw. "Cerebral, my ass."

His free hand slid lower and lingered. "Your ass is many things. Cerebral is not one of them."

And they'd moved full circle back to sex. Outside the rain was bearing down, isolating her from the rest of the world, isolating them.

She rose up on his chest, inviting his eyes to wander over her bare skin. This, sex, she could handle.

"I like the rain," she whispered.

The amusement fell from his face, leaving behind lust…and something not so easy.

He pulled her closer, took her face, took her mouth, and it was far from easy. His kiss wasn't hot passion or casual sex or mind-screwing play.

Without thinking, Ashley found herself sinking into this

new kiss. The storm rolled across the Atlantic. She loved the rain, loved the feel of his body under hers, feeling his cock stir with carnal intent. But his heartbeat was firm, sure. Those powerful arms were tight, secure. He wasn't letting her go.

Ashley lifted her head, stared into eyes that were not so simple, not so casual.

"Don't think, Ash. Just go with it," he urged.

He wanted her to step in the airplane, push away from everything she knew was smart, rational and logical.

And he called himself an analyst? Shameful.

However, smart, rational and logical weren't currently invading her head. The storm outside, the storm in her head had drowned them out.

Her mouth hovered lower, her eyes not so simple, not so casual.

Just go with it? She would.

IT WAS ALMOST SEVEN when they met with Mariah, just as the woman was closing up her studio. The place was blazing with psychedelic colors and a chaotic mix of fabric and textures that defied description.

Very chichi with a head rush.

The clothes were arranged in disordered, yet strategic piles. It was organized anarchy, which suited the owner, because Mariah D'Angelo was as intimidating as leg warmers, circa 1983. Her hair hung in a long, kinked black braid down her back, and she wore blue jeans, an artistically ripped black T-shirt, her feet sporting polka-dot high-tops.

Hard to believe, yet true.

David took up an innocent bystander stance against the far wall while Ashley launched into her spiel without a sweat. "I want you to add your designs to the event. I'll do two challenges. Casual and cocktail, and look, I'm even telling, so it'll be easy. You know what they are. Just give me your best stuff, and we let the customers decide. No secrets. I don't have a big operation. Only four stores, and they're not even…"

David coughed once, soft yet effective. Uplifting, not down-trodden, was the mantra of the night.

"But we get a lot of traffic and the media coverage has already started." It was true, *Chicago Fashion Weekly* had put two paragraphs in the September calendar. "It's a golden opportunity."

"What about my expenses?" asked Mariah, cutting to the heart of the matter.

"All covered," promised David, who had no idea of the balance on the Ashley's Closet credit card.

Mariah looked at David, then Ashley, then shrugged in a completely naive, trusting manner. "I'm in."

Ashley hugged her, until Mariah—not that trusting—pulled away.

"I'm sorry," Ashley apologized. "I'm working to recharge my…"

Another cough from David.

"Revolutionize the stores. Transform the fashion design landscape in Chicago," she finished, flashing David a relieved grin. There. That wasn't so hard after all.

The best part was that Mariah looked excited. "Do you want to check out the studio?"

Ashley examined the day-glo colors, the cottony soft fabrics, and sighed. "I think it's my destiny."

In the end, Ashley walked out wearing a newly purchased bijou pink bandeau top, with a matching sarong skirt with the sheerest of chiffon layers that danced around her thighs. To complete the frivolous ensemble—très Miami—she wore a white hat with a big, floppy brim. *Beach Blanket Bingo* meets Jackie Onassis.

She and David strolled through the open-air plaza, the summer breeze rippling through the skirt. She felt dramatic, alive, confident. She was the Ashley that she'd always dreamed of being.

"Can you believe it? She was entranced, like I was, you know, fabulous."

"You were good," he told her, and this time she didn't mind

the warm light in his eyes. She was even holding his hand, a daring move rife with untoward possibilities, but tonight she was walking on ocean air, with a salsa beat accompanying the marcato of her blood.

Couples cruised the square, doing nothing but enjoying life—what a concept.

"I had her eating from the palm of my hand."

"Especially after you bought the clothes."

"Oh, fine, burst my bubble, you big lug. Whining to me about how you're all sensitive. You've got all the sensitivity of a razor blade."

"Look at you. Giving back, a jab, jab, cross, and then wham, the body blow."

Ashley stopped and stared. "Boxing!"

He shot her a confused look. "What?"

Ashley patiently explained to him the significance. "You box."

He nodded, still not grasping the genius of her analytical skills.

"I bet you want to know how I figured it out. Don't you? You are dying to know."

Obviously sensing—finally!—the importance of this moment, he nodded again. Smart man. "Go ahead. Share."

"Your arms," she told him, her fingers trailing over his bicep in a brazenly uninhibited move.

"My arms?"

"It now makes perfect sense. Your biceps are too big for swimming, you don't have runners' legs, your thighs are too thick, runners' are like matchsticks. But boxing…it fits."

"You've been studying my body in some detail, haven't you?" he asked, stroking his chin, very Sherlock Holmes.

"Embarrassed when a woman expresses admiration for your physiology?"

"Not at all. I thought it was my awe-inspiring sexual prowess that drew you, but this, too? My ego is growing by leaps, bounds…inches."

Ashley knocked at his arm. "Pervert."

He didn't even try and deny it. "Busted."

She studied his face and grinned. "I did great, didn't I?"

"You were great."

"It's going to work, isn't it?"

"It is," he answered with complete confidence.

With one finger she flicked back the brim of her hat, pulled him close. "That was the exact, correct answer."

His hand slid over the bare skin of her back, gliding underneath the thin material of her top. "I really like this. Very practical. Accessible. Sexy."

"You think?"

"I think."

"We should go back," she suggested.

"We should," he replied, giving her a long kiss. Then he took her hand and they walked briskly to the hotel.

"I have to be honest. I cannot lie," she confessed. "It really is your sexual prowess."

"Now who's the pervert?"

"Busted," she said, tucking nicely under his arm.

David only laughed.

IT WAS THREE in the morning, but outside the hotel it didn't matter. The beach was still alive with Friday-night noise. The moon was full and golden, a brilliant orb that cast the room in its magical embrace. Inside the bed, it was warm and comfortable, a secret place.

"Tell me about your wife," asked Ashley, daring to venture to secret subjects.

David propped up one elbow, and even in the faint light she could see the requisite jaw-clench. "There's not a lot to say. We were married out of college. She's a perfectionist."

Ashley smiled and David, being overly sensitive, glared. "Why is that funny?"

She tried to keep a straight face and failed. "You can be a little stilted when you're not happy. I can't imagine two of you."

"I'm not stilted," he insisted.

"You're not relaxed," she pointed out, avoiding mention of the locked shoulders or the fisted hands.

"I'm relaxed." His jaw clenched even more.

"Do you truly believe that?"

He winced and fell back in bed. "No."

She thought to carry on, now that she had wandered into the deep end. "I think you have suppressed anger issues." After dealing with her sister, understanding the ins and outs of the human condition, such as it was, she had learned to spot the signs.

"I don't."

"It's because of her, isn't it? You can't forgive her. Not that I can blame you, but it still eats at you."

He propped back up on his elbow. "Don't analyze me."

Obviously David didn't take to psychobabble as easily as Val. Still, Ashley was curious about his marriage, the marriage he didn't want to talk about, and curious about the bitch. Ashley couldn't help her feelings. Whoever had worked over David, well, the word *bitch* fit, and Ashley was nothing if not accurate.

"I don't want you to hurt," she told him, and the deep truth in those words surprised her. She didn't like him locked-jawed and locked-mind. She understood that sometimes he needed to be that way, but she didn't have to like it.

He leaned closer, and the locked jaw disappeared. She reached up a hand to tame his hair, and inadvertently her body curved into his.

"You're too soft, Ashley Larsen." David looked at her, then looked away, staring intently at the same wall that Ashley had studied only hours before. Sometimes studying a wall was easier than studying the mess of your own life.

"I'm sorry she hurt you," she said, pressing a kiss over his heart, her fingers tracing initials there. Her initials.

David caught her hand. "Are you trying to heal me with the magic sex energy?"

So, he wanted to make a joke now? At least he wasn't

looking at the wall anymore. Okay, she'd wait. "Very perceptive. My vagina is a powerful thing—full of ancient medicine."

At that, David moved over her, pushed deep inside her, and
his eyes locked with hers. Her breathing changed, slowed, and
her hands clutched at his back to hold him there. This time,
there was no frantic coupling, no pounding rain, no mundane
chatter, no jokes. There was only this unshakable thread
between them. An odd connection that she once believed must
be the pull of hormones, and the feel of his thick cock filling
her. Ashley had assumed that this void that he filled was the one
between her legs. She was wrong.

The void he filled was the one in her heart.

All her life, especially when reading fairy tales, she had
believed in love the old-fashioned way—you had to earn it. But
this felt like a gift. Some shimmering chalice that the gods had
handed her on a misguided whim. All she had to do was drink
from it. All she had to do was swallow the taste of this. All she
had to do was accept the gift that she had been given.

Without hesitation, David knotted their fingers together like
pieces of a puzzle locking into place. Each time he pushed
deeper, she rose up to follow without question. There was no
choice, not here, not now. Later, she would think. Right now,
slow pleasure built inside her, each wave of sensation larger than
before, growing outward, farther, seeping into places far
removed from the apex of her thighs. It was so much easier
when it was nothing but lust, but now her feelings were muddled,
woven into a knot that she had no desire to untangle. Not now.

This man, the one who overturned the world without
thinking twice, pulled at her.

The candles hissed, their glow falling to dark. His seductive
mouth grazed her lips, her neck, and she gasped at each gentle
touch. A trail of unshakable dreams followed in the wake of his
kiss, a trail of purposeful hunger followed in the wake of each
insistent thrust.

"Ashley," he whispered, and her heart skittered in fear.

He wanted to ruin this perfection. Words, once said, could never be unsaid. Deeds, once done, could never be undone. Ashley loved this drive within him, the need to push harder and higher, but not here. Not yet. She wanted to drink it in, sip at the taste. But to think about it, worry about it, was to ruin it.

Fears could be conquered, not easily, but it could be done. Worries could be dismissed, put off for another day. But loyalties and responsibilities—those pieces of herself that made her who she was—could not be so easily set aside.

"Ashley…"

Her lips pressed against his to trap his words, her thighs clenched tightly around him.

"Don't think about it," she murmured. "Just go with it."

David, being the smart man that he was, didn't say another word.

AT 7:00 A.M., THE PHONE RANG. Ashley's cell.

She untwisted herself from David, and reached to the nightstand.

"Hello?"

*"Ashley? It's your mother."*

"Mom?" Her mother's voice was shaky and afraid. Instantly, Ashley knew.

*"It's Val. I don't know what to do. Last night…"*

Ashley's heart stopped because this wasn't fair. She had reconciled herself to her own happy ending. She wanted to believe, she wanted to hope.

Her mother's words rushed out in one frantic sentence. *"Shedidn'tcomehome."*

# *10*

ASHLEY DIDN'T BOTHER to shower. It would have taken too much time. She threw her clothes in her carry-on, stuffing the floppy hat on her head.

David sat up. His eyes were full of concern. "What's wrong?"

Ashley jammed her toiletries into the side pocket of her carry-on. "Nothing. Nothing is wrong. I have to get home."

"Is something wrong with your mom?"

"No." She glanced down, realizing that she wasn't dressed. God. Furiously she unzipped the carry-on and pulled out some shorts and a shirt. She had worn them before, and they would be wrinkled. Screw the wrinkles.

"Is it your niece?"

"No."

He stood and calmly pulled on his jeans, as if he knew exactly what to do. No panicking. No caring about wrinkles. "Your sister?"

She didn't bother to answer. She was too close to tears.

"Ashley."

She looked up. "I just need to be home. Okay? Where's my feet?"

His eyes darkened with pain, and she didn't want to be the cause of it, but right now, that wasn't her concern. Tomorrow it would be. But not today.

"Feet?" he asked, all pain gone, the careful mask back in place.

"Slippers. I need my slippers." She saw the pink fur bulging from the side pocket. There. She was ready.

David pulled a shirt over his head. "I'll drive you to the airport."

"Don't worry about it. Get some sleep. I'll catch a cab."

"I want to drive you to the airport," he said again, being a gentleman, being stubborn, being David.

"I don't need your help," she nearly shouted. She knew she could handle this. She always handled this, always taken charge when Val disappeared—for days, weeks, months at a time. Today was different. She couldn't juggle David and Val at the same time, they were both too demanding, and she wasn't that good.

David merely stared, and this time there was no pain, only the icy coolness of a man who knows that unfeeling is wiser.

Ashley looked away, found the brown walls, the gutted remains of the candles. "I have to leave."

His eyes raked over the room, the rumpled bed, and then he looked away as well. "Sure. I had a great time. Loads of fun. Call me."

HER PLANE LANDED at O'Hare at one in the afternoon, and the first person she saw when she entered her house was Val. Apparently, she was no longer missing.

Ashley, nonviolent, marshmallow Ashley, threw her carry-on across the room.

*"What the hell did you do?"*

Val's face crumpled because Ashley never yelled, never cursed and never got mad. No, Ashley let people beat on her over and over again.

"I was helping someone from AA. She called last night. I'm her sponsor. She needed help, Ashley. I could help her."

Ashley pulled a hand through her tangled hair. "Why didn't you call Mom and tell her? Val, you know what Mom will think if you disappeared. You know what I would think if you disappeared."

"My phone wasn't charged. I forgot." It was typical Val. Life with a recovering alcoholic was like having another child. No, that was an overstatement. Brianna was easier.

Ashley swore. "Where's Mom?"

"I don't know. I guess she took Brianna to school this morning and then left for work."

"Does she know you're okay?"

"Not yet."

"Don't you think you should tell her, Val?"

Val scuffed at the floor with her bare foot. "She'll be mad."

"No, Val, she won't get mad at you." *Not like I'm mad at you.*

Reluctantly Val called their mother, and there were quiet murmurs as Val reassured her. Now that the crisis was over, now that Ashley knew that her sister hadn't been drinking, she collapsed, exhausted, into a chair. Her hand covered her face, partly because her eyes hurt, and partly because she didn't want to look at Val right now. Her family had always been her first concern, and Jacob hadn't minded. No, that was part of the problem in their marriage. Honestly, he hadn't even noticed. But David noticed. David cared. He wasn't a man who liked being left alone in a Miami hotel room. Divorce did that to you—made you see everything as a betrayal.

Ashley understood.

"Ashley?" There was Val. Though she wasn't looking at her, Ashley could imagine the neediness on her face. Val wanted to know that everything was all right, but it wasn't all right.

After years of thinking Val would be okay, and instead Ashley rescuing her over and over again, gullibility had transformed into a protective sort of paranoia, mostly for cause. However, Val needed to know that disappearing all night was not acceptable behavior. She had to teach Val to be responsible.

Her hand fell from her face, and Ashley let Val see years of anger in all its rawness. Val flinched. Ashley barreled on. "You couldn't borrow a phone? Didn't you think we'd worry?"

"I didn't think. You're mad at me, aren't you?" Val socked her fist into the couch. "Even when I'm doing something right I still screw it up."

Ashley sighed, resigned to the unteachable. "You're not screwing up. We didn't know. We worried."

"You don't trust me. Thirteen months sober, and you still don't trust me. I have worked my ass off to get you and Mom to stop looking at me like I'm going to raid your wallet, or wreck the car, or call from jail, but it's never gonna stop, is it?"

Brianna would be home soon. Their mother would be home soon. Ashley was still wearing the bunny slippers and the smell of David. She couldn't fight this battle. Not now.

"Val…"

Val socked the couch again. This time, a lot harder. "Shut up, Ashley." Val stalked off and Ashley, resigned to having hurt the entire world, turned on the television. Her eyes processed a new method for making homemade pierogi on the Food Channel, her mind blessedly blank, until she heard Val's footfalls on the wooden floor.

Softer footfalls, not nearly as mad.

Ashley immediately noticed the tear stains, the swollen eyes that looked full of hurt, and she wished the medical community had some pill, some shot that could take away Val's pain and give her confidence.

"I'm sorry," muttered Val. "Of course you're not going to trust me."

"I trusted you."

Val laughed with heavy scorn, and no humor at all. "You flew home because you thought everything was fine? No, you flew home because you thought I was out drunk, throwing up vodka at some shithole bar, and you knew Mom couldn't handle it by herself."

"I didn't think that, Val." Actually, she had thought it, but she wanted to be wrong. That should count for something.

All her life Val had been searching for strength. Sadly, the only place Val found strength was in her sister. "You shouldn't have to put up with this. I'm sorry. I don't want to let you down, Ash."

Ashley closed her eyes. She was tired and hungry, and now she wanted a hot, cleansing shower, so that the tangles from her hair would disappear, so that she wouldn't smell David on her skin. She had left Miami for nothing. The wanting was still there, a painful ache, and she didn't need those wants, nor those aches. Well, at least now, she, David and Val could all be miserable at once.

Slowly she uncurled from her chair and accepted the world she had, not the world she wanted. She noted Val's tortured eyes and her patience snapped. Self-misery didn't set well with her.

"You don't want to let me down? Then don't!"

THE FLOPPY HAT stayed hopelessly slung on the chipped, wooden four-poster. The bunny slippers stayed neatly lined up in the closet, breathlessly awaiting their next outing.

Ashley's days were spent coaching Sophie on the ins and outs of the radically diverse Lakeview clientele, which was a talent unto itself. The women of north Chicago weren't Gold Coast socialites, needing the latest from Nordstrom. No, they wanted retro and ripped. And if a man wanted to buy himself a dress, you didn't blink twice, and told him his hips definitely did not look too fat in that skirt.

At the Wicker Park store, Scarlett was going great guns. When Ashley had first goggled at the graffiti window display, Scarlett had brandished her spray-paint can proudly, not sensing the property-insurance-rate-hike fear in Ashley's risk-management heart. However, to give the woman her due, instead of looking trashed, the place now had an urban feel that actually mixed well with the street's other businesses.

Alas, sales at the Naperville store were down three-point-seven percent. Probably the latest in nonwrinkle fabric that Ashley had embarrassingly gone overboard with. Altogether her bottom line was slowly sinking into the red.

Each day, after she got home, she punched the numbers into her computer, and her spirits fell a little further, so much so that she almost stopped doing it, but David had taught her to follow the numbers—no matter how bad.

If the numbers were bad, the nights were the worst. Sitting up in her bed, cell phone in hand, willing it to ring. He didn't call. No surprise there.

She had seen the damage in his eyes when she left the hotel room, and she knew he didn't like to hurt. Honestly, who did? He'd show the pain for a flash of a second, and then it would disappear behind that brick wall of stubbornness, as if he wanted to be somehow impenetrable to pain.

Hence, no call.

It took her seven days to call him, which sounded like a long time, but she had to carefully plot out what she wanted to say. David deserved to know about Val. He deserved to know about Val's issues, but Ashley had never liked discussing her sister. Val's skeletons were firmly wedged deep in the Larsen closet right next to Ashley's slippers.

Talking about Val's problems felt vaguely traitorous, like laughing at someone else's bad haircut or discussing a fashion-don't behind a friend's back. But she knew she had to tell David the truth. Their relationship was no longer causal, something more than stranger sex. She didn't know exactly what, but whereas she had a certain loyalty to her family, now she had a certain loyalty to him as well.

He picked up on the fourth ring. Either he was in a meeting, or else he was upset. Considering it was a Friday night, 9:00 p.m. on the east coast, she was betting on the latter.

"Hello?"

"It's Ashley."

Silence.

Okay, he was angry. He didn't know her problems because she had not shared with him. And if she had shared her problems, he wouldn't be mad.

"Why are you mad?" she asked. It didn't seem right to blurt out, "My sister is an alcoholic." Some things needed buildup.

"I'm not mad," he answered, which was nice because it helped to provide the necessary buildup.

"You're mad."

"I'm mad," he said. Look how easy they fell into the same rhythms, the same arguments, the same routine. The consistency only made her sad. Seeing her hat, she took it off the bed post and perched it on her head. It made her feel better.

"I had a family emergency," she told him, still working on the buildup.

"I get that, Ashley. I understand that. But don't you think you can tell me why you left? I was worried, I was thinking, why won't she tell me? Is it because it's awful, or because it's nothing? For all I know, your sister had a hangnail and that's why you ran."

"It wasn't a hangnail."

"Then what was it?"

Ashley gathered her courage and prepared to tell her sister's worst-kept secret. Slowly the tongue got it together, the lips formed the right sounds and the words haltingly emerged. "She drinks. Drinks too much. She used to drink. She doesn't anymore. But it hasn't been very long."

"How long?"

"Thirteen months, seven days. It wasn't fun."

For a moment, he was quiet. "Why did you leave Miami?" he asked, as if she hadn't just told him that her sister was a recovering alcoholic, and still wasn't in a good place.

"My mother called. Val was missing. She's found now."

"Sober?" he asked crisply, as if they were checking off boxes on a survey.

"Sober. She'd just left her phone off. No big deal," she said. "Now do you understand?" With restless fingers, she played with the brim of the hat. Letting it droop down in her eyes, pushing it off to the side. Nothing seemed right.

"How old is your sister?"

"Thirty." And they were back to the survey questions. "She has a daughter. Eight years old. There was no one to take care of Brianna, that's my niece, except for Mom, and she's, oh, I don't know, but it's not a good idea. I had to be here." Ashley stared at herself in the mirror, and the floppy hat didn't seem so jazzy anymore.

"Does she do this a lot?"

Ashley didn't know what to say. Over the past thirteen months, life had been fairly quiet, especially compared to Val's bender that had lasted through most of Brianna's second year. That had been followed by three years of sobriety. But then Val had tried to go to community college, and instead spent most of her afternoons skipping class and sitting in the pub. Neither Ashley nor their Mom had known about that lost semester until the grades showed up in the mail. "It comes and goes."

"You shouldn't put up with it. She's an adult. She's capable. She is, right?"

"She's my sister, David," she whispered, in case anyone could hear.

*I can hear fine.*

"And that means she's not capable?"

"No, she is."

"You're not tough enough, Ashley. You have to be strong, and say, not my problem. They own that problem. And if they make stupid decisions, you can't let it ruin your life."

"She's not ruining my life."

"All right. Rephrase. You can't let it hurt you, you can't let it affect you."

"She's family."

"Trust me, that's not an excuse. Your family can hurt you most of all."

"David—"

"Stop. I'll drop it. You have to do what you think is right. I'm only the innocent bystander, not my concern. Who's the last designer gonna be?" he said, and obviously they were finished talking about Val and her problems. Business was easier for both of them.

"I'll stick to Chicago. There's a guy in Wicker Park. I need to give one to the home team."

"You want me there?" he asked, a completely stupid question for such a smart man.

"Of course. I want you. In Chicago."

"I can't," he said, his voice hoarse. Ashley stopped playing with her hat, frowned at the phone.

"I didn't say when," she said to let him know that she could see through his little denial tactic. "You don't want to come here, do you? You're still mad."

"It's not you."

"It's my *family?*" she asked incredulously.

"It's something else, Ashley."

"Like what?" He was so clever about keeping his secrets. Now, he wanted to know every detail about her life, and like a gullible idiot, she had told him, but when it came to opening up, he was a clam. A tongueless, noiseless, speechless clam. Ashley hated clams.

"I don't want to say anything," the clam answered.

Furiously, Ashley jumped up from the bed, and began to pace. David needed to hear this. Oh, he needed to hear every word.

"That doesn't work for me, and let me tell you why. I just spent seven days beating myself up because I didn't want to tell you about my sister. It's not an easy subject to talk about, and it's not my story to tell, so I have issues with saying anything about it. Big issues. But I knew I had to tell you because it wasn't right to leave like that. It's not me. And because I knew I had to tell you, I stopped beating myself up, practiced my words—several times, mind you—and I called and I told you the truth. So I don't want to hear, 'I don't want to say anything.' I have laid bare my soul here, so you can suck it up, and bare yours as well. What the hell is the matter with Chicago?"

There was a long silence and she stopped pacing, afraid she'd been too rough. Sure. From the closet, her slippers were busting a bunny-gut. But at least she'd done what needed to be done. Or at least, she'd thought she'd done what needed to be done.

What if she'd been wrong? What if she had moved this relationship up a level, and he hadn't? What if they were still having stranger sex and she didn't know it?

*What if she had betrayed Val's secrets to a man not worthy of knowing them?*

*Gee, thanks, sis.*

*No, I don't believe that.*

*Ha.*

She waited, feeling uncertain, not even sure if he was still on the line.

Finally, he spoke. "My ex-wife lives in Chicago."

*That was it?* Ashley began to pace again. She had assumed it was something bad. Something heart-twistingly awful. "I'm wanted for a felony there." "I was once mugged on the South Side—the memories get to me at night." Or even, "I have a love child roaming the streets, I can't bear the guilt."

*This was it?* She stopped her pacing and sighed loud enough that he could hear.

"It's a big city, David. The third largest city in the United States. I guarantee you won't see her."

"I know. It's weird."

"You *should* see her. Confront your fears head on."

"That's a really bad idea."

"Only because you're terrified."

"I'm not terrified."

"Liar."

This time, he sighed, a frustrated sigh tinged with overtones of "you don't get it"—much like hers had sounded. "Ashley, it's complicated."

Ashley wasn't deterred. "How long since you've seen her?"

Silence.

"You haven't seen her, have you?" she asked, and it killed her that he was still so busted up over his ex. Studies had shown that men had a much harder time than women. Ashley had never believed it—until now.

"There's no reason for me to see her. She's married. She's got a new life."

"And so do you," she reminded him softly. Ashley was some part of that new life, she knew that without a doubt.

"Then you come with me."

*Come with me.* It was definitely moving their relationship into a level beyond stranger sex. Meet the ex-wife. And she wanted to be there for him. She wanted to meet the bitch in person, possibly glare at her when no one was looking.

But then what the heck would they talk about? And what about the questions?

Sure, come with him, meet his ex, explain that yes, they met on a plane and live half a nation apart, but their relationship transcends such obstacles. Oh, God. This was a bad idea. They'd have to lie.

"I don't know," she told him, staring at herself in the jazzy white hat. She looked like a woman who tackled the world head-on. Hats could do that to you. Fool you into being something you aren't.

"Terrified?"

"Yes," she answered truthfully.

"Would you do it for me?" he asked. It was a terrifically cheap shot because there was guilt involved in this equation, since she had left him stranded in Miami alone *and* there were few things she wouldn't do for David. The list was growing smaller daily. He was not the world's most perfect man, he was not the world's easiest man, but he was constant and loyal and he cared about her dreams when sometimes she ignored them. He got big bonus points for that. Dreams were very fragile things.

"When?"

"I'll set it up. Two weeks from now, last week in June. Christine's schedule is flexible."

Christine. His ex-wife was named Christine. It was a nice

name, an elegant name. Not as elegant as say, Ashley, for instance, but a name was only a set of letters arranged in some arbitrary order.

"You're sure this is a good idea?" he asked.

*It's an awful idea. A god-awful idea, Ash.*

"You want to borrow my bunny slippers?"

"Only if you're still attached. Preferably naked."

She plopped onto the bed, smiling for the first time in days. Seven days to be exact. "I could be naked now."

"Jeez, Ashley, do not tease. Fourteen days is killer…. Are you really naked?"

Her smile shifted into a grin. She shed her Hello Kitty sleep shirt, slid her panties down her legs and looked in the mirror. Something was missing. She pulled the brim low, low over her eyes. Trampy, vampy. Better. This was the way a woman should look when she's talking to her lover.

"Now I'm naked. Except for the hat."

"You're wearing a hat?"

"The white one we got in Miami. It makes me daring."

"How daring?" he asked, the words sounding wonderfully strangled.

She merely laughed, then fell back against the pillows. The cell was at one ear, her free hand sliding over her breasts, taking a short moment to get to know her ever-tightening nipples on a close, personal basis. She'd never been much for self-exploration, either the physical or mental kind, but honestly, it did have advantages. Being eight hundred miles away from sex could make you creative.

"Ashley, what are you doing?"

"Touching my breasts," she told him in a hushed voice. "I have very sensitive nipples, did you know that? Little buds that perk up at the slightest hint of a cool breeze, or a playful finger, or a hungry tongue."

"Oh, jeez."

"I wish you were here to see."

"I do, too. I didn't know my imagination was this vivid, but gawd, you wouldn't believe the stuff in my brain. I didn't even know I had this stuff in my brain until now."

"Do you like my breasts, David?"

"They're perfect. Soft and plump. I love the way they fill my hands."

She checked her breasts and smiled. "You have nice hands," she whispered, sliding her fingers down her body in a little dance. "I like when you touch me between my legs."

"You're touching yourself, aren't you? I'm a dead man. Tell me you're touching yourself. No, don't tell me." He coughed, his voice deeper, huskier, and she felt an answering shiver skim across her breasts, her skin. "Go ahead, I can take it."

"Now I'm touching myself. It's so nice and warm and comfortable. Taking all the time in the world." It was the hat, she kept telling herself. It was the hat that made her voice sound different, sensual, aroused…turning her on even more.

Her old quilted bedspread was soft against her bare skin, but it felt odd to be lying here in her room, naked, pleasuring herself. She'd always kept her love life, her sex life, separate from the house, spending the night out if she needed, but this felt forbidden.

David's voice urged her on, and her body responded as if he were there, as if they were his hands on her, not her own. Between her thighs, she was wet and swollen.

"I want you here. In Chicago. Touching me. Tasting me. Filling me."

"A plane… I could get on a plane…now."

"But then what would I do? That'd be…hours. No, I think you're going to have to talk me through this one."

To please her, he talked about her body, how he loved to plunge inside her. He told her that her skin was soft, the taste of honey against his tongue. As he spoke, her fingers danced with more talent than before. When he talked of her breasts, she heard awe. *Awe.* His words stroked over her, as surely as his hands, and her eyes drifted shut because she no longer wanted to stare at four walls. She wanted him in her head, taking her body.

His voice grew more ragged, his whispers more intimate, and when he took himself in hand, he told her, her fingers stroked even faster. Over the phone line, he couldn't see her blushing skin, or the way her feet dug into the covers, needing a place to hide.

There she lay, on her old bed, her fingers buried between her thighs. Her heart skipped forward, the beat of her blood matching each slide of her hand. He asked her to show him this when they were together, and she wondered whether she had the courage. She thought for a moment, smiled, and said yes. It was a stranger's voice that was talking, and her hand moved faster.

"I need to come, David," she breathed, and her hips rose, higher and higher, until she felt as if she were flying. Her hand tightened on the phone, and she could hear David, she could feel David.

*At last.*

"David?" she asked, because he had gotten so quiet.

"I think I died."

"I'm sorry," she said, apologizing for more than this.

"You shouldn't apologize so easily. I was a bastard." His voice was soft and warm, softer and warmer than her hand, softer and warmer than her old quilt, and she wished the sound of it wasn't quite so appealing. It made all the wants return, and as valiant as her hand was, as familiar as her quilt was, they were a poor imitation, and she knew it.

"Spoken like a man who just got his rocks off," she joked, because it would be two weeks—at least—before she saw him again.

"I'll call you when I set up the dinner," he continued, still in that same appealing tone. Ashley sighed as the wants returned.

"I miss you," she told him reluctantly.

"I miss you, too," he said. "I'll call tomorrow night."

Ashley hung up the phone and stood up to stare at the naked

woman in the mirror, wearing the floppy white hat and her heart on her sleeve.

This was the woman who hadn't drawn a paycheck in four years. This was the woman who was going to lure some of the brightest designers in the country to her boutique, as if it were some great privilege. And this was the woman who was going to have to introduce David to her family. More specifically, Val.

Ashley frowned because she hadn't wanted to go there yet. Val wouldn't like David. Ashley knew it. Actually, Val would be fine with him until she learned he lived all the way in New York City. Then she would hate him. And proceed to tell Ashley about it in many detailed lectures. Telling Ashley how he wasn't good enough for her, that she should hold out for someone better.

*I wouldn't do that.*

*Yes, you would.*

*Only because it's true.*

Sometimes families sucked.

# *11*

DAVID WAS HAPPY now that he knew about Ashley's sister. Not happy, as in, he was glad her sister is an alcoholic, but that was a better option than the thought of some man—Jacob?—calling her back to Chicago, and putting the wariness in her eyes. Ashley didn't realize that he couldn't stand to see her hurt. He wanted to protect her, to keep the wolves away, but he was too far away to do a great job of that. So, he had to trust her, to believe that she could manage on her own.

Still, that wasn't always enough, and sometimes he found himself calling her just to hear her voice, just to make sure. When he heard her breathy, nervous rambles, he would get instantly hard, feeling the insistent urge to plunge his cock inside her over and over again, while watching her face, that reckless mouth. She had no idea how much he thought about her, embedded between her thighs; if she did, it would probably scare her. Hell, it scared him, and he was a guy.

They didn't have phone sex again. He didn't ask, and she didn't ask, and since he wasn't sure if he would survive another night like that again, he was almost glad. Almost.

The ache in his cock, the tightness in his balls, kept him from thinking about Chris and Christine. Ashley did that. She made some of the hurt go away. The trip to Chicago was a few days from now, and he was excited, aroused and ready to punch his brother's face, all at the same time.

He would land in DC on Monday, then fly through

Oklahoma City on the trip back, but before he got to Chicago, he had one thing on his calendar. Lunch with Martina's ex, Barney Burdetti.

THEY MET AT Raw, a sushi place near Church. On a normal day, David wasn't a big fan of sushi, but today, it wasn't about sushi, it was about pretending to be Martina's perfect man. It wasn't that he wanted to be Martina's perfect man, it was merely that he wanted to teach the jackass that had cheated on her a lesson.

Martina's actual perfect man wasn't hugely tall, a couple of inches shorter than David, and his face had that pinched-fox look, that some women might have considered attractive. Whatever. And as he listened to Barney drone on about his accomplishments, talk about the multitudes of women in his life, David came to the realization that Barney was more clueless than most men.

They discussed the markets. Barney and David's friend Tony bitched about the slowdown, while David smiled, perhaps more arrogantly than he should, but hey, what the hell. And when Barney began to talk about how much he loved books, how he used to sleep with a hot little editor from midtown, David saw the opportunity he'd been waiting for.

"No, kidding, I've been seeing a lady in the book biz. I've always had a weakness for cool blondes. Tiny, with crystal blue eyes. God…" He wiped his brow. "Sorry, I just start thinking."

Tony nearly cracked up. "David works a little too hard. Sex does a number on his brain. He'll be cruising along at the gym, and then, boom, you can knock him out. I ask, what happened? He shrugs. Getting laid though, he gets more excited than most."

"She's good, huh?" asked the weasel.

"I don't like to talk about that."

Tony busted out laughing. "Since when?"

David glared.

Barney was intrigued. "You're among friends. You don't need to be shy."

"Nah, she's different," he said. "I mean, don't get me wrong, she definitely keeps me up at nights. All night, sometimes. Gawd, just the other night…" David trailed off meaningfully, sipped at his martini, and smiled as any well-satisfied man would.

Tony shook his head. "I think it's getting serious."

David nodded. "Right, she wants to settle down. She's only twenty-four, I told her that she was too young to think about that sort of thing, but her sister just had a kid, and now she's an aunt, and she goes on and on about little Jameson. Who names a kid after Irish whiskey? Apparently, in her family, they do."

David knew the exact moment that Barney started putting the pieces together. It was like watching gears click into place. He nodded slowly. "Sounds like she's thinking about marriage."

"Maybe," answered David, shrugging in a perfectly casual manner. "I don't know. I'm not ready. I got divorced a few years back, and I want to relax, sow some wild oats, plough some fields…"

The man leaned forward, waving his chopsticks like a drunken samurai. "You can't lead her on like that. What if she gets hurts? You can't hurt her," protested the guy who had slid a knife right through her heart. David frowned, and studied Barney more carefully, the pinched lines in his forehead, the anger in his eyes. When he'd first met this guy, he'd wanted to punch him in the face, but now…not so much. Did the man have a living, beating heart after all?

"I don't want to cause any problems," David began, watching Barney's face as he talked. Testing the waters. "Honestly, she hasn't said anything, so I'm probably assuming. But you know, a guy can't be too careful." He put an extra dose of jackass in his laughter just to see what Barney would do.

"She's probably just jumping into another relationship too fast. You know, I've seen women who break up with a guy, get their heart broken, and then boom, they stick to the next guy like glue."

"That could explain it."

"Has she said anything about this other guy?"

"What other guy," asked David innocently.

"The guy she just broke up with. I bet she's still hung up on him."

"I don't know."

"Well, what did she say?"

"Geez, Barney, don't get yourself so worked up here. David's a nice guy. He's not some shark among women," Tony said.

"Seems like an asshole to me."

David looked at him, hurt. This shouldn't be so much fun. "Hey, I don't know how I've offended you here. Let's change the subject."

"I want to know what she said."

"She's never mentioned another guy, okay. Why should you care?"

At that moment, Barney took a long sip of his drink and started lying his ass off. "It's happened to me before. I was seeing this woman who was talking about how special we were, and how things were so perfect, and I was thinking, hmm, maybe, and then suddenly, she mentions the guy she used to be in love with, the asshole she's still in love with, and before I know it, I show up at her apartment, and who's there?"

"The asshole," answered Tony.

"It's happened to you, too?"

"Nah, I just figured it out."

"So she really loved that guy? She went back to him?"

Barney nodded once.

"He must have loved her, too. In that asshole way of his," said David.

Tony laughed, and David shot him a look. Tony stopped laughing and shrugged. "I thought it was a joke. It was funny."

Lunch broke up shortly after that, Barney leaving with a thoughtful look in his eyes. As for David, he felt strangely...touched. Maybe the bastard loved her after all. Maybe next time the man wouldn't cheat. Maybe pigs would fly. But Martina seemed to have a thing for him, so who was he to judge?

He'd have to tell Ashley about this one. She would laugh, and maybe, she'd think a little better of him. She'd seen a lot of his bad sides, and not too many of the good.

"So, who's the babe?" asked Tony, as they headed toward the gym.

"Ashley," he answered.

"She's a book editor?"

David shook his head. "She owns clothing stores."

"You're doing a book editor, too?"

Tony was such a novice about some things. David rolled his eyes. "Nah, I made all that up."

Tony slapped him on the back. "You had me going. I was nearly hating you."

"We spar. I beat you. You can hate me again."

"You are one-hundred-percent triple-A asshole."

David grinned. "I know."

DAVID'S PLANE TO Chicago touched down six hours before they were supposed to have dinner with his ex-wife. Ashley was anxious to see him. To calm her nerves, instead of sitting bogged in traffic, she took the train to the airport and met him outside at the arrivals area. The sunglasses were to keep her eyes from giving away too much, but the hat gave away more than her eyes ever could. He saw her, grinned, and she started to laugh.

It felt so marvelous to laugh.

He flicked at the brim, took off her sunglasses and nodded once. "I will never look at this hat the same way again." Then he was kissing her, and she was kissing him back, and she wanted to laugh again. He did that. Made her happy inside. His mouth tasted like airplane coffee and too many lonely nights, and she could feel the hunger growing inside her. Fourteen days shouldn't have been that long for a woman who once had a dry spell last a year and a half. Now fourteen days was more than a lifetime. *And fourteen nights.* What she would give for fourteen nights with this man. Against her thigh, he was thick and more than ready, and she rubbed—only once because she wasn't that cruel. David groaned nicely.

"Where's your hotel?" she asked, because she wasn't that cruel, either.

He gestured toward the shuttle bus.

Ashley looked up, surprised. "Here? *Our* hotel? You got a room at O'Hare?"

He shrugged, a flush on his face. "I know. It's goofy. You don't need to remind me."

Something inside her melted to goo. She would have wagered he didn't have a romantic bone in his body. She would have lost. "I don't think it's goofy. I think it's cute."

"Cute? Oh, God. I don't want to be cute," he said, but his eyes held a dark liquid green that warmed her.

The shuttle was slow, the airport was packed, and the waiting was interminable. His hand crept out, his fingers curled around hers, and she didn't mind. The shuttle driver wanted to chat. He thought they were on a layover, headed to some tropical vacation spot for honeymooners.

"It was the hat," the driver told Ashley. "And you have that look."

She blushed, not wanting to blush, but doing it anyway. David was different. She was different. The world was different. Ashley told herself that it was a rehearsal for meeting Christine the bitch, when she would need to act the part of devoted lover, right now, though, there wasn't any acting involved.

When they got to the hotel, it was different, too. Oh, sure, they didn't get that far into the room, but this time, David lifted her, the hat falling helplessly to the ground. With his hips, he pinned her against the door, and she wrapped her legs around him like the hussy she was. One hand fisted with hers, holding it there between them. The other hand grabbed tight at her waist like an anchor. His mouth locked with hers, kissing her as if it'd been a lifetime since they'd been together. For three heartbeats he held her there, hands joined, mouths joined, and then she could feel the length of him, thick and hard between her thighs, and she wanted to be joined there as well.

"Hurry," she murmured against his mouth, her hips already starting to grind because she knew the fast rhythms of their sex. It was the rhythm of her blood, her heart.

David raised his head, stared into her eyes, and her body stilled. This was different.

His eyes were raw with passion and something far more damning. Today she could see herself reflected in his eyes. The way he saw her. The tenderness, the love simmering there. Today he was changing things. Since Miami, he had waited, but he wasn't a patient man, and she knew it. He wouldn't wait anymore. Truly, he didn't need to. The world was shifting, tilting, and it seemed appropriate that she wasn't standing on solid ground. No, her entire being was balanced solely on him.

Her blood bubbled with it, forgot the worries, forgot the doubts.

Ashley smiled.

Gently he feathered a kiss against the side of her mouth, pressed another to her lips, and then the hand at her waist slid down, lower, pulling her panties to one side, until there was a line of cotton cutting along her already overstimulated sex. The pain was exquisite, and she whimpered, pleading for him. At this moment, she was at his mercy.

Thankfully, he didn't make her wait long. His thrust was slow, stretching her, filling her, until she didn't dare move, didn't dare breathe, and she didn't dare look away from the insistent demand in his eyes. She worried that he was going to be the death of her, this stubborn man laying claim to her heart, but she was more worried that he was also going to be her life.

He was waiting, waiting for an answer. Slowly she pressed a single kiss to his mouth, it was the only answer she could give, and only then did he begin to move.

It wasn't supposed to turn out like this. Today he was so sure,

so gentle, so far removed from their usual overheated matings.
She'd never seen this side to him, he'd kept it too well hidden,
or maybe she hadn't wanted to see. Against her skin she could
feel the burn of his body. Strong thighs that would never let her
fall. Strong arms that held her easily.

Outside, the planes were taking off, roaring overhead,
defying gravity. Inside, the world was spinning out of control, defying gravity as well. It wasn't supposed to turn out
like this.

The shadows of the sun cast a dark flush on his skin, a drop
of sweat beading against his neck, and she licked it away,
tasting his salt, tasting him.

"I missed you," he whispered. The simple words pulled
at her heart.

"You make up for it nicely," she answered back, her body
moving so perfectly with his. There wasn't any humor in the
words. She had tried, she had failed.

His mouth nipped at the side of her mouth, once, twice, and
then he was kissing her again, and Ashley was lost. It was so
perfect it hurt.

Her free hand curled tighter around his neck, bringing him
close, bringing him deeper inside her. It was supposed to be a
long-distance affair. It was supposed to be hot and torrid. They
were supposed to have lost this passion once the newness
wore off, once she got to know him better. Oh, God, she liked
him even more.

David touched the corner of her eye with his mouth. "Don't
cry. I would never hurt you."

"I know."

He unlocked their hands, held her and took her to bed. Then
he bent and began to undress her. "I'm not going to take you
against the door," he said, and her shaking hands moved to the
buttons on his shirt, the fly of his pants, until he was bare. Thick
arms, a hard chest and a cock that jutted out impatiently. All hers.

He lifted her shirt over her head, slid her skirt down her

legs, exposing the thin gossamer of her bra and panties to his hungry gaze.

She expected a bold compliment, a lusty remark, but he didn't say a word, only the jerk of his sex betraying anything at all. Silently he moved over her, his mouth covering her breast through the thin silk. His lips pulled slow and hard, and her head fell back, her mind too drowsy with the feel of him, the scent of him, the touch of him.

Sure fingers tossed her bra aside before his mouth returned to hers. He used his tongue, his teeth, all to leisurely drive her insane. This intoxicating new rhythm was killing her. Her legs spread wide, wantonly wide, slid up and down the length of his and the fine curve of his ass, which only seemed to increase the heavy pressure of his lips.

Only once did he look at her. Her hand reached out, smoothed his hair, and she knew he was going to destroy her carefully ordered life.

Their eyes met, and then he lowered his head, proceeding to do just that.

It was a thorough seduction, coaxing her hands to wrap around his back, his waist. Eventually his mouth tarried lower, playing with the hollows of her belly, his fingers taking the band of her panties, pulling them down her legs, her skin burning, her nerves frayed.

His mouth followed, dallied too long between her thighs, and she whimpered, and then moaned, and fisted her hands in the blankets, dragging the covers apart.

In her entire life, Ashley had never been so thoroughly adored. There was no other word for it. He demanded so much from her, but he gave infinitely more. Now he knew her so well. He knew where to touch, where to tease, his hands soothing her hips, as he loved her so carefully.

The hotel room felt like magic this day. The orange covers shimmered to gold, the late afternoon sunlight glistened against the walls like pearl. The thundering jets outside were only matched by the silent thundering of her heart. He took her hand, joined it with his and brought her entwined hand to his mouth. Then he slipped inside her, and quietly she gasped.

*I love you.*

She didn't want to say the words, but they tumbled out before she could stop them.

"Good," he whispered, and took her mouth once more.

Afterwards, when he had decimated the last of the feeble denials in her heart, he pulled her to him, and she stayed curled there. When she was this close, she could smell the crisp musk of his cologne, so slight, so subtle, mixed with the heady scent of David. Her nose tickled with the scent, with the crisp hair on his chest, and she wanted to stay here all day. To watch the moon play silver on his dark hair, to watch the sun bloom across his skin, to watch the rise of his breath as he slept. She'd never watched him sleep. They never had the chance. Tonight she would watch him sleep.

Under her hand, his heart was steady and strong. He didn't speak, and she was glad there were no probing questions, no insistent pushes. Not now, not today. Maybe he knew he had already won, and she had never clued in they were locked in a battle. It was the way of her life. Too much awareness, one day too late.

So they both lay there, not speaking to each other, not looking at each, not bearing to be too far apart. The minutes ticked past, until his watch beeped once.

"We need to go," he told her. "The train leaves in half an hour."

Ashley nodded, and slipped on her clothes. "David?" she asked. The room was heavy with so much left unsaid. Normally, it wasn't her way to ask; normally, it was his way to tell, and these new rules muddled her head.

He buttoned his shirt, and came to her side, not touching her, but his eyes were the softest shade of green. "Let's get through this. We'll figure it out. I'm a smart man, did you know that? You should know that."

She smiled, slipped her hand in his, and nodded once.

# *12*

---

THEY TOOK THE Northwest line to Norwood Park. Not one of the most monied neighborhoods in Chicago, but a nice one with trees and tidy lawns. One for blue-collar families who shopped at Sears, not at boutiques, and Ashley wondered about Christine's new life. This wasn't tony Manhattan. Not by a long shot. Ashley dropped the bitch label, only because now she felt a tiny bit sorry for Christine.

As the train rumbled along the tracks, and the clock ticked closer to six, David grew more and more still. The locked jaw was back, the shoulders were so straight she swore he'd grown five inches, and his eyes had turned to ice. He wore a jacket and tie, as if this were business, rather than personal, but as a woman who donned bunny slippers and floppy hats in order to buck up her courage, she understood.

"It'll be fine," she told him, with an encouraging smile.

The smile he gave her was tight, and not so fine, as he vacantly stared out the window.

*He's a coward. I knew it. Can't take facing a little woman. What sort of man is that?*

*Shut up, Val. You're not going to do this to me.*

*He's still hung up on her. That's the problem. Get over him, Ash.*

Ashley wished that David would talk, if only so she wouldn't have to listen to Val's voice in her head. It was a few blocks from the station to the house, but Ashley didn't mind. The warm summer air was cool, and she made one-sided small talk, trying to ignore the pebble that was fast turning into a boulder in the pit of her stomach.

The house was in a long line of homes that sat behind Kennedy Expressway. The noise of the cars was constant. There was a neat yard, lined with bright yellow and pink flowers, and a Subaru parked in the drive. As they approached the door, it opened, and a lady walked out. Tall, elegant, dressed in jeans and a sweater that was the pure vibrancy of Carolina Herrera. Possibly secondhand, but still jazzy. This woman was exactly what the name Christine implied, but she was smiling and waved happily, as if this were old home week. Whatever.

What was odd was David's reaction to her. His smile grew less cold, his shoulders relaxed and while the greetings were still somewhat stilted, it wasn't nearly as bad as what Ashley had anticipated. Apparently, it wasn't nearly as bad as what he had anticipated, either.

"Come inside. Chris is out back, working on the lawnmower. It breaks down weekly."

And she left David for a man who drove a Subaru, and whose lawnmower broke down weekly? Okay, Christine was just flat-out stupid, thought Ashley, because there was judgmental and then there was factually correct.

The house was tiny, a living room with dark paneling, a kitchen that was tidy, but locked back in the '70s. However, Christine had left a mark. The artwork was top-notch, and there were fresh flowers in every room. In fact it was so nice that Ashley began to relax, David began to relax. Everything was fine until the man walked in through the back door, and then the locked jaw returned, the shoulders tensed, and David's smile was gone like the wind. He didn't even try to pretend to be polite. Ashley stared, confused.

"David," the man said.

"Chris," David answered with a tight nod. Then he seemed to remember his manners. "This is Ashley. Ashley, David, Christine."

Chris was nearly as tall as David, with dark hair and hazel eyes. Obviously Christine stayed to a certain physical type. "My brother hasn't said anything about you," Chris said, taking Ashley's hand, shaking it in a gentlemanly way. Exactly like David.

*His brother?* Ashley froze, removing all traces of anything from her face.

Christine, exquisite hostess that she was, broke the silence. "Let's go to the living room. Ashley, would you like something to drink?"

"I'd love one, thanks."

"What do you drink?"

"Whatever you have." Tonight wasn't the night to be picky.

The inside of the house was tastefully shabby. The furniture wasn't new, no Ethan Allen here, but it was obvious that Christine had a good eye. Apparently two. *Oh, God.*

Ashley finally dared to look at David. He should have told her this. He should have prepared her, but unfortunately, David was too preoccupied with not looking at his brother.

Oh, God.

Ashley took a seat on the couch, David followed, and she grabbed his hand, her fingers digging into his flesh, not as much in anger as panic. They would get through this, they would get through this. If she repeated it often enough, it would be true.

Christine, bless her, started to talk, and it took a moment for Ashley to register that she was talking to her.

"So, how long have you and David been seeing each other? I mean, coming all the way from New York. That sounds fun, honestly. But serious, too." Then she shot David a relieved look. "I'm glad to see it."

So Christine assumed that Ashley lived in New York, near David. It would be easier if Christine thought that, rather than trying to explain that Ashley didn't live in New York. The whole plane thing. The whole travel thing. Ashley opened her mouth.

"Ashley lives here. We met on a plane." David obviously didn't intend to keep things simple.

"You met on a plane to Chicago? Today?" Christine looked shocked, and Ashley started to explain, but David got there first.

"No, it was a while back. It works for us," David said curtly, and that was one way to end that conversation.

Chris sat silently, sipping his beer. Christine, still polite, bless her heart, was not deterred. "So, what do you do, Ashley?"

"I own some boutiques in town. Ashley's Closet. Naperville, State Street, Wicker Park, Lakeview. I'm in fashion," she added stupidly.

"I haven't heard of it, but I love to shop," said Christine, completely unnecessarily.

"You should visit," answered Ashley, completely unnecessarily.

"I will," Christine replied, and Ashley prayed she was only being polite.

Meanwhile, David and Chris hadn't said a word. Ashley glanced at David and then smiled at Christine. "Do you mind if I go outside for a minute? I get a little claustrophobic sometimes. I have so many phobias, sometimes I can't keep track. David, can you come with me?"

He flew off the couch, and they walked briskly outside, down the three steps to stand under the lone elm tree in the yard.

"You're claustrophobic?"

"No," she said, leaning back against the hard, stabilizing bark of the tree. She needed support right at that moment.

"I'm sorry," he blurted, and while she had been ready to give him a large piece of her mind for dumping her in this unprepared, the apology stopped it at once.

She pulled once at his tie. "I'll live. Will you?"

David nodded once, but his eyes still hurt, and now she knew why. It wasn't Christine that had sliced him in two. It was his brother. She couldn't imagine the betrayal, but the pain she understood all too well. With a husband or a wife, you could sign a paper, and they were no more. With a brother, or a sister, the pain cut deeper, the anger more cold. It was blood.

Ashley didn't like to think about the years that Val had drank herself into oblivion. It was so much easier to pretend it had never happened. Apparently David dealt with his pain the same way.

Not caring who was watching, Ashley slid her hands around his neck, and kissed him. His broad arms wrapped around her like a lifeline, and she liked being needed. He'd bailed her out a few times, for once, she could return the favor. He rested his forehead against her own. "I'm sorry," he repeated.

"You have nothing to be sorry about. We'll get through it." Then she would chop his brother into small pieces, but that would be left for another day. And honestly, she did like Christine. The woman was back to being a bitch, albeit a stupid bitch, because she had picked the wrong brother, but Ashley wasn't about to complain.

"Are you okay?" she asked.

"I'm fine."

"Should I kill him for you?"

He laughed, a rough, awkward sound, but it tugged at Ashley's heart just the same. "You'd commit capital murder for me?"

"In a heartbeat."

"I love you, Ash."

She grabbed his hand and squeezed, and they went back to confront the evil bitch of an ex-wife and David's back-stabbing son-of-a-bitch brother.

*He's calling you Ash? That's my nickname. I don't like him, Ash. I don't trust him.*

Ashley smiled at David, pushing the voice aside for now. Sometimes procrastination could be a very useful thing.

FOR DAVID, it was four hours in the bowels of hell, but he survived, and actually by the end of the night, he had talked with Chris about the apartment, and they agreed to split the proceeds in half. David didn't feel the need to be petty anymore. Ashley did that to him—kept him from being juvenile and vindictive.

The anger was still there, the rage, but it didn't burn so hot anymore.

In the last four years, Chris had changed some. There was a cut of gray in his hair that hadn't been there before, and there were neat lines bracketing his mouth, but when Chris looked at Christine, there was something in his eyes that should have made David hurt, but didn't. Maybe he should have visited here earlier, he wasn't sure, but he was here now.

Okay, they would never be as close as they had been, but maybe…

As the evening went on, Ashley stuck to him like glue. Almost—dare he say it?—flagrantly possessive. It surprised him, that protective streak within her. He'd never seen it before, except maybe once, when she took off from Miami to find her sister. It was just one more reason that he loved her. Every time he was with her, he found new reasons to love her. New things about her that pleased him, comforted him. He'd never thought about needing someone. In a lot of ways, he hadn't needed Christine, but at that time, David didn't need anyone. He was so sure that he owned the world.

Now he knew better. Now he knew that he could need.

With Ashley, things would be different. Ashley loved David. David loved Ashley, and he was going to do everything in his power to make this permanent. She'd love it in New York. All he had to do was convince her to move with whatever means necessary, and David was nothing if not creative.

He found her eyes, Christine was showing her the latest in art deco vases, and Ashley moved across the room, coming to sit on the arm of his chair. "You about ready to go?" he asked, because he'd done his duty, he'd made his peace. All he wanted to do now was get back to the hotel, bury himself deep inside Ashley and make up for fourteen days lost.

*She loved him.*

Her smile was slow and wicked, and made him catch his breath. Suddenly, he couldn't wait to leave.

"Let's call a cab," he suggested.

"You don't want to take the train back?" she asked, and obviously people in Chicago weren't as efficient about their transportation as New York.

David leaned closer, pitched his voice low, but he didn't care who heard, he was more interested in tasting the side of Ashley's neck. Right below her ear, where the skin felt like silk. "We're not far. The cab will be faster."

Ashley, his wonderful Ashley, jumped up from her seat and clapped her hands together. "All right. I bet you guys have to get up early tomorrow. I know I do." She took Christine's hand, pumped once. "Great to meet you. Come by the store." Then she looked at David, her smile falling a few points. "It was nice to meet some of David's family. I can see the resemblance. You're lucky to have him."

Chris stared at the carpet, and after one phone call and ten minutes of waiting, the cab honked outside, and thank God, that was over.

Christine waved them off as if everyone were the best of friends.

Once Ashley and David were safely in the cab, speeding away from Christine and Chris and Norwood Park, David dove in and took Ashley's lips. She curved into his arms, her mouth opening, her tongue teasing his. He shouldn't be making out in the backseat of a cab, but these were desperate times, and he was a desperate man. Her fingers grabbed his thigh, moved higher to cover the bulge at his fly, and began to move in the most supremely confident way.

Oh, hell, yes. "Tell me you're going back to the hotel with me."

Ashley slapped the seat, not the reaction he wanted. "Crap. I need to call home. They don't know where I am." Quickly she plucked her phone from her purse and punched in a number, and David sat silently willing his cock to be patient.

"Val, hey, it's me. Listen, I got tied up at the store. It's going to be late. I probably won't make it home tonight."

*At the store?*

"I know, it's a pain. I hate inventory."

*He was inventory? It was the middle of June. Who did inventory in the middle of the month? She didn't need to lie about this. And if she was going to lie, she needed a better lie.*

"No, no, I don't need your help. I've got the staff here. We'll finish up, and I'll just sack out in the back. No need to worry. How was your day…? Excellent. Give Brianna and Mom a kiss, and I'll see you in the morning."

She clicked off the phone and David told himself it didn't matter. Then he promptly asked her, "Why didn't you tell them?"

Yeah, it mattered.

Carefully she shrugged. "They don't need to know."

There was something strange in her face, something evasive, and it bothered him that she needed to keep their relationship secret, as if there were something wrong with it. There was nothing wrong with it, and everything right with it.

Still, she was an adult, she knew her family better. He should let her handle it the way she needed to handle it.

And still he couldn't shut up. All right, it bothered him. He wanted to be understanding and sensitive, and all those "good" qualities, but he wasn't. She had told him that he didn't like to admit things, so fine, he admitted things. It bothered him. He turned to Ashley and tried to reason. "You're an adult now, so who cares? It's no big deal. If you don't tell them, it makes it a big deal. You should say something, Ashley. Tell her the truth."

"I'll do it when the time is right," she told him, which did nothing to make him feel better. In fact, it only made it worse. "I just wanted to get through tonight…and we did."

"Yeah," he said, and he settled her against his shoulder. "We got through it."

Still she didn't relax. He could feel the tension in her shoulders, her neck. He only wished she would trust him to fix what was wrong with their being together. He could, he knew he could. All he had to do was convince her family he was the perfect man. A challenge? He was up for it. For Ashley, he would do anything.

WHEN THEY GOT BACK to the hotel, Ashley felt oddly unprepared. He loved her, she loved him. Okay, fine, now what were they supposed to do about it? The first second he entered the room, he put away his jacket, and pulled at his tie. Ashley blinked twice, noting what was obviously his evening ritual. How odd; she had never known. Fascinated, she sat in the black leather desk chair, and watched David proceed with his life. He was heading to the bathroom before he noticed.

"What?" he asked.

"This is new."

He thought for a second. "It is. I like it. You like it?"

"I do."

"Good," he said, wandering off to the bathroom.

Eventually he poked his head around the corner of the room. "You didn't bring pajamas, did you?"

And he was nervous. "No."

"Okay. I'm fine with that."

She thought for a second. "David, do you sleep in pajamas?"

"Not since the divorce, but I'm usually alone. I packed some tonight."

"Why?" she asked, because she wanted to understand how his mind worked. It was a mystery all unto itself.

"It seemed rude not to," he explained.

Ashley giggled. "Now you get shy?"

"I'm not shy. It just doesn't seem right. What if you get offended or something? Women and men, they're different. They think about things differently."

She curled her feet up under her. "Yeah?"

"Fine. Laugh at me, but I'm telling you, there're men who aren't so sensitive." He pushed at his hair, and the cowlick reared up in the back. "Do you mind if I check in with the office? I'm expecting an answer on something. It won't take more than two to three minutes."

Ashley shook her head. "I don't mind."

He unbuttoned his shirt and pulled the laptop from his case and settled down to work. While he sat there, she watched him contentedly. She'd never seen him work before. His eyes were always moving, and he was fast on the keys, his fingers flying, which didn't surprise her at all. She'd seen those fingers in action—on her.

He hadn't been kidding about the time. No more than three minutes later, he shut the lid and stowed the computer away. "Thanks. We're in the middle of earnings season. It's a zoo."

Then he held out his hand, sat down on the bed, legs splayed and pulled her between them. "Thank you for staying."

"Well, you're in my town. It's the least I can do."

He kissed her once. "I appreciate it." Then his mouth moved to her neck, tickling her with his stubble. She giggled and he raised his head. "Do you want me to shave? I can shave."

"No, I like it." And she liked this. He was new, too. Strange to see such an arrogant man so unsure about domesticity. Domesticity. She had been worried about it, now it sounded like bliss. She settled in between his thighs. "How was it tonight?" she asked, when his mouth returned to nuzzle her neck.

"Fine."

Ashley sighed, frustration and pleasure mixed together in one disjointed sound. "You don't have to tell me 'fine.' I was there. It was miserable. I want to know how you were feeling."

He raised his head. "Can we not talk about my feelings?"

And now he was ruining all her fantasies of what domestic bliss should entail. "Why don't you want to talk about your feelings? I like talking about your feelings."

Long, efficient fingers worked the buttons on her shirt. "I

think you secretly delight in other people's misery. You're a closet sadist."

"How did you know?"

"It was the beady gleam in your eyes that gave you way, Marquise de Sade," he told her, then he took her blouse and hung it up in the closet, right next to his jacket. David McLean was a tidy man. She liked that. She liked having a man to pick up her socks, not that she would throw down her socks, but it was comforting to know that if she did, he wasn't too proud to pick them up.

She stood, stripping off her pants, a straight-line pair that she had bought from a tiny shop in Galena. They were elegant, looked pricey and wrinkled like the devil. She handed them to him, just to test her theory. "I don't have beady eyes," she told him, watching as he headed for the closet.

Ashley grinned when he returned and his hands lifted her face to the light. "Let me see. Definitely beady. Shifty even."

His fingers unhooked the clasp on her bra, his hands gliding over her breasts, his sigh pure male satisfaction, like a cold beer in August, or a win in extra innings. For a moment, she surrendered to the lovely idea of being the cause of said satisfaction, but there were bigger things to consider. Namely, whether passion and domesticity could be wrapped up in one package. "You know what's on TV tonight?"

"I admit I didn't check." He shucked the last of his clothes, began to put them all away, and as she studied the irrefutable evidence of his arousal, she realized that yes, passion and domesticity could coexist nicely.

"The original *Halloween* is on television. Can we watch it?"

He turned, hanger in hand, wearing only a disconcerted frown. It was truly a lovely picture. "I'm in town for twenty-four hours, and you want to watch television?"

Ashley considered pointing out the three minutes that he had spent working on his computer, but decided that would be small of her. "Stay another day," she offered instead, laying out on the bed, a not-so-virginal sacrifice clad only in a demure scrap of innocent white silk.

David took a long, hard look, considered the offer, scratched the dark stubble at his jaw. "I'd have to juggle things."

"Juggle. You're a good juggler," she told him, watching with a pleased smiled as he climbed into bed. "Besides, we have to talk to Horatio Moore tomorrow. He's the guy in Wicker Park."

"Oh, God. I had forgotten," he said, stretching out next to her.

"Already you've forgotten your mission?" Ashley tsked, her avid gaze wandering over the exquisite easy-to-wear lines of his body. Highlighting the collection were strong, masculine arms that were never too big, never too rough. The broad chest was iconically male, accentuated by two sharply defined whirls of hair that trailed low in a fanciful temptation that drew the eye lower still. The long, lean legs were an eye-pleasing frame to an ass that belonged in a Calvin Klein ad. Completing the look was the bold design of his cock, long and thick with classical styling, the perfect combination of both form and function.

He made her silly with lust. Her nipples perked, her demure scrap of white lace now thoroughly damp. As an analyst who evaluated things daily, David noticed…and caught her wrists, pulling her closer. "My only mission is to pleasure you."

"Then you have to stay another day," she insisted, and he slid the demure scrap down her legs, tossing it over the side of the bed. Obviously there were limits to his orderly nature.

Her mouth grew dry with anticipation. He sat up against the headboard, pulled her back against him, skin to skin, and his hands traced over her breasts, flirting with her thighs. "I'm supposed to be in San Jose tomorrow."

"San Jose?" She blew a raspberry. "They don't deserve you. Chicago deserves you."

"I can be persuaded," he said gallantly, and against her back, the long ridge of his erection bucked in agreement.

With lazy eyes she watched them in the mirror, his body

blocked by hers, except for the warm hands cupping her breasts, the unwavering thumbs at her nipples that stoked a pulse between her legs. "I accept that challenge," she offered, brave words from a woman being steadily seduced into submission.

His mouth played with her neck, her ear, and she cocked her head to one side. "Introduce me to your family," he whispered, and instantly she stiffened.

"Not this time. Maybe next."

"Scared?" he asked, his mouth still against her neck, but his hands were still.

"No."

"Yes?"

"Yes," she admitted, her posture hardening from happily distracted hussy to not quite so stupidly distracted anymore.

David's busy hands resumed their task, and Ashley relaxed again. "You don't have to be. Honestly, I'm not that intimidating."

"It's not you I'm worried about."

"Who are you worried about?" he asked, showing an apparent fascination for the sensitive skin below her ear. Happy sensitive skin.

"It's Val. She won't like you."

In the mirror, she could see the stubborn lock to his jaw. "And why not?" he protested. "Come on, that's ridiculous. I'm nice. I'm polite, even chivalrous at times. I can bring you to orgasm six, seven times a night, and God knows, that should count for something."

"It merely says I'm easy," she told him, opening her glistening thighs to illustrate the point—and perhaps distract him as well.

David wasn't that easily sidetracked. "Why won't she like me, Ash?"

"She's just quirky," she said, pulling away, turning her back on the inviting picture in the mirror, and this time, David didn't seem to object.

"Does she like any of the men you go out with?"

"I haven't dated a lot. The stores have kept me busy. It was just easier that way."

"Is this going to be a problem? If it is, I'd rather know about it."

He talked as if everything was so simple. And if she admitted to him that it was going to be a problem—which she did—what did he expect to happen? What did he think he could do about it? Ashley couldn't fix the problem. David couldn't fix the problem. Only Val could fix the problem, and she was trying. Honestly, she was trying.

"Is this going to be a problem?" he asked again, and she knew it wasn't Val he was asking about. It was more a question of whether Ashley would have a problem if Val had a problem.

"Like the issue with your brother, and how you told me about that one?" she shot back, avoiding the answer nicely.

David ran his hand over his face. "Exactly like that one. Damn, you're going to make me talk, aren't you? Fine. You want to know, I'll tell you. Tonight wasn't so bad. Christine didn't faze me at all. At first, I wanted to hit him, not because of what he did to her, but what he did to me."

After that, he shut his mouth tightly, as if he had fulfilled all obligations of discussing his feelings. Not by a long shot. Ashley was diving in.

She pulled a pillow from the bed, and lay on her stomach, her feet kicking up in the air. "Were you two close? Has he always been in Chicago?"

She could feel his eyes touch on her ass, but he didn't reach for her. Obviously passion and domesticity could exist, but passion and families couldn't. Made perfect sense to her. "They moved here after the divorce. He said they needed a fresh start. He was right."

"He loves her," she said softly.

He gave her a cold look. "I don't care. That's his business."

"Sorry. Tell me what it was like growing up. You never talk about that."

"Well, since all of my memories involved my brother, I didn't want to talk about it."

Past tense. She noticed. "You could now?"

David thought, mulled it over and pulled her back against him. His hands moved over her, not as much to seduce her, as to soothe him. She didn't mind. She liked that she could do that. Soothe him. "I can talk now."

And he did. He told her about the time that Chris had skipped school to go to the Yankees game, and David had lied for him. But then their mother had found out, and they were both grounded for two weeks, which David thought was tremendously unfair since he hadn't skipped school. He told Ashley about the Christmas that their father had taken them camping up at Lake George, and Chris had told David that the shadow creeping in the darkness toward their tent was a bear—not a raccoon. All his life, he and his brother had been together, until one day they weren't. Families shouldn't be split apart like that; it wasn't right. Someone always ended up hurting, and in this case, it was David.

After he finished all that talking, he looked at Ashley and smiled. "You know, I'm sensing a trend. All my life, my brother has given me the crappy end of the stick."

She covered his hands with her own. "Except with Christine. You are so lucky to be rid of her," she told him.

His fingers slid lower, tempting, tempting… "You're jealous, aren't you?"

"Am not." One long finger slid inside her, and Ashley's back arched high in relief.

"I don't mind. I think it's kind of sexy," he said, his thumb finding her most suggestive spot, and circling there, until she forgot about planes, forgot about television, forgot about her sister, and focused on nothing but the insistent torment of his hand.

In the mirror, she saw them together, saw the heavy darkness of his eyes, saw the swollen flush of her body milking his hand, and for the first time in her life, she saw herself come.

Later, her lungs remembered to breathe, and she turned her head to kiss him. When kissing wasn't enough, she turned in his arms and slid over him, her lips tasting the skin of his chest, sampling the taut lines of his abs, and then, with serious intent, she slid lower, her hands sizing his cock.

"What about the movie?" he asked curiously.

"Maybe later," she told him, before her mouth closed over him. There was domesticity, and then there was stupid.

# *13*

EARLY THE NEXT MORNING, before the sun even thought about getting up, the airplanes resumed roaring overhead. David didn't open his eyes. He simply lay there, with Ashley curled up, half on the bed, half on him. It was pretty much the best blanket ever. Airplanes weren't so bad. They had given him this.

For a few minutes he stayed there, not daring to move, sure this was all a dream. Her leg stirred, sliding against his own, and his cock really didn't care if it was a dream or not. Gawd, he was a goat.

Her head was pillowed on his chest, and he pushed back the hair from her face. He had thought she was the weak one, vulnerable, letting everyone walk over her. David was wrong about that. Yesterday, she'd gotten him through the worst dinner in his life. He shouldn't wake her, he should let her sleep, but this was his last day. He never told her how hard it was to leave. He didn't even tell her that he was thinking about moving to Chicago. It wasn't a bad town. They had banks, they had the Chicago Board of Trade. No, it wasn't New York, but Chicago had one very important thing that New York didn't. Ashley Larsen. The woman he loved.

He couldn't help but sigh.

The outside lights filtered in through the sheers, casting the room in a dim glow, and Ashley lifted up on one elbow, sleepy eyes met his own.

"Good morning," she said. "Welcome to O'Hare, the airport that never sleeps."

"Hmm," he answered, kissing her once, pulling her fully on top of him, then burying his face against her hair. He liked the soft smell of it, one more thing New York didn't have. "I'm sorry we didn't get to watch the movie."

"No, I think my movies will always lose out to your sex. I can read the writing on the wall."

He lifted his head to stare at her. "*My* sex?"

"Fine. *Our* sex."

"I like that. Our sex." His head fell back again, and he stroked her arm. The condoms were on the nightstand within reach. If he just stretched…

"You want to go see my stores?"

He lifted his head, squinted. "Now?"

"No, this morning. We meet with Horatio at two. We have lots of time."

David looked at the box of condoms, examined the valley between her bare breasts. Come on, this was important to her. This was her dream, and all he could think about was sex? Hours and hours of sex? That was his dream. But no, this wasn't about David, this was about Ashley.

"Sure," he told her, even managing to smile.

"We don't have to," she said, obviously sensing his hesitation, or perhaps the morning wood that was happily finding its home between her thighs.

"No. I want to," he insisted, now feeling extreme guilt. But she was naked. And her nipples were starting to go dark and pouty, and her eyes were laughing at him.

He watched as she reached for a condom. "We could do both."

"Both?" he asked innocently.

She took the packet in her teeth and ripped. His eyes narrowed. She did that on purpose.

"It won't take long," she answered, busy fingers at work.

"It might," he shot back.

"I'm talking about the stores," she said, and he felt less guilt mainly because she was impaling herself on him and thus, guilt was impossible.

"I want to see them. I really do. I'm here. We should—" she lowered herself in one sharp move "—see them."

David couldn't speak if he tried.

Her arms slid up his chest, curled around his neck, and oh, damn, he was staring down the valley of her breasts once again.

"Later," she said, kissing him, riding him, pleasing him.

THEY ENDED UP sleeping through the morning runway traffic. David knew the right thing to do was wake her up, then they could get dressed and he'd see Ashley's Closet in person. His hands curled over her shoulder and shook her awake. Sleepy eyes looked at him.

He was definitely moving to Chicago.

"We should go."

"Okay," she murmured, and then promptly fell back against his chest.

He propped her up a bit. "I want to see your stores, Ashley. It's important."

"We can sleep."

"We can sleep tonight. You should get up." If she didn't get up now, they weren't leaving, and then he would not be the supportive man he wanted her to see. Last night, he wasn't watching her movies, now they weren't visiting her stores.

"Hmm…"

David flew out of bed before he could change his mind. "I'm going to take a shower," he announced, eyeing the silky skin of her back, the way her ass bumped high in her sleep. That bump was so cute, so curvy, so intensely…inviting. He could just fit into that bump. "I'm going to take a cold shower."

She rolled over, and David froze. The ass was safely stowed away, but now there were breasts. A shadowy triangle of hair beckoned between her thighs. Perfect thighs. He could sense his willpower disappearing. "You're not being fair to me. You know, first the movie, now this. I'm trying to be good. I'm trying to show you I'm not a horndog. You're killing the image, Ashley."

She threw a pillow at his head.

"I'm taking my shower," he stated for the record, turning his eyes away from the bed.

The box on the nightstand torpedoed soon after, condoms flying out like rain.

Obviously Ashley Larsen wasn't a morning person.

David turned on the shower and smiled.

God, he loved her.

THE SOUND OF the shower killed her libido, and Ashley sighed. Oh, fine. She flung her legs over the side of the bed and raked her hand through her tangled hair. When she moved to stand, her legs wobbled—only for a second. But she and David didn't have long. One more day.

Not quite in her happy place, she trudged to the bathroom, ready to hit the bracing spray, and maybe seduce David in the process. Halfway to the door, the phone rang.

It was Val.

"I have a problem."

Ashley sank back on the bed, and clutched a pillow to her chest. "What sort of problem?"

"I'm sorry."

"Don't apologize, Val. Just tell me what's wrong."

"I didn't know."

"You do know. Tell me."

There was a long silence and Ashley waited. "I wrote some hot checks. I thought I had more money in my account, and Brianna needed some new clothes for school, and I knew payday was coming up."

"How much?" she asked.

"About seven hundred dollars."

"You spent seven hundred dollars on clothes for a little girl?" Ashley swallowed. For a sober Val, that was a lot of money.

"I knew you'd be mad," Val whispered, and Ashley could hear the panic in her voice.

"I'm not mad."

"You're mad, Ash."

"I'm not mad."

"Where are you? I called the stores. You lied to me. Why are you lying to me?"

"We don't need to worry about this now. One thing at a time, right? Where's Brianna?"

Ashley looked up, found David leaning against the wall, hair wet, a towel wrapped around his hips. His eyes were waiting to see what she would do. The hard bent in his jaw said he thought she would cave. A test. Ashley hated tests.

"She's at school. Mom's at work. I didn't tell her. She'll worry. You can help me, right?"

"I can't help you now, Valerie." Coolly she met his eyes. *There. See? She could do it.*

"You don't understand, Ash. They called and wanted me to come down. They told me it was a special sale. It was a trap. So here I am at the mall, and they aren't happy with me. They're going to call the cops."

*Cops? Oh, God.* "They don't call the cops for bad checks."

"They do if there's more than one bad check."

*There was no way that Val could get out of this on her own.* Ashley looked at David. *No, Val could get out of this on her own.* "Valerie, I'm not going to do this." Her voice was firm, unwavering, as steady as the hard line of his jaw.

"Please."

"No," she answered, her voice not quite so steady.

"You can't leave me hanging like this." Now Val was doing the angry-pleading thing, and Ashley had never responded well to that. She didn't like it when people were mad at her, she didn't like it when she felt guilt. Feeling both at the same time was guaranteed to kick her butt.

"I have some business to take care of," she stated, not letting her butt get kicked.

"You're with somebody, aren't you? You're out fucking some guy, and you don't give a damn about me. I need you."

Slowly Ashley's gaze drifted away from David. "I can't do this right now."

At that, Val hung up.

"Problem?" That was David. Master of the obvious.

"No. No problem," she replied.

Five seconds later, the phone rang again. David looked at the phone, looked at Ashley. Ashley waited, but then eventually jabbed the talk button with a lot of extra force. She was going to tick somebody off here. If it wasn't Val, it'd be David. But David was the tough one. Val, not so much.

"Yes?"

"I'm sorry, Ashley. I don't mean to yell at you. I don't know what to do. I don't have seven hundred dollars."

She couldn't look at him. Not now. When she looked at him, she couldn't focus, couldn't concentrate, and she needed to keep her wits about her. "You get paid on Monday?"

"Yes. I just need a little money until then. And you might need to talk to these people."

"Where are you at?" Ashley asked, defeat in her voice.

"Nordstrom."

*Nordstrom.* Yes, when it came to her daughter, Val spared no expense. "I'll be there in about an hour."

"Could you get here any sooner than that? You know I don't handle this stuff well."

"It'll be an hour. I need to get my car."

"Thanks, Ash. I'd be dead without you."

When she hung up, she tried to smile at David.

"Are you okay?" he asked.

Anger would be so much better than sympathy. If he was

angry, she could be mad at him for being angry. With sympathy, there wasn't a lot she could do except analyze her own shortcomings, and wonder if she was doing the right thing. The only problem seemed to be that there never was a right or a wrong thing. There was only two wrongs. Ashley sighed. "I'll be fine."

"You're going to go?"

"Yeah." It wasn't the answer he wanted, and she knew it.

"Do you want me to come with you?"

She stared balefully. "I don't think it'd be smart."

"No, probably not. What about Horatio?"

"Who?"

"The designer guy."

"Damn."

"Want me to reschedule for you? Might as well do something useful."

"No. I can make it there by two. Don't worry about it." She met his eyes, wished she could read his mind. "Are you mad at me?"

"No. I could never get mad at you. Sometimes I get mad for you, but that's a different thing."

"Thank you."

"Don't mention it. You should tell your sister about us. She might actually think twice about calling."

"I will. It's just not the right time."

"There won't be a right time, will there?"

*There never is, Ash. Never will be.*

*I don't need to hear this, Val.*

*That's you, not me. All you, sis.*

"I have to go," she told David, and then quietly, efficiently, she got dressed. She'd had enough of that voice in her head. She'd hear the live version later, and that wouldn't be as easy to shut out.

DAVID WAITED FOR Ashley until one-fifty, by which time he decided that she wasn't going to show up for her meeting with the designer. Four times he had called, not wanting to interrupt, not wanting to yell, but merely to know if he should reschedule the damn meeting.

Four times she didn't answer.

Finally, realizing that Ashley wouldn't be there, he made a command decision to see Horatio himself, betting on a large position of negative consequences with absolutely no capital to back it up. In the biz this was appropriately named "naked short."

Maybe she'd be mad, maybe she'd be happy, but at this point, somebody needed to worry about her livelihood, and apparently it wasn't her.

Hell.

It wasn't that he was angry at her. He wanted to help her, make her life easier, fix things. When he got frustrated, anger seemed to be the emotion du jour, and in this case there was no one to receive that anger, except for one poor client from the vinyl flooring company, and honestly, if it had been some other company, he wouldn't have lashed out, but today, he didn't have the patience for anything.

He took a cab to Wicker Park, finding the shop on a well-trod street of one-named shops and understated bars. There was money here. It was there in the window displays and the polished signage. But the neighborhood was not built on flashy cosmopolitan dollars. This was "I'm too cool to be rich" money.

David opened the glass door to the shop, and stepped inside, only it wasn't a store, more of a workspace. There were a few long tables piled high with fabric, and a maze of clothes racks on wheels were parked with absolutely no respect for traffic flow. As he stepped around one, a man appeared. A Pillsbury Doughboy type, mid-thirties, with a tape measure in his teeth.

"Horatio Moore?" David asked. Then he pulled out his business card, trying for European fashion flair. Ha. Whatever. Today he'd be lucky to pass for Yankee asshole.

The man pulled the tape measure from his mouth. "Who are you?"

*Oh, yes, who was he? International man of fashion. Right.*

"We represent Ashley Larsen, she had discussed the…fashion event for her stores? Chicago's Next Big Look. She had selected you to showcase your designs in her boutique. It's a great honor."

Horatio squinted in confusion. "You're from New York?"

"We manage a variety of interests."

"I didn't realize this show was this big."

Using two fingers, David pinched his forehead in what he hoped was egotistical ennui. "Big is not what we want. We want exclusive."

"And you want me?"

"Ashley wants you. We're merely the bank."

"Sure, I'll do it," Horatio said with a nod. Apparently being an overbearing ass was the key to success within this world. There were certain parallels with Wall Street. "What's the plan?"

"In September, over the Labor Day weekend, she'll have a set of two challenges. Cocktails and the everyday sort of clothes."

Horatio laughed. "Cocktails? You mean cocktail wear."

"That's it." Jeez, this was clothing, not the GDP. "You make the designs for the show, and the audience will decide which designer represents the Next Big Look for Chicago."

"Who am I up against? Probably Lorenzo. I hate that prick. You know how many times he's stolen designs from me? More than I can count." He pointed to the striped dress in the window. "See that? Admire the slim cut. Look at the way it moves. Sometimes, I swear, I can only stand in awe."

David looked at the dress, frowned. "I can see that."

"The dress is my masterpiece, my signature. Lorenzo ripped it off, and—oh, God, strike me dead now—he added a belt! It's like putting a moustache on the Mona Lisa. Bastard."

"There's no Lorenzo. There's a lady from Miami, Mariah…" He struggled for the name, and gave up, settling on the singular alone. It made her sound more important. Whatever. "And then there's a guy from New York."

"Out-of-towners? Whoa, that'll be awesome. Hey, you want

to look around? I've got a great brown cashmere that would go so well with those shoulders of yours," he said, sweeping his glance over David in a purely professional manner that still made him nervous. This was so not his world.

David took two steps back. Two steps closer to freedom. "No. I have a call with Milan in five minutes. Another time."

"You're sure? I can do some great things for you."

David waved, fleeing the place. *Fashion.* Captain Kirk would have never been caught dead in a boutique, not even if the entire universe was at stake.

Ashley was going to owe him for this one. Big-time.

IT WAS NEARLY MIDNIGHT when Ashley got to the hotel. She thought about calling first, telling him the crisis was over, but sometimes it was easier to duck the bullet, rather than take it straight to the heart. When she slid the key card in the locket, she peeked in, found the lights on and David at work at his computer.

"Hello," she said cautiously, trying to gauge the mood. He was shirtless, in blue jeans, quite casual except for the tense line at his shoulders. And of course, no look of impending emotional eruption would be complete without the severe cut of the jawline. Ashley forced a smile.

"Welcome back."

"I'm sorry," she offered, getting the apology right out there in the open, before the real accusations started to fly.

"Is everything okay?" he asked, his voice concerned, but his eyes bothered her, like Miami before the afternoon storm. Miami was so much easier than Chicago.

She wanted to go to him, touch him, wanted to soothe the rigid shoulders, but that was more ducking. Needing to get this over, she cleared the tension from her throat. "Yes. It was a mess. We had a fight with the bank, had to trudge to ten stores. And you know, they really rip you off on checks. The first one actually would have cleared, but no…they had to put the biggest check through first. Sneaky jerks." Her smile wobbled a bit, but she was steady. She walked over to the desk and leaned against the corner, trying for casual, too.

"I'm glad you got it worked out."

A long silence followed, and she didn't like the silence, so she rambled on to fill it. "How was your day? I'm glad you didn't fly back to New York."

"I thought about it, but I'm booked on the first flight out in the morning."

She knew he would have thought about flying back, was almost surprised that he was still in Chicago. Ashley would have sat in the hotel for days waiting for him. David wasn't her. "I'm sorry I didn't call."

"I assumed you had a reason."

"I couldn't get away," she offered, not a great reason, but partly the truth.

"Here," he said, and handed her a card. *Horatio Moore, Designs by Horatio.* "He's in for the show. You'll have to call him, but he agreed."

Oh. My. God. She stared at the card, stared at him. "You met with him?"

"Somebody had to. I tried to call and see what you wanted, but you weren't answering your phone."

Her smile started to wobble again, and she bit her lip, hard, preferring the pain to the guilt. In her life, her dreams had always been pushed aside to take care of other things. More important things. It wasn't that she was walking away, no, but sometimes you had to do what you had to. While she had been busy cleaning up Val's mess, she hadn't expected him to clean up her own.

"I'm sorry," she repeated. Maybe if she kept saying it, he would believe her. He didn't look as if he believed her. He'd barely lifted his eyes from the screen. "We were talking to the cops," she babbled on. "I didn't think talking on the cell would be smart."

"No, I'm sure it wouldn't have been smart. Polite, yes. Sensitive, yes, thoughtful, yes. Smart. Obviously not."

"You're mad," she stated, then went to sit on the bed, then immediately stood, because she didn't want to argue on this bed. There were too many good memories here. She didn't want to spoil it with bad ones, and there would be bad ones now. She braced herself against the wall, hands behind her back and waited. She didn't have to wait long.

"Hell, yes, I'm mad," he blurted, but his voice was eerily calm. She liked it better when he yelled, but he didn't yell, he only swiveled the chair around toward her. "When you left, I was furious at your sister. At the garbage she was dragging you into. But now, my anger has moved beyond that. You could have told me what to do, could have clued me in a bit. If I had known you wouldn't show until midnight, I would have flown home. I like this hotel room, but not that much."

Yup, the truth hurts, but the cold look in his eyes was worse. Ashley wanted to stay calm because now wasn't the time to fall apart and prove everybody right. "All I needed to do was get Valerie in a better place, talk her down from the ledge and then get back here to you."

Apparently that was the tipping point because finally he stood with his arms folded across his chest. Neatly hidden beneath his arms were twin angry fists.

"Do you hear how you talk about her? You sound like she's a four-year-old, Ashley. She's thirty years old. Let her grow up."

In David's mind everything was so easy. Damn the consequences, just do what you needed to do. Life wasn't like that. Ashley took a lingering glance at those arms, wished he would tug her close, wished his hazel eyes weren't so troubled. But no, they were going to have this out. Damn.

"You don't understand," she started, but she'd never been good at educating herself nor anybody else, yet it was important for him to understand this: that there were no good choices here.

"Why don't you explain it to me, Ashley. Explain why you have to play nursemaid. Explain why you put your shops on hold, why you put me on hold, why you put everything on hold when she calls."

She shot away from the wall and started to pace. It was so easy for him to criticize, to point out how to do everything better. Yes, she was prepared to eat crow for screwing up the day, she should have called, but she wouldn't let him do this to her. This, *this,* she didn't deserve. "You don't know."

David cocked his head, a challenge in his eyes. "Tell me."

She glared, opened her mouth to yell, but then she began to speak, carefully, absolutely, so he could follow her. "As bad as you think this is—with the bounced checks, the needing to find lost permission slips for Brianna, the stupid arguments—it's a cakewalk now. I go to bed at night, and I don't have to take a pill to sleep. I don't have to ask the bail bondsman how his kids are doing. I don't have to check my purse in the morning to make sure all the money is there. I don't have a pit in my stomach when the weekend rolls around and I'm not sure if Brianna's going to see her mother or if Aunt Ash and Grandma are sitting primary. This is easy, David. This is *good.* I've been to hell. I don't want to go back. If babysitting and holding her hand keeps me out of hell, I'm all for it. You don't know. People that don't go through it— they don't know. You're all Mr. Tough Love, throw your brother out, throw your ex out, throw Val out. I'm not you. I can't be you. Sometimes I wish I could be like that, but I can't. I'm sorry if that disappoints you and I'm sorry I didn't call today, and I'm sorry that you don't approve of the way I treat Val, but it's what I'm going to do because it works. You think I'm stupid for putting up with this, but *it works,* and nobody, nobody, can argue with that."

He stood there, impassive, a hard wall of stubborn. "You have a right to be happy."

Oh, that was underhanded. He wasn't supposed to be thinking of her. He was supposed to be all mad, and selfish, the manly man who knew it all. That, she could stand up to. This, she wasn't sure. "I am happy," she said, and she wished her voice sounded more certain.

"I want to kill her, Ashley, and I'm not a cop, or a soldier, or somebody that deals with violence on a daily basis. I'm an ordinary guy. I work with *spreadsheets*. Financial models, return on investment, and I want to kill her. I want the problems gone. I want your shops to run in the black, but I can't fix it if you don't want me to. I want you to be happy, and she makes you unhappy. I don't like to see you unhappy. I hate it."

"I'm sorry," she said, apologizing again. She was sorry she hadn't called, she was sorry her sister was a walking reality show, she was sorry that she hadn't been there to meet with Horatio, and most of all, she was sorry because he was flying out early in the morning, and she had wasted a good fourteen hours. Ashley didn't want to waste any more time.

"Are we okay?" she asked him. David looked so frustrated, and she understood, but anger and frustration, those emotions didn't solve anything. She'd gone through that when Val had turned up both drunk and pregnant, an especially awkward situation. From then on, Ashley's decision-making changed forever. It wasn't so easy to be all tough and hard like he wanted her to be. Still, she wished it were easier on him. He was getting a painfully quick lesson on the realities of living with a recovering alcoholic. Yeah, welcome to the club.

His arms dropped to his sides. Helpless. Yes, she knew that look, too. "I want us to be okay," he told her, his voice low. "I want everything fixed, but I don't think everything is fixed."

Of course it wasn't fixed, but Ashley took happy when she got the chance. "Could we pretend? Just until you get on the plane?"

"Until the next crisis?"

"Yeah, until then."

"I'm not very good at pretending, Ashley." She already knew that. She loved that he saw the world so simply, could look at the bad and label it for what it was. When it came to her business, she needed that simplicity, that honesty. She'd learned from it, and was stronger for it.

But the other thing that David had done for her—her aspirations were getting bigger, and they almost seemed obtainable. At one time, she had been ambivalent about doing much more than keeping Val sober. Now, her wish list was longer. She still wanted to keep Val sober, but she also wanted to do right by Ashley's Closet, and most of all she wanted to keep David in her life. It shouldn't be impossible, and if it was, she didn't want anyone to tell her so. Not even him. "Please try. You want me to be happy. Make me happy. We don't have a lot of time, David. I don't want to spend it like this."

David gave her a smile, and she wished it were more certain. Then he came to her, and pulled her close, and for a few moments, his cheek rested on her head and in his arms, she found the very happiness he said she deserved. "I'm very happy now," she whispered. "You make me happy." Surrounded by everything she said she wanted, Ashley smiled to herself, and she wished it were more certain, too.

THE BEDSIDE CLOCK said five-thirty, and outside the sky was turning the first shades of gold. Halfway between 2:00 and 3:00 a.m., David had closed his eyes, but sleep remained out of reach. Theoretically, lying here with Ashley, his fingers skimming through the soft waves of her hair, he should have been one happy man, but something was off. Probably the way she was frowning in her sleep.

Gently he pushed at the twin lines above her eyes, but they wouldn't disappear, no matter how much he willed it. Ashley's frown remained, so David's frown remained as well.

Twenty-four hours ago, he had everything in his life mapped out. He would move here, there would be no more planes, no more tiny hotel shampoo bottles, no more Do Not Disturb signs. Every night he would pull her close, and every morning, she would wake up against him. Like this.

It used to give him hives to think about living in the same city with Chris and Christine. Now, he could even stomach the idea of seeing them—occasionally, and Ashley would have to be with him. That anger he could put aside.

Val? No, that anger wasn't going anywhere as long as she treated Ashley like her own private punching bag.

He shifted, uncomfortable in his skin.

Warily, his free hand fisted, and he increased the pressure until his skin paled white. David was an absolutist. He was paid a decent salary in order to be straight and upfront. He didn't look the other way, he didn't pull his punches—in his job, in the ring, in his life. He never had, and it was probably one of the reasons that Christine had left him.

What Ashley wanted was for him to look the other way. Now, truthfully, there were a lot of things that he would avoid doing to make her happy, but he couldn't stand still and watch her hurt, or watch her frowning in her sleep and then cluelessly pretend that he was okay with this plan.

But that's what she wanted. She put her needs second, her heart second, her life second to someone not nearly as worthy.

And while she was busy saving her sister, she didn't want him to judge. But every day he went out and judged. It was who he was.

Ashley shifted, her warm skin brushed his, her breast pillowed against him. His cock rose, wanting to take her. His heart pumped, wanting to take her. But this time it was his obstinate mind that stood in the way.

He didn't even know how to look the other way. Sure, he could try. David lifted his fists, twisted them in the air, studying the compressed power within. Slowly he released the pressure, wanting to ease the taut burn inside him, but it didn't go away. No, pretending only made it worse.

David's frown deepened, and finally, abandoning all pretense of sleep, he climbed out of bed. His plane took off for New York in a couple of hours. Home. Where was home anymore? He wasn't sure.

Quietly he headed for the shower. After he was dressed,

carry-on packed, he kissed her once on her sleepy, furrowed forehead, trying one last time to make her worries disappear.

"I love you, Ash." His words were whispered and for his ears alone. Then he slipped out of the room before she woke.

# 14

FRIDAY PASSED and he didn't call. Ashley kept herself busy making plans for the upcoming show, telling herself not to borrow trouble. A reporter from *Chicago News Daily* had promised coverage and the *InStyle* columnist from the *Tribune* was intrigued. In the afternoon, she pulled off the PR hat, donned her manager hat, and smacked some sense into Evelyn, the manager of the Naperville store, who horrendously believed that a midnight blue blouse should be matched with a set of royal purple silk capris.

At first Evelyn was surprised because Ashley wasn't usually such a bossy boss, but Ashley's tolerance level was zero. Eventually Ashley whipped her into shape, giving her a lengthy diatribe on the subtleties of color, how a sophisticated scheme did not let the gradients run into each other like a smash-up on the Kennedy. No, they must flow, and wash together until they are as one. Evelyn was suitably humbled, the purple capris were back with the white blouse where they belonged. Fashion crisis averted.

By the time Ashley pulled into the driveway it was late, she was exhausted and David still hadn't called. Not even an "I'm in New York" call, and she told herself it was not a sign of the end, or even worse, that he was trying to teach her a lesson on phone etiquette, which she didn't mind so much, but David really wasn't the "teach you a lesson" sort of man. So that left her back at "the end" conclusion. Sadly, she was starting to look at the world with harsher eyes which, in a time like this, really stank.

She opened the door to the smells of Val cooking supper, and Ashley smiled at the sign of normalcy. Day one after the great meltdown, and all is well. Yay. She hung her bag on the hall tree just as Brianna barreled forth from her room, and began insistently tugging at her hand.

"You hit the jackpot, Aunt Ash. Come look!"

Sure enough, in the middle of the living room, were three big boxes, and one tiny one. Val looked at her expectantly. "What's going on?"

"I don't know," answered Ashley, completely truthful, but she liked surprises, the good ones, not the bad ones—she wasn't stupid. This looked to be a good surprise, and she hoped against hope that the surprise provider was the one man who hadn't called. If he hadn't called and sent her stuff instead, well, she would be big and forgive him.

"Can I open one?" asked Brianna.

"Sure," Ashley replied, hoping it wasn't anything unsuitable for an eight-year-old, or more likely, something unsuitable that Brianna hadn't seen yet.

Brianna tore into a box and pulled out a small LCD television, then a DVD player, a can of buttered popcorn, and one gift-wrapped box, labeled, Do Not Open Until 11 p.m.

Brianna was entranced. "Who're they from, Ashley?"

Ashley made a goofy face as if this was no big deal, but Ashley was entranced as well. "A friend."

Brianna wasn't swayed, neither was Val. "A TV is always a big deal."

"It's a little TV. Almost tiny."

"Can I have it?" Brianna chirped, in her extra-angelic voice.

"No," Ashley said, clutching the package close, choosing now to impart discipline, mainly because David made her headily selfish.

Brianna scowled, not used to Aunt Ash saying no. "Please?" she asked, blinking her big puppy-dog eyes ever so sweetly.

Ashley stood firm. "Sorry, kid. This is all mine. Someday you'll be grown up, and you can selfishly deny the small children in your life. It's the circle of life. Get used to it now."

Brianna made a face, but she knew she was beat. "Fine." She stomped to her room with extra force. That little bit she had inherited from Val.

Before the really difficult questions began, Ashley gathered her boxes. "I'm going to go try this out," she said, scooting the tower of cardboard down the hallway.

Whistling to herself, she cleared a spot on her dresser for the TV and DVD and stared way too long at the single gift-wrapped package. There was a hesitant knock at the door, and Ashley stowed away the gift, surprised that it was Val, and not Brianna. Hesitant knocks weren't usually her style.

"So, quite a haul there…" Val started, waiting expectantly for Ash to chime in with the answer.

"It's not a big deal. A bet I won a few weeks ago. I had forgotten," Ashley lied like there was no tomorrow. Once the truth about David was out there, there wasn't much she could hide from Val, and for a few more days, a few more weeks, maybe a few more months, she wanted to keep her and David's relationship simple and reduce the chance for failure. Having Val know that David lived in New York increased the failure-quotient possibility by a factor of a gazillion.

"You were never a good liar, Ash."

"I'm not lying."

"Lying, much?"

Ashley stared at the three boxes, and knew that it was the moment that she had dreaded, but it was the moment she couldn't put off any longer. Val should know, and hopefully, if there was a merciful God, it wouldn't be a problem. "It's from a man. I've been seeing him for a while."

Val rolled her eyes. "That's it? Why didn't you say something? I think that's awesome. You need to get out more. Get laid. Relax. I'm very happy for you."

And wow, that was so much easier than she had expected. "Thanks."

"Tell me about him," Val said, pulling up a chair. "What's his name, what does he look like, and most importantly, does he fully understand the nuances of a man's pinnacle role in a woman's sexual fulfillment?"

"David. He's tall, brown hair with a cowlick in the back. Good eyes, smart eyes. Nicely built, and yes."

Val laughed, and it was so nice to hear her laugh. "Sox or Cubs? Which is it? If he goes for the Sox, I'll have to change my mind."

"I know he's not a Sox fan. Not sure about the Cubs, though."

Her sister shrugged it off with a wave of the hand. "Well, I like his taste in presents. Now Brianna can watch cartoons and I can come back here and watch my movies with you."

Oh, peachy. Ashley smiled. "Sounds great."

Val stood up, she knew about David, and all was still right with the world. One day at a time, and today had been a great one. "You don't have to hide these things, or skulk around. Honestly, I'm good, and I'm glad that you're good, too. It's nice we can all be at a good place, together."

"It is nice," she agreed.

"Thanks for the help yesterday, sis. I'm so clueless about these things."

"You're not that clueless, Val. Sometimes you know exactly what you're doing." Her gaze lifted, met her sister's evenly. "You have to start taking charge. I won't always be there to bail you out."

Immediately Val panicked. "What are you saying, Ash? Are you deserting me now? Thirteen months sober and time's up, I'm on my own—"

Ashley held up a hand. "That's not what I'm saying."

"You're giving me a heart attack," Val muttered. "On some days, I think I've got everything under control, and then, it's like the devil whispering to me. You're my role model, you know? I look at you, and think, if I screw up, Ash's going to be mad, and it helps me walk the line. You're my rock."

Ashley withheld her sigh, resigning herself to the role of the rock. "You're doing great." Then, because even rocks needed their alone time, she rubbed her eyes. "How much longer before dinner? Maybe I'll take a nap. I'm beat."

Val was not fooled. "Phone sex with the new dude, right? You don't need to protect me. When do I get to meet him?"

"Soon. I think he'll be here for the show." She hoped.

"Okay, as long as he treats you right."

"So far, so good. Call me when dinner's ready."

"Thanks, Ash. Every night I tell God I don't deserve you, but I'm so very glad you're here."

AT ELEVEN O'CLOCK, her cell rang, just like she knew it would. It was David, mysterious giver of presents.

"Hello," he said, his voice filled with anticipation. He was waiting for her to acknowledge his generosity.

"Hi. How was your day?" It was torment mainly because she liked to know she was keeping him on the edge. David McLean, on the edge, was pretty much the most fun she'd had all day, and today had been a great day.

"I had a good day. Yours?" Now, anticipation was morphing into something more challenging. Avid curiosity. Ashley nearly laughed.

"Good," she told him calmly. "So, anything new?"

"No. You?"

Oh, he was near to breaking. She could hear it. Just one more minute. "How was work? What city are you in?"

"A large metropolis known as Manhattan."

Finally, she stopped, because it seemed cruel to go on. "I got the boxes."

"What happened to soft-hearted Ashley? I miss her, she would never tease me like this. So, did you open them?"

"Only the ones I was supposed to," she answered primly.

"Obedient little minx, aren't you?"

"Not that obedient. Don't get crazy."

"So you opened the little one?"

"No," she admitted, since deep in her heart she was an obedient little minx.

"Ha. You can open it now."

"What's the magic word?"

"Please."

She smiled and tore off the paper, finding her very own copy of a *Halloween* DVD, the original. "That's so sweet. It's not every man that gives a woman a movie about a knife-wielding serial killer."

"That's your bloodthirsty taste, not mine."

"Still, I think it's nice. Thank you."

"Well, go ahead, put it in the player."

"I'm not going to watch it now. I'm going to talk to you."

"No, you can watch it. I owe it to you."

"That's no fun, David."

"No, I bought a copy for me, too. We can do movie by phone. I've never seen this."

"You've never seen *Halloween?* That's un-American."

"I actually purposefully avoided it up until now because I consider myself a sensitive man."

Ashley smothered her giggle. "You're really going to watch it?"

"I am. For you, my darling, anything."

She put the DVD in the player, and pushed the play button. "I want you to know that I told Val about you today. She took it well."

"I told you. You should listen to me more. I'm always right."

Ashley popped the lid on the popcorn as the eerie theme song filtered through the room. "I know. Okay, we're on...." The credits flashed by, and the opening scenes began to show a young couple making love, caught in the throes of forbidden teenage passion. Ashley had forgotten about the opening of the movie, and she coughed twice.

David, of course, was not as discreet. "Oh, now wait a

minute. This is so unfair. I have to sit here and watch someone else get laid? Oh, not the shirt, not the shirt, she's taking off the shirt, Ashley. This is completely unfair. I'm alone here, and while I love my hand, it's to be used only in case of emergencies. This should not be an emergency. I'm doing this for you."

Slowly she lifted a piece of popcorn to her mouth. "Shh… They're about to get whacked."

"Really? Good. There is some justice after all."

*One more reason to love David McLean.* "You talk during movies, don't you?"

"No, I don't. Not usually. I'll shut up now."

THERE WERE THREE LONG, torturous weeks before she could fly out to New York, in which time she had:

1) Outlined and communicated the show's challenges to Horatio, Mariah and Enrique, who were "stressed," "wowed" and "underwhelmed," in that order.

2) Lined up ongoing coverage from *Chicago Today* and *Chicago This Morning, Chicago Tomorrow* and *Chicago At Night.*

3) Increased sales at the State Street store by an eye-boggling thirty-three percent.

4) Got Val on a budget.

5) Helped Brianna with her school project on global warming and catastrophic climate change—i.e., a tornado in a plastic soda bottle.

6) Watched *Friday the 13th,* parts 1, 2, 3 and 4 remotely with David.

7) Had unsatisfactory phone sex on what was becoming a nightly basis.

David was right. A hand could only go so far. Ashley had upgraded to a vibrator, a turbo-charged device with seven attachments, which did nothing to alleviate said frustration. So by the time she got on the plane to New York her entire female parts were in such twisted misery that she didn't need the bunny slippers. Amazingly, severe sexual frustration and lurid fantasies could kill most phobias, or at least push them aside in favor of bigger, rawer, more stimulating thoughts.

The flight was total misery when she imagined him naked, pounding into her, over and over. If she kept her thighs clenched tight enough, it was almost—*almost*—enough. By the time he picked her up outside the arrivals gate, she was a package of C4 just waiting for the right fuse.

Her hands jerked him close, planted a long one on him, and soon, he *was* getting the vivid picture that her tongue was painting in long, meaningful strokes. She could tell because he was expanding nicely between her thighs. Men could be so shamelessly easy, a completely hypocritical thought, but she was too sexually frustrated to care about being honorable. There was a time for honor, and a time to get laid.

"I need sex, David. I've sat scrunched in that tiny seat, and all I wanted was to have you naked, buried between my legs, hammering inside me, over and over and over and over…."

The very smart man stared, and then took a big, cleansing breath. "I have an idea," he said, grabbed her hand and pulled her down three flights of stairs. Eventually, they were in the long hallway of an international terminal filled with passengers.

"Where are we going?" she needed to ask, not seeing how this was going to help her painful situation. "Isn't there a bathroom or something?"

"Security," he answered. "Trust me."

After passing El Al, Aeroflot, Aer Lingus and some other airline she didn't recognize, they were at the end of the hall, a lone gate proclaiming Pan Pacific. The kiosk was deserted, a high wall keeping the gate partly out of view.

His mouth took hers, and he lifted her on the ticket counter, but Ashley wasn't convinced.

"Are we alone?"

"As good as it's going to get. Pan Pac, they tanked." His hands climbed under her shirt, shoving her bra aside. "Overpriced. Price of fuel killed them," he said, and then his mouth settled on her breast.

"What about cameras? Aren't there cameras here?"

He lifted his head. "I don't know. I don't care. Do you care? Please don't care."

She smiled wickedly and he lowered his head. From that moment on, Ashley closed her eyes, her blood pumping to the even pulls of his mouth, his tongue. Her hips started to clock in rhythm, and he spread her thighs, pressing two fingers inside her.

Oh, yeah.

She grabbed his jaw, pulled his mouth against hers and locked her legs against his waist, pressing, rubbing, doing whatever it took to make her body feel better. He groaned, angling her legs down until she was poised right…right…there.

Magically, efficiently, gloriously he had brought a condom, and with one hard thrust the world turned bright rainbow colors.

"I missed you," she mumbled at one particularly poignant thrust, and David grunted in acknowledgment. Sometimes words weren't necessary. His hands slid beneath her ass, pulling her off the counter, their bodies coming undone, and she moaned until he turned her around, pressed her stomach against the counter, and oh, oh, oh, this was so much better. So perfect. He was hard and thick and she could feel his body hot against hers, his skin slick with sweat. In the distance, the announcer was cancelling someone's flight, but here, Ashley was starting to fly.

His hands slid up, cupping her breasts, squeezing her nipples tight, not gentle. The blunt shove of his hips was not gentle, but the hard bursts of pleasure were killing her in the best way possible.

"There. Faster. Need to do. Faster." Her voice was almost to breaking; Ashley was almost to breaking.

"Faster works," he murmured against her neck, and that was the last rational thought she had. Her hands dug into the smooth plastic of the counter, finding nothing to grip but a hard ledge, and she held on, absorbing the rippling power that was breaking her in two.

Her eyes drifted closed and she could feel his hands, his cock, holding her, filling her, and just as her orgasm was about to…there, she shoved her hips back, forcing him deeper into her womb.

For a minute her body absorbed the shock waves. He covered her with himself, his mouth pressed tiredly beneath her ear. His chest heaved in great waves, and she smiled, exhausted. Marvelously sated, but exhausted.

"We've got to stop meeting like this," he whispered, his breath slowly adjusting to normal. When the last of her climax faded, and her legs could actually support her weight, she turned.

Discreetly, she adjusted her skirt, and tucked her hair behind her ear. David was fixing his clothes, but the shirt, it still wasn't right.

Ashley reached out, tucked in the side, then admired her work. "It was too obvious," she said.

"Men know anyway."

"Really?"

"Trust me. Guys know. Where to?"

"Your apartment," she stated firmly.

"This is new. Sex at the gate, sleeping at my place…" He took her face in his hands. "From bunny slippers to a dominatrix whip. Could be fun."

Ashley wagged a schoolmarm finger at him. "Don't get crazy."

"This isn't my crazy face. This is my optimistic face. So why the change, assuming you don't have peekaboo leather hidden in your carry-on."

"State Street is up thirty-three percent over last month. I'm basking in the glow of my own success. I felt you deserved to bask in my success as well."

"I'm completely unsurprised."

She liked his unsurprisedness, the way he was looking at her with what a less confident woman might consider pride. "Yes, I'm completely unsurprised, too. Let's go home. You can pleasure me more."

LATER IN THE AFTERNOON, they took a cab over to Brooklyn and David watched Ashley work Enrique over with disturbing enthusiasm. There was something new about Ashley today. Something that kept drawing his eye. She was more sure of herself, she didn't have the shell-shocked post-divorced look anymore— one that he suspected he still carried around inside. Even Enrique was sucking up to her, and when she told the designer about the deadlines and shipping arrangements for the show, Enrique began talking about his newest idea, a liquid jersey dress with a keyhole twisted-bodice, whatever the hell that was.

When Ashley nodded and smiled, Enrique sighed.

Yeah, David knew how he felt.

After they left the store, Ashley's fingers curled over his.

"He's eating out of your palm. If your top had been cut half an inch lower, you could have turned him sexually."

"Are you jealous of a gay man? That's so sweet."

David gritted his teeth. "It's not jealousy. I understand how the male brain thinks, what its priorities are."

"Even the homosexual male brain?"

"They have a dick, they have sperm. Some truths are universal. And don't call me sweet."

She didn't call him sweet, but her smile said it. Honestly, he didn't mind. "We going to walk across the bridge, or take a cab home?" Home. He liked the way the word rolled off his tongue.

"No walking. We're cabbing it, today."

"Feeling wimpy?"

"Nope. Just happy."

IT WAS SOMEWHERE long after midnight, and they were still awake. The Ring DVD was playing, but David didn't really care who got killed or how much blood was spilled. There was no sight that could be better than the one before his eyes. Ashley Larsen in his bed. He liked the feel of her there, the new scents that came with her. She was leaving on Sunday, but the pictures in his mind, the memories in his brain, would stay.

Her legs curled into his, silk into rough, her hands stroked his chest, soft and small, her hair fell over his shoulder, and this time, she didn't brush it away. He loved the feel of her hair, her hands on his shoulders, her bare skin against his.

He wasn't a man who stayed for days in bed, but here, with her…he could stay in bed for a lifetime.

When she was here, when they were together, sleeping, talking, making love, everything was at peace. Everything slowed down, and the world felt like such a safe, marvelous place. He liked the peace, he liked the way the anger disappeared, the way happiness stirred.

Ashley was not a woman you doubted. When she loved, he knew it, the world knew it. It was there in her face, her movements, the way she touched him, the way she loved him. It wasn't that David had gone seeking that sort of love, it wasn't that he even thought he required it, but there was something so easy about it.

So simple, so peaceful.

Come to New York. Stay here.

She turned her head and he stroked her lips with a gentle finger. "Come to New York. Stay in New York, Ashley."

Her smile was everything he needed. The light in her dark eyes gave him hope. "It sounds like a lot of fun. And think of all that flying I wouldn't have to do."

Already his mind was jumping to the next part of the plan. "We'd set you up with a boutique in…I don't know, Brooklyn or the Lower East Side, maybe. Soho or the Village, the rent would be nuts, so I wouldn't do four. Start small, work your way out."

"You've thought about this?" she asked.

"Yeah." And he had. It had been bubbling in the back of his mind. He had their life completely mapped out. This could work.

"What about Ashley's Closet?"

"Sell 'em."

She rolled her eyes. "After all this work? Are you crazy?"

"I guess so." He wasn't crazy. He was happy. He was in love.

"You're not crazy. If things were better, I would do it," she said, curling toward him. He could feel the warm weight of her breasts, the gentle slide of her thigh against his own, almost distracting him from his perfect idea, but not quite.

"You would?"

"I would," she told him.

That was all he needed to hear. "So do it. Now that you say it, it doesn't sound so crazy."

"I can't leave Chicago. You come there."

*Chicago?* "I did sort of consider it, but I live in New York, the financial and fashion capital of the world, home to the New York Yankees, which you could eventually grow to love. It's like God planting a sign. David and Ashley belong here. I don't believe in signs, but Ashley, sometimes it's stupid not to see the obvious."

"Don't do this to me, David." Her smile dimmed and she shifted, not much, but enough that their bodies were no longer touching.

This time he didn't try and pull her back. There were fights he could win, and some that he couldn't. "How long do we stay like this? Forever?"

"No."

"Then what do we do? What are we supposed to do?"

"Come to Chicago."

He gave her a hard look. "Do you think that's a good idea?"

"No. I'll figure out something," she said, and it disappointed him that she couldn't see the truth in the matter. She wanted the world to be one way, and it wasn't. The world didn't bend to you; you had to bend the world.

"No, you won't," he told her, wishing that just once he could be smart enough to keep his mouth shut.

"What's that supposed to mean? I'm not smart enough?"

Frustrated, he rubbed his eyes, not liking the hurt in her own. "You can't leave your sister. She's thirty years old. You can't mother her your entire life."

"I don't want to," she whispered, and her voice was so sad, so sorrowful that this time he did pull her close.

"I know. I'm sorry. I just want you here with me. All of the time. Or even most of the time. I'm tired of sleeping alone. I'm tired of eating alone. I now hate my cell phone because the reception is never good enough to touch, and thankfully jacking off doesn't cause blindness because I'd be pulling disability if it did. I love you, Ash. I thought I could do this. I didn't think I'd fall in love."

Her mouth pressed against his. "I know."

"Come live with me and be my love," he whispered. It was his last, best shot.

"Let me think about it," she said, and then he covered her, sliding into sex, and he loved her as if this was forever. But it wasn't. It was only one night.

In the morning, the sun rose, the alarm clocked blared and Ashley took off on a plane for Chicago. After she was gone, David looked up at the bright golden sky, and wondered how one night could seem so damn short.

# 15

LABOR DAY weekend was the ultimate shopping holiday in the fashion business. Friday, the fun and breezy spring fashions reigned supreme. Come Monday, the darker, more somber styles of the fall season had taken over. Ashley hated Labor Day, hated all the rigid rules that dominated a business that proclaimed in a very cosmopolitan accent that it was free of rules and lovingly dwelled in organic chaos.

Never trust a fashionista.

However, it was the number one weekend for people to peruse the racks, the number one weekend for people to consider what the new world of style should look like, and ergo, it was the perfect weekend for the Next Big Look for Chicago.

The night before, she hadn't slept, spending the hours alternately stressing between whether anyone would show up—or even care—and then praying that David's plane wouldn't be late, since today of all days, she didn't want him to be late.

There had been a live segment on *Chicago This Morning—Friday Edition,* in which Ashley was interviewed before the entire hypercritical Chicago metropolis, or at least that's what it felt like. It had gone well, except for the one moment when she fumbled with an extra "err," the ultimate media don't, but she had recovered nicely.

Val had been a trooper, possibly—probably—feeling guilty, but whatever the motivation, Ashley welcomed the help. Even their Mom and Brianna had been there, shoving banquet tables right and then left, then back to right. Three generations of Larsen women doing what they did best—undeciding.

The designers were there at the State Street location of Ashley's Closet. Enrique in a Haight-Ashbury, clubbish look of black leather paired with a silver paisley vest. Mariah had chosen a beautiful rose-organza skirt and Christian Louboutin heels that made her tower over most everyone, and Horatio had chosen a staid black tux, with dark tortoiseshell nerd glasses, complete with a cigar that he used like a conductor's wand, pointing and directing and condemning at will.

Now *this* was organized chaos.

Ashley, on the other hand, was a disorganized mess.

At 10:00 a.m., Christine McLean McLean, aka the bitch, showed up. Sadly, she wasn't there to gloat, she was only being sweet and supportive, which only made Ashley—who was a wreck—hate her more.

Ashley dodged the caterers who were setting up the warming trays, and casually, carefully introduced Christine to Val, which was like introducing Bonnie to Clyde, Thelma to Louise, and Leopold to Loeb.

Brianna, the little traitor, was entranced by Christine's matching hair barrettes and shoes. "That is awesome. Are they fuchsia?"

Christine preened. "Why, yes, what a clever child," she said with a mother-to-be stroke of her still skinny—hate you, hate you—womb.

"You're expecting?" asked Val, and suddenly there were the likes of Thelma and Louise discussing the ins and outs of morning sickness, at which point, Ashley left for the storeroom where she threw back a couple of antacid tablets to calm her stomach.

She was there for half an hour when Val arrived and sat down on a stack of boxes. "So, that's David's ex, eh?"

Ashley held up the tag gun and smiled. "Yes."

"You should have told me, Ash."

There were so many sins of omission that Ashley had failed to mention that she wasn't sure exactly what Val was referring to. "Yes, I'm sure I should have," she said, pricing with nervy restraint.

"He's not Chicago stock. What are you doing?"

Ah, yes. The big sin of omission. Ashley put down her tag gun and pulled out a box of sweaters. Quickly she folded them, face down, arms across, one side to the middle, other side to the middle, and voila, everything meets happily in the middle. "I'm not doing anything, Val. Everything is fine. Don't worry."

"She's his ex?"

"Yeah."

"Divorced men. There's gotta be something wrong."

"I'm divorced, Val."

"I rest my case." And then she grinned, no harm, no foul. "You know I'm kidding. But seriously, I mean, how well do you know this guy. Just met him, and he's sending you TVs and stuff."

Ashley took a deep, calming breathing, feeling the bubble-gum taste of the medicine coat and soothe her stomach. She picked up her tagging gun once again. There was nothing left to price, but she needed the feel of it in her hands nonetheless. "I've been seeing him for a while," she told her sister with easy casualness that she couldn't believe she'd managed to pull off.

Val's eyes sharpened because Ashley's sister was no fool. Yes, they loved to live in denial, but deep inside, nothing got past them. "How long's that?"

"Since April. We don't get to see each other that often, but we meet up. Chicago, Miami, sometimes New York. It works."

"But you can't build a permanent relationship like that. You're thirty-two, Ash. Now, that's not old, but let's say you stick with him for another four years, because you know that women stay in these relationships that aren't good for them for a long, long time. Then, after four years, he runs off and marries his hot, twentysomething secretary. There you are, now thirty-six, and officially S.O.L. Statistically, do you know what your chances are? Go out and get hit by lightning, why don't you?"

Ashley put the gun down and chose her words carefully. "Val, don't." Short, but effective.

"Look. I love you. You're my big sis, and you're the smart one. Usually. But this time... Seriously, it's a recipe for disaster, and I say that as someone who has written many disasters all her own."

"Don't make a big deal out of this, Val. Not today. Not now."

Val sighed, and not in a good way. "Okay. Go ahead, wet your proverbial whistle, have a fun time. I'll be there when you need me, Ash. And you will need me."

Ashley managed a pained smile. "I know."

THE SHOW WAS scheduled to start at two, it was noon, the store was starting to fill, and there was still no sign of David. It was official. Ashley was panicked. Christine, bless her heart, was greeting everyone. Enrique and Horatio were stalking around each other's still boxed-up clothes with a disdainful sneer.

Ashley had hired four models for the day, and they swooshed in with both style, grace and those huge dark sunglasses that were perfect for covering up last night's excesses. Not that she was being catty—oh, God, she was being catty—but honestly, where was David?

In the back, Ashley had marked off a curtained area where each designer could work with their models in secrecy—Horatio had insisted, Ashley didn't care. As each went to their respective corner, Ashley went back into the tiny storeroom and tried to find the voting ballots where each customer could pick their favorite within the categories. She pulled out empty box after empty box, when she felt a familiar, bold, yet comforting hand on her rear.

She knew that hand, she knew that smell, she knew that man.

David.

Ashley turned and clung to him with all the neediness of a woman who had officially given up a lot of phobias in the last four months, but was still, in the deepest parts of her heart, terrified.

His arms came round her, his mouth found hers, and she forgot about the scary parts. After a good, blood-pumping interval, she pulled up to breathe.

Man, he looked good. Edible. He'd ditched his khakis and Brooks Brothers shirt for something a little…dare she say it? Dashing? The jacket was a slouchy, soft, tweedy brown-green that perfectly brought out the earthy tones in his eyes. Underneath he had picked a sexy ivory fitted poet shirt sans collar that was unbuttoned casually low, displaying an eye-catching hint of chest, a finger-tempting splash of chest hair. It was entirely too sexy, entirely too strategically packaged, and she knew without a doubt that someone else had picked it out for him. But the pièce d'résistance? The traditional David McLean jeans—well fitted, well-worn, well filled.

"Someone went shopping."

"You don't like it, do you? It's too artsy, isn't it? I told the guy, give me a suit, something nice, but he said that nobody went to a fashion show in a suit. I told him he was wrong."

"He wasn't wrong, David. You look awesome. Tasty, even, and I'm saying that not only as the woman who wants to bed you, but a fashion professional as well."

He grinned, glanced over her deceptively simple little black dress with its come-hither neckline and heels to match. "Listen to you, sexy shop owner. And did you see all the people out there?"

All those people. Hungry people. Thirsty people. "Have the caterers started to serve yet? It's a mess. The press is pouring through the door, and I have no champagne. Do you know what a show is without champagne? It's a dry heave, that's what it is. It's worse than a dry heave. Gawd, this is going to be a bust."

He rubbed her icy-cold hands with his. "Hello, Ashley. You're going to do fine."

"I'm glad you're here. I didn't think I'd be this nervous."

"You can show me exactly how glad, unless I'm interrupting your regularly scheduled crisis already in progress?"

Temptation was never easy to resist. Ashley didn't even try.

She tugged at his jacket and ran her fingers up over the tweed, loving the texture of fabric and well-muscled man. Then his mouth was on hers, the taste of mint and coffee and lust...much lust. Much unslaked lust. Her hands lowered to his waist, finding the back pockets of his jeans. Digging her fingers in his pockets, she felt the muscles clench under her hands.

"Oh, damn, Ash. Don't seduce me now."

"It's the nerves," she whispered against his mouth.

He pulled free. "Oh, honey, I love your nerves. I love your breasts...." She ground her hips against him, and he stopped fighting the inevitable. His hands searched under her skirt. "Wow, you are soaked. Two minutes. That's all we need."

He pushed a finger inside her and her heart nearly exploded.

"And you must be David. Nice to meet you."

At Val's voice, Ashley's heart did explode. She jumped back, David jumped back, and there stood Val, eyeing him curiously.

Okay, maybe this wasn't going to be so bad. "David, this is my sister. Val."

Politely he held out his hand, shook hers and look at that... It was like nothing. "Nice to meet you," he said.

"Sorry to interrupt, but the champagne is here. They need to know whether to open it now, or wait until the winners are announced."

Damn. Ashley stared at Val. "Are you okay?"

Val waved a hand. "I'm fine. You're the one who looks like she's falling apart."

Ashley smoothed her hair, and glanced at David.

"What do you want me to do?" he asked.

Val smiled at him. "We've got it under control. Kick back. Look pretty."

Ashley shot David another look because sometimes Val didn't say exactly the right thing, but then, sometimes David didn't say exactly the right thing, either. Maybe he didn't notice.

His smile turned a little tighter, and his jaw clenched.

It was going to be a long, long day.

"LADIES AND GENTLEMEN," Ashley paused for dramatic effect. "The winner of Chicago's Next Big Look is…Horatio Moore."

Horatio whooped and Enrique glowered, and Mariah's face fell a little, as the cameras flashed and captured the moment for all eternity. Poor girl, but Ashley wasn't worried for Mariah. She'd seen the offers to manufacture all three of the designers' entries, and today there were no losers.

Nope. Not a one. She examined the store, noted the packed crowd, noted the continuous tap of the cash register and grinned happily.

"Ladies, can you bring those gorgeous looks out one last time?" And the models appeared wearing the cocktail dresses. Personally, Ashley loved Mariah's the best, a neon-blue silk with a fitted waist and a pouf flounce at the knee. But as much as she loved the blue silk, she could see why Horatio won.

The black dress had beautiful beadwork not seen since the '20s. It didn't have the sleek lines of Mariah's, instead it was a graceful drape that forgave many flaws and made every woman look beautiful. In short, it was the perfect dress for the not-so-confident woman.

As for Enrique, he had designed a hideous concoction of red poppies gracing yellow fabric, and it looked more like a two-year-olds' crayon drawing than a dress you wanted to wear for a night on the town, but still there were people wanting to buy from the New York designer. Somehow, between the three, she had found the exact perfect mix.

She, Ashley Larsen.

After two hours of hand-shaking and smiling, and photo ops and answering questions, and another fifteen minutes of soothing Enrique and bolstering Mariah, the sun began to set, the store cleared out, the caterers cleaned up, and Ashley congratulated her four managers on a job well done.

It was over.

Now all she had to do was keep peace between her mother,

her niece, her sister, and the man she loved. Her fingernails dug into her palms. Ha. A piece of cake.

IT WASN'T SO AWFUL, David thought to himself. Ashley's sister seemed much nicer than he had imagined. She looked like a more sharply cast version of Ashley. The same dark hair, the same nose and the mouth, but the eyes were a study in contrasts. David had seen eyes like Val's—the hard-boiled cynics' on Wall Street for instance.

Their mother was another story. Completely different from what his own mother had been like when she was alive. And as he watched Ashley's mother peering out at the dark streets, her hands clamping nervously on Brianna's shoulders, he could see exactly where Ashley got it from.

As for Ashley, she looked exhausted. There were shadows under her eyes that weren't usually there, and strands were starting to escape from the bun. All he wanted to do was get her home, tuck her in bed, not even needing to jump her, which was testament to how tired she looked. He walked over to her, running a hand over her neck, feeling the tense muscles there. "How much do you have to do tonight?"

Her gaze moved across the store. "That's enough. I think I want to celebrate."

Val stood. "Great idea. You deserve it. I didn't think you could do it, Ash, but hell, you did. I'm proud of you, sis. We can hit Paradise Pup. Brianna loves the burgers, don't you, sweetie?"

Brianna, hearing her name, broke into the conversation. "I'm all for that plan."

It wasn't exactly what David had planned, but okay, he was the guest. Ashley needed to decide this one.

She stared at him, and he wished she wouldn't stare at him like that—as if she didn't want to go to dinner with her family because she knew that he knew she was going to cave, and then he'd be disappointed with her, and today of all days, he didn't want to be disappointed with her, and then…

"I don't think I want to go," she was saying. "You take Mom and Brianna if you want to eat there. I'm going to go with David."

Hell had just frozen over. He knew it. David was so shocked that he forgot to smile, and he wanted to smile. Val frowned ominously. "I thought you wanted to celebrate."

Immediately, Ashley realized her mistake. It was there in the wariness in her eyes. "Actually, you know, I don't want to celebrate. I want to go…somewhere quiet."

Val's heavy sigh could be heard in Wisconsin, and her gaze cut to David, death in her sights. "You know, Ash, you're always there to celebrate my special days—the anniversaries, the birthdays, and tonight, I wanted to return the favor because you've done a great thing, but okay, if you feel that way…go away, do your little thing."

Carefully, David studied the pink necklaces in the display case because as much as he wanted to open his mouth, he knew that'd be a mistake.

"Thanks for understanding, Val."

"No problem. Listen, I got this letter from the district attorney this afternoon, and it made me nervous. Can you take a look tonight when you get home?"

Ah, so the battle wasn't over yet. Val was much more effective than he gave her credit for.

"I won't be home tonight, Val."

Holy shit. David's hands nearly drove through the glass. Not only was Ashley holding her own in the ring, she was going for the knockout. Ashley was turning into a fighter. He'd never been more proud.

"Where'll you be, Aunt Ash?"

Ah, the voice of innocence.

"You're too young to know about this," answered Val. "Mom, can you take Brianna out to the car. There's one other thing that I need to talk to Ash about, and then we'll take off. And yes, Brianna, we'll get the burgers."

After they left, David gave Ashley a weak, yet hopefully encouraging smile. She was doing great, just one more round, and then victory was hers. Immediately Ashley took the offensive. "Leave it alone, Val."

"You don't even know what I'm going to say."

"I know exactly what you're going to say. You're going to tell me how I'm making a mistake, and this is a time for family, and how the only people you can depend on are your family, and then you're going to remind me how Jacob was such a mistake, and you think David is a mistake, too, because he lives in New York, and you can't see me in New York, and why even waste my time and his, and now that you've met his ex-wife and seen what a total bitch she is, you can't think he's that smart, and he's probably just using me, or even worse, he's got some squeeze back in New York, and how would I know since I live in another town, because honestly, how can I trust any man. Did I get it all?"

"Very good. Although you missed the important part. Do you love him, Ash?"

"Yes."

"Are you moving? Are you leaving this town and haven't said a word?"

The room got dangerously quiet. David perked up his head, watching Ashley with interest.

"Maybe."

Val looked at David, then looked at Ashley. "I'm wasting my time here, aren't I? Do what you need to do, Ash. Have a nice life." Then she stalked out the room, the bell at the door jingling behind her.

Ashley turned to David, and her face crumpled a bit. "I think that went well."

David gathered her close, but Ashley not only looked exhausted, now she looked beaten. "One day at a time, Ashley. She'll come around."

He hoped.

IT TOOK EXACTLY seven hours for the full effects of the crisis
to be known. David and Ashley were both fast asleep in the
hotel room when Ashley's cell rang.

Ashley opened one eye, stared at the clock. 4:37 a.m. She
didn't want to answer the phone. For the first time in her life
she actually considered letting the goddamned phone ring, but
she didn't.

"Ash, I need you to come get me." It was Val, stumbling
through her words without a care in the world.

"Where are you at, Val?" The words came out of her mouth
by rote. She knew the routine. She knew her part.

"How the hell should I know?"

"O'Malleys on Addison?"

"No."

Ashley rubbed her eyes, praying this was a bad dream, but
she knew it wasn't a bad dream. Or if it was, she was stuck in
it—the same bad dream, over and over and over and over. "Ask
the bartender for an address."

Val started to laugh. Vodka did that to people. Made everything funny.

"He's not the bartender, he's the police."

# 16

DAVID KNEW the answer to his question before he asked it. "I have to go," she told him, already sliding out of bed, turning on the light, pushing her hair from her face. All the excitement of yesterday was gone.

"You don't have to leave."

Mechanically she pulled on clothes—a yellow skirt, a red-flowered shirt and a beaded blue necklace because apparently bright happy apparel was the best way to pretend you weren't dying inside. The dark hollows in her eyes gave proof of the lies.

Those hollow eyes shot him a desperate glance. "Don't do this now," she pleaded.

"I'm sorry, but look at you, Ashley. What are you going to do? What are you supposed to do to help?"

"My sister is drunk at the Cook County jail. I'm going to go, post bail, take her home, throw her in the shower, try and keep the shit from Brianna and Mom, and carry on. That's what I'm going to do."

David rubbed his eyes, feeling the helpless anger burn inside him. He'd never liked helpless. "Do you want me to go?"

This time, she pulled her hair back into a ponytail and didn't even bother to answer, instead she focused on packing to leave.

David grabbed his jeans and shoved his legs into them. While she stuffed her toiletries in the case, he pulled her clothes out of the closet, realized what he was doing, and shoved them back on the hangers that jingled like bells. *No.*

He had tried to stay silent, tried to let her do this, but he couldn't. He could not sit this one out. "When will you stop? When is she going to call, and you say, 'not today?'"

"Not today." Her smile was sad, and David swore, and then her smile got a little more sad. "Do you know what I love about you, David? We have known each other for a few months, but you encourage me to do things, encourage me to take risks, and I do it. Do you know why?"

"Why?"

"I feel safe with you. I know that if I'm with you, no matter what I do, you'll always be there to catch me if I fall. Is that true?"

David didn't like having his motives twisted, his emotions twisted, his heart twisted, and he wanted to lie to her, but in the end, he couldn't. "Yes."

"And I love my sister," she told him, shutting her suitcase, zipping it firmly closed, "and I want her to feel safe with me, David. I want her to know that as long as I'm alive, I will always be there to catch her if she falls. Is that wrong of me? Is it wrong of you?"

"It's not the same thing. What you're doing…with your business and all, that's the good stuff. That's positive. With Val, it's not healthy, Ashley. Sometimes you have to let people make their own mistakes and learn from them."

"You think that if I bail out Val, I'm making a mistake?"

"Yes."

"What are you going to do, David?" she asked him, as if she was absolutely sure she was right. As if there was only one way to deal with the people you love.

There it was. Put up or shut up time.

Furiously David began grabbing his clothes from the closet, not caring how he did it because he wanted the world the way he wanted it. He wanted Ashley to be harder. But it seemed it didn't matter what he wanted. In the end, it was Ashley who got the 4:00 a.m. wake-up calls, Ashley who patiently paid the fees for NSF checks, Ashley who did it all. There was a pattern here, and she didn't mind the pattern. David did. She had worked so hard, and it was all for nothing because she would never get anything *she* wanted, and he'd have to stand there with his thumb up his ass, seeing her sad smile, and seeing the glow fade from her eyes.

*No.*

"I can't watch this, Ashley. I can't watch you handing her your heart and watching it burn. You sound like you're going out to pick up her laundry, but it's four-thirty in the morning after one of the best days of your life, and you're going to a police station. Doesn't this hurt you? What about you, Ashley?"

"I can handle it. I can help her."

"This is not help."

She pulled her shoes from the closet, then sat down in the chair, seeming oddly composed. She was going to go. Oh, man, she would need a cab. David picked up the phone and dialed the front desk, ready to get her a cab.

There was a knowing smile on her face as she watched.

Before the operator answered, David hung up.

Ashley slid her feet into her yellow heels. It wasn't even 5:00 a.m., and she was wearing yellow heels. The world was not a nice place. "Do you know what pushed her off the ledge, David?" she asked, and deep in his soul he had known that they were going to reach this point eventually.

His hands flexed, then fisted until the knuckles glowed white. "Oh, no. She might want you to believe that our relationship killed her sobriety, but the only person who pushed her off the ledge was Val."

"Action, reaction. Thirteen months she's been sober, David." She stood, smoothed her skirt. Then she met his eyes. "Are you going to be here when I get back?"

She wanted to know what he was going to do. This moment was more than calling her a cab, more than packing her clothes. *Of course I'll be here,* he thought to himself. *I could never leave you.*

His breathing stopped, his lungs not sure what they were supposed to do. He hated this. He hated his goddamned principles. He hated that he couldn't be like her. His eyes drifted shut because he didn't like that sad, knowing smile. When had Ashley gotten so very smart?

Carefully he exhaled, opened his eyes.

"I don't think I should stay. I think I would get very mad, and I would yell at you, and you don't need me to yell at you. You need me to be supportive and say you're doing the right thing, and that's not even close to who I am."

She nodded once, a tiny jerk of the head, and that was the end.

A MAN DIDN'T NEED to be in an empty hotel room. He found the shirt she had left behind and he neatly packed it into his carry-on because he couldn't stay here, and he couldn't simply leave her stuff out there for the maid.

It was five in the morning, the planes were just starting to take off, and David sat on the bed. He had never imagined this moment. He'd never even contemplated it. From the first second on that airplane ride to nowhere, he'd known he'd never met someone that he felt so comfortable with—someone that made him lust, someone that made him laugh.

No point in laughing now.

His case sat on the bed, staring at him, telling him to go home, but David wasn't ready to go home. There wasn't anyone there, and he didn't want to be alone. He picked up his cell and made a call.

CHRIS DIDN'T ACT surprised or weird. He acted as if this were no big deal, and for that, David loved his brother even more.

They ended up sitting on the back deck, drinking a beer and watching the sun come up. As he looked out over the fenced yard, the old picnic table, the flowers beneath the kitchen window, it occurred to David that his brother had created the house their father had always wanted.

"What did you expect her to do, David? You know it's so easy for you to cut people off and never speak to them again, but most of us aren't like that." Chris rested in the lounge chair because this was his home turf. This was his domain, his castle. Here, David was the outsider.

"You picked love over family, why couldn't she do it?"

That was the hard part. David expected the ultimate sacrifice. There was pride involved here. Ashley had a choice. Once again, David had lost.

"I didn't pick love over family."

David drained the last of his beer. Reached for another. "You want to make it sound prettier, Chris? You fucked my wife."

"I loved your wife," Chris answered, sounding hurt that David was mad.

"Geez."

"Don't do that. I loved her more than you ever did. Christine was an ornament to you. You never talked with her, you never even knew what she wanted."

David thought over some of the conversations he'd had with Christine. "She wanted matching clothes and a maid."

Chris shook his head. "She wanted a home. She wanted a kid. She wanted a husband who came home at five and listened to her whine about the day."

It all sounded neat and domestic, and not a thing like the marriage that David and Christine had had. "And that's you?"

"It is. It was never you." His brother looked at him as if David were the alien. As if he were the one who was being a fool, as if the world had swapped sides, and somehow he was stuck alone.

"What am I supposed to do, Chris? Do I have to start going to see a therapist to figure out how I'm supposed to be a man? Do I stock up on self-help books?"

"I don't think so, David. I don't think Ashley thinks so, either."

"She's wrong about this, Chris. I know I think I'm right all the time, and a lot of the time—but not all the time—I'm right. But this time, I'm right."

Thankfully, his brother nodded. "I think so, too."

"Do you really? You're not just saying that because my life sucks at the moment?"

"No, I think you're right. Maybe she'll realize it, too."

David remembered Ashley's smile. She knew David was right. She knew she was doing the wrong thing, but she couldn't help herself. "I don't think so." He stood, tossed the beer can in the garbage that was right behind the grill. Their father had a grill exactly like that. "Why don't you take all the money on the old apartment, Chris. I don't need it."

Chris's jaw shifted into a hard line. "No. We go half. You keep thinking there's something wrong with my financial choices, David, but there's not. I don't need what you need."

At that, David sighed. He'd tried, he failed. "Fifty-fifty it is. I should go."

"You could stay. Christine could make pancakes."

"That's too much. Maybe you could come out to New York some time and we could be brothers for the weekend. I think I'd like that. That, I think I can do."

Chris nodded. "I could do that, too."

# 17

"HELLO, MY NAME is Valerie, and I'm an alcoholic."

The room was half full. It was an old Lithuanian church with long wooden pews, and the October sunlight pooling in through stained glass. The scent of pine cleaner filled the air, nearly obscuring the scent of humility. This was where people came to wipe out the darkest stains inside themselves.

At this meeting, there were no businessmen in well-cut suits, or women with two-thousand-dollar bags. That was Lincoln Park or Lakeview, not here.

Here was what families left behind, what the nightly news left behind, what the world left behind. Ashley had never liked sitting in these meetings. When Val was outside this place, she was hard and tough and ready to face the world on her own terms. Inside her group's circle, Val's eyes lost the hard edge. Here they were filled with fear. Seeing that fear always reminded Ashley of her own weaknesses.

After everyone had gotten up to speak, after the last of the stale coffee was gone, Ashley waited for the room to empty, because this was the perfect place to talk.

"I'm proud of you, Val." And she was. She knew her sister battled dragons that she would never understand, and she also knew this wasn't easy.

"Thanks. Thirty days isn't long." Nervously Val's hands slid up and down her jeans, her nails short, bitten to the quick.

Ashley smoothly folded her arms, covering her own polished

nails in the process. "Thirty days is a step. A good step. And every day, you take another step."

"I'm glad you're here," her sister said, and the hand-sliding stilled.

"I am, too, but this is it, Val. I won't do this again."

"Do what again? Come to a meeting with me?"

Ashley smiled gently. "The next time I'm not going to answer the phone. The next time you bounce a check, you're in charge."

"I'm not going to do that again."

"Then that makes it much more easier for you."

"What's got into you?"

"I'm kicking ass and taking names. The biz is doing great, but I'm going to sell it. I hope I'm going to New York." Ashley put the statement out there. She wasn't going to dodge anything anymore.

"You're deserting me?" The fear was back in her sister's eyes, and Ashley felt the familiar urge to reassure her, to tell her that she wasn't deserting her, that she would always be there, but David had been right.

"No. This is what you need."

Val grabbed her hand, her fingers digging into Ashley's skin, but Val didn't know what she was doing. That was always the problem. "I can't work this without you."

"That may be, but you're not working it with me very well, so I'm not sure it makes a difference."

Val stood and started to pace. There were certain similarities with David. She'd never tell him, but it was probably a lot of the reason it was so easy to fall in love. These two people whom she loved most of all. These two people who needed her most of all.

"These aren't your words. You've been talking to him, haven't you?"

"No, I haven't talked to David since he left, but he's right. I've been there every time you've had a crisis. Always ready to prop you back up, and when that happens, you don't think you can prop yourself back up, and you have to know that. You have to know that you can do this. I'm your bunny slippers, Val. Sometimes you have to fly without them."

"You can't do this to me." Her sister's voice was louder now. Her hands were on her hips.

Ashley looked away. "I have to."

"What about Brianna?"

This time, Ashley turned back because this was Val the manipulator speaking. This time, Ashley would fight back. Her voice was low and calm, but for nearly two weeks she'd practiced these words in her head. "Ah, yes, your daughter. Think about her, Val. Think about your daughter. Next time, Aunt Ash won't be there. Grandma will, but I wouldn't count on Grandma. You need to count on Val." It was hard talk for Ashley. The tone and words felt foreign to her, but it was time.

"I can't do this."

"Yes, you can. You've told yourself that you can't for so long that you believe it. Go to your meetings. Go to your job. Take care of your daughter. You'll learn something. You'll learn that you can."

Val stared at her, expecting Ashley to give in because Ashley always gave in, but this time Ashley wasn't, and eventually Val figured it out. "You're leaving?"

"Yeah."

"When?"

"I'm getting on a plane tomorrow. I don't know what'll happen, but I have to try. I love him. I'm going to be with him. I'm going to be happy. That's my dream. I want my dream, and you're not going to take it away."

Val's face paled and she took a step back. "I'm sorry. I didn't mean to do that to you."

"I know. But you did. And we're fixing it."

"LADIES AND GENTS, it's bad weather in New York. The fog on the east coast is killing visibility, and we're waiting on the plane to get here. It's in the air, and should be here within half an hour. I apologize for the delay, and appreciate the patience. Sit tight, and I promise we'll be boarding within the hour."

With a cautious eye, Ashley surveyed the family across the gate area. The toddler looked especially deadly with the sugar-infused, "I haven't had my nap" laughter. If there were justice in the world, Ashley would be on aisle seven and the family would be on aisle thirty-seven. It wasn't that she hated kids—some day she would probably want them—but squishy hormones didn't automatically translate to the apocalyptical desire to spend more time in the terror-filled skies.

She leaned her head against the back of the hard chair and closed her eyes, blocking out the noise and chaos that was O'Hare. Today's hellish air travel conditions seemed the price she was going to have to pay for being too cowardly to call. But how did you pick up the phone and explain this new, tougher Ashley? It seemed…wimpy and undetermined. This was a conversation she needed to have in person. She wanted to look in his eyes, watch them melt to an earthy green or freeze to an icy black and then she would know where they stood.

"Ladies and gents, the flight is in. We'll let the New York passengers depart, and then we'll send in the maintenance crew, and before you know it, you'll be on your way."

At last. The doors opened and the passengers streamed out. Ashley watched them emerge: one woman in a clever royal-blue shirt dress with great lines, a teenager in a leather jacket, boot-cut jeans tucked into boots, a woman in a suit, circa 1940, totally *Casablanca,* with a cinched jacket that would be killer uncomfortable. While she pondered whether style should trump comfort, she nearly missed the next passenger, but her heart knew, her mind knew, and her eyes widened at the man in khakis and a blue button-down shirt.

There was a lined crease in the khakis because it took a seri-ously neat man to iron his khakis. The soft brown hair was longer than before, badly in need of a trim, and that cowlick on the back...her fingers ached to soothe it.

His gaze met hers, dark brows arched in surprise, but he didn't smile, and she wished he would smile. Her heart pinched with something easily identified as fear, but now there was something new. Hope. David was here. Surely that had to count for something.

He took the seat across from her, legs splayed, his hands hard on his thighs. "You're arriving or departing?" he asked, still not smiling, and there was an intensity in his face that gave her a nervous chill.

She licked her lips, his eyes followed the movement, her body lit like a match, and she wished they could simply fall into bed. Everything was so much easier when it was only passion. When this had first started, passion was her only purpose. It was fun, pleasurable, and she didn't have to worry about getting hurt. Somewhere along the way, her heart had started taking risks again. Following the lead of her brave heart, Ashley took a deep breath. This was it, do or die. "I was flying to New York."

"For business?" he asked, in a voice that indicated he wasn't taking risks yet. Okay, fine.

"No."

"You didn't call."

"I was afraid you wouldn't talk to me, that you would think that I wasn't serious. I thought if I got on a plane, and left my life here, you would know I was serious."

"That's what you're doing?"

Still he was forcing her farther out on the ledge. Ashley raised her chin. "I have a broker who's looking for a buyer for the stores."

"Wow."

He didn't look happy, only shocked. She didn't need shock, she needed agreement, concurrence, some sort of sign that she had not just jumped out of the airplane without a chute.

"You were right," she told him, and that caught his attention in a way that store-selling and Ashley's potential relocation plans had not.

"About what?" he asked, his eyes curious, and maybe, hopefully, thawing just a little.

"I told Val that I was moving because I thought I was holding her back. As long as I was there to protect her, she wouldn't trust herself, and she needs to learn to trust herself. To know that she's strong enough solo."

"You told her that?" He was surprised. She could hear it, and she was inordinately pleased that she had surprised him. He didn't know how much he had taught her.

"I did."

"How'd she take it?"

"Better than most anyone could have imagined," she said, glancing down at his carry-on. The same tidy black hard-sided Samsonite that she knew by sight. She'd been so caught up in her own worries that she'd neglected the obvious. "Why are you here?"

For a second he hesitated, his eyes reluctant. "I thought you might need me," he said, his voice low, nervous. So, Ashley wasn't the only one who didn't like standing on the ledge.

"Even though you thought I was making a mistake?" Perhaps there was some cockiness in her tone.

He nodded. "I stayed away as long as I could, but I need you, Ashley." As he talked, the words ran faster. "You should know that I'm a very responsible man, but can be stubborn when I know I'm right. Yes, I have taken defensive driving, but sometimes, a lot of times, sensitivity escapes me, and I have only picked up strange women in airports once, and it was the best day of my entire life." When he looked at her with pleading eyes, everything fell into place. David was terrified.

Her mouth twitched into almost a smile because honestly, standing out on a ledge was so much nicer when you had someone to share it with. "Twice."

"What?"

"You have only picked up strange women in airports twice."

"Are you toying with me, Ashley Larsen?"

"I am."

His chest heaved with a visible sigh. "I brought you a present."

"I love your presents."

"I know," he said, holding out a small box wrapped in gold. She ripped off the paper to reveal… "*Aliens*. Look at you."

"It's horror, yet sci-fi as well. I felt it was symbolic." He was blushing. She loved that he blushed. He was so strong, and so arrogant, and so stubborn…and yet, then he did these foolish things that pulled at her heart.

"How many copies did you buy?" she asked, not wanting to admit that her heart could be bought with such a trivial gift as classic-horror DVDs.

"Only one," he answered, his voice amused.

"I like the sound of that. No more long-distance television co-watching."

"Nope. If I want to grab you, I have that right."

At that moment, she wanted to touch him, but some invisible hand held her back. Always before they had jumped to the physical first, but this time there were things that needed to be said.

"I love you. You should know that there's baggage in my family and it will probably always be there."

He took her hand, stroking his thumb over her palm. "I love you, too, Ash, and we'll work through it with Val."

"Maybe, but for now, I want to see how she does."

"Maybe she'll do fine."

"I don't know, but I haven't tried moving away before. Maybe it'll do good."

She could feel his strength flowing through her, into her. Someday she would tell him how very desperately she needed him, but not today.

"I found a place for you," he offered, and she was immediately insulted.

"I thought I could live with you. What was all that, 'come live with me and be my love'? No, buddy, once those words were out, you were tied to me for life in ways you could not imagine."

"Not an apartment. A shop. It's in Brooklyn, not far from Enrique because I think your sartorial sign is very Park Slope. All new moms and a more sophisticated palette. Chelsea, Soho? That's not you."

"I could be Chelsea," she told him because she didn't want to be Brooklyn. She wanted to be *über*Chelsea, the cutting edge of style and aesthetic.

David launched a defense of his own position. "I don't know, Ashley. Chelsea? Do you know what happens there? It's pencil skirts and stilettos and red-lined capes and finger-cut opera gloves that come up to the neck, and lots of gold chains. Very avant-garde. It's not your signature. Your style is very traditional. Never argue with your style."

Ashley looked down at the trademarked Ashley Larsen flounce skirt, now pleasingly paired with boots—albeit classical ones—and a V-neck buttercup sweater that was best defined as "traditional."

She gazed at him, he gazed back with his trademark "I'm right" eyebrow-quirk, and at that moment, all was perfect in her world.

"Flight ten-eighty-seven to New York is now boarding. First class, or passengers with small children are now invited to board."

Ashley perked up at the announcement. "That's my flight."

Instantly David frowned. "You don't want to go on this flight. Did you see the sadistic gleam in that kid's eyes? He's going to scream the whole way, and I swear those were Cheerios in his hands that he was firing like missiles. You'll end up with a splitting headache that no aspirin can cure, and who wants to start off in New York with a splitting headache and cleavage full of breakfast cereal?"

"You have a better idea?" she asked, surprised. She had suspected that he would want to depart Chicago as fast as he could.

"Oh, yeah. Here's the deal, you miss the flight, and the airline will honor the ticket later, possibly charge you a change fee, but if you have the right connections, they'll even waive that."

"And you have the right connections?"

"I can be persuasive. I know, it's hard to believe, but yes, the airlines love me."

"You want to go with me back to the house?"

David looked at her with horror. "Are you kidding? No way." He picked up her carry-on, slung it over his shoulder. "I know this room. Honestly. It's great. There's some noise from the planes, but you get used to it really fast."

She got up, left the crowded gate area and began to follow him. She was going to follow him anywhere. "Twice. This is definitely twice."

He glanced over, his eyes were earnest. "So this is working?"

"Like a charm." They passed the newsstand, and familiar memories came rushing back, but this time, there wasn't any nervous reaction, no worries. This was right. This was fate. "Do we need to stop for supplies?"

He turned to stare, disappointment covering his face. "Do I look like a man who comes unprepared?"

"No."

"You keep underestimating me, Ash."

"You are so full of yourself, David," she said, catching his hand. He bent low, whispered into her ear. "I want you full of myself."

"Pervert," she whispered back.

"I'm a guy. Sue me."

"I love you, David."

"Love you, too, Ash."

And from somewhere behind them, the passengers boarded the plane, departing Chicago for New York. Tomorrow Ashley would worry about the flight. Right now, she only needed one thing, and she had him.

*David.*

# *Epilogue*

IT WAS A SNOWY Chicago day in January, the very first day to be exact, and there was a small rental truck parked outside the Larsen house. The truck was loaded with boxes, mostly containing an assortment of shoes, skirts, sweaters, shirts and hats. These were Ashley's belongings, and she was torn between needing to organize both her old life and her new one all at the same time.

"Prudence Mayhew was telling me about Saks," Brianna chirped, trailing behind her aunt, while Ashley shuttled boxes from her bedroom to the front hallway. "I want to shop Saks. I could get some new boots, like yours, Aunt Ash. Those are killer boots."

Val shook her head ruefully. "Those are your genes, Ash. Not mine."

Every now and then, Ashley would stop and study her sister, waiting for her to crack or fall apart, but she never did. Val was holding up fine. Maybe this would work after all.

From the living room, David hefted a box on his shoulder. As the muscles rippled in his arms and his back, Ashley found herself feeling a little flushed.

Val sighed. "Nothing like watching a strong man do good physical work."

"Play your cards right, little sister, and you, too, could win one for your very own."

Their mother stepped into the room, carrying one of Ashley's old photo albums and handing it over. "Let's not put the cart before the horse. Val has a lot of work to do—"

"Which she will," Ashley assured her sister.

"—before she's ready to tackle a man."

Wisely, David ignored the women and kept hauling boxes back and forth. This took longer than it should due to the fact that Ashley's mother kept finding old boxes of Ashley memorabilia tucked throughout the house.

While her mother went to retrieve another of Ashley's boxes, Ashley took the time to go over her final instructions.

"Brianna, you have the folders all organized for your mom?"

"Bills, reminders, school junk and important papers."

Ashley nodded. "Very good. Now, Val, if you need to find something, ask Brianna, and she'll know where to start looking."

David came back into the house, snow dusting his hair and the shoulders of his coat. "Last box," he said, and Ashley noticed the look that passed between him and Val. There was a truce, although Val still had issues with him, but David had been…dare she say it? Sensitive.

Of course, Val had been on her best behavior, making a meeting every day, showing up for work early and keeping Brianna up-to-date on school to-dos.

Feeling brave enough to leave them alone, Ashley pulled Brianna back into her bedroom, which looked sadly bereft without her pictures, her collection of hats and the pile of magazines strewn by her bed. She ducked into the closet and pulled out a shoe box.

Solemnly, she put a hand over the lid before Brianna could lift it.

"This is a very, very important secret, Brianna. I'm going to make you give me the world's best promise that you will keep it."

"I'm very bad at secrets, Aunt Ash. I open my mouth and the truth flies out."

Ashley's mouth quirked at the corners. "Yes, I know, we all have our weaknesses, but you have to promise. It's for your mother."

At that, Brianna nodded once. "I swear. What am I swearing for?"

Ashley patted the box. "Sometimes your mother might have problems. You know, big problems, and her voice will get extra screechy, and when that happens, and she's using a lot of really bad words and you're worried about her, I want you to come in my room, grab the box and give it to her."

"Like a present?"

"Exactly."

"What's in the box?"

"You can keep it quiet?"

Brianna considered the question, chewed her lip, then finally nodded. "I can do it."

Ashley lifted the lid.

Brianna gasped. "Those are your bunny slippers. You're giving them to Mom?"

"She might need them. Bunny slippers are a magical thing. When you slip on the power of these puppies, there's not a lot you can't overcome. When Val gets upset, you make her wear these, and tell her that Aunt Ash is watching, and she's right there. Can you remember all that?"

"I think so."

"Are you scared, Brianna?"

"Nah. Not as long as you promise to take me shopping at Saks. Prudence would really kill to shop there, she told me."

"Not only courageous, but mercenary as well. I don't know where you got those genes, Brianna, but treasure them. They will get you far."

David poked his head in the room. "The snow's really starting to pick up. We should leave."

Ashley's niece studied him with somber brown eyes. "We're going to miss her."

David smile was apologetic. "I know. I'm sorry."

Eventually Brianna shrugged, because to an eight-year-old, the world was a simple place. "We'll be okay."

Ashley gave Brianna a quick hug. "I think so, too."

It was another hour before all the goodbyes were said, and finally Ashley was taking a step off the curb.

New York.

She was moving to New York. She swallowed hard, took a good long look at David. She loved him, she trusted him, she knew him, but this was huge, this was...

*Ash, he's not a serial killer. I will never ever say this aloud, but he's good for you. He's holding your dreams safe. That's worth bonus points.*

Ashley stared hard at her sister, who was waving, managing a smile, all while blinking furiously.

*You're right, Val.*

*I know I'm right.*

The snow began to fall faster, the ground turning from icy brown to pristine white, and Brianna picked up a patch of snow and threw it at her grandmother. Ashley smiled. They would be fine.

David opened the door, watching her closely. "You're sure?"

She gave him her hand and climbed in the cab. "Positive."

Outside was cold, the wind starting to pick up, but the heater was running on high, and here she was warm, safe.... Fearless. She waved out the window, hoping her mother would remember to keep the oil changed, hoping that Brianna would keep up with her homework, and hoping Val would stay strong.

"She's going to be okay. Those Larsen women, honestly, they don't know their own strength." David gave her shoulder a comforting squeeze before starting up the engine and pulling away from the curb.

"You're right, David."

"I know I'm right."

Ashley leaned over and surprised him with a kiss.

"What was that for?"

"For letting my family fly out to visit over spring break." The darling man didn't even looked shocked. "I think they'll really enjoy seeing the city, and Brianna, she's got a great eye for fashion. So are you shaking with fear at the prospect?" she asked, eyeing him carefully.

"Not even a quiver."

Ashley's smile was slow, but sure. "I'm feeling a quiver. Do you want to know where?"

"Seven hundred and ninety-two miles, and you're going to torture me the entire way?"

"It's the new me."

"Don't make me stop this car."

Ashley laughed and rested her head on his shoulder, no bunny slippers necessary. Yes, indeed, everything was going to be just fine.

# millsandboon.co.uk Community

## Join Us!

The Community is the perfect place to meet and chat to kindred spirits who love books and reading as much as you do, but it's also the place to:

- Get the inside scoop from authors about their latest books
- Learn how to write a romance book with advice from our editors
- Help us to continue publishing the best in women's fiction
- Share your thoughts on the books we publish
- Befriend other users

**Forums:** Interact with each other as well as authors, editors and a whole host of other users worldwide.

**Blogs:** Every registered community member has their own blog to tell the world what they're up to and what's on their mind.

**Book Challenge:** We're aiming to read 5,000 books and have joined forces with The Reading Agency in our inaugural Book Challenge.

**Profile Page:** Showcase yourself and keep a record of your recent community activity.

**Social Networking:** We've added buttons at the end of every post to share via digg, Facebook, Google, Yahoo, technorati and de.licio.us.

## www.millsandboon.co.uk

# 2 FREE BOOKS
## AND A SURPRISE GIFT

We would like to take this opportunity to thank you for reading this Mills & Boon® book by offering you the chance to take TWO more specially selected titles from the Blaze® series absolutely FREE! We're also making this offer to introduce you to the benefits of the Mills & Boon® Book Club™—

- **FREE home delivery**
- **FREE gifts and competitions**
- **FREE monthly Newsletter**
- **Exclusive Mills & Boon Book Club offers**
- **Books available before they're in the shops**

Accepting these FREE books and gift places you under no obligation to buy, you may cancel at any time, even after receiving your free books. Simply complete your details below and return the entire page to the address below. You don't even need a stamp!

**YES** Please send me 2 free Blaze books and a surprise gift. I understand that unless you hear from me, I will receive 3 superb new books every month, including a 2-in-1 book priced at £4.99 and two single books priced at £3.19 each, postage and packing free. I am under no obligation to purchase any books and may cancel my subscription at any time. The free books and gift will be mine to keep in any case.

Ms/Mrs/Miss/Mr_____ Initials _____

Surname _____

Address _____

_____

_____ Postcode _____

E-mail _____

Send this whole page to: Mills & Boon Book Club, Free Book Offer, FREEPOST NAT 10298, Richmond, TW9 1BR